Nadine

Mama!

    Love jon NE Way

Thanks For your Support

"AUGUSTA NIGHTS"

Let make Hollywood Smile!.

    Hugs & Kisses !!,

        Dana Mitchell

    Smith K. Green

Published
2/2010

"Augusta Nights"

"The Saga of Armstrong Prentice"

David K. Drew II

COPYRIGHT © 2010 BY DAVID K. DREW II.

LIBRARY OF CONGRESS CONTROL NUMBER: 2009914271

ISBN: HARDCOVER   978-1-4500-2135-7

               SOFTCOVER   978-1-4500-2134-0

               EBOOK   978-1-4500-2136-4

This is a work of fiction. Names, characters, places and incidents either are the product of the author's imagination or are used fictitiously, and any resemblance to any actual persons, living or dead, events, or locales is entirely coincidental.

This book was printed in the United States of America.

To order additional copies of this book, contact:

Xlibris Corporation

1-888-795-4274

www.Xlibris.com

Orders@Xlibris.com

73577

To: Mom, Dad, Konica, Tse'lani and Cheryl but most of all, for all of the wonderful people of one of the greatest cities in the world, my home town, Augusta, Georgia.

"Taller cotton than most men will ever see and the kind of cotton that most men would kill or die for, and somebody said that pimpin wasn't easy."

Armstrong Prentice

Acknowledgements

First and Foremost I'd like to thank God the Creator, whose unconditional love and eternal forgiveness never cease to amaze me.

Thank you Father for my wonderful daughters, Konica Avery-Drew (Boss Lady), and Tse'lani Sekoya Drew (Mini-Me) whom I live for, and who have taught me that the most wonderful word and the most beloved sound in the English language is Daddy!

I want to send out continued love and respect to my parents, the late Flora and David Drew, and to my grandparents the late Benjamin and Eleanor Walker of Warrenton, Georgia and the late Arthur and Mabel Drew of Portsmouth Virginia.

Myriad accolades and praise go out to my Sister, confidant, and best friend, Cheryl Drew Allmond and her crazy crew Vera, Mona, Kimberly and Evelyn of Silver Spring, Oxen Hills and Columbia, Maryland respectively, I continue to pray for you all.

I will never know how to properly thank my cousins Irametta and Yvette Cherry or my cousins, who are the closest things to brothers I will ever have, Donovan "Muffin" and Keith "Dirty" Cherry of Augusta, Georgia, along with my Aunt Thelma Holmes of Warrenton, Georgia, whose stories about my ancestors made this book possible.

To my support network, the Human Resources and Directorate staff of the WJB Dorn VA Medical Center in Columbia, South Carolina, Phyllis, Anthony, Therese, Valerie, Dianell, Tamara, Nadine, Becky, Sheri, Martha, Jean, Pat, Faye, Celeste, Adrienne, Tatanya, Chee'Tara, John, Buffy, Tamika, Jeannette, Effie, Ruth, Benjamin, and my confidant Tammy, as well as our leaders Patricia and Thomas, who have shown me that laughter is the greatest healer of all and thanks for what you do for this county's Veteran's such as myself.

To my lifelong friends, Cheryl and Anthony Leakes of Atlanta, Georgia, Teddy Taylor and family, Darius, Valerie and Robin Key, Wanda and Angie Samuels, Jessie Spurlock, Cecelia McGruder Dunbar, Cynthia and Barbara Emanuel, Ida Clark, Debra Salley, Bernard Reese Cunningham, Charles Wardy and my straight up partner from the 2nd Infantry Division Artillery at Camp Stanley, Korea, Lester Philpot all of Augusta, Georgia, Douglas and Alice Young of Ellenwood, Georgia, Linda, Doris, Barbara, Deloris, Debra, Jackie, Janet, Eric, Sam, Keita, Beverly, Dot, the late Joseph Moore and the rest of the crew from Perry Avenue and Ervin Towers, thank you and I love you all.

To my surrogate family, Carol, Judy, Jody, Chip, and Geoff Grant, their spouses and children, thank you so much for believing in me and especially Geoff for my God-Son Connor David Grant and to his late Grandfather and my mentor Robert "Bob" Grant.

For words of wisdom and advice I would like to thank my friends Rosa Rice, Tina Mitchell, Opal Fulwood, Nikki Wilson and Sharon Hoggard for giving me their perspective on this book from a female point of view.

To the cast of "Love Always Charleston", its Director, visionary and my Business Partners with BJG Productions, Bob J. and Marlene Gaye, who had a dream that we have brought to fruition over the course of the past ten years and we continue to be the longest, "on the air" Soap Opera in the South. To my Business Partner, also with BJG Productions, and co-Executive Producer of the show, Benjie Anderson, thanks for your belief in me man, loved you and Michael Angelo in "Jack Squad" and I can't wait for the sequel. To the Actors: Michael Angelo, it's great to see what you are doing now in movies, looking forward to the premiere of "Single in Atlanta". To Dana Soto and Reggie Lovelace, Erica Cole, Keisha Oates, Will Parks, J. Adonis, Nikki Lashay, Angela Hester, Kanya, Prieska Outland (the Jet centerfold was breathtaking), and the entire crew, thanks for all your support and let's make the next ten years memorable as well. The website address is *www.lovealwayscharleston.com*.

And last but not least, those of you that have always believed in my potential and stood by me even when the skies were dark and the rains persisted, Felicia Drew, Nikki Parks, and Richard Powell of Atlanta, Georgia, Sandra and Beatrice Milliner, of Baltimore, Maryland, Uncle Johnell and Aunt Barbara Sykes of Richmond, Virginia, Uncle C.P. and Aunt Fran Sykes of Bowie Maryland, along with Uncle Eli and Aunt Liz Bracy of Roanoke Rapids, North Carolina, and who could forget Aunt Daisy, Kim, Keith and Karen Sykes of Brooklyn, New York. Thanks for all you did to ensure that regardless of anything else, I would become a man among men, your plan worked and I thank you.

Augusta, Georgia

Augusta's racial makeup has long been largely African American. Its African American citizens have contributed greatly to the rich tapestry of the city's history. A number of listings in the National Register of Historic Places reflect the role of African Americans.

The State of Georgia initially banned slavery during earliest colonial times, but eventually the Trustees allowed it, giving in to pressure from colonists who saw slavery providing economic benefit to their neighbors across the Savannah River in South Carolina. Remote Augusta worked gangs of enslaved Africans brought over from South Carolina even before it was legal to do so.

The production of cotton required intensive labor to grow and pick, as well as to prepare to sell and send to market. Cotton's potential for making high profits accelerated the desire of Southern planters to own more slaves in order to grow more cotton, and slavery grew ever more prevalent after the invention of the cotton gin in 1793. Augusta area farmers joined in the frenzied rush to plant more cotton, which almost completely supplanted the previous cash crop, tobacco.

By 1787 a large group of African Americans, who had been slaves on the Galphin Plantation at Silver Bluff, arrived in Augusta and settled in the then adjacent village of Springfield. Mostly free, they formed Springfield Baptist Church there, which was an offshoot of the Silver Bluff Church that the Galphin slaves established before the Revolution. Displaced by the British invasion of South Carolina, former Silver Bluff slaves formed Springfield in Augusta and another church in Savannah that are among the oldest independent African American congregations in the nation.

Cedar Grove Cemetery in the Pinched Gut Historic District has been the burial place of Augusta's black population, both slave and free, since the 1820s. Burials began there after the St. Paul's churchyard closed in 1817. At that time, Magnolia Cemetery was founded for whites and Cedar Grove soon thereafter for African Americans. By an act of the legislature, authorities removed the remains of African Americans originally buried at St. Paul's and re-interred them at Cedar Grove in 1825.

Augusta had five black churches before the end of the Civil War, in an era when formalized assembly of African Americans was frowned upon, if not illegal, in most parts

11

of the South. In addition to Springfield, Thankful Baptist, Trinity Christian Methodist Episcopal, Central Baptist, and Bethel African Methodist Episcopal Churches all had their own buildings.

After emancipation Springfield was the center of educational and political activities for Augusta's black citizens. The Augusta Baptist Institute was founded in 1867 in Augusta's Springfield Baptist Church, eventually moving to Atlanta to become Morehouse College. The Georgia Equal Rights Association was founded in Springfield in 1866. This association evolved into the Republican Party in the state.

African American churches initiated efforts to educate Freedmen after the Civil War, first at a former wagon factory turned shoe factory by the Confederate government on 9th and Ellis Streets. Other notable African American educational institutions established in Augusta after the Civil War include Reverend Charles T. Walker's Walker Baptist Institute; Ware High School, Georgia's first public high school for African Americans, built in 1880 by the Richmond County Board of Education and later the subject of a Supreme Court case that legalized the practice of segregated education; Lucy Laney's Haines Normal and Industrial Institute; and Paine College, a joint effort of the black and white Methodist churches. Shiloh Baptist Association founded Shiloh Orphanage in 1902 to provide housing, care, and education for black children without families.

After the Civil War, African Americans, not yet legally segregated from whites, gradually gravitated to the neighborhoods south of downtown. This area, now known as the Laney Walker North Historic District, was formerly an area settled by Irish immigrants known as Dublin. Trinity Christian Methodist Episcopal Church, Central Baptist Church, and Bethel African Methodist Episcopal Church all had been in Laney Walker since before emancipation. All three congregations have moved away from the neighborhood, and only Trinity CME's building still stands. Afterwards a number of other churches came to the neighborhood. Tabernacle Baptist Church, which has a national reputation, moved to the district to its present building in 1915. Laney Walker became Augusta's principal African American neighborhood and the location of important black owned businesses such as the Penny Savings Bank, and Pilgrim Health and Life Insurance. It was also home to noted black educator Miss Lucy Craft Laney. Another neighborhood developed outside the original city limits known as The Terri and Nellieville, parts of which became the Bethlehem Historic District.

Still another African American neighborhood, originally called Elizabethtown, developed north of the affluent suburb of Summerville. Today the neighborhood is the Sand Hills Historic District. The Cumming Grove Baptist Church and Rock of Ages Christian Methodist Episcopal Church were among the earliest congregations founded to serve its residents.

Amanda American Dickson's acquisition of a large house on Telfair Street in 1886 is a notable exception to the trend toward segregation of housing and neighborhoods. Amanda Dickson was perhaps the wealthiest African American woman of her time, having inherited the entire estate of her white father, David Dickson of Hancock County,

Georgia. She lies buried in Cedar Grove Cemetery under an imposing monument, a contrast to the modest grave markers on surrounding lots.

Preservation efforts in the African American community have centered on specific landmark buildings, including Springfield Baptist Church on 12th Street, The Lucy Craft Laney Museum of Black History and Conference Center on Phillips Street, and the former Penny Savings Bank on James Brown Boulevard. In addition, Historic Augusta, Inc. is restoring the Union Baptist Church.

It was in this bastion of African American pride and upward mobility that spawned what would become an institution in not only the State of Georgia, but in the Southeast as well. You see Armstrong Prentice would become the South's first African American Senator since Reconstruction; his election in 1962 would do more than just break the color barrier at the Capitol in Atlanta. Armstrong Prentice went on to secure his legacy by rewriting the dreaded Literacy Test and Poll tax that had become an immovable object for blacks seeking voting rights.

For over thirty years Armstrong Prentice would be the color of African American politics in the Southeast. After this he retired and faded into the sunset, or did he? The one thing that didn't fade was his influence; the people who were indebted to him, and his power. It was the kind of power that ordinary men would die for, and the wealth, wealth that had been accumulating for over three generations, old money, and money made from the sweat of black and white men alike, man sweat.

1

"Telephone ringing in the background"—

Armstrong Prentice doesn't make a move because he knew that Constance would answer the phone no matter what time of night it was and he guessed it must be around five in the morning. Hell, when he thinks about it he hasn't answered a ringing telephone in his house in over thirty years. He only uses the cell phone contraption his kids gave him so that he can look almost hip nowadays, he still can't get the hang of that blue tooth thing however.

Papa, Papa, wake up it's the Atlanta Journal Constitution and they want to know if you have anything to say concerning the death of David Franklin! Papa, Papa wake up!

David Franklin, who the hell is "hello", yes this is Armstrong, I mean Senator Prentice, David Franklin, oh lawyer David Franklin of Atlanta, the Mayor's ex-husband? Well yes I have known David Franklin and the Mayor for years. They were recently at my birthday party held at the Augusta National, with difference guests of course. Yes I knew him well; he handled some business for me and my family years ago when he was an advisor for Maynard. Yes the late Maynard Jackson, the first black Mayor of Atlanta. As I remember it he handled some deed and trust work concerning land I owned near the old Airport. We have remained in touch for all of these years; yes I did quite well on that deal, thank you. My condolences go out to him and his lovely family and to Shirley and the kids; yes you can quote me on that.

What was that all about Papa?

Well I'll be, David Franklin passed away last evening. He could've been no more than about sixty five years old I guess. Doesn't surprise me a bit after going down the way he did, he was once one of the most powerful political advisors in the State and when after divorcing Shirley and going through that airport concessions scandal, it's a wonder he didn't lose his mind a long time ago, they say a stroke got him. All that he put Shirley through and you can see where she ended up. He laid the very groundwork that got her Maynard, Andrew, and Bill elected to office. Hell Lomax may have been in that group if he hadn't pissed David off, they eventually ran him totally out of State politics. He landed at Dillard University as its President and from there to Chairman of the United Negro College Fund. What things you do in the dark will eventually find their way back to the light Connie it's such a shame. David Franklin, let's be sure to take him off the guest list, maybe Shirley too, what do you think?

Whatever you think would be best Papa.

Might want to give her a call and inquire about the funeral, we will definitely need to clear our calendars for that one. I can still rub elbows with the best of them if I do say so myself besides I am still considering that offer Governor Purdue made me. Who would believe that after all these years the Governor, a Republican one at that, would still need me to keep the peace in this part of the State? I just might consider heading the State Department of Democratic Studies at the University of Georgia or even that seat in Washington Connie, I just might. However I will not cross party lines no matter how good he sweetens the deal. I am almost tempted to run for State office again especially now since Charles Walker shot himself in his political foot. Who do we have now Carver? Funny, Carver is not a pimple on the ass of Charles Walker, on second thought keep Shirley on the list there might be a Senate seat in her future; I might just be able to use her later on.

So sorry to hear that Papa, I will give Shirley a call later on today and ask about the arrangements, its time I did some shopping anyway. I haven't really spent any time in Atlanta since Coretta passed. Speaking of Coretta I will be so glad when those kids of hers and Martin's get their act together, did you hear that they are suing each other? It's all about money, Martin died almost penniless and since they got a little bit of money now they have just lost their minds. I do miss her coming down to spend time with us; nobody even knew she was here in Augusta. Remember the time her, Oprah and Mya came down so we could play bridge? I really miss those days Papa, I really miss those days. I might as well get up now, don't feel much like sleeping anyway. You need anything? Papa, Papa . . . . well at least one of us can sleep.

2

His Dodge Charger made a left turn off of Interstate 520 onto Laney Walker Boulevard just below the Omega House where he watched both of his brothers' growl, bark and make absolute fools of themselves during and after their college days, what characters . . . . to his right is what remains of the legacy left by one of Augusta's original Gangsters, the infamous Charlie Reed and Son's Funeral Home, last stop for Augusta's Godfather of Soul, James Brown, and to his left is one of the last bastions of debauchery still left in Augusta, the infamous Cool Spot and College Bowl Lounge where he knew you could still get anything your heart desired either right out front or on the inside. He is amazed that they still have these places open where you can buy a bottle of your favorite elixir on the front and then take it around the side or the back to enter the place where the only amenities were a table and a bathroom, a bathroom that even the devil's imps would find offensive, but the scabs of society still make their way there day in and day out looking for a friend and a free drink. As he passes East Boundary he can remember when, on the right side of the street, there was an Arthur Treacher's Fish and Chips joint not far from Forsyth street where they once lived and where they brought you your food on what was supposed to be newspaper the way they did it in England, and who could forget the Cemetery where even in death you were segregated. He makes a right turn and then another left to pass May Park where as a youth he played Tennis and came to watch Softball games. Welcome to the Augusta Richmond County Law Enforcement Center where you can go to court and do long or short time and never have to leave the building to do it.

Good morning Sir,

Morning Captain Prentice.

He is handed a newspaper and a copy of last night's blotter report as he enters an office with familiar surroundings. The first thing he notices is the name etched on the door. Captain Armstrong Prentice II. On the wall is a faded photograph of him graduating from Paine College and then from the Police Academy, then there is the one of the entire family at a congratulatory party at Pendleton King Park. But the one that he is most proud of is the picture of him and his parents taken when he graduated from Special Operations Training at the FBI Headquarters in Quantico, Virginia, my dad, the man, not the myth but the real Armstrong Prentice. The one man he admired the most in the entire world. The man who wielded the real power in this State and he carried the same name as this giant, Armstrong Prentice II. He was named the second because his father did not want the nickname, Junior, to stick. He never wanted his son to be called anything but who he was, Armstrong Prentice II, as if the first was never enough.

As he sits down at his desk he glances at the lovely picture of his wife Cheryl, the one of him and his brothers and the one of his baby sister Tammy next to another copy of the article about her arrest, trial, and acquittal. He wonders what her day will be like today and if she can ever escape the demons that dwell in her psyche.

How are you feeling today Tammy, how's my baby sister?

He also wonders how it all became so unraveled. He can still remember the day he was called into the Chief's office and told that he was no longer on the case due to his emotional attachment to it. He remembered the night he received the frantic phone call from Tammy saying that she had just shot Tony and was terrified wondering what she should do. He also remembers how he found her in the parking lot of Richmond Academy almost out of her mind. He remembers how he escorted her unnoticed into his office to avoid the News people and how he defied his father who insisted that he drive her to Sandy Grove, the family's Jones Creek estate. He then remembered the countless sleepless nights that he spent wondering just how shocking the entire case had become and how it had electrified the town and galvanized the masses into pro Prentice and no Prentice factions.

He also remembers how it all just went away . . . . Armstrong Prentice had a way of making things just go away. But why was he kept in the dark about the back door deals and agreements and even today . . . . two years later why the files have remained sealed. More importantly there are still rumors about how justice comes with a price. The rumors will not just go away . . . . the last thing he remembered about the case was how Judge Henry J. Ruffin, one of his dad's best and oldest friends, looked as he closed his briefcase and shook the hand of the District Attorney as the door was closed from within, but why was Judge Ruffin there? He was no longer a criminal lawyer in fact he had been appointed Judge by Governor Zell Miller. He was the first African American Superior Court Judge for the Augusta Judicial Circuit. He never knew who was standing behind the door to close it but he always wondered . . . .

3

Cheryl exits the bathroom with the early pregnancy test held firmly in her left hand, a feeling of frustration engulfs her as; once again, her desire to produce an heir to the Prentice dynasty goes unfulfilled.

I must remember to talk with Strong about seeing a fertility doctor, here I am forty five years old and I have yet to bring another Prentice into this world. But how will I get him to go? He would never agree that there could even be a remote chance of the great Armstrong Prentice II having inadequate soldiers. I need to solidify my position in this family no matter what the cost. Kelvin and Maria already have two children and I am not mad at my girl Maria at all, she knew what to do and how to do it, slang it girlfriend. Get in where you fit in and tie the knot tight. Lord knows if something happens to Armstrong I could be left out in the cold with no links to this family and there is no way in hell I am going back to New Orleans. Rebuild my ass, Katrina taught me that I can't swim nor drink all that water, okay! If I wanted to see the ninth ward in New Orleans again all I have to do is drive through Sunset Homes or is it Cherry Tree Crossings nowadays, anyway that's all I would need to remind me of those good ole days, okay, enough about New Orleans. I pray that nothing happens to my husband in the line of duty but a sista gotta take care of a sista and I am not getting any younger. We all know that king playa Martin Prentice has no plans to settle down any time soon, not as long as there are still some women in this town that he hasn't slept with yet and Ms. Tammy can't even give away no pussy after killing her last boyfriend. Let me go on line and read today's paper to see what is going on in this "Garden City" as they call it.

Cheryl can still remember when she first met Strong; she was in Atlanta in the lobby of the Hilton Suites on Peachtree Dunwoody hoping to get a glimpse and spend some quality time with one of the Boston Celtics who were in Atlanta to play the Hawks that night. This was their hotel and as she waited amidst the other "hangers on" or "gold diggers in training" at the bar, she noticed a nice cultured gentleman who she thought must be affiliated with the team in some manner. She remembers watching as the bartender poured him a shot of Hennessy then she waited until he was done with that and had the bartender send him another one on her. She can still remember the first glance he shot her way after asking the bartender where the drink had come from.

She remembered that distinctly because she had never seen a man hang a suit the way he did as he almost floated to the seat next to her to thank her for the drink personally. And the way the brother smelled, damn, the faint scent of Paul Sebastian cologne and coconut bath oil, and those shoes had to be Fendi, a woman can tell a lot about a man by the quality of the shoes he wears, as well as his watch and this man wore a Movado and smelled like money, old money and Cheryl knew the smell of money. Sadly all she knew about real money was its smell.

Her only regret was that she had lied to him about why she was at the hotel. She told him that she worked for the agent of one of the ball players and was in town to have him sign a contract for a new endorsement and then after a few more drinks and the exchange of phone numbers her Greek God was gone. But he did leave his business card, Captain Armstrong Prentice II, Chief of Homicide, Augusta Police Department. Armstrong Prentice, where had she heard that name before?

She never really expected him to call, hell he could have had her that night, right there on the bar if he had the notion. But he did call, and that's when she told him that she too lived in Augusta and was just performing the duties of a notary that night in Atlanta. One date led to two and two led to three, and the rest is history and what a lovely history it had been thus far.

Although she wondered why this brother had never been married and wasn't a "baby daddy" she was intrigued at his "devil may care" attitude and he did treat her right, he treated her as if no other woman on the face of the earth existed. There was never any pretending with Strong, he said what he meant and meant what he said.

After dating him for about three months he finally took her to meet his parents at Sandy Grove and what a day that had been. Sandy Grove was the kind of place that only existed in her dreams back in New Orleans, the "Big Easy" had its mansions and immaculate cottages but this was the cream of the crop, this was phenomenal and one day this could be home.

She never knew just how much Strong was worth financially because he never talked about money, he never seemed to look at money the way the average person did and after visiting Sandy Grove she knew why. He was the namesake of a retired State Senator and a retired Associate College Dean, so that meant money on top of money on top of the man on top of her and he would spend his entire life in that position if she had anything to do with it besides they didn't call him Strong for nothing.

If the folk back in New Orleans could take a look at her today, if her friends could only get a glimpse of how far she had come, only Millicent, her partner in crime and closest friend and confidant, knew the real story. A story that the rest of the world must never know, especially since Cheryl Ryan Prentice had arrived, she had really arrived.

4

"Alarm blaring in the background".

Kelvin reaches over to the night stand and turns off the alarm then looks over at his young bride Maria and wonders what he had done in a past life that has made this one so wonderful. Here he is at the zenith of his military career with a lovely wife eleven years younger than he was, and two smart and healthy children, Boregard and Eleanor who were both named after his ancestors.

I knew that volunteering for Afghanistan would punch my ticket to the big time, I just hate that I put Maria through all that anguish wondering if she would ever receive the visit that so many of her friends received notifying them of their husband's death and now with this plum assignment with the Defense Information Systems Agency headquartered in Mclean, Virginia with duty at the Pentagon, who could ask for more. I only wish dad had approved of my volunteering. I can still remember the conversation, or was it a lecture "no son of mine will ever have to fight for this country, the Prentice family has paid enough dues and I have not worked my fingers to the bone to build a name for myself and this family just to have a son of mine risking his life in some far away land under the guise of democracy. I forbid it Kelvin, I utterly forbid it. Democracy, that's another word for de money and if you got de money you don't have to go fight and by God my name is Armstrong Prentice and I got de money".

Colonel you will have to be just a little bit quieter when you get up in the morning I am not in the Army and do not need to get up at this ungodly hour, can't you get one of those watches that have an alarm in it? Wake me up when you get back from your run so that I can get your offspring up and atom. Sir, yes Sir . . . and all that crap . . . . love you sweetie.

Love you too grouchy. I have loved you from the beginning back when you were starting your career as my secretary during my tour in Texas. I was a young Captain then and can remember how difficult it was just trying to get your attention without violating any fraternization rules. Fate has a way of making the right things happen. He remembered that her Mazda 323 broke down right after leaving the main gate at Fort Hood and how he just so happened to be right behind her. His main issue was how to ask such a lovely creature to dinner knowing that the first obstacle to get over would be the age difference. But Maria never made that an issue they just had fun together. He fondly remembers the weekends in Dallas and San Antonio and vacations in Galveston and how could he forget the weekend lunches in the park and the smile that won his heart. Yes Maria, he did deserve you and he also deserved Boregard and Eleanor. His input to the family legacy was now complete, his destiny was secure.

No Children or boy or series?

5

Pulling into his driveway on Castle Rock Drive, Martin glances at the car clock reading five fifteen in the morning.

Damn I should have stayed at Wanda's house; at least I could have gotten another thirty minutes of sleep. Okay, just go inside get a shower, get dressed and hit Huddle House on Walton Way for breakfast. I just hope Augusta's finest can get along without their Principal being one hundred percent today. I will be there physically but mentally I should hit the wall at about two this afternoon, I have to remember that I am not as young as I once was and these late nights or should I say early mornings are gonna catch up with me sooner or later . . . . Looks like it's gonna have be later cause a playa gots to play . . . ya heard , , , a playa has gots to play. Besides who is the coolest Principal in the Central Savannah River Area . . . . I know, I know . . . . ya heard. Nothing but the dawg in me . . . . why must I feel like that . . . . why must I chase the cat . . . . nothing but the dawg in me . . . . QK9—in full effect.

Yep the life of a playa is an intriguing one especially when you come from the most prestigious family in the South. But this lifestyle gets old real quick and what Martin Prentice really wants to do is settle down. He wants to find what his brothers have already found and that is a soul mate to spend the rest of his life with, he is tired of the early morning risings especially from places unfamiliar to him. But that comes with the game and there has never been a better player, and the women, even they become a blur after a while. Yes, Martin Prentice wanted to find that one special someone, that someone that he could spend the remainder of his days with, Martin wants to find his soul mate, his Queen.

Augusta has its share of eligible women but the ones that he always found himself with always seemed to have a hidden agenda. It's not that he hid his pedigree or pretended to be less than he was, besides just the name Martin Prentice would turn heads and cause finger pointing outside the VIP sections and yes he always commandeered the VIP sections, in some clubs like "Private Eye" they even called it Prentice's row. Augusta may be slow but not that slow, it always had a steady supply of the finest women in all of Georgia and even the South for that matter and it was his duty as a gentleman to ensure that they were all pleased and satisfied beyond their wildest dreams. Playa, playa, play on.

6

(Augusta Chronicle Herald)—Tamlar "Tammy" Prentice was an aspiring Beauty Queen who shot and killed her boyfriend when she learned he was having an affair with another woman.

Prentice, 26, was crowned Miss Augusta in August 2006, four months later, in December, when Prentice discovered her boyfriend, Anthony Leakes of Savannah, was cheating on her, she went to the other woman's house in Augusta with a gun to set things straight, said Richmond County District Attorney Darius Key.

Prosecutors claim Prentice drove to the home of Nikki Parks, to confront her about her involvement with her boyfriend of three years. When Leakes arrived, the State contends, Prentice argued with him and shot him in the chest with a gold-plated semi-automatic handgun she had received as a gift from her father.

Leakes died from the wound two days later in the hospital.

Defense Attorney Chip Grant portrayed the 5-foot-10, 210-pound Leakes as a violent abuser of women who was high on drugs the night he was shot.

Grant said Prentice only fired in self-defense because she knew Tony always kept a gun in his car.

During his opening statement, however, Key pointed to the path of the bullet that went into Leakes' chest, he said Prentice vindictively shot at her boyfriend to ensure his demise."

Prentice is charged with one count of murder, assault and felony use of a weapon, if convicted she faces life in prison without the possibility of parole.

Prentice is the daughter of former State Senator Armstrong Prentice and former Associate Dean of Paine College, Constance Walker Prentice both of Augusta Georgia.

Prosecutors called their only witness Wednesday, Nikki Parks, who said she and Leakes had been engaged to be married.

Parks described her fiancé as a "big teddy bear", but admitted that he was once arrested for assault following a night club incident at "Club 3000" in Augusta.

24

Parks told jurors how Prentice, a former beauty queen, came to her house on River Ridge Road on December eleventh, to confront her about the man they both thought they were going to marry.

Parks said the confrontation escalated when Leakes arrived and started yelling at the beauty queen. She testified that then Prentice got a gun from her car and pointed it at Leakes as he ran behind his car. The witness said she was able to calm Prentice down, and Leakes finally returned to his car to leave.

Then, walking toward her house with her back to the street, Parks said she heard a shot rang out and turned and saw Prentice pointing a gun from her car window. She said Leakes stumbled toward her in pain.

"Nikki, that bitch shot me, call 911," Leakes yelled, according to Parks.

Tammy wiped the tears from her eyes realizing that she had read this article almost every day since her acquittal. She still finds it hard to believe that it happened, she misses Tony and wishes it would all go away . . . . make things go away, that's what her father always promised her he would do if things in her life went awry. Go away is what she made Tony do, go away is what her father made happen to her dreadful case. Go away is what Armstrong Prentice always did to problems concerning his family, concerning his name, and especially concerning the love of his life, Tammy his little angel and only daughter.

But how long could he make things just go away, how much power did he still wield in local, as well as, State politics? How could a mere retired State Senator wield so much power?

But they didn't know the real Armstrong Prentice. Armstrong Prentice was a man among men way before he was, should we say, voted into political office? You see Armstrong Prentice was the most powerful black man in the State of Georgia and could make all things and even some people just go away.

25

7

Good morning Papa, I got your coffee next to the newspapers on the balcony. I thought we could sit and talk for a while. You have been so busy lately that we haven't had time to catch up and there are quite a few things that I need your input on. I just got off the phone with Shirley and they still haven't finalized David's funeral arrangements but she promised she would call and let us know as soon as they did. It's going be a big affair so I will have to get me a new dress.

Not a problem, it will be good to see some of the old crew that I haven't seen in a while, I'm sure that Joe Lowery will be there and Juanita. I was glad to hear that her son finally got his life back together; I guess spending time behind bars has a way of getting your attention. Can you imagine all that nonsense going on with them and the King children? Martin, Coretta and Ralph, all of them are spinning in their graves over them kids. I also want to visit Maynard; you know they buried him in Oakland Cemetery right downtown overlooking the city, that is such a fitting place for a man of his stature.

Yeah I know Papa, and speaking of kids, we will have our entire brood over for Thanksgiving this year. It's been so long since all the family has been here at the same time. Kelvin is finally back on American soil, thank God, and Martin promises not to go back to Rio again this year, I wonder what is in Brazil that keeps that boy on a plane Papa I really wish I knew.

Ahem . . . . well you know there is a lot of history in that place and I'm sure it has something to do with the curriculum there at the school.

I hadn't realized that today marks seven years since the World Trade Center bombings and all that nonsense, and they claim they still can't find Osama Bin Laden.

If they really wanted to find him they would have already, if they can find Hussein in a hole in the ground in the middle of the desert they can find Bin Laden's tall lanky ass. Don't get me to speaking on the subject. Did any of the children call? Is everyone alright?

As far as I know everybody's fine, I've talked to all of them in the past week and looking forward to seeing Boregard and Eleanor, I really miss my grandbabies.

So do I, I need to spend more time with Boregard and let him know what it is like to be a Prentice. We Prentices have been the staple of this city for over three generations;

we have fought and bled in the very soil of this city. He needs to know his place, he is the only grandson of Armstrong Prentice and he needs to know his place.

I know Papa but he is just a baby, he just made five years old, give him time Papa give him time.

I will give him time but who knows how much time I have left, somebody needs to know the story Connie. Somebody needs to know from where we came and how we derived our power base. Somebody needs to know why the name Armstrong Prentice is feared as much as respected in this city and in the South for that matter.

Armstrong there will be time for all that, besides isn't that what you have been sharing with Tammy? I thought she was the chosen one?

I wish Connie but it has to be a male child that has always been made perfectly clear, it has to be a male heir.

I wonder if Tammy would like to come to Atlanta with us, it would be a plus if she were to be seen at the funeral with all the newspapers and photographers. What do you think Papa? She could use the exposure; God knows she isn't getting any younger.

Now Connie, you know that I do not go for all of that society stuff the way that you do, she's your daughter and you know what's best. Besides anything to put that boy's death behind her would be a benefit to her and our name. She is a Prentice after all, give her a call and tell her it was my idea if you have too.

8

Phone Rings.

Hello honey, how is your day going?

I'm fine Strong, listen I was looking in the paper and the Mayor's White Ball is next month and I was wondering if we could get a better table this year. Your mother knows everybody and I just thought it would be nice to sit at the main table with them.

You mean rub some of the same elbows as them right? Sweetie I go to those events just because of the position that I hold at the department and nothing more, the only reason we get decent seats at all is because of my last name and you know it.

I know Strong but I just thought it would be a good thing to have someone to talk with, mom and I do need to talk about the holidays and I just thought this would be a great time for that, you know how boring it can become towards the end of the evening. So tell me what do you think?

I think between you and my mother I am going to be doing what you all dictate anyway. So the least you can do is get my Tux ready I'll talk to Dad myself.

No Strong, let me talk to your mother about it first, then you can talk to your Dad, we need some girl talk anyway. Besides every time I talk with her I am reminded about just what it means to be a Prentice woman . . . . and I am a Prentice, so would it be okay?

Go ahead; by the way what do I get out of all this?

You get me and some special attention tonight how does that sound?

It sounds like I will be home early if at all possible.

Meowwwwwwwwwwwwwww.

Not the cat whisper, don't start something that you can't finish.

I never do Strong, I never do, bring it home baby.

9

Maria Prentice is relaxing on her deck having a quiet breakfast after getting the kids off to daycare. It's still a blur to her how she met such a wonderful man who, for the first time in her young life, made good on all his promises to her. The only thing he ever asked her for was her loyalty and even though he is eleven years her senior, he had become her everything.

She actually enjoys the military lifestyle, everything but the extended absences. The travel doesn't bother her at all, as a matter of fact after about three years in one place she automatically gets in the mood to move. What she could not understand was the politics of the military, how could her husband who had been a Battalion Executive Officer just a couple of years ago get to the Pentagon and spend most of his time making coffee for guys with stars on their collars, she just didn't get it. The only thing she was sure of was that Kelvin enjoyed the duty and said it was just a stepping stone to greater things.

What she couldn't understand was why he never really talked about going home to Fort Gordon, why he never mentioned wanting to go back to Augusta.

Another thing she didn't quite understand was the secrecy that was so prevalent in the family about anything having to do with their heritage. She distinctly remembered when she hinted about building a family tree at Thanksgiving dinner three years ago and how the entire room got quiet and everyone seemed to have their eyes on her. What was the big secret, it was just another American family right?

Anyway she had to hurry so that she could make it to the Pentagon to view the dedication of the 9-11 Victims' Memorial, Kelvin said that the event would be something that she would remember for the rest of her life. He said that there would be one hundred and eighty four benches engraved with the individual names of those who died that day and besides this was an opportunity to pack a lunch for her husband.

I have done this a hundred times but still feel a little awkward riding the train to DC. I know to park the car at Glenmont, take the Red to Metro Center then get on the Blue and get off at the Pentagon; Kelvin said he would meet me at the entrance.

I had almost forgotten how beautiful Washington is in the summer, I don't get the chance to get down here that often but when I do I so enjoy it. The Museums, the

Monuments and the Dogwoods and just the atmosphere of being in the Nation's Capital makes it all worthwhile but today is 9-11 so I'd better be careful. I don't really like the idea of being on public transportation today but everything beats trying to find a suitable parking place and the traffic today in DC will be a Bear. I hope everything is okay, I wonder what Kelvin is doing, I love you sweetie.

10

Good morning Dr. Prentice

Morning Doc.

Well Mr. Clean has finally arrived, brand new Steve Harvey suit with a fresh pair of Gators and a Hermes silk butter cream necktie with my Klaus Kobec imported wrist watch and a fresh Blount and Sons haircut, what can a brother say I mean the Blount's on Brown street go back two generations and know what to do with a brother's hair. Any man with any prominence in the entire CSRA got their haircut at Blount's at one time or another. Not to mention the Lexus in the private parking space that reads Dr. Prentice—Principal. Good morning Mrs. Bradford and how is the luckiest secretary in the world doing today?

That's Executive Assistant, and I'm good Dr. Prentice, I'm good and why, may I ask am I the luckiest Executive Assistant in the world?

Because you happen to be mine Mrs. Bradford, you happen to be mine.

You definitely haven't changed much since high school Martin.

Oh no Mrs. Bradford, not Martin, Dr. Prentice . . . . that's Dr. with a D.

I heard you were out on the town last night.

Who me?

Yes you Dr. Prentice and you know you can't hide in a town this small besides how many brothers in Augusta drive a 2009 Midnight Black Lexis IS with that QK9 license plate?

Oh, did I tell you it has blue tooth capabilities and a V6 performance tuned suspension?

Anyway, here is your list of appointments and that Mr. Rice called again, as a matter of fact he will be here at 3:00 pm today, he said that it was important.

Who is this Mr. Rice? Call him back and find out what company or student he represents, I really am not feeling any rowdy parents today.

Ok Dr. Prentice will do.

As Martin enters his office he can't help but notice the name on the door. Dr. Martin Prentice, Ed. D.

Yes the hard work has finally paid off and who could have picked a better spot to land in than as Principle of one of the most prestigious school in Augusta, Georgia, Lucy Craft Laney High School.

It always hits Martin hard in the chest when he reads the inscription on the wall as you enter the door.

Lucy Craft Laney—Educator. Born on April 13, 1854, in Macon, Georgia. Daughter of former slaves, Laney was taught by her mother to read at a young age. She grew from an eager reader to a dedicated educator who spent much of her life teaching African American students. At the age of 15, she enrolled at Atlanta University where she graduated in 1873 and then spent several years working as a teacher before opening her own school in Augusta, Georgia, in 1883.

Laney's school, which later became known as Haines Normal and Industrial Institute, started out small with only a handful of students. By the end of the second year, there were more than two hundred African American students enrolled. Over the years, Laney made many improvements and additions to the school's offerings. In the 1890s, the school was one of the first to offer kindergarten classes for African American children in the South. She also opened a training center so that black women could train as Nurses. The school's curriculum provided the students with traditional liberal arts courses as well as vocational programs, which was ground-breaking at the time.

Laney died on October 23, 1933. A pioneering educator, she led the way for many other educational leaders, including Mary McLeod Bethune and Charlotte Hawkins Brown.

Then there is the Museum next door which even today is the only African American Museum in the CSRA. And the new mega-stadium across the street is dedicated partially to Coach Dupree who did almost as much to steer young men onto the right path as Mrs. Laney herself.

Who would have known that this area would look as great as it does today? Well one man knew because he provided the finances to make this happen. He envisioned this over ten years ago prior to the death of his old friend and Augusta's only African American Mayor Ed McIntyre.

Yes his father Armstrong Prentice and Ed would discuss the revitalization of this area while sipping coffee with Dr. Blount in the Dentist's office that was in the next block. Martin remembered Dr. Blount always had a lollypop and a kind word for the children, I mean anybody who was anybody had Dr. Blount for their Dentist. There weren't many black Dentists in this area at that time, none as prominent as Dr. Blount anyway.

I again wonder if this is what Mrs. Laney had in mind, I would like to think she did anyway.

11

I am so tired of reading about this upcoming election that I can't wait until November to have this nonsense over with. Obama should win but don't think for a minute that the white folk in this country are going to sit by and watch a Negro move into 1600 Pennsylvania Avenue unscathed. It just won't be that easy. Trust a sista okay!

Wait a minute, must not forget the Mayor's White Ball is next month. Has it been a year already? I gotta give it to the man, he may be the poster child for real white boys but he gives some slamming parties. Deke might have some soul brother in him after all. Besides if I am ever going to get Armstrong into the Chief of Police's office I got to get closer and rub elbows, among other things, with the Mayor, but how? I refuse to just blend into the background.

I will not be denied, calm down Sista calm down. You must first understand who you are? You are married to a Captain in the Police Department who just so happens to be the son and namesake of the most powerful man black or white in the State, Armstrong Prentice. If anybody can make this Chief thing happen maybe it's my father in law. So let's see what kind of juice daddy in law really has. But Armstrong must never know. I have got to get Strong and me a seat at the main table with mom and dad next month. It shouldn't be too much of a problem; I'll just make sure it seems as if it was her idea.

12

So honey how did you like today.

Actually it was a little sad Kelvin, just to look at all those flags and the brand new benches with the names of all those who died was amazing. It took me a while to realize that the people that were searching were looking for the bench that was made for their loved one that they lost on that day. There was even one woman who I overheard trying to explain to her son that the bench they were sitting on was named for his father. Oh Kelvin it was so sad and I am so glad you invited me to the ceremony; I'll remember it for the rest of my life.

I'm glad you enjoyed it; I just thought this would be one of those Oprah moments for us and today the eyes of the entire world were here on Washington and on the Pentagon. I just can't imagine what must have gone through most of their minds when that plane hit. I'm just glad that as a country we are doing something about it instead of just turning the other cheek.

You are the most patriotic man I know Kelvin Prentice and I am beginning to understand why you went back to Afghanistan after your first tour. Just know that I will always be here to support you no matter what. But understand also that your family needs you as much as this government, actually even more, so you promise me that you will be careful. Promise me Kelvin.

I promise Maria I will take care of myself.

Okay, and because you are so patriotic, I wonder if I can find a red, white and blue teddy for later on, think you'll be able to salute.

I already am sweetie, I already am.

See you at home Colonel and don't be late, I'll have Vera watch the kids.

13

Ok, now what am I going to do with myself today? I guess I should go look for a job but why? I am the only daughter of Armstrong Prentice. Dear old Daddy. But I do need to do something with my life I can't live under Daddy's shadow forever, can I?

(Telephone ringing.)

Hello,

Oh hi Mama. I was just thinking about you and Daddy, how is Mr. Armstrong Prentice doing this morning?

Stop teasing your father, everything on this end is okay, I was just calling to ask you to come to Atlanta with your father and I to attend David Franklin's funeral.

Mama who is David Franklin?

Not sure you remember him child, he is an old friend of your father and I, and former husband to the current Mayor Shirley Franklin. Anyway he passed away last night and we are waiting for firm funeral arrangements but I assume it will probably be this Saturday so I thought it would be nice for you to join us, besides I haven't been shopping in Lenox Mall for a while and I am dying to visit Atlantic Station. So I figure we can leave tomorrow and drop your father off at Paschal's after we've checked into the Ritz and you and I can do the town . . . . on your father of course!! So I will expect you at Sandy Grove no later than noon so that we can head to Hotlanta as they call it now. Oh, bring something outstanding for the receptions and whatever else may be happening in the city.

You mean bring an empty suitcase so that we can buy new outfits for the entire weekend?

Why of course sweetie, we are Prentices you know!

14

Armstrong sips at his coffee and glances at the newspaper then gazes from his second story balcony over the vastness of his Jones Creek Estate. He never knew that his land would be as coveted as it had become over the last few years. He never imagined that this would be the site they wanted for the new Jones Creek Golf Course. The land was passed down to him on his eighteenth birthday and he let it sit for almost ten years before building his estate on the lower two hundred acres and now sitting on what was once prime farm land sits the premier Golf Course of the South just walking distance from his back meadow. The course itself sits on a five hundred and twenty acre site; it's almost as prestigious as the Augusta National, the Palmetto or the Reserve Club over in Aiken. They would pee their pants if they knew they had purchased this land from a black man for top dollar, and not just any black man but Armstrong Prentice, the black man. Maybe one day they will understand why I named this place Sandy Grove.

Sandy Grove Estates sits on 480 acres of prime real estate on Jones Creek right outside of Augusta in Evans. The main house is 80,000 square feet with twenty five bedrooms, fifteen bathrooms, and eight formal dining rooms along with six formal living rooms complete with 60,000 square feet of living space not including the three sub basements, a riding stable, lake, helicopter pad, nine car garage and a thirty thousand foot servants quarters with ten bedrooms.

Armstrong continued to gaze over his vast estate then remembered the dream that he has had almost every night for the past two weeks, the dream that takes him back to his childhood and a meeting in the woods that he overheard as a child. This meeting took place somewhere on a dirt road off of the Gibson Highway in Warren County years ago. The meeting was between his grandfather and Mr. Johnson who was a huge landowner in this area. Mr. Johnson was screaming and shouting at his grandfather "the truth must never be made public Prentice, it must never come out!" "There is no way in hell I will allow you to destroy what was built with the blood, sweat and tears of our ancestors right on this very land". "Look around you, look around at land that has been in this family since the beginning of time and I will die before I let the truth be known". "Land is the only real wealth Prentice because God is not making any more of it". "This land was earned by sweat, man sweat Prentice". "Sweat more from your people than from mine but that is in the past". "Now we must take up the mantle and decide how to move forward from here. We can't move backward not even if it means that one of us will have to die here tonight".

Armstrong always wondered what the secret was all about but would have to wait another thirteen years before his father, in his happiest moment, confided in him and set the very foundation for what had transpired in the annals of this State and this City over the past two generations. Prentice indeed kept the secret because of the sweat of his ancestors but that wasn't the only reason. For to divulge the secret would not really destroy the Johnson clan, it may devastate them for a while but not destroy them. But it would definitely destroy his clan. Oh yes the truth back then would have destroyed them for sure.

15

That sure was a nice send off they gave David Franklin wouldn't you say so Tammy?

Yes it was something to see, even the haters showed up today and look at Daddy, Mama he has not closed his mouth since the service ended.

Honey your father is in his element, he is with the most influential black people in this State right now. He will get back to us later but believe me, if I know your father, and I do know your father, he is making plans to solidify his place in the history of this State, plans that would blow your mind. Most of the guest today didn't come here to see David Franklin put away, they came here to see each other in order to rekindle old friendships and some came to make new ones. They also came to see who is still alive and to find out who still has the juice as they call it, but never mind that, it's just your father doing what he does best Tammy being Armstrong Prentice. Quite a few of them came out just to see whose ass they could kiss and make a profit from it and your father washed a special spot for them this morning. He's probably got more lip prints on his ass right now then I've been able to put there in the last thirty years and believe me I have contributed my share.

Laughing—Mama you ought to stop.

Let's get out of this heat; your father will meet us back at the Ritz this evening. In the mean time I will have the driver take us to Gladys and Roscoe's Chicken and Waffles on Peachtree; I heard that is the place to be for brunch even if it is Saturday. Driver! Driver!

16

I still say Andy; there is no way they will allow Obama to just walk into the White House unscathed. I expect them to find some dirt on him any day now, they already attacked his wife, his minister, his friends and anybody else they thought might have a story to tell.

Not so sure about that Armstrong, I think if there was something to find on him they would have found it already. The problem with him is that he is too clean.

But how did he get where he's at without showing up on the establishments radar screen? Can somebody tell me that?

You must first understand where the guy came from Armstrong; he engineered a grass roots campaign on Chicago's South side and garnered their support by making things happen in their communities thus solidifying his name recognition on the streets. He did a lot of things to bring life back to those impoverished neighborhoods and he used that influence to grow from local politics and get himself elected to the Senate, hell he could have been Mayor of Chicago but he aspired to a higher calling and you must admit that he has a powerful team behind him. Nobody expected him to run for President so they weren't paying much attention to him, their mindset couldn't conceive a junior Senator from Illinois with aspirations to become President of the United States after spending less than two years in the Senate, which was unimaginable. In other words Armstrong he played politics from the old book, a book that you know so well. He got out on the streets and went door to door and actually woke the masses up even those that had become disenfranchised with our electoral process and had become convinced that their individual votes wouldn't count, well he convinced them that their votes did count and gave them back the pride that voting itself once meant to our people. Does that sound familiar?

And he did all of this in Jesse's back yard? They can't ignore him now. Can we get some money into his campaign or do you think he'll need it.

Actually I don't think he can win Georgia no matter what happens at this point, unless you can call in some of your markers and get the white vote to swing his way. What do you think about that Armstrong?

Are you asking me for a favor Andy?

No Armstrong, not at all, I will wait until I really need something amazing to happen before I ask you for anything, your pay back policy is a little too steep for me.

Not really Andy, I just believe in what the Romans called the "*Virtue of Gravitas*". Meaning I value, discipline, strength and loyalty in my friends as well as in my enemies.

Well I am fortunate to have always been a friend; I've seen what happens to your political enemies. How long are you going to be in town Armstrong I would like to set up a meeting between you, myself, Joseph, Tyrone and Martin III and I hope John is back in town, we need to try and see if we can put an end to this family squabbling and bring some honor back to the King name.

I would consider it an honor Andy; I'm staying at the Ritz in Buckhead and can stay in town as long as I am needed, just say the word and I am at your disposal. Connie and Tammy are here with me and they would love to spend some time with you, it's been a while and Tammy has grown so much since you last saw her, she would love to see her Uncle Andy. So tell me Andy how does it feel to have a street named after you? I saw that statue in the plaza and I was impressed my boy, I was impressed, it was well earned and even more deserved. I am proud of what small part I may have played in making all of that happen.

Thanks Armstrong, none of it could have happened without you but lest not we forget whose footprints I followed, as I remember correctly you were the first black man to have a statue erected in his honor and to have it placed on the Capitol grounds in this State was a true accomplishment, you paved the way for all this and most of what we politicians have accomplished for the past thirty years. I'll call you tonight.

I'm looking forward to it Andy.

17

Daddy, thank you so much for inviting me to come to Atlanta with you and Mama, I have had a ball and I hope we didn't spend too much of your money at Lenox Mall today but you know how Prentice women are. We just had to have the best so what did you and Uncle Andy have to talk about last night that we ladies could not hear? I must admit I am impressed at what he has achieved since last I saw him. Well let me get back to my room I must get ready to go out tonight, I think I'll head over to Club 112 but first I have to see if Cassandra is at the Urban Grind, maybe she wants to hang out with a sistah. And if I get lucky I might just have a date to take me there, that guy I met at the funeral looks kind of promising so don't wait up I am a big girl and can handle myself.

Be safe Tammy and let the driver know where you are going just in case he has to come and pick you up.

Okay Mama.

Papa, what did you and Andy have to talk about that was so important you had to meet with him and all those guys late last night? Is there anything I need to know about?

No Connie, I got it all under control, Andy just wanted to have a word with me and the guys about the upcoming election and a few other things, you know, man talk. We just had to catch up on a few things and look ahead on the horizon and see if there is someone we might just be able to help get into the White House, that's all. By the way, I won't be coming directly home with you and Tammy tomorrow; I need to make a stop in the country to visit a few people.

Is it that time again already?

Yes Connie but not to worry I should be home later on Monday or by Tuesday early afternoon at the latest.

Okay Papa, but I always worry every time you have to go back to Warren County.

Well it happens to be a necessary evil Connie, don't let it bother you, besides by now you should be accustomed to it, I do it every year and it has been a year.

Okay, see you when you get home but be careful Armstrong.

Yes, Concierge please can you order me a car? Yes this is Senator Armstrong Prentice in Penthouse 2; yes I want to drop it off in Augusta probably Monday or Tuesday afternoon. Yes, no can't do the compact thing, can I get a Cadillac or that new fangled Chrysler 300. No the color is not important, thanks I will be down to pick it up in the morning.

18

I almost forgot what traffic could be like leaving Atlanta, I hope the girls are okay but I have got to get this piece of business done.

Interstate 20 hasn't changed much except for that new Mall they put up, Stone Henge, Stone Crest, Stone something and Conyers and Covington have grown so much it's almost like they are a part of Atlanta now.

I can remember my father bringing me up here visiting Daddy King and Mr. Dobbs right after I graduated from college, seems like yesterday, it's hard to believe that it was over fifty years ago and so much has changed. I must remember the next time to go back down on Auburn Avenue and see if it even resembles itself, it seems to me that with all the renovation going on that the black elite in this city would ensure that Auburn Avenue gets back to its old self. If it hadn't been for Auburn Avenue there wouldn't be a black elite in Atlanta, the ground work for their success was laid years ago along that very corridor. Maybe one day my people will understand the value of history.

The one thing that hasn't changed is the prestige of the Prentice name. It was good to see Joseph, Tyrone, John, Andy and the others while in Atlanta, I don't get to rub elbows with black royalty that often but I still got the juice, I still matter. Or is it that my money still matters? It's not really important anymore as long as when Armstrong Prentice gets a cold, the black elite in the State of Georgia still catches the flu.

Wow, the Oconee River, I can remember when this would mark the midway point between Augusta and Atlanta for me. I can't count how many times I've passed it going in both directions, who would know that less than twenty miles from this very spot lies the infamous Reynolds Plantation where President George Bush resides when he visits Georgia. It's funny how the most powerful man in the free world sleeps on a plantation when he comes to the South, if only he knew that Reynolds Plantation was originally known as "Crackers Neck".

Highway 278 welcome to Warrenton, not much has changed here in Warrenton, the Knox Theater is still standing and I can remember when blacks weren't allowed in there, years later they were only allowed in the balcony, white folks never knew that the best seats were up there anyway.

I see Mrs. Jane's Restaurant is still operating, I can also remember when blacks weren't allowed in there either except to cook, but today if you want country cooking at its best anywhere from Atlanta to South Carolina, this is the place to get it.

Well I can't show up until after sundown so I might as well drive around town for a minute. I think Granddaddy's land was around here; yep there it is Bray Street, there it is what is left of Granddaddy's place. It looks the same just a little smaller than I remember, or was I small then? I remember Mr. Chunk had a small store right across the street.

As kids we would run up and down this street, can't remember whether or not it was paved then, I actually think not. I remember there being no street lights and it would get so black you couldn't see your hands in front of your face. I can close my eyes right now and remember the smells of the cranberry, plum and peach trees that surrounded the yard, I can still taste the sour grass.

It's been an entire year; I may as well get this over with, this is my turn right here.

Armstrong drives back, deep into the woods to a little hut that looks as if it's misplaced in the middle of what was once a huge cotton field. The lights are dim and he can make out the silhouettes of two other cars, he recognizes the first one right away as belonging to Walter Johnson, the head of the Johnson clan and a friend of the family from as far back as he can remember. He and Walter once played together as kids while their fathers attended meetings in this same little hut years ago, the only thing that has changed is that he and Walter are the family representatives now. The other car must belong to his son.

Knock, knock, knuckle, knock, knock.

The door opens and Armstrong is greeted with a smile and the fragrance of aged Cognac and Cuban Cigars.

Come in Armstrong, come in, you remember my son Franklin, come on in and rest yourself let me get you a drink and a stogie. How has the year been treating you?

Armstrong embraces Walter and as they look into each other's eyes they know that there has never been and can never be any bullshit between the two of them not if their lives are to remain the same.

Welcome home Armstrong.

19

I'm sorry Dr. Prentice but I tried to reach Mr. Rice to get him to reschedule but he states that it's a matter that demands your attention and he has already arrived, what shall I tell him?

Send the man in Sonya, I'll speak to him but after fifteen minutes interrupt us and tell me that I have another meeting to attend.

Will do Dr. Dr. Prentice, this is Mr. Rice.

Good afternoon Dr. Prentice and thanks for taking a minute out of your busy schedule to meet with me.

How may I be of assistance to you Mr. Rice, do you have a student here at Laney?

No, Dr. Prentice not at all, this has nothing to do with the school, it's actually a rather private personal matter sir.

Go ahead Mr. Rice, what are your concerns?

Well, Dr. Prentice, my name is Jamie Rice and I was in the area from Savannah and happened to pass by the school, saw your name on the marquee and was wondering if you were related to Mr. Armstrong Prentice?

Yes Mr. Rice, Armstrong Prentice is either my father or my brother and may I ask what that has to do with me?

Well Dr. Prentice, I am a private investigator looking into the Anthony Leakes murder case and everywhere I turn the name Armstrong Prentice, your father, seems to surface. It just seems a little odd that his name invokes more than a little passion when mentioned in Savannah or here in this city.

Well Mr. Rice, if you were any good as a private investigator then you would know that my father is a very important man in this town and in this State for that matter. But I don't get involved in my father's affairs so will that be all? Besides the Leakes case has been closed for over two years now, why the inquiry?

Well Dr. Prentice, my client.

Who is your client Mr. Rice?

I am not at liberty to say.

Well I am no longer at liberty to waste my time with you; I'll see you to the door Mr. Rice.

Dr. Prentice, may I please have another two minutes of your time so that I can put this matter to rest for my client?

Go right ahead Mr. Rice . . . . you have two minutes.

Well, it seems that there has been talk of a possible civil wrongful death lawsuit that, as you know, does not have to meet the same burden of proof as the criminal case did, and I just thought the family might want to be informed.

Okay Mr. Rice, consider us informed and thank you for being so kind but I am a very busy man and your two minutes are up.

Where can I find your sister Dr. Prentice, I believe her name is Tammy?

Mr. Rice, I will say this one time and one time only and I really insist that you ask around town and find out exactly what tree you are considering climbing, the fall will be much worse than the climb I can assure you. You are speaking of my sister Mr. Rice and Tammy has been through enough anguish where this case is concerned, I forbid you saying anything to her, as a matter of fact Mr. Rice, this meeting is over and you will forget about my sister and anything else having to do with that case. Please take this kind advice and back off, you need to remain in your league.

Dr. Prentice I do believe you may be making a mistake.

No Mr. Rice, you made the mistake by coming here, now please, have a good day sir. Sonya, see Mr. Rice out.

(Dialing the phone)

May I speak to Captain Prentice please, it's his brother Martin.

Just a minute sir.

20

THE CIVIL WAR

Washington wants me to move my men through Alabama and capture Mobile; however since Admiral Farragut closed Mobile Bay the port is no longer of any military significance, instead I am going to proceed Southeast from here toward either Savannah or Charleston. My first obligation is to my men and I must ensure that they can be fed and that the livestock can forage. President Lincoln has just won the election and General Grant has finally given us permission to proceed.

Sir, we just got word that General Hood has abandoned Atlanta and is headed towards Chattanooga.

I already anticipated his move, General Hood hasn't the guts to enter Tennessee; he just wants me to spend another six months fighting over land that I have already fought for and won, that's the main reason I sent General Thomas to Nashville so that he could deal with General Hood if he was foolish enough to go there. No, General Hood will not go to Tennessee he would rather abandon the entire State of Georgia; I predict that he will head towards Alabama, which is why we will head South.

General Howard, I want you to take the Fifteenth Corps under Peter Osterhaus and Francis Blair's Seventeenth Corps and General Slocum I want you to take Jefferson C. Davis' Fourteenth Corps and Alpheus Williams' Twentieth Corps with Judson Kilpatrick's Cavalry and the Gold train. We will split into two wings and proceed by different routes but will stay no more than forty miles apart.

General Howard, gather your men and head towards Macon, and General Slocum I want you and your men headed towards Augusta. Keep your sentries' alert because I just might decide to take the Capitol at Milledgeville. General Slocum may I have a word with you sir? General Slocum we have been through a lot during this campaign and will probably go through a lot more, there is no way the South can prevail during this war. This is about more than slavery General; this is about President Lincoln's new vision for the South and for this Country. General Kilpatrick's cavalry must get through with the

Gold no matter what. Load the rails at the rail yard and have his men ride alongside it until it reaches your contingent in Augusta then wait for further instructions from me. I haven't exactly figured out how to get it back up North unless we can get it loaded onto a frigate in Savannah. Do you understand General? This is your primary responsibility, get the Gold Train through. What is your plan?

General Sherman sir, look at this map, I can take the rail from Decatur, through Greensboro, and then to Washington, Georgia which is only a day and a half ride from Augusta. I can hold up in that area until I hear from you and determine the next move.

Sounds good General, we move out at zero four hundred hours, send General Kilpatrick to the rail yard to load and guard the Gold, I want them to move out at zero three hundred hours. Have them wait in Washington until you get word from me to proceed.

21

JOHNSON PLANTATION

I never thought I'd live to see the day that I would take arms up against my brother and other members of the Johnson clan, this civil war will continue to go on until it has destroyed every family in the South.

Massa Johnson, Mordicai was on the train with Missy coming from Richmond when dey heard that General Sherman was on his way from Lanta and was burning everything in his path, what we gone do Massa?

Go fetch Mordicai; I want to know what all he heard.

Yassa Massa.

Mordicai, tell me what ya heard on the train wit Missy.

Well Massa I was in the back with the other niggers and theys all talking bout Lincoln freeing da slaves and all, and dey says General Sherman was already in Lanta and coming dis way, said he burnt all along the way and dat dey was coming on horseback, by train and walking. Is we gonna be free Massa? Massa what dat mean us being free?

Go back to your chores Mordicai; I need to think right now, I need to think, tell Boregard to come and see me in the big house.

Yassa Massa.

Boregard, I want you to get on your best horse and go tell Mr. Roberts, Mr. McGregor, Mr. Warren and Mr. Burkhalter to meet me at the Mason Hall right away, its important.

Yassa Massa.

22

Quiet down, quiet down, we're all in a panic right now but we have to quiet down so we can think this thing out. Now I just got word from outside Atlanta that General Sherman is indeed on the way and that he is destroying everything in his path. Hear tell they are stealing all they can get their hands on and raping women and carrying on something fierce. We must have a plan. Now I can hide all the womenfolk in the woods on my plantation, we have enough food and supplies for them and the chillun. I can also hide most of the slaves but I hear some of them in South Carolina and Tennessee are joining the Union forces and helping them kill white folk. Now I know we been treating our slaves like part of the family all this time and I don't anticipate nothing like that happening here but we must prepare none the less. I hear that they have a train headed this way supported by about two hundred or so men. My question is why are they headed this way and what is on that train that's so important that they got to have it guarded by so many soldiers. There's nothing of strategic value in this part of the State, why are they coming here? Anyway my services are available to you if you need it for your families and your property, just let me know, in the meantime if you hear anything else contact me immediately. We are in this together and we did not work so hard for this land to watch it destroyed by a bunch of damn Yankees.

Boregard get the horses and let's head back home. Gentlemen we will meet here again tomorrow night to see what we can come up with, God be with all of you, the South will rise again.

23

Boregard Johnson was more than just a slave to Massa Johnson, I mean the two of them were both nursed and taken care of by Mammy Brown who raised them both from suckling babies. They had seen a lot together and trusted each other more so than any outside man could understand. These two had a special bond and that bond would transcend through their descendants and through decades of turmoil. Yes these two were as close as brothers, as close as brothers ever were.

Boregard, you heard what was said back there, do you have any ideas about anything?

No sir Massa.

Forget the Massa crap Boregard we are alone now.

Well no I don't sir. But I did find it interesting that they would be sending a train this way guarded by so many soldiers. It really doesn't make any sense, if they are heading south it would seem like they would be headed towards either Augusta or Savannah. Warren nor Wilkes County has nothing of any strategic value to offer any combat hardened General.

I see, well spoken Boregard, Fessa Brown taught you more than any school could have thought of Boregard, thanks to him most of the slaves and white folk on Johnson Plantation can spell their names, cipher and read, I never understood why they fight so hard against teaching slaves anyway, the more education a man has the more valuable he is as well.

That's just it sir, we are not seen as men just property sir, mere chattel.

I'll never be able to understand that Boregard, but the law is the law, however I must say that I do miss Fessa Brown, he was the smartest black man ever heard of in these here parts. There should be something tangible to remember him by, actually when I hear you talk with understanding that within itself is something tangible, but as usual nobody must ever know that most of you are educated so again, we have to keep that to ourselves.

Tell you what Mr. Johnson, I have some kin up near Greensboro on the Oconee River, which is where the train would have to make an overnight stop, I have some kin up there that work as stable hands at the train station that just might be able to listen in on that train. Who knows they might be able to give us some information we can use to decide what our next move should be.

Good idea Boregard, how long would it take you to get up there and back?

Well it's a good two days ride but I can make it in a day if you let me take my boy Prentice with me, he's much younger and could get the information back to you much faster, time is of the essence.

Ok Boregard leave tonight, that should put you on the river before the train arrives. Take this pass for you and Prentice and get Mammy to fix you some food from the big house, but be careful Boregard, be careful.

They shake hands and look deep into each other's eyes . . . . be careful Boregard . . .

24

Captain Prentice

Hey Strong! What's up man?

Nothing, little brother just keeping the city safe as usual, what's up with you, it must be important for you to call me here at the office?

Well, I just had a visit from a Private Detective from Savannah by the name of Jamie Rice and he calls himself warning us about a possible civil suit against Tammy in that Anthony Leakes murder case, he also seems to be fishing in a pond that may include you and Daddy.

From Savannah, man I thought that was a done deal, have you mentioned anything to the old man yet?

Nope, thought I'd touch base with you first.

Good, don't say anything to him just yet, let me see what I can find out about this Jamie Rice.

This Rice fellow also mentioned that he wanted to talk to Tammy, I let him know that she had been through enough and that I forbid him speaking with her but I don't think I was convincing enough, he seems to be a little stubborn, anyway you got the ball now Captain Prentice but let me know if you speak to the old man about any of this, I'd really like to be kept in the loop this time.

Okay Marty, I will see to that, I just want to look into the background of this Jamie Rice, I got some connects in Savannah and I promise to keep you looped, peace.

Jamie Rice, I know this is not happening all over again. Who is this guy and why is he searching for information concerning this case? I know I have Teddy's information somewhere in this rolodex. Yes here it is, Detective Teddy Taylor, Jr., Chatham County Police Department.

Yes, may I please speak with Detective Taylor; tell him it's Captain Prentice from Augusta.

Hello, well I'll be damned, Strong, man it's been a while since I've heard from you, how long has it been, two years, how's the family and how is Tammy doing?

Actually Ted, that's why I'm calling, the family is fine but there is a Private Detective snooping around here by the name of Jamie Rice, does that name ring a bell with you?

Unfortunately it does man, a couple of years ago Mr. Rice and I had a few issues if you get my meaning, he's a Private Detective but kind of on the shady side. I thought he was here in Savannah, why would he be up there in your neck of the woods?

That's what I need help with man; he stopped by the school and talked with Martin about a possible civil suit concerning the Anthony Leakes case and Tammy, have you heard anything?

Nope not at all, if I had you would have been the first to know man and you know this. Besides that case is old news, Anthony was from Savannah but I don't know if he still has family here, no one showed up at the trial that I can remember.

Yep that's the way that I remember it as well could it be the other woman, what was her name Nikki Parks?

I don't think so she had no claim to him except for being his alleged fiancé.

Look Teddy, I need a favor man, I need to talk with this guy while he is here on my turf. Can you get with someone that might be able to get me a description of the car he might be driving and if possible the license plate? I really need to find out what this guy is up too and who is behind this mess.

If it were anyone else man I would say not no, but hell no, but we go all the way back to second grade man and loyalty means something to me. I'll see what I can come up with so chill until I hit you back, and man, sorry to hear that you are going through this crap all over again, stay up and kiss Tammy and Cheryl for me.

I will man, peace.

25

Hey Strong, Teddy, I got that information you asked for earlier, I also put the word out that I need information concerning who might be behind all of this and right now I keep coming up empty but I will continue to look.

Did you find out anything about the vehicle he might be driving?

Yes I did, he should be in a Beige Mitsubishi Diamante with Chatham County, Georgia license plate FAM 357.

Thanks Teddy, I owe you one man, I really owe you on this one.

Keep me informed man and let me know if you need anything else, peace.

Mrs. Hammond, get in here I got something for you.

Put out a silent all points on Mr. Jamie Rice, he should be driving a Beige Mitsubishi Diamante with Chatham County Plates FAM 357. Do not apprehend, just locate and have them get back to me personally, oh, and let them know that I do not want Mr. Rice to know he's being followed, thanks Faye.

Okay Mr. Rice you wanted to meet Armstrong Prentice well you get your wish.

Captain Prentice?

Yes Faye.

The vehicle you are looking for has just pulled into the Harvest Table restaurant on the Gordon Highway.

Thanks, I know exactly where it is, I will be out for a while but you can reach me on the radio, inform the squad car to notify me if he leaves before I get there.

It shouldn't take me but a few minutes to get to the restaurant, just make this left on Gordon Highway at Red Lobster, pass the old bowling alley, pass Southside Terrace and bam, I'm in there. I'm actually a little hungry myself come to think about it but the Harvest Table has been the main reason Augusta is gaining weight. That must be his car over there. I have no idea what this guy looks like, so I will have to do a little police trick I picked up somewhere along the way.

Yes sir, I am Captain Prentice and I need you to announce that there is a Mitsubishi Diamante with Chatman County plates that has left his lights on.

But sir those lights turn off automatically it's a Mitsubishi Diamante.

I know that man, just make the announcement and I'll take it from there.

"To the owner of a Beige Mitsubishi Diamante with Chatham County tags, you left your lights on. To the owner of a Beige Mitsubishi Diamante with Chatham County tags, you left your lights on".

Excuse me, Mr. Rice?

Yes sir I am Mr. Rice, who are you? Wait I need to check on my car.

Not so fast Mr. Rice, there is nothing wrong with your car, I just wanted to take a minute to have a word with you, I am Captain Armstrong Prentice, we haven't met but I think you have been inquiring about me and my family.

If you don't mind Captain can we go back inside and talk, you can't get chicken like this everywhere you know.

Actually Mr. Rice, this is not a social call, I need to know what business you have with the Prentice family, who is behind your inquiries and to inform you that my sister Tammy is off limits for you and anybody else's questions. Do I make myself clear?

Well Captain Prentice, I see that bad news travels fast in this town, I was just with your brother a couple of hours ago, he seems to have a problem with me speaking with Tammy as well, can you explain that?

Listen Mr. Rice, I don't answer your questions you answer mine, now I have spoken with an old friend of ours in Savannah, a Detective Teddy Taylor and he has already given me the 411 on you and your sleazy operation, now what is this all about Mr. Rice?

I see you've done your homework Captain, I still think we need to either go back inside and talk or at least have a seat in the car, this is very important Captain Prentice, it's very important.

What is it Mr. Rice?

Mr. Prentice I represent an interest who is considering filing a civil suit against Tammy Prentice and for that matter the Prentice family for the death and cover-up concerning the Anthony Leakes murder case.

What cover up Mr. Rice? Or is this some conspiracy theory that you and some fool have come up with to extort money from my family.

Mr. Prentice, I promise you this has nothing to do with extortion I'm just representing my client here and thought it would be wise if I made my way back up here to Augusta to meet with Tammy personally and get her side of the story.

Her side of the story is in the public record Mr. Rice and unless you can come up with a miracle Tammy has nothing to say to you, as a matter of fact Mr. Rice, I don't want her to even know that you exist, do I make myself clear?

Well she is already aware that I exist but that's of no importance right now, look Captain Prentice I know that we can communicate on a much higher level than this, don't you think? We are two reasonable men here so there is no need for the threat of any type of violence.

Mr. Rice I wasn't threatening you, I don't have to threaten you and at least one of us is being reasonable, now I will need to know the name of this client of yours because I am sure we can come to a meeting of the minds on this matter and how does my sister know about you Mr. Rice?

Sorry Captain Prentice I am not at liberty to divulge that information, however since you claim to represent Tammy I have been authorized by my client to make you a small proposition.

And what might that be Mr. Rice? I however need to remind you that extortion is a Federal crime and I am an officer of the law, my oath states that I may have to arrest you if I were to witness a crime being committed, but to put it bluntly Mr. Rice I don't give a hot damn about my oath right now. What I need you to know is that you are screwing with my family and there is no way in hell I am going to allow that. This is not television Mr. Rice, I am Armstrong Prentice II, Chief of Homicide, and just so we understand each other, I can make your small ass disappear without a trace.

Would that be because you are a Prentice or because you are Chief of Homicide? Look Captain Prentice, I have been authorized to request a onetime payment of, should we say, two hundred thousand dollars and my client will just go away, my client will literally disappear off the face of the earth and if not I can also promise you that they will file a wrongful death civil suit against your sister and your family, by the way I don't scare easily Captain Prentice, you have 24 hours to consider my proposal I'm sure you can find out what hotel I am staying in so have a nice day Captain, remember you have 24 hours.

26

JOHNSON PLANTATION

Prentice I think we ought to leave the horses here, who knows what might be going on in the woods of Greensboro? Aunt Shines' cottage shouldn't be that far.

Paddy . . . . Paddy, it's Boregard, Paddy . . . . Paddy.

What are you doing up here cuttin Boregard, its black dark, your Massa know you done gone?

My Massa the one sent me up here, I needs to speak with Pokey, he still work the horse stable at the rail yard don't he?

Yep he still does blacksmithing work up yonder.

Get him for me Paddy, this is important.

Hey cuttin Boregard, how you and the missus doing?

We fine Pokey but I ain't got time for chattin right now have you heard anything about a train on the way from Lanta coming this way? I hear it ought to be here in a couple of days, you heard anything?

I heared a couple of white folks speaking on it while I was shoeing dey horses, but how did you know?

Don't worry about that Pokey, what else did you hear?

Not much really, dey talking about da Gold dats all.

What Gold?

I heared the train was fulla Gold, the Gold dem soldiers from the Noff done tuck from everybody, it's spose to be headed toward Washington County for to wait to hear from General Sherman hisself . . . .

What else Pokey, is they anything else?

Naw cuttin Boregard, but da train spose to be coming wit a lot of soldier's dats all, lots of soldiers with dat train.

Thank ya Pokey.

Look yall, me and Prentice gotta go now. And remember you did not see us tonight, you have not seen us at all, I'll tell the missus that I saw yall and that ya doing okay and I hope we get through this Sherman thang in one piece. If yall need to run you know where to find us, yalls family so ya always welcome. Prentice you got the information now go and head on back, ride like the wind boy; I will be right behind you but get back to Massa Johnson as soon as you kin.

27

Massa Johnson, Massa Johnson

Who is that?

It's Prentice Massa, Boregard on the way but he sent me on ahead with the information Massa.

Shhhhhhhhhhhhhhh, be quiet boy, it's got to be midnight, did everything go okay?

Yassa Massa.

Where's Boregard?

He coming Massa he sent me on ahead so I could get back to you faster.

Okay Prentice, head over to the hut at first light.

Yassa Massa.

(Later).

How far is Boregard behind you?

Should be here any time now Massa, my cousin Pokey, the blacksmith at the rail station, said he heard white men talking about a lot of Gold being on dat train, the Gold that the soldiers from the Noff done tuck for everybody, dats why the train is coming dis way so that it can wait in Washington County till General Sherman decides where to send it after that, it should be here in a few days, deys a lot of soldiers spose to be wit da train too Massa, a lot of soldiers.

Shhhhhhhhhhhhhhh, I hear a horse.

It's me Massa Johnson, Boregard.

Come on in Boregard, so did you find out anything else about the train?

Just that it's full of Gold and will have about two hundred soldiers guarding it once it get to Washington County, right now they have about fifty soldiers riding along with the train.

How you know that Boregard?

When Prentice left I went to the train station and nosed around a little, I overhead the station master telling a white man that the normal route would not be available until further notice. He said that the train had been taken over by the Yankees and he had no idea when normal travel would resume if it ever resumed, he then said that Yankee soldiers were on the way with the train and about fifty soldiers. The rest of the soldiers are supposed to meet up with the train in Washington County to guard it at the station.

Fifty soldiers, which would mean at least fifty guns . . . . Gold, Confederate Gold. There is no telling how much Gold is on that train. How many people have General Sherman killed for it and how many lives have been lost to his greed? Boregard go and round up the other Massas and have them meet me at the Mason Hall, we got some planning to do, we have to move quickly, so you get ready. Before you leave go get some food at the big house, you have earned it I'll see you when you get back.

28

MASON HALL

Gentlemen I have some information concerning that train that's on its way down here from Atlanta, my sources inform me that the train is supposed to be filled with Confederate Gold, Silver and other valuable items that have been stolen from our brethren and taken all the way from Richmond and everywhere else during General Sherman's march. Now I have it on good authority that the train will wait in Washington County until they receive word from General Sherman as to where to go next. Gentlemen I think we need to meet that train and show General Sherman's men some southern hospitality Warren and Washington County style is anybody with me?

You done lost your mind Johnson you are talking about a train that is probably being guarded by trained cavalrymen, there is no way we can win and if we did what would we do with the Gold, turn it back over to its rightful owners?

Yes that would be the plan to turn it back over to those that it belongs too, that would be the Christian thing to do. I am sure that General Sherman has other plans for that Gold other than turning it in to the Union, that's blatant thievery and we should do something about it.

By the way Johnson, where does your information come from? How do we know that what you say is the truth? I don't mind dying for Dixie but I at least want to know whether it's a Yankee or a Confederate bullet that gets me.

I promise you that the information I have comes from a very reliable source.

I need to know the source Johnson before I stick the rest of my neck out for a dream; I got my wife and kids to think about. All I got in this world is my land and I can't take a chance on losing it because of a pipe dream, I hope you understand Johnson but I can't be with you on this one.

Neither can I Johnson.

Neither can I, sorry Johnson.

As the room clears only Massa Johnson and Boregard remain.

They don't understand Boregard, they don't see the future here, and sometimes a man has to risk everything in order to make a better life for his family and there will be no better time than right now.

I know what you mean Massa, I may have an idea.

What are you thinking about Boregard?

Well Massa, one of the reasons that I went on and sent Prentice back here was because I wanted to survey the situation myself, first hand, I wanted to have a look at the landscape between here and there so I rode the train tracks back instead of taking the most direct route. I figure that if we wanted to take the train ourselves, the best place to make that happen is when it stops in Crawfordville to take on water, I figure it will be late and the men and horses will be tired as well, they would probably stay overnight in Crawfordville before making their way into Washington County. Besides they don't seem to be in any hurry to arrive here, if that was the case they would have ridden straight through. Before I left I asked my cousin to keep an eye on the train from a distance and to let me know when they leave Greensboro.

What scares me about you Boregard is that we think too much alike and it can never be good for a white man and a nigra to think alike but right now you have the best idea I have heard.

Boregard, Boregard,

Who dat?

It's cuttin Pokey.

Massa can you go in the next room for a minute, come on in Pokey.

I heard the train will be leaving Crawfordville on the way to Camak instead of Washington County. What dis all about Boregard, why yo Massa so interested in dat train?

Don't worry bout dat Pokey, thanks for the news, any idea when they will be arriving in Camak?

I hear da day after tomorra, they staying overnight in Crawfordville den on to Camak, be careful Boregard, be careful.

You too Pokey, now gone on ya way fore your Massa misses ya.

Thanks for erything.

Massa Johnson, Massa Johnson

Yes Boregard.

Massa we need to talk away from dis house.

Okay Boregard, go get the houses and let's take a ride.

What's got you riled Boregard, what is it?

You heard that they are planning to arrive in Camak instead of taking the train to Washington County, whatever we gonna do we got to do it soon, they are expecting the train Friday morning. We only got tonight and tomorrow night to do whatever we're going to do. I can get a posse of folks together and we can bushwhack the train before it gets to Camak.

How do you plan to do that Boregard?

I don't Massa; I'm just going along with whatever you plan to do, you know we can't get our hands on no guns or nothing like that and that's what we will need to pull this off. I know I can get at least thirty men that I can trust to keep their mouths shut but there is no way we can move unnoticed without some white men with us. Now the real question is how many white men can you get to go along with us that you can trust?

Not many Boregard.

Well you gonna have to get the ones that you can, trust me and get your hands on all the guns you can; we will have to keep this between my family and yours.

You know I trust you with my life Boregard, we've been attached at the hip since birth, there is no man I trust more than I trust you, white or nigra.

Then let's call a meeting tonight and decide how to make this happen, I think the perfect spot to take the train on its way to Camak would be in Barnette but we will need some sharp shooters, some high ground and a whole lot of luck.

Get everybody together and meet at the hut in two hours, remember Boregard they have to be family and we have to be able to trust them.

29

Mr. Johnson the train's on its way, they got about fifty riders with it. About ten riding ten miles ahead on the track, thirty with the train and bout ten are riding about five miles behind the train.

Boregard, you got your men set up to take the ten in the lead, hopefully with as little fire power as possible. Send Prentice and his crew to get those riding behind the train and with the rest of the family we ought to be able to take the train right before it gets into Barnette, be careful Boregard, be careful. I probably won't speak to you again until we get back to the hut. You sure you can trust your men with half the Gold?

No problem Massa, can you trust your kin?

Stupid question Boregard, I guess both of us are a little jittery, well let's get it done so that we can get it over with and move on past this night.

The first shot took the right side of the face from the rider and made it a permanent part of the railroad tracks. The second shot was never heard by his partner, no one could tell where the shots were coming from but the ten were now down to eight when the yell went out.

Before the bugler could make a sound his breath was cut short as a bullet pierced his throat and all that could be heard was a gurgling sound, the last sound that he ever heard. The eight were now seven. The remainder quickly made a futile attempt to find cover but still had no idea where the shots were coming from or could ever imagine that tonight they would dine in hell.

They had no idea that Boregard was more than just a crack shot he could shoot the wings off a butterfly in mid flight at more than fifty yards. Training gleaned from squirrel, raccoon and possum hunting. Boregard knew this hillside and knew it well, it wasn't far from here where he did some of his best hunting and fishing.

Boregard also took pleasure in doing his part for the Confederacy; he would do all he could to ensure that Mr. Johnson did not lose anything, besides they were like brothers.

As the other men fell Boregard could only wonder how Prentice was making out with the men at the rear. He hadn't much to worry about, he had taught his son well and they had planned their part in this down to the letter. The both of them knew it would alter not only their lives, but the lives of their children's children as well.

Boregard knelt down and placed a learned ear on the train tracks and could hear no movement, he knew this to mean that they had already stopped the train, he also heard nothing from the men he had left in the rear to alert him if something was amiss, he and the rest of his men galloped down the tracks toward the train.

Upon their arrival they could see that Mr. Johnson's men and Prentice had almost emptied the train and was placing the Gold and other valuables on the backs of nine plow mules.

Mr. Johnson glanced up at the sun and guessed that it was only about another twenty minutes till sundown, he knew that he would need the cover of night to get the Gold back to his plantation.

Boregard, take four of the plow mules and take the long way back, go around Brier Creek and enter the land from the lower forty acres and then meet me at the hut but when you get there don't bring the Gold to the hut, leave Prentice with it hidden in the woods, I will take the other mules with me and we will enter from the south on the Norwood road. Make sure we account for everybody, the last thing we need is somebody running their mouths right now. We will wait a while and make sure all these Yankees are dead and buried. They will begin to miss the train I figure sometimes later on tonight and I plan to be back on the land and well rested when they come to inquire, now get a move on and be careful Boregard, be careful.

30

How did things go Boregard, we okay?

Yes Massa Johnson, I left Prentice with the mules and he will stay there until I get back with your instructions, now how do we plan to keep anybody from knowing what we did tonight Mr. Johnson? They gonna know about the train after a while, what are we gonna do?

Well the way I got it figured Boregard is that they still think the train's going to Washington County, well we will just let them keep on thinking that and I will show my face at the Mason Hall to them tonight during our usual meeting, that way they will know that I had nothing to do with the robbery if it comes to that.

But Mr. Johnson what happens when we start buying things and such like that?

That's the beauty of it all Boregard, we didn't do this for us, we have always taken care of each other and I see no reason for that to change. Tonight after I get back from the Mason Hall I want you to bring your son Prentice to the hut and I will bring my son Franklin. Boregard this move wasn't for us but for our kin, we will continue to live the same way we have always lived. I plan to have both of our boys bury the Gold somewhere that only they know about and have them promise under a bond from God that they will continue to be as close as we are for the rest of their lives, and another thing Boregard, tell Mammy Brown to be there too and tell her to bring the secret.

What secret Massa Johnson, what secret?

Mammy Brown will know.

Mammy Brown, Mammy Brown, Massa Johnson wants you to come down to the hut tonight and he wants you to bring the secret with ya. I don't have any idea what he is talking about but he told me to tell you to meet us down there and for you to bring the secret.

My Gawd, my Gawd, I prayed and prayed that I would live to see dis day, thank you Jesus, dey is a Gawd.

Mammy what you going on about?

Don't sass me boy, just gone and let me be I tell you, let me be. Lawd it's been near bout fifty years since the old Massa made me keep dat secret, I told him I would take it to my grave unless the young Massa wanted it known. I don't know what done happened to make this day come but I thanks Gawd for it. I gotta get cleaned up and make sure I looks my best, that way if I get struck dead I'll at least be already dressed to meet Jesus.

31

I'm surprised to see yall back here at the Hall.

One matter has nothing to do with the other Mr. Johnson, this is our regular meeting night and we are still Masons, we don't have to agree on everything but we do have to show love and respect for one another.

Thank you brethren for coming tonight and let me be the first to apologize for the words and attitude we had here during our last meeting. I don't know what I was thinking when I spoke about that train but I still think it would have been a good idea. So what's on the agenda tonight?

I pledge that we go off the agenda tonight Johnson and try to make some sense about these Yankee marauders that will soon be in this area. What are we going to do about the looting and things?

Well I think what we ought to do is find somewhere to hide our valuables and get the women and children hid either on my plantation or someplace else. We don't know how many men are coming or from what direction, we don't even know if they are coming this way or what's going to happen but we need to be prepared for the worse I reckon. I still have my place available and think we should have sentries posted in all directions maybe twenty or thirty miles outside of town to alert us if they see masses of troops coming our way. They can light some hay to warn us or send one of their men back, whichever we decide, the last thing we need to do is sit on our hands and wait for the inevitable.

I think the sentry idea is the best, we can send four sets of three men in all directions and have them stack hay in the highest points and then if they see them coming they can light the hay and we will know what direction they are coming from and to get the women and children hid.

That sounds like the best idea for the moment so let's go with that.

All agreed!!!!!!!!!!!!!!!!!!!!!

All opposed!!!!!!!!!!!!!!!!!!!

Okay the motion passes and I pray that real soon this nonsense will be over.

32

Boregard, this is what we have to do, we have to bury the Gold in a safe place and hold it for the next generation, in the meantime we will just continue on like we've been doing, that way we won't have to answer too many questions when they find what's left of that train.

What you mean what's left of it Massa Johnson?

Well Boregard, I had some of my men drive the train almost up to Washington County, that way when they find it they will assume whatever happened to the Gold happened there and have no idea that we got it hid right here in Warren County. Here's my plan, we keep it hid for now then we can sell off some of it to expand the land here in Warren County and east of here in Richmond and Columbia County, my plan is to buy up as much land as we can so that it will always be in the family and Boregard I mean your family as well.

But Massa they ain't gone let no slave own no land in Columbia and especially not in Richmond County.

I thought about that also Boregard, I will buy the land and nobody will ever know that the land actually belongs to you, then one day when times are a little better, maybe not in my lifetime or yours, but one day things between our races will get better Boregard and then I can see to it that your land is turned over to your kin at no cost to you.

Massa Johnson, Massa Johnson, Mammy Brown said she is ready at the hut, told me to fetch you and Boregard.

Thanks Prentice, tell her were headed that way now.

Did you bring the secret Mammy?

Yassa Massa but what call for that information now? Your Pappy wanted me to keep this information and take it to my grave with me if you never asked to hear it yourself. I sho don't want no trouble Massa but a promise is a promise.

Mammy Brown you knew that from the very beginning there was a bond between Boregard and I and I can remember my Pappy telling me that one day I would need to know the truth. Today is that day Mammy, now is the day when I need to know the truth that my Pappy was speaking on. I need to know now Mammy, I need to know now!

Lawd a mercy, well Massa, you wonder why you and Boregard ain't ever been apart since you was birthed? I suckled the both of you like you was my own, yall have always been close and played together all ya lives. I've watched the both of you grow into strapping men and I know now that your Pappy was right, he just didn't want anybody else to know about it being the truth. There has always been talk but I know the secret and now the both of you will know it. Massa Johnson, you and Boregard is half brothers. You both gots the same Pappy which means you have the same blood flowing through your veins. I knew that when I buried both of your Mammies' that it would be left up to me to share the secret with you and I hope by your Pappy that I done the right and honorable thing. This information was to bring you closer together not separate you now especially now when you gonna need each other more than ever with dat General Sherman and his burning mess. Yall gonna need each other more than anything. Now I'm quine head back to the big house Massa and get ya supper ready.

Thanks Mammy and, if you don't mind, set another place at the table for my brother. Well what do you think Boregard?

I don't exactly know what to think Mr. Johnson. I mean what does all this mean?

It's simple Boregard, it means that everything you see, as far as your eyes can behold is land that is partially yours and your families, and I'm gonna see to it that we do the right thing. Regardless of how this war turns out, we can always stay right here on this land and live out the rest of our lives, we are blood Boregard and I am honored to have such a man as yourself as my brother.

Well thank you kindly Massa Johnson; I must say that I am pleased as punch to have you as kin myself.

But again, let's keep this a secret between you and me and one day soon we will share it with our most trusted man child. I know how you feel about Prentice and I must admit that Franklin has represented himself quite well too; I just might make him my heir.

Same here Mr. Johnson, Prentice has become quite a man, he is so ambitious, let me know when the time comes.

I will do that and remember that only one heir must ever hold deed to the land Boregard, that way we can keep the secret safe and only between the families, when the time is right we will know it, until then we'll just keep on as if nothing has changed.

33

(Doorbell ringing).

Now, who could that be at my door this time of the morning, well actually it is afternoon, but why are they beating on my door like they five-0 or somebody. What tha , , , , I know I heard somebody beating on this door just a minute ago but I don't see anybody around . . . what's this? Somebody left me a letter.

Dear Tammy: Its been such a long time since we've talked and I just wanted you to know that I forgive you and that I miss you so much, I also what you to know that I have been watching over you and that I am always near you and the love we shared stays on my mind, love Tony.

That signature, that cologne, Oh Tony, Tony . . . . wait a minute, is this someone's idea of a joke. Who would do something like this? Who could be that trifling?

Yes, this is Tammy Prentice and I need to speak with Captain Armstrong Prentice.

Just a minute Ms. Prentice.

Hey Tammy, what up Sis?

Strong, somebody left a letter on my doorstep and it has Tony's signature and smells like his cologne, what should I do, I am about to lose my mind, what do I do Strong?

Just put the letter down Tammy I'm on my way out there. Just make sure your door is locked and don't destroy any of the evidence, I am on my way.

Ok Mr. Rice, so you want to play hardball I see, well batter up!

Officer Lankenau do we still have a line on that Jamie Rice?

Yes sir we do, last check he was parked on upper Broad Street near Harrisburg.

My sister lives in Harrisburg, have a patrol car bring him in, I want to have another talk with this Mr. Rice.

What's the charge Captain?

Haven't thought of one yet but I will, just have him brought in, the hard way and make sure he feels it.

34

So Mr. Rice, it seems that we meet again.

Good try Captain but it will take a little more than being arrested to intimidate me.

Nobody is trying to intimidate you Mr. Rice, I thought I made myself clear when I said do not go near my sister.

What do you mean? I haven't been anywhere near Tammy and I don't take orders from the likes of you.

Mr. Rice, someone left a letter on my sister's doorstep a couple of hours ago, of course you wouldn't know anything about that now would you?

No, I can't say that I do Captain, and by the way, with regards to our earlier conversation the price has now gone up to two hundred and fifty thousand dollars, you see a brother does have expenses.

Mr. Rice lets understand each other, I mean lets really understand each other, the first thing I want you to do, if you haven't done so already, is to ask around town and inquire exactly about who it is you are attempting to extort. I have no doubt that you are way out of your league, now here's what's definitely going to happen, you are going to get up from this table, walk out of that door, and head back to Savannah or whatever outhouse you slivered yourself away from and I am going to forget that this day ever happened. How does that sound and let me promise you something else, if I see you again anywhere in this town I will automatically consider you hostile and well, you get the idea. And just to make sure we understand each other Mr. Rice, two of Augusta's finest will escort you out of Richmond County, officer get this scum out of my station.

I'll see you soon Captain Prentice and be sure to tell Tammy I said hello.

Why you . . . . get him out of here now!!!!

35

Hello Mom is Dad around?

Sure son, how are you and Cheryl?

We are doing just fine; as a matter of fact I thought she would have called you by now to talk about the Mayor's White Ball, are you guys ready for this year?

Of course dear, your father and I got the invitation but haven't really slowed down enough to think about it, I know it will be fabulous but you know your father. Thanks for reminding me, Cheryl called and I was too call her back, thanks son, here's your father.

Well, to what do I owe this pleasure, it's not every day I get to talk to the future Chief of Police, and how are you son?

Ok, Dad let's take a break on the Chief of Police thing; there are quite a few other guys with more seniority than I have.

Yes son, I know that but you are the only Prentice in the bunch and that still carries a lot of weight in this city. Now I know you didn't call me to discuss politics what's on your mind Strong?

Dad, its Tammy.

What, what do you mean its Tammy, is she okay!

Well Dad, there seems to be something coming back to haunt her from that Tony Leakes thing, there is a Private Detective in the city from Savannah stirring up a little trouble, he actually had the nerve to try and extort two hundred and fifty thousand dollars from us in order to keep a civil suit from being filed against Tammy.

What do you mean civil suit. Well I never . . . . who is this guy son? And more importantly where is he? I am Armstrong Prentice and I refuse to be meddled with, where is he Strong?

Dad, dad calm down, I am on my way over to Tammy's right now and I had some of my people escort Mr. Rice out of Richmond County with a stern warning that if he returns here there will be hell to pay.

Well you told him right son, does he have any idea who we are? Does he know what the name Armstrong Prentice means in the State of Georgia and the entire South for that matter? Hell if a mosquito bites me in Georgia six people on Capitol Hill get malaria. Do I need to handle this one son or can you?

I can handle it Dad, I just wanted you to know.

What did you say his name was again?

Jamie Rice.

And he's from Savannah you say?

Yes Dad, but I said I can handle it.

I know you did son I just want to know who to erase if you find out you can't.

36

Yes, yes this is Armstrong Prentice and I need to talk to the Mayor.

Just a minute Mr. Prentice I'll see if he has time for you.

Has time for me! I am Senator Armstrong Prentice and by God he will make time!

Yes Sir Senator Prentice.

Hello Senator.

Yes, how are you doing Otis.

I am doing fine Senator . . . ah, sir, what can I do for you?

Well Otis, I missed you the last time you were in my fair city, actually it seemed that you were trying to avoid meeting with me, now tell me that it ain't so Otis.

No sir Senator, of course not sir, I remember what you did for me during my campaign for Mayor and the good deeds you have done throughout our great State sir.

Stop kissing my ass Otis I got enough people here in Augusta and Atlanta doing that already. I got a problem that I need corrected as soon as possible; I need to know that you can handle this for me.

Sure Senator, anything.

Does the name Jamie Rice mean anything to you?

No sir but I can look into it if you need me too.

Listen Otis, he is supposed to be some type of big shot Private Detective who is snooping around in the wrong backyard if you know what I mean. A couple of years ago my youngest, Tammy, got herself caught up with a rascal named Anthony Leakes that she ended up having to shoot dead. I'm sure you know the rest of the story since he was from Savannah; anyway it seems that here we are two years removed from that tragedy and now out of the blue this private dick says that he is representing an individual who is considering filing a civil suit against my baby for wrongful death. Now what I need to know is who the hell he is and who has brainwashed him to think that he can go up against Armstrong Prentice in the first place and have a snowballs chance in hell of being successful? I need to know who he represents and the best way to handle this debacle. I promise to remember what you are doing for me Otis and I mean that sincerely, I need you to remember that it's good to know a man of my means if you ever decide to graduate your political acumen from the City to the State level. Tammy is my baby Otis and everyone knows how I feel about my children. Tammy is the youngest and the only girl; there are no limits to where I will go or what I will do to protect her. Do you get my meaning Otis?

Yes sir, and thank you sir for contacting me personally, I will be talking to you shortly Senator.

Thanks Otis, I knew I could count on you, have a nice day.

Mrs. Hostos, get me the Chief of Police.

On the phone sir?

Hell no Valerie I want that son of a bitch here in my office now!!!

37

JOHNSON PLANTATION

Mammy Brown can I speak with you a minute? I got something weighing mighty heavy on my mind.

Sure Boregard, I knowd you would be by here foe long, what on your mind son? You know you can always talk with your Mammy Brown.

Well Mammy, its goes back to what you and Massa Johnson was talking about being the secret and all. I always wondered why old Massa Johnson and the new Massa Johnson always treated us different from a lot of the other slaves. When we go to town I can see a major difference in how wese is treated. We gets to eat just as good as the Massa hisself and sometimes right here in the big house. Why dat Mammy?

Well Boregard, you gots to understand that old Massa Johnson had a lot of respect for an old uncle of yourn; the one you hear bout called Fessa Brown. Fessa Brown was a free man who worked up Noff for part of the year and worked right here on the plantation for the remainder of it, that's cause he loved your Aunt Eleanor enough to work right long side her here on the plantation until the day she died. He was also considered to be the smartest nigra in all dese parts and he was sponsible for the Johnson clan learning to read and cipher and work the plantation in order turn a profit. Boregard at one time old Massa Johnson was just a little more than white trash hisself, the only thing he had that was worth anything was his slaves. When Fessa Brown come down here from Philadelphia he walked right up to old Massa Johnson and presented hisself like a fancy dan, a real man son, an equal. Old Massa Johnson respected him for the way he carried hisself he told old Massa Johnson that he would come down here for six months out of the year so that he could be next to your Aunt Eleanor and dats what he done.

You mean to tell me that Fessa Brown was a free man and not a slave?

Yes boy, Fessa Brown was a free man with all the papers to prove it. Old Massa let him come down here and work and he was responsible for this farm finally turning a profit. He taught old Massa how to irrigate the crops and how to plant different crops in different pastures so not to take all the minerals out the ground and he taught old Massa's daughter Elizabeth how to read and cipher and she went on to be the belle of the ball when it come to education. It was Elizabeth who convinced old Massa to let all his slaves learn to read and write, she taught them herself at that one room school house that we used as a church. Elizabeth and Fessa Brown is responsible for all dat and old Massa appreciated him for being the man that he was. Even white men in town respected Fessa Brown. Yep boy your uncle was quite a zample of a man.

But what I need to know Mammy is how can old Massa be my Pappy? I thought my Pappy was Armbruster Brown?

Armbruster was your Pappy boy, let the world know it. But your real Pappy was old Massa. Armbruster left this earth never knowing the truth, that was just how things was done in those days Boregard. Ain't anybody to fault for it, it is what it is and you remember that slaves did what dey had to do to survive. If it hadn't been for Fessa Brown coming down here courting Eleanor who knows how we would have turned out as a family. The Lawd works in mysterious ways, you hear me boy, it's the Lawd's work, you just be proud of your blessings. I mean what I say, word coming from up Noff that they fighting this here war cause of us, kin you imagine dat? The whole country fighting a war just so that we can all be free. I don't know what it mean to be free but I want it. Crazy folks in town talking bout leaving the County and going up Noff and such to live but not me. I'm gonna stay right here on Johnson Plantation for as long as the Massa say I kin, I know what side of my bread gots the butta on it besides I'm too old to go anywhere. Massa Johnson is a good white man and we all gots it better dan most. Nope, if the Lawd wanted me up Noff he would have had me birthed up dere.

Why did old Massa ask you to keep this secret for so long Mammy, why he ask you to hide the truth?

I don't know Boregard; it's just dat old Massa knew that the day would come when you and Massa Johnson would get so close that it come necessary for the both of you to know. I believe Massa Johnson always figured it to be true but never said anything until now but tell me Boregard what has happened to make him want you to know now?

Gotta go and find Massa Johnson Mammy, thanks for the talk.

Boy did you hear me? Why now Boregard?

Massa Johnson, Massa Johnson, can we talk sir? I'm just a tad bit confused.

In a minute Boregard, I got an idea what we can do with the Gold. Mammy Brown has been talking about wanting a slave church build next to the old school house on the other side of the slave quarters. How you feel about that?

Well sir, you know Mammy Brown, she never asks for much but she has mentioned wanting a slave church back there for quite a while now.

Yes, it has been quite a while and I thinks we need one closer to the plantation for the while folks in this area because sometimes the rain gets so heavy that it's hard to make it to the church in town and I'm sure the Parson wouldn't mind coming all the way out here as long as we keep the collection plate full. Boregard, my plan is to build both churches and bury half the Gold in the white church and the other half in the nigra church. I mean to split this between the families but we can't do anything until we know how this war is gonna turn out, so the only thing we can do now is start construction on both the churches so we don't have to have somebody standing guard over the Gold back at the swamp. How does that sound to you Boregard?

Sounds great Massa but as I said before ain't no white man gonna let no slave own no land no time soon Massa.

Just let me worry about your family getting your share Boregard, as long as I continue to breathe it's gonna happen the fair way, remember that Boregard, always be fair, the secret is to buy land; land is the only thing that God is making no more of, land will sustain our families Boregard, both of our families' both nigra and white.

38

Mayor, Chief Cherry is here.

Send him in Mrs. Hostos.

Well Mayor, to what do I owe this honor sir.

This is not a fucking social call Donovan; I had a call from Armstrong Prentice earlier today. Do you know who Senator Armstrong Prentice is Chief Cherry?

No sir I can't say that I do.

Well you will after this meeting, Armstrong Prentice is the most powerful man black or white in the State of Georgia and was the first black man elected to the State Senate in the entire Southeast; he was also one of the movers and shakers who put me in this office.

What does he need from you sir?

I need a line on some low life by the name of Jaime Rice; he is supposed to be some Private Detective who has no idea whose cage he is beginning to rattle. He would stand a better chance of surviving if he went to Atlanta and jumped off the top of the Bank of America building. That same Armstrong Prentice decided to call in a little favor and he is not the type of man that you say no too.

Prentice, where else do I know that name from?

That Leakes murder case a couple of years ago.

Oh, you mean the one where the debutante ended up killing her cheating boyfriend?

Yes that's the one, well the debutante, as you say, was none other than Tammy Prentice, Armstrong's daughter.

Ouch, but that case was closed Mr. Mayor and if I remember correctly she got off on self defense, so what's the problem now?

Well this private dick Jamie Rice claims to be representing someone who is considering filing a wrongful death civil suit against Ms. Prentice. He won't reveal who, if anybody, he may be working for. For all we know he could be pissing in the wind but even that fool has to know that you don't play around in a snake pit without getting bit. Senator Armstrong Prentice can be a Pit Viper when he needs to be, what I need is for you to find out all you can about this asshole and find out why he has decided on such a lovely day to screw up my afternoon.

39

(Phone Ringing).

Hello, Prentice residence.

Hi Consuela, this is Cheryl is Mama Constance around?

Oh, Mrs. Cheryl, it's been a while, how have you been?

Just great Consuela and how are those twins of yours?

They are doing just fine Mrs. Cheryl, thanks to Mr. Prentice they are both enrolled at the University of Georgia, hang on I'll get Mrs. Constance for you.

Thanks Consuela and congratulations.

Hello Cheryl, my goodness I was just thinking about you, how have you been girl?

Just great mom I had you on my mind as well, I know you watched the debate last night and I am so tired of all this mess. John McCain knows that he has no idea what this economy is going through right now, what does he have eight houses and thirteen cars?

At least child, nobody seems to want to talk about that crippled wife he left somewhere in Virginia I believe, he probably can't remember her himself with his old ass and don't get me to talking about Sarah Palin, you have got to be kidding me. He would have stood a better change choosing Barbara Walters or even Oprah to run with him, at least they know how to answer questions. My Lawd, we are in the last days for sure. What's on your mind Cheryl, got me blabbering on and such what's up with you child?

Well nothing really I was just talking to Strong and trying to get next month planned and all, you know the holidays are coming up and I just wanted to make sure we don't have any slip ups this year, I thought I would get with you and start making plans now rather than later, are Kelvin and Maria still going to make it this year?

Well, you know I haven't spoken with Maria this week but I'm sure they will make it. They better bring my grandbabies to me for the holidays; they are getting so grown nowadays. And yes it is a good idea for us to get together and make the plans earlier rather than later, we will have to do most of the cooking ourselves this year because I have given Consuela that time off since her kids will be home this year. Besides there's nothing like cooking holiday dinner in your own kitchen with both of my lovely daughter in laws and Tammy, I really love the holidays.

Yes me too, I was just reading the paper and saw that the Mayor's White Ball is next month; I can't believe it's been a year already. We had a great time last year and I remain so impressed with our Mayor, what do you think mom?

Well I haven't seen Deke in a while, well not since the dedication of the Jessye Norman Amphitheater anyway; you know they donated a building downtown to her the other week, I saw him but didn't get the chance to speak with him, and he was being all Mayoral.

So much has happened this year in the city that I still wonder what the theme of the Ball will be, I'm surprised that they haven't put it out there yet.

Well I was up to Paine College the other day and spoke with Dr. Bradley and he thinks maybe we should present the Mayor with an Honorarium for his community service, possibly during the Ball; he has done so much for the city since taking office from that traitor Doug Young. Armstrong seems to be pleased with his leadership and I can't find any fault in the man, to my knowledge he hasn't decided on a higher office yet but I'm sure he may be talking to Armstrong about that in the near future.

Do you miss the college Mama Constance? You could've been Dean yourself if you wanted the job.

I was content being the Associate Dean dear, my primary responsibility is to Armstrong and this family but if I had wanted to be Dean I would have been Dean, primarily because of my credentials but more importantly because of whom I am married too and I would never admit that to anyone that wasn't family you know what I mean? Being Mrs. Armstrong Prentice is a full time job anyway and I cannot argue about the benefits package.

Strong and I haven't really talked about it yet, he will have to be there and all but when those men get to talking they seem to forget that they did not come to the Ball alone.

Sweetheart you must understand that this Ball and all the other Dog and Pony shows are all about powerful men rubbing elbows, telling lies, getting drunk and making promises that none of them can afford to keep. A woman's place is on his arm and in his shadow during those charades. You should know that by now Cheryl, you and Strong definitely have been to enough of them to know which role to play and don't get it twisted sista; it's all about playing roles. Earn your Emmy girl I already have my Academy Award.

I know Mom but sometimes I get so bored just waiting at some obscure table in some forgotten corner of the Ball. If Strong were Chief of Police maybe we would get a better table.

That's true but I never knew Strong had that ambition, I thought he was content being in charge of Homicide. Hmm, I never thought about having a Prentice as Chief of Police but that's not a bad thought I must admit, I wonder how his father would feel about that? I tell you what Cheryl, why don't you and Strong plan on sitting at the head table with Armstrong, myself, the Mayor, his wife and a few other prominent people, how does that sound?

Oh Mom, that sounds great, but you have to do me one favor.

What's that dear heart?

Don't mention to Strong that I spoke with you about him and the Chief of Police thingy ok?

I'm sure you have your own reasons for that but, okay sweetheart okay, the Ball will give us a lot of time to plan for the holidays anyway. Talk to you later about what styles will be appropriate as soon as we know what the theme is. Gotta go sweetie, Armstrong will be missing his Tea.

Goodbye Mom.

I wonder what Cheryl is up too, I know that child did not think she was manipulating the conversation. I had already pegged Strong to be the next Chief of Police and that was the primary reason I tried to see the Mayor last week, anyway I'll talk to Armstrong about it now that I know there is an interest. Hmm, Armstrong Prentice, II, Chief of Police, that does have a nice ring to it.

You go girl, you just got invited to the main table at the main Ball of the year and won't have to worry about Strong coming down on you for pestering his mother. And who knew that I would be able to bring the Chief of Police thing up too. I think this calls for a bit of Chardonnay and a major or should I say Mayor Celebration? I can't wait for Strong to get home tonight and show me again why they call my baby Strong.

Purple teddy for a wildcat . . . . where did I put Strong's handcuffs I'm feeling like becoming a detainee, and as Bernie Mack can say "Ta Night", but what if he water boards me . . . . that's why I do Pilates, it is what it is.

40

Strong, thank you for coming, I don't know exactly how to handle this.

Don't worry Tammy, from now on I will have two plain clothes officers watching your place and they will be here twenty four hours a day until we can make some sense out of all of this madness. I just got off the phone with Dad and we will figure this thing out. Can I see the letter?

(Knock at the door).

Captain Prentice, Jody Grant from the crime lab is here.

Send him in officer, Jody this is the letter that my sister just received, get it to forensics and see what they can dig up.

Tammy have a seat and tell me everything you can remember.

Well, I was just, oh I don't remember exactly what I was doing but I know I heard the door bell and I also heard someone knocking on the door like crazy, so I looked out of the peephole and didn't see anybody. Then I opened the door and found this letter on the welcome mat. Strong what's going on? It is Tony's handwriting and it smells just like that Sean Jean cologne he always wore, I know the smell because I gave it to him Strong, I am so scared.

Don't be scared Tam if this is somebody's idea of a joke I promise you that I will have the last laugh. Is there anything else that you can tell me, has anything else seemed strange here lately?

Nope, just some hang ups on the phone and all but that always happens at one time or another. Strong, what did Daddy have to say about all this?

Now Tammy you know Daddy, he's just concerned about your safety and your state of mind; you were a mental case for a while after all that crap went down. So he's going to be Daddy regardless. It just so happens that he is the great Armstrong Prentice but any father would be concerned at this point. Now listen, I don't really want you going anywhere, if you need anything use this walkie-talkie to talk to the guys parked outside and around the corner. I don't want you just arbitrarily leaving the house just yet. I think I may know whose behind this, agreed?

Okay Strong thanks for coming over, I feel much better now.

No problem, of course you could always go out to Sandy Grove and spend some time with our parents, Mama will be worried about you as well. I don't know whether Daddy has told her already, probably not, but she always worries about you anyway. Glad you guys got a chance to do Atlanta the other week, must have been nice, and anyway gotta run. I will be checking on you later and Martin will probably be over so I'm Audi five thousand.

No you didn't say Audi five thousand, somebody just had an eighty's flashback you would always tell me that when I was a kid.

You will always be a kid to me Tammy; you will be my kid sister always and just know that I love you and there is absolutely nothing you can do about it.

41

Quiet Down.

Quiet Down.

Chief?

Good morning men, I just wanted to take a few moments this morning to come down and meet with you personally so that we can understand the matrix of what's going on here in Savannah. I just left the Mayor's office and he is extremely impressed on the progress we are making in keeping the crime rate, not only below the national average, but below where we were last year at this time. As you all may know, violent crime is down but we are still having a problem with burglaries of person and property. These home invasions are a direct result of the poor economic crisis that is prevalent in the country right now. I am not making an excuse for any of it; I still want the perpetrators prosecuted to the fullest extent of the law. I guess I came here to say thank you all for a job well done, by the way, anyone of you who has had any contact with a Private Detective by the name of Jamie Rice I would like to see in interrogation room number two immediately. I will be there for the next two hours. Sergeant Cook a couple of years ago a scumbag by the name of Anthony Leakes was murdered in Augusta by a young lady by the name of Tammy Prentice. The case was closed over two years ago when Ms. Prentice was acquitted due to self defense. I need that case file on the table in interrogation room two immediately.

Right away sir, help yourself to some coffee Chief.

Don't mind if I do, have any Krispy Kreme doughnuts?

Sir there is a Detective Taylor to see you concerning Mr. Rice.

Send him in.

So Detective what can you tell me about this Jamie Rice?

Well Chief, I attended Paine College in Augusta with Armstrong Prentice II who is the Captain in charge of Homicide for the Augusta Police Department; anyway I received a phone call from him just yesterday concerning this Jamie Rice, he stated that Mr. Rice was in Augusta stirring up trouble concerning his sister's murder case.

His sister, oh yes I see Tammy Prentice.

Yes sir, he asked me to find out what I could about Jamie Rice, actually sir, I have had a few run-ins with this Rice character myself and thought I'd help an old college roommate out a little so I sent Armstrong information concerning the type of car he drove and his license plate number. I was just doing a friend and professional colleague a favor sir, I had no idea it would escalate all the way up to your office. If you don't mind my asking Chief what's going on?

Never mind that detective, what else did he ask you about our friend Jamie Rice.

Well sir, he was concerned with the fact that Mr. Rice claims to be representing somebody that is threatening to open up a wrongful death civil suit against Ms. Prentice and he asked who he might be representing. Honestly sir, if I may say, this Jamie Rice is no better than an ambulance chasing Lawyer. I wouldn't be surprised if the client he is claiming to represent is Jamie Rice himself, he has a record a mile long; I am surprised he still carries a license in this City.

Thank you detective, if you think of anything else you know where to find me. It's okay to come to me direct, and I'm sure you will keep this conversation between us?

Sure, thanks Chief.

Well, well, well, okay let me get this straight in my head; Jamie Rice is stating that he is representing someone who is considering bringing a civil law suit against Tammy Prentice. The Chief of Homicide in Augusta is Armstrong Prentice II, and the thorn in the Mayor's ass right now is Senator Armstrong Prentice. What in the hell is going on and how did this fall in my lap. I see the court transcripts are missing, I vaguely remember the case.

Officer, catch detective Taylor and send him back to me, also send in Captain Sykes.

Yes sir Chief, you wanted me back.

Listen detective, this may sound a little bit strange which is why I asked your boss Captain Sykes to join us. Now C. P. and I go back to high school in Roanoke Rapids, North Carolina ourselves so I can understand why you did what you did with Captain Prentice in Augusta. I have no problem with that but right now I need to know that I can trust the both of you on this. Now C. P., you heard me this morning mention this Jamie Rice, well what really brought me down here today is a phone call the Mayor, my boss, received from Armstrong Prentice in Augusta.

But Chief, why would he call the Mayor, I just spoke with him yesterday.

No detective, I think you mean your old college buddy; I'm talking about his father Senator Armstrong Prentice.

Oh, the old man.

What can you tell us about him Taylor?

Well sir, Senator Armstrong Prentice is still the most powerful political machine this side of Washington, D.C., and nobody is going to challenge that, I've only met him a few times when I was at Sandy Grove with Strong, that's what we call his son, my college roommate sir.

What is this Sandy Grove?

Well sir, Sandy Grove is the Prentice estate just outside of Augusta, it actually sets on about four hundred and eighty acres of prime real estate, right outside the city.

Four hundred and eighty acres, now that's what I call living Chief.

Anyway sir, in Augusta there was always mystery surrounding old man Prentice; he was the first black man elected to fill a State Senate seat in the entire Southeast and could have been the first black Governor of Georgia some say. Instead after thirty years at the Capitol he retired and became involved with local politics and was the machine behind getting his friend Ed McIntyre elected as the first black Mayor of Augusta. Then Ed disgraced the office and was arrested and served some time for corruption, afterwards the old man just blended into the background, but believe me there has not been an election in this entire State that he hasn't had a major hand in. He is believed to be the most powerful man politically black or white in the South.

Wasn't that his daughter that was caught up in that Leakes murder case?

Yes Captain Sykes it was.

That was the strangest case I have ever seen in my life, she was never officially arrested, and the trial lasted less than two days and even today no one can locate a copy of the trial transcripts or even remember who was actually on the jury. Some big shot attorney from Atlanta represented her and it's my understanding that some back room shenanigans went on.

I noticed that too Captain, I have the police report right here, it's marked closed but there isn't a copy of the trial transcripts here either.

Okay, okay, so the man has a little juice and can make things happen, my question at the moment is what does Jamie Rice have to do with Armstrong Prentice and the Leakes murder case?

Detective, where is Jamie Rice right now?

Last I heard Captain he was still in Augusta, I have his home and office staked out already but there has been no sign of him yet.

See if you can find out who he has been associating with here lately, maybe if we can find this invisible client we can head off some of this mess. Right now Jamie Rice is the key and I want to get the Mayor out of my ass, my mouth is already beginning to taste like shoe leather. Get on it and keep me informed.

42

Augusta's finest; you must be kidding Captain Prentice. I know what went down the night Tony was shot, I was there! Tammy had the nerve to go to Nikki's house and confront her about Tony. While she was talking to Nikki, Tony pulled up and began cursing her out, that's when she ran to her car and got the gun. I gotta give it to Nikki though; she was able to calm the situation down by talking to Tammy. Then just as Nikki turned to go back towards the house a single shot rang out and Tony stumbled towards Nikki and eventually died from his wounds.

I was parked across the street hoping to spend a nice romantic evening with Nikki. Actually Tammy and I pulled up at about the same time. When I saw what was going down I was amused at first but nobody knew that fool would have a gun. Hell I thought I would just get to see a good cat fight. After the cops left I was the one who comforted Nikki. What nobody really knew is that I loved Nikki more than life itself and she is still crazy about a man who has been dead for two years. I will never forgive Tammy for ruining not only my life but the life of the woman I love. Now that I have lost her forever it's time for you to lose also Tammy Prentice. Yes you will lose and your family will lose too. Your family will lose the same way that I lost, the way I lost the family that I never had the chance to have with Nikki.

That little note she received was just the beginning, I plan to put you in the same Georgia State Mental Hospital in Milledgeville where Nikki has been since the trial. It's only a matter of time Tammy, I may be leaving Augusta today but I shall return, you can bet on that.

Since I am this close to Milledgeville I may as well stop by and see how Nikki is doing. I hate to see her in an institution but it's the best place for her right now. She really went ballistic when Tony died and that farce of a trial just sent her over the edge. I wonder if she will know me today.

43

Yes, I'm here to see Ms. Nikki Parks.

Are you on her visitation list sir?

Yes I am has she had many visitors?

Your name sir?

Mr. Jamie Rice.

Mr. Rice she hasn't had any visitors sir; yes here you are, I see it's been a couple of months since your last visit.

Yes I know, she wasn't feeling well then so I thought I'd give her time to rest and get her thoughts together, is there anything that I should know?

Let me get the Doctor Mr. Rice.

Mr. Rice come with me, I am Doctor Trina Boyce, thanks for coming. Mr. Rice you are not family so I probably shouldn't be talking to you about the patient but since you have been her only visitor there is something I think you should know. Nikki has repressed all memory of that faithful night a couple of years ago. In fact according to her this Tony person is still alive and I think she is too fragile right now to know the truth. Therefore I would appreciate it if you didn't dispute her mental place right now. If she speaks of him in the manner that may not be true, remember that it's her truth she is dealing with right now and we need her in a good place mentally, do you understand?

Yes Doctor I do, thank you.

Nikki, you have a visitor sweetheart, it's your friend Jamie, and do you remember Jamie?

Yes I remember Jamie, how are you Jamie? Did you bring Tony? Did Tony come with you?

No Nikki, ahhh, he is going to come with me the next time; he's still at work but will be up here to see you soon okay.

Okay Jamie, thanks for coming to see me. You know I have a birthday coming up; I'm going to be thirteen, I'm going to be a real teenager. Mama said I could wear makeup then and probably some lip gloss, are you coming to my party?

Yes Nikki, I would love to come to your party.

Do you like birthday cake? Mama said I could have a birthday cake, or some cupcakes, I don't know exactly what I want to have but it gonna be either cake or cupcakes and kool-aid. You gonna bring me a present?

Yes Nikki, what would you like?

I want some Naruto books and maybe a Zune so I can listen to my own music and not that elevator music they play in here. I got some Beyonce CDs and some Mary J. Blige and Anthony Hamilton CDs I could listen too. I'm gonna be thirteen. Are you coming to my party? I gotta go take a nap now Jamie, thanks for stopping by to see me. What was your name again? Do you know Tony? He's my boyfriend but don't tell my Mama okay? Don't tell my Mama that I got a boyfriend. I gotta go take a nap now . . . . bye.

Bye Nikki, see you the next time, take care. Excuse me Doctor, how long has she been like this?

Go ahead and cry son, tears have a way of cleansing the soul, how old was she today?

Twelve, but what's happening to her?

We're not quite sure yet, we have been examining her for the last couple of weeks, she was fifteen yesterday which is why I asked you about her age.

But Nikki is twenty six years old, what is happening to her?

Nikki is finding a place in her mind to hide all the pain, in her mind today being twelve is a safe age and place for her, who knows what age she will find comfort in tomorrow?

Will she ever be the Nikki I knew again?

That's hard to say young man but we do keep the faith, it would help if you prayed for her. She is suffering from what they call Post Traumatic Stress Disorder among other things. Just pray for her, that's all any of us can do right now, just pray.

Yes, I will do that; I'll be back in a couple of weeks. Thanks for your help Doctor Boyce, I really appreciate it.

Have a safe drive home Mr. Rice.

44

Captain Prentice, this is Officer Kimo Carrington, sir Mr. Rice is leaving the Mental Hospital right now, should I keep trailing him?

Yes Officer, trail his black ass all the way back to Savannah, I want to know where he lives, understand?

Yes Captain I understand sir.

Milledgeville, who in the hell could he be visiting in the Mental Hospital in Milledgeville? This is getting more complicated as the day goes on. May I speak with Detective Taylor please; tell him it's Captain Prentice from Augusta.

Hey Strong, what's up man, what the hell have you gotten me into? I just had a meeting with my boss and the Chief of Police, all of this over that phone call I got from you earlier. Who has Jamie Rice shitted on to make me have to smell it all the way down here in Savannah.

I don't know what you're talking about Ted, how did the Chief of Police get involved?

He is speaking on the Mayor's behalf Strong, the fucking Mayor man!

Damn, if the Mayor is in the middle of this my father has to be behind it, I'm sorry man I had no idea he would be running things all the way from Sandy Grove, I had to tell him what was going on because Tammy was involved, so what else is going on at your end?

Well I have his office and his house staked out, I will need to have a face to face with him if his ass ever turns up.

Well he just left the State Mental Hospital in Milledgeville I had an officer trail him to make sure he left Augusta and he was at the hospital for almost an hour, any ideas why?

Nope, not a clue man but I will look into it; if he just left Milledgeville he should be back here in a few hours, thanks for the tip man and I promise to keep you informed. Oh by the way, get my ass out of this Strong; I don't need the Mayor's office bringing me the heat man. My last name is not Prentice, its Taylor and it didn't get to be Taylor sewing motherfucking clothes, holla back at me dawg.

Okay will do. Hello may I speak to Dr. Prentice, tell him it's his brother Strong.

Yeah man, what's up?

Well I promised to keep you in the loop over this Tammy situation and I don't think we have a problem, I'm still doing some investigating and I had to inform Dad but looks like I may have it under control, at least for the moment.

So the old man knows, now you know Strong that could mean this could easily be blown totally out of proportion with him being involved, you know he is a fool when it comes to Tammy man.

Don't worry about it Martin, I got a couple of my best men keeping an eye on her right now and Mr. Rice is on his way back to Savannah, I made sure of that. What are you doing later on?

Well I'm gonna stop by and see Tammy for a minute but I got a date with an angel tonight.

What angel is it this time Martin?

You remember Cynthia Emanuel?

Yep, and?

Well we had a thing years ago and I have been smitten with her since Junior High School, she's always been the one that got away.

Whatever man, take care and remember to put a hat on the head without the brain man, don't want any illegitimate Prentices walking around.

No couldn't have that, the old man would have a coronary, holla at me later man.

Be careful little brother, I remember how you felt about Cynthia, she was the one that had you singing "In The Rain" by the Dramatics outside Allen Homes, handle your business Martin, I'll holla.

45

Detective Taylor, this is Officer Jay Jones; Jamie Rice just made it home.

Put him in cuffs and bring him to me officer.

Yes sir.

Mr. Rice, I think you remember me, I am Detective Taylor and I need to know where you have been hiding for the last couple of days.

I do remember you, where have I been? You're the cop, tell me.

I see you haven't changed your attitude towards law enforcement at all.

Who could forget you detective, now as always, if you don't have a warrant I am free to leave and I plan to exercise that right.

Sit down Mr. Rice, what were you doing in Augusta and who are you working for on this Tammy Prentice thing?

I don't know what you are talking about detective, Tammy who?

Don't play games with me Mr. Rice, you will talk to me now or I will lock your ass up for so long you will forget how to talk, do you understand me Mr. Rice, syllables will escape your mental existence, now can we talk?

You got nothing to hold me on detective.

Is that a fact Mr. Rice, well let's see, how does attempted extortion sound, and how about trespassing onto private property, driving without a seat belt, busted tail light, should I continue?

You have no jurisdiction in any of that mess that happened in Augusta.

Maybe not Mr. Rice but I can always hold you for extradition back to Augusta all it would take would be a phone call from me to someone I think you know, a Captain Armstrong Prentice II.

It would be his word against mine detective, his word against mine and I plan to take my chances on that.

Sure it would be Mr. Rice, a sleaze bags word like yours against a Captain in the Augusta Police Department who just happens to be the Chief of Homicide now let me see how I would vote on this one. Officers put him in the holding tank for a couple of days and let's see if his lips loosen up.

You can't do that detective.

Sure I can Mr. Rice, by law I can hold you for forty eight hours on suspicion alone and right now I suspect you of committing more crimes than I can name. Now do you want to talk with me or would you prefer spending some time with the dregs of society back there?

All right what do you want to know?

Who you're working for would be a good place to start.

I'm sorry but that's privileged information something like lawyer client confidentiality.

You are not a lawyer Mr. Rice, you're a scumbag, now is there anything called scumbag client confidentiality?

Cute, detective, real cute.

We still have room for you in the back Mr. Rice.

Okay, okay, I am not working for anybody, what now?

Why go and threaten Tammy Prentice?

Excuse me detective, is this Jamie Rice?

Yes Captain it is; ok go ahead with your interrogation.

Why go and threaten Tammy Prentice Mr. Rice?

I have my reasons detective, I have my reasons.

Do you even know Tammy Prentice?

That's not important.

Why her?

Look detective I have done nothing wrong and I want out of here.

Mr. Rice, I have all night, as a matter of fact I have both nights.

Has Captain Prentice filed any official charges against me?

No he hasn't as of yet but I can give him a call, do you want me to make that phone call Mr. Rice?

I know my rights and I want out of here right now.

Officer put this piece of crap in lockup.

Did he share anything before I barged in?

No Captain, nothing we were just getting started.

Sorry detective, I should have stayed out.

Well he did tell me that he was working alone but I still don't know whether or not to believe him. You know he is right I don't have anything to hold him on; there haven't been any formal charges.

Call Captain Prentice in Augusta and see how he feels about us having this prick in lockup.

Hey Strong, Teddy here, listen we just picked up Jamie Rice, he isn't doing much talking except to let it slip that he was working alone, I have no idea how he fits into this mess but I plan to find out. Do you need me to hold on to him for a couple of days? I can come up with something on this end to justify it?

No Teddy, let him go for now but I would appreciate it if you kept a tag on him for me. Did he say anything about going to the Mental Hospital in Milledgeville? Any idea what he may have been doing there?

Nope no idea at all, I'll let him stew for a couple of more hours then call him back in, maybe he'll talk then.

Tell him that if he comes clean I won't press the extortion charges.

Will do man, peace.

46

DAY OF JUBILEE

Mammy call all the slaves together out by the church, I want to have a word with them.

Yassa Massa.

No more Massa, Mammy Brown, Mr. Johnson is good enough from now on.

Whatever you say . . . . Massa.

I want every slave that resides on this plantation to hear me and hear me good. As you all know Warren country was spared the horrors of General Sherman's Army last year and we have all heard rumors that yall was one day going to be free. I would like to think that I have been a pretty good Massa to all of you and I want you to know that the day you have waited for has now arrived. On this day December 6, 1865 the 13th Amendment passed by Congress to the United States Constitution has been ratified by the States, in other words slavery is no more and all of you are free men and women. Now you have a decision to make, you can stay on here if you want to and although I can't pay you much I will agree to share all that you grow in the fields with you in exchange for yall staying on here to work or if you decide too you can leave like I understand quite a few others are doing. As I said before I think I have been a good Massa to all of you, I may not have been right all the time but I have tried to be fair to all of you. I want you to take the rest of the week to decide what you plan to do and if you plan to go or stay let Mammy Brown know and we can move on from there. Your Day of Jubilee has arrived and I plan to go to the big house right now and have a drink and celebrate for you myself. This day has been a long time coming. Thank the Lawd.

Mammy, have Boregard and Prentice meet me and my son at the hut, we have a few things to talk about.

Yassa Massa.

Well Boregard how does it feel to be a free man? This is the day you have all waited for. The four of us here in this room must promise from this day on that nobody ever knows about the confederate train or the Gold. General Sherman and nobody else ever knew what happened to it, they found the remains of that train up there near Washington in Wilkes County. We must make a sacred bond right here and right now, who knows tomorrow there might not be a slave left on this plantation but I need to know that our bond remains. This is the plan Boregard, I have already spoken to a broker in Richmond County and he had agreed to sell us one thousand areas of prime farm land and another one thousand acres to add on to the plantation here. The farm land in Richmond County will be yours Boregard for you and your family to do with as you please.

Massa I told you time and time again that dey ain't gone let no black man own no land in dese parts.

Times are changing Boregard and I know what you told me and I know you are right but they will sell it to a white man, a rich white man who they think will be from up North, a man by the name of Armstrong Prentice.

Who is Armstrong Prentice Mr. Johnson?

Armstrong Prentice is your great grandson Boregard.

My what?

Armstrong Prentice is your great grandson; he is your son Prentice's unborn grandson, that's the way I got it all planned. To keep people from connecting our families we will change your kin's last name from Johnson and Brown to Prentice and his first name honors your pappy Armbruster.

My son here will see to it that the land is purchased and when the smoke clears and Armstrong turns eighteen my son's heirs will see to it that the title is deeded to Armstrong. As far as anybody will know some man from up North will own the land outright. When Armstrong is old enough Franklin's grandson will handle the transfer of deed to him. What happens to the land is your great grandson's choice at that point Prentice. I know neither you nor I will live to see the land change hands but I promise you that it will be done fair and square, I promise that my will shall dictate those exact terms. The only thing I ask is that our heritage remain our secret and that once a year on my birthday our chosen man child will meet and discuss the progress and the future plans for the Johnson clan both the white side and the nigra side. Nobody outside of the people in this room and the one designated to replace us in this covenant shall ever know this secret. Nobody must ever know where our power base is derived from. Our power comes from the land and the bond that we have as a family, is that understood? Until that day comes when the land is turned over to Armstrong Prentice we will work your thousand acres in Richmond County and my fifteen hundred acres here in Warren County and continue to accumulate all the land that we can. That's how we will accumulate and sustain wealth and power Boregard, understand?

Yes Mr. Johnson that is understood.

I brought this knife so that we can draw blood and share this oath between the four of use. This little blood that I draw from each of our arms will be mixed in this Mason jar; after it's mixed this jar will be the symbol of our bond. The blood in this jar will remain with a little more added from each generation; this will bond us forever and keep the family line pure.

Remember only one of your sons must know of the secret. Only one son can be designated to replace you in this covenant; however we must not wait until it is too late to pass the secret on to the next generation. We must ensure that this is done as early as possible after the boy reaches adulthood and begets a male heir. He must dedicate his life to keeping the secret no questions asked!

47

Armstrong awoke startled as he remembered his meeting with the two members of the Johnson clan at the hut along the Gibson highway. He realized that it was past time for him to name his successor in the covenant as Mr. Johnson's heir had already named his son to succeed him. But who, I mean Armstrong II was in line to possibly become the next Chief of Police in Augusta and Martin hadn't acted his age in years although he has thrived academically he was still a kid at heart. The one person he really wanted to share the secret with and the one person he knew he could trust unconditionally was Tammy but she was a girl. No, the covenant would never go for that. A woman's place was on her man's arm or in his shadow, that's the way he had heard Constance say it time and time again. Could he trust this to Kelvin? They barely talked anymore, especially since he was so against Kelvin volunteering for the Army. Or at least that's what he wanted Kelvin to think; actually he was proud as a peacock that the boy stood his ground like a real Prentice, a man among men. His heart told him that he could trust Kelvin with this information, besides he was the only one of his children that had children of his own. He would carry on the family legacy, but how would he convince him to move back to Augusta? Who owed him a favor at the Pentagon up high enough to make this coincidence happen? Maybe afterwards he could convince Kelvin that the family business was more important than the business of the country. At least he had to try, he needed his entire family around him and he needed Kelvin now. Besides he missed his grandkids, he really missed his granddaughter Eleanor and his grandson little Boregard. And then he remembered who owed him a favor. He remembered a young junior General who he steered to become selected as the Chairman of the Joint Chiefs of Staff years before his time. Although he has since retired Armstrong figured that he still had a lot of juice inside the beltway and the fact that he as a Republican didn't come close to complicating matters.

Connie, Connie.

Yes Papa?

When was the last time you spoke with Sandra Milliner?

My God Papa it's been a while, I think the last time was during that reception in the White House for Nelson Mandela back in, when was it gosh, Papa I do believe that was in 2005.

Wow, has it been that long?

Yes Papa it has, what's on your mind?

Did we send them a Christmas card last year?

Yes Papa we always do.

Did we get one from them?

Yes Papa we did, what are you up to?

Well Connie, I'm not getting any younger and I want my entire family here with me. I was thinking about asking the General to help me get my boy stationed here at Ft. Gordon and away from that mess in Washington, D.C. I need him especially Constance. It's time.

It's time for what Papa?

I think it's time for him to formally replace me on the covenant, it's his legacy and then he can pass it on to Boregard.

Papa, I don't usually get involved in these matters but Kelvin will lose his mind if he knew what you were up too. I want them home too but if he knew that you had any hand in a transfer he might not ever speak to you again.

He is a Prentice Connie and its high time he started to act like one, I will not be denied!

Consuela.

Yes sir.

Get me General Colon Milliner on the phone right now.

Yes sir.

Well good afternoon General, and how's the weather inside the beltway?

Not sure Armstrong I'm actually in New York right now, Sandra and I are up here visiting some friends. To what do I owe this pleasure?

Well General, I need for you to do me a small favor. You see my health hasn't been the best in the world over the last year and I was wondering if you could call in one of your many favors from your Pentagon days and get my youngest boy transferred from there to Ft. Gordon here in Augusta. I kind of want my kin around me to help with the family business.

I see Armstrong but shouldn't he submit a transfer request through the channels? I can ensure that it gets approved, that would be no problem. What is his rank and how long has he been at the Pentagon?

He's a Light Colonel, General and he's done two tours in Afghanistan and has been back for a little less than a year.

When will he have a year Armstrong?

Now sure General, can you help me?

Armstrong you and I go a long way back, even during my days as the Commander of Forces Command at Fort McPherson in Atlanta. I really miss driving down to Sandy Grove and spending time out on the lake with you. Do you still have that cook, what's her name Consuela?

Yes General, she has been a part of the family for over twenty years; as a matter of fact her twins are at the University of Georgia. I am proud to have had a hand in that myself.

Armstrong, his name is Kelvin right the middle boy?

Yes General.

I can't make the move happen until he has been at the Pentagon for at least one year. But if he is on the south end of those twelve months I can get orders in his hand within thirty days, how does that sound to you?

That's great General that is just terrific. If you can throw in a Command for him that would be gravy as well.

I'll see what I can do Armstrong. Kiss the wife for me and tell her that she sends the most beautiful cards that Sandra and I have ever seen. Hope to hear from you both real soon.

Hey General let me ask you a personal question before you hang up. Were you surprised that you did not get the call to be the Vice Presidential nominee from John McCain?

Well Armstrong, I can share this with you if you keep it under your hat.

I promise.

Actually I did get the call but I couldn't see myself running against another brother, have a great day Senator.

Thanks again General.

Connie.

Yes Papa?

When did Kelvin get back from Afghanistan this last time?

I believe they got back in March Papa, why?

There is a good chance they may be moving back to Augusta in March of next year.

You have got to be kidding me; you mean my grand babies are going to be here with us. Armstrong Prentice I love the way you move old man, I love the way you move.

Tell Consuela that whatever she made for the General when he and Sandra were down here the last time to make it again and put it in the overnight for him at his Brooklyn address.

This will be a glorious holiday season Papa, I just can't wait.

Connie, I have brought the Prentice clan all together again and under one roof. A roof called Sandy Grove.

Papa since you seem to be in such a jovial mood have you given any thought to going to the Mayor's White Ball this year?

Connie you know that I look forward to that party with the Mayor every year, the best one we had was when Ed was Mayor. The Mayor's Mansion has never seen so many collard and turnip greens in all its born days. You think they ever tore down the barbecue pit that Ed and I built in the back of the Mansion? Man those were the days, I sure do miss him Connie, Ed McIntyre was the pillar of the black community back in those days, but money has a way of corrupting many a man or should I say the lack of it. It would seem to me that our illustrious former senior State Senator would have learned his lesson from all that mess, and then he had the nerve to try and get his son elected to a position that he was nowhere near qualified for. I'll tell you one thing; a Prentice will never be broke as long as I have something to do with it. My ancestors made sure of that and I think I have carried the torch a pretty respectable distance myself. Now I just have to convince Kelvin to take over the reins, it's not going to be easy, he's almost as stubborn as I am and he got it honestly but I need him now, for the first time I need my boy.

Well Papa, I think he'll come around, the children not only respect you for being the patriarch of this family but they generally like the old man as I hear them call you. You have done a great job with those boys, its Tammy that I'm still working on. Another thing Papa, do you think Strong is ready to be Chief of Police? I think he's pigeon holed as Chief of Homicide, he's held that same position for going on four years now, I was kind of hoping that one day he might even consider running for Mayor. Chief of Police can be used as a stepping stone, what do you think about that Papa?

Well Connie to tell you the truth that thought has crossed my mind a time or two and Deke is in his last term but this wouldn't be the year. The world is already in an uproar because Barrack is running. We definitely don't need to give the political landscape an overdose of color right now, maybe after the next election is over with we can think about it again. Chief of Police, now that's a possibility, do you think he would want the job? It's not down and dirty police work it's mostly a political position and Strong enjoys being down there where the rubber meets the road. Remind me to ask him about it. It does have a nice ring to it though Armstrong Prentice, II, Chief of Police. I must say it does just roll off your tongue.

Oh Papa, you are a card, you are definitely a card.

48

Good morning Mr. Rice.

How were the accommodations for you last evening, you know the city of Savannah prides itself on its charm and Southern comfort.

Ok detective you made your point.

Let's cut the shit Mr. Rice.

What beef do you have with the Prentice family or is your beef just with Tammy?

Look detective, I was up all night and I'm really kind of tired, can this wait?

Oh no Mr. Rice, I've waited long enough, spill it or you can have lunch back there with the fellas, now what is your interest?

Do you remember the Anthony Leakes case detective?

Yes I remember it quite well Mr. Rice, is that what this is all about? That case has been closed for over two years and as I read the case file I didn't see your name mentioned anywhere. Is there some new evidence that you have uncovered, anything that we should know?

Not really detective, you see I was seeing Nikki Parks.

How do you mean seeing Nikki Parks, wasn't she supposed to be Tony's fiancé in all of this?

That's what the newspapers said but Nikki and I had a thing going on, she was actually about to break it off totally with Tony when this thing went down. She was leaving him because she found out about him and Tammy. Tony was a playa but not a very smart one, what he didn't realize is that when you date someone like Tammy Prentice with her pedigree and background it's bound to get out. You see Nikki had some AKA sorority sisters who knew all about Mrs. Tammy Prentice so when they would see Tony with her or when they would kick it on the down low here in Savannah word eventually got back to Nikki.

Did Tammy know Nikki?

Not sure if she knew Nikki or if she just knew about Tony seeing another woman.

How did you get to know her?

Well that's where it gets a little complicated; I was initially hired by Tammy Prentice to follow Tony Leakes. We connected on the Web because she couldn't use a local private detective without word leaking back to her brother on the police force. She had an idea that Tony was cheating on her but had no way of proving it; she hired me about six months prior to the incident. During my investigation I observed Tony and Nikki on a number of occasions and then just so happened to bump into her down on River Street one evening while here in Savannah, we struck up a conversation, downed a few oysters shooters, enjoyed a couple of additional shots of Patron and had a nice walk.

You have got to be kidding me man, so you fell for the woman who was dating the man you were hired to keep an eye on? This sounds like some movie of the week shit to me.

It gets even more complicated, after that night Nikki and I became just casual friends, she felt comfortable enough with me to tell me all about what was really going on in her life and things like that.

So you are telling me that she knew that Tony was cheating on her?

Yes she knew but had no way of proving it, like I said things get even more complicated. After she found out what line of work I was in she hired me to trail Tony as well.

And you took the assignment?

Why not? This was the best of both worlds, I was a little strapped for cash at the time and this way I could double dip for a minute if you know what I mean. It also gave me an excuse to spend more time with Nikki. Did you ever get to see her detective? Did you ever meet her? She was the most beautiful woman I had ever laid my eyes on and the last thing she deserved was to be played by Mr. Anthony Leakes, she deserved better than that, she deserved me.

Go on Mr. Rice, so now you are developing feelings for a client of yours, how professional, how exactly did she feel about you?

Like I said after that first meeting we spent quite a bit of time together, weekends in Charleston and down on Hilton Head, she didn't want to be seen out in Augusta for obvious reasons but we had our moments there too. As a matter of fact on that dreadful night we had planned a nice rendezvous at her place, that's how I became a witness to the entire scene that night.

You were a witness? But you are not mentioned anywhere in the police reports.

I know, I was parked across the street and saw the entire thing go down but I stayed behind the scenes until the cops left, then I stayed with Nikki for the next three days. She was a mess and we got closer over the next eight months waiting for the trial. It's funny, she always said that Tammy would get away with murder, she was convinced that Tammy would walk and it drove her into a state of paranoia that I have never seen before, she was actually afraid for her life. Then after that farce of a trial she just lost it.

What do you mean Mr. Rice, just lost it? Where is Nikki Parks Mr. Rice? Where is she?

Nikki is in the Georgia State Mental Institution in Milledgeville detective and has been there since the trial.

She has been there for two years!! What's her prognosis?

Well they keep telling me that her situation may improve and it may not. She suffers from PTSD and is also quite delusional and schizophrenic. She is actually convinced that Tony is still alive; I can't stand to see her in that state detective. She has digressed to a young child and doesn't remember anything about that night. You see, that's why the Prentice family must pay. Tammy Prentice has gotten away with murder and no one seems to give a damn. I was then and I am still in love with Nikki, Tammy Prentice ruined my life and I think she should pay for that, she should pay for what she did to Nikki.

Mr. Rice calm down, you may need a little counseling your damn self. Do you know what you just said? You have just threatened Tammy Prentice in the middle of police headquarters.

I don't give a damn detective, the first amendment gives me the right to say what the hell I choose too and you can't hold me on intent but I will promise you this much, the Prentice family has not heard the last of me, you can take that to the bank.

Officer, take Mr. Rice back to holding.

You can't hold me forever remember that, you can't hold me forever.

Sir, I need to talk to you.

Yes detective, what is it; do you have any additional information on Mr. Rice? I still need to get back to the Mayor on this.

Yes sir, that's why I'm here, I just completed my interrogation of Mr. Rice and I think we may have a major problem. This thing is more involved than we could have ever imagined. I also think I perceived a direct threat to Tammy Prentice and the Prentice family.

You see Captain Sykes, Mr. Rice was a suitor of Nikki Parks and was there the night that Tammy Prentice shot and killed Anthony Leakes.

What do you mean was there, I didn't see his name anywhere in the police report?

I know sir but according to him he was sitting in his car on the other side of the street when it all went down. He was actually there to see Nikki on a personal basis, here is where it gets complicated; he was working for both Tammy Prentice and Nikki Parks. The both of them hired him to track Anthony Leakes.

Get tha . . .

Yes sir, as a matter of fact, he met Nikki while working for Tammy. Anyway its gets even deeper still, it seems that Nikki Parks lost her mind after the trial and is currently at the Mental Institution in Milledgeville and is as crazy as a loon. Mr. Rice was and is still in love with Nikki Parks and has sworn revenge on Tammy Prentice and her family.

Damn, this thing is not going to go away quietly is it detective.

Not the way that I see it sir, not the way that I see it.

Okay thanks Taylor; the next question is how to explain this to the Mayor? What are you doing for the rest of the afternoon detective?

No sir, I don't like that look on your face, this isn't fair Captain.

Let's go and see the Mayor, I'll drive.

49

Be seated gentlemen.

Thank you Mr. Mayor.

Now what can you tell me about what going on? Wait a minute; let me get Senator Prentice on the phone, is there anything he shouldn't know about this gentleman?

That's your call sir.

Well I like to lay all the cards on the table, that way our friend the Senator can't come back and say that we didn't disclose everything.

Get me Senator Armstrong Prentice on the phone.

Sir the Senator is on line one.

Senator?

Yes, Otis, and thanks for getting back to me so soon, I was almost about to fly to your office and have lunch with you.

That won't be necessary sir, I have you on speaker phone and I have Chief Donovan Cherry, Captain C. P. Sykes and Detective Teddy Taylor here in the office with me, they have Mr. Rice in custody and have completed their initial interrogation. We thought this was something you should know so I asked them here personally to bring you up to speed on this.

Great Otis, let me hear it all, don't leave anything out, remember this is my daughter we are talking about and I don't want any loose ends.

Chief?

Captain?

Senator Prentice I will let Detective Taylor speak since he conducted the interrogation himself.

Is that Teddy?

Yes sir, it is.

My Lawd, how have you been Teddy, I haven't seen you since the last time you and Strong were here at Sandy Grove, I was a great friend of your parents, are you doing alright son?

Yes sir, Mr. Prentice as well as can be expected sir.

Glad to hear it, glad to have you on the case for me Teddy, I know that I can trust you.

Yes sir, anyway Mr. Prentice is seems that Mr. Rice was a witness to what happened that awful night with Tammy and Nikki Parks. It also seems that Mr. Rice was a suitor of Ms. Parks and was working in the capacity of a Private Detective under hire from Tammy and Ms. Parks as well; they were both paying him to spy on Anthony Leakes as each suspected him of cheating.

Wait a minute Teddy; let me get this straight in my mind, this scumbag was hired by my daughter Tammy and then hired by Ms. Parks to spy on this Leakes fellow?

Yes sir, while working for Tammy Mr. Rice met and fell in love with Ms. Parks. Subsequently after Anthony died, and after the trial, Ms. Parks had a nervous breakdown. She has been institutionalized in the State Mental Hospital in Milledgeville since the trial. She suffers from paranoid schizophrenia and PTSD as well as other ailments. This is the reason Mr. Rice is seeking revenge, he blames your family for what has happened to Nikki Parks.

But we had nothing to do with that mess Teddy, how serious is he about these threats?

I am a little worried Mr. Prentice; you should have seen his eyes, from the looks of things he could use some counseling himself.

Otis, Otis, you still there?

Yes Senator.

Otis how long can we hold this fool, what can we charge him with? What about the extortion he tried on my son? How long can we hold him on that?

Well sir, we can legally hold him for another twenty four hours without charging him with anything, the problem is we can't hold him on intent. We could press the attempted extortion charge but he would still be out on bond within twenty four hours. In addition to that we could hit him with a restraining order that keeps him away from your family. Other than that Senator there's not much else we can do, he has actually committed no crime.

So your plan is to wait until he hurts my daughter or does something to my family. Otis I expected more out of you, I want results, do you hear me? I want results Otis, Chief, what is it, Cherry or Sykes, whatever, dammit, if you can't run that damn police department I can get someone who can run the damn thing. Now Mayor I put you in office and . . . .

Excuse me Chief; Captain, and Detective Taylor wait outside.

And I can put you out!

Senator, Mr. Prentice, sir please listen to me.

No you listen to me Otis! I want this scum held indefinitely; at least until I can figure this thing out, can you hold him for another forty eight hours?

I will see to that Senator.

Then so be it, that's far enough time for me to deal with this situation myself. I will stand for no interference from you nor that motley crew of misfits you call a Police Department Otis, am I understood?

Yes sir, you are understood sir.

Do I make myself clear Mayor?

Crystal, Senator.

Have a nice day Otis and enjoy what's left of your tenure!

Pompous Ass, Chief Cherry, Captain Sykes, both of you and Detective Taylor get back in here.

Yes sir Mr. Mayor.

I want the three of you to go out and get the best shovels you can find and dig me up enough dirt on this Mr. Rice to keep his ass in handcuffs, I need him to remain locked up until I can figure this thing out, if it extends pass the forty eight hour period, then let him walk out of the front door, than lock his narrow ass up again immediately and keep doing that every fuckin forty eight hours until I can get this thing figured out, do you understand? I want you to go out and turn over every fucking leaf until you find something that will keep this asshole locked up. The last thing we need right now, is for Armstrong Prentice to think he can call shots here in Savannah, am I understood?

Yes sir, but Mayor may I ask one question sir, why are you worrying about him calling shots here in Savannah?

Because when Armstrong Prentice cashes a check here the entire city of Savannah could go bankrupt, that's why Captain, any more stupid ass questions?

50

Mr. Johnson, glad you could take my call.

No problem Armstrong, I knew that if it was you on the line then it had to be important, what can we do for you?

Well Mr. Johnson I have a small problem and need to use one of my challenges.

What does this challenge consist of Armstrong?

Well, there has been a threat to the family and I need the threat removed without getting my own hands dirty, I'm sure you understand?

Armstrong that's why we had this means of disposal developed for moments such as this, we must ensure that there is never a threat to the sovereignty of either one of our families, besides turnabout is fair play and we owe you one.

Thanks man, I appreciate it.

When can we expect you?

I should be there by dusk tonight and is one hundred fifty thousand still the going rate?

Sure, that would be fine, have you decided upon your successor yet?

Yes sir I have, I'm putting the wheels in order to make that happen this year hopefully.

Good Armstrong, because as soon as he is in place the both of us can retire and enjoy the fruits of our ancestor's labor, I'm actually looking forward to that day.

So am I, so am I, see you tonight.

51

Hey baby sister.

Sup baby brah, Strong told me that you were going to stop by but knowing you it could have been next week, so what up with the pimpin Principal?

Hey, cut that out, I'm not here to talk about me, how are you doing sis? I saw those keystone cops parked outside protecting and serving, so they say.

I'm cool Martin, the situation just had me a little startled for a minute, I just knew that it was Tony's signature on that letter but there is no way it could've been his, it was just somebody playing a very stale joke I guess, anyway I got big brother Captain Dudley Doo Right on the case so it's all good. Now tell me about those skeezers I hear you've been hanging around with, you better be careful man because I ain't trying to go to another funeral, ya heard.

Look, Sis, I got it all taken care of, ain't no way in hell I'm gonna let Killa go swimming without his scuba gear on, wet suit, flippers and all. If it can get though neoprene we better name him Hercules.

That's not my worry Martin, Hercules is ok, I just don't want him to have the initials HIV.

Aright, so what you got to eat up in here?

I made some of my world famous white chili and beans and some quiche if you want to warm it up.

Quiche, you mean cheese and eggs in a little bourgeois ass biscuit cup? When did you become a gourmet? Never mind, I still go for the regular food like bologna and ramen noodles and a rib eye every now and then. You can keep the quiche for you and your valley girl girlfriends and speaking of girlfriends, can you hook a brother up with that tall friend of yours?

Who do you mean Martin, Tameka?

Yeah Tameka, the one that drives the red Benz, with that chest that can make a sweater smile for days, I mean those have got to be some double D's, and the legs, good clawd the legs, lawd the legs, man as you follow them up they make a perfect ass out of themselves.

You mean Tameka? Leave her tits and ass alone, she ain't got time for you Martin, besides everybody knows you are the biggest playa this side of the Savannah River.

Maybe I'm a playa because I haven't found my queen as of yet. Besides I always lay my cards on the table then they can decide if they want to be the playa or get played. I always give them options, besides after dating me not only does their stock as individual ladies go up, but they are seen as having hit the jackpot and their chips always turn blue.

You got issues Martin.

No for real Tammy, look I do not even try to keep it a secret. I am Martin Prentice, the most eligible bachelor in the south. I come from the best pedigree; drive the smoothest ride, got the deepest dimples, still got all of my sexy and to top it off, a pocket full of dead presidents. What more can a woman ask for?

You mean what more can a skeezer ask for? You are a trip man but you have always had your game down tight just don't slip up, remember there is a thin line between love and hate and with the economy the way it is today Martin sisters out there trying to get paid, makes that line even thinner and I don't want to have to kill a . . . . damn.

What wrong sis?

Martin you know that it was an accident right, I was just protecting myself. I did not mean to hurt Tony, I loved him Martin and now he's gone because of me and I just can't seem to get my life back on track, I just can't seem to find firm footing again.

Look sis, nobody is blaming you for what went down, so you have to learn to forgive yourself. You have got to forgive yourself for what happened because there is no way to go back in the past and rewrite that script. Everybody knew that Tony was always packing heat; he always had a piece on him. Remember when dad would go hunting over in South Carolina with Dr. Blount? Remember he said to never point a gun at anybody unless you planned to pull the trigger, so just by him reaching for it was reason enough for you to bust a cap in his ass, it was self defense Tammy, you have to live with that, I love you sis. You want me to hang around tonight? Maybe we could watch a movie the way we did when we were kids, you want to try and find "Dark Shadows" with Barnabus Collins and Angelique or what was it called "Shock Theater" with Count Justin Sane? Remember when we would lie on the floor with the blanket and as soon as a scary part came on we would duck under it? Well you would duck anyway.

Stop lying Martin, you ducked too.

I was just faking it so you wouldn't develop a complex when you grew up that's all, however looks like I failed because you are definitely complex.

Right, no Martin but thanks for asking but you can go ahead and enjoy your weekend. Let's see its Friday night; you'll probably hit the Private Eye or Club 706, then when it starts getting late you will probably hit The Velvet Rope or Room and then top it off at Club 3000, especially if you can hook up with Keith, or what did they call him "Dirty Cherry", yall were a trip man . . . See I know you like a book Martin, we were too close growing up man, I know you.

Tell you what sis why don't you come with me tonight so that I can give some of those lovelies a break. I mean that way they don't have to wonder all night whether or not they have a chance with me, know what I mean?

I'm just not ready to get back out there yet Martin; I tried when I went to Atlanta with Mama and Daddy. I hit Club112 and stopped by the Urban Grind and hollered at Cassandra, I know you remember her, the owner that you had that mad crush on? They had 2dimplesdaPoet performing that night and it was standing room only, that big brother knows he can spit some rhymes and some knowledge and I even got a signed copy of his book "Can You Hear the Drums", believe me by the time the night was over I was hearing some drums okay! I had a nice time but I just felt that everybody knew what had gone down with Tony, and I felt like I had a million eyes on me.

You probably did have a million eyes on you Tammy, you still look aright and all.

Just aright Martin? Look I am still the shit okay, you might be the baddest playa in the game but you forgot who I got my skills from man. I am still the baddest chick so don't get it twisted.

Okay, okay, I guess you were my best student, look I gotta bounce I love you Tammy and there is absolutely nothing you can do about it.

Get out of here crazy man.

52

Officer Taylor please . . .

Hey Strong, what brings you to Savannah man?

You know damn well why I am here, where is that piece of shit and can I get a sit down with him?

Not sure about that, I already talked with him and when I called your office they said you were out but never mentioned that you were on your way here. The Chief, the Captain and I had a great time in the Mayor's office this morning. Guess who else was in on our conversation?

Who?

None other than the great Senator Armstrong Prentice himself.

You have got to be kidding me what is my old man up too Teddy?

Well, to tell you the truth, he tore the Mayor a brand new asshole and said that he would take care of the matter personally if we couldn't. The only problem with that is we have nothing concrete to hold the guy on. He is certifiable on the real but still legally unless you want to press charges we will have to let him go tomorrow and if you do press charges any half way decent attorney would have him back on the streets before the ink on the court order dries. It is quite clear that he has a personal interest in your sister's case and has been stewing for the past two years; we need to keep an eye on him man.

Keeping it real Teddy right now, with my Dad on the rampage, this jail is the best place for him. What did you mean he has a personal interest?

Well, I'll give you the short version and a copy of my report, it seems that he was hired by Tammy to spy and get the goods on Anthony Leakes. In the meantime while Rice was doing his private dick thing he got close to Nikki Parks with whom he had some type of fling with, and then she hired him to spy on Anthony as well. Anyway, the bottom line is Nikki Parks is in that mental institution in Milledgeville you asked about the other day and this asshole is still carrying a torch for her. It seems he blames Tammy and your family for ruining his having a life with Nikki.

Man that sounds deranged.

It is but from what I saw when I looked into his eyes, he is serious about that man.

If that's the case why try and extort money?

You know Strong, I've been wondering about that myself. I don't think he was serious about that, two hundred and fifty thousand to a Prentice is like two hundred and fifty dollars to me and if he was just half ass good at his job he knew that already. I think he was just trying to get under your skin or maybe put together some skip town money. Other than that I don't believe he had any intention of collecting and if he did it would have just been icing on the cake for what he may really have had in mind. Honestly I think he needs a shrink his damn self.

Can this cat be serious? I have got to get back to Augusta to my old man before he starts tripping like only he can, thanks for the copy of your report.

Still Strong, there remains some questions about that trial man, I know you are going through enough right now but when I look at the case I can see a whole lot of questions that I could really use some answers too.

Like what Teddy?

Well first of all there aren't any trial transcripts anywhere to be found and nobody can remember or has a record of who was even on the jury. The fact that Tammy was never officially arrested is strange enough. I don't mean to step on anybody's toes, you know me and you go all the way back man, but someone is bound to want to know some of the answers to these questions, don't you?

You know Teddy I have been wondering about that case since it went down. How could I honestly wear this uniform knowing that there has been, quite possibly, a crime committed here and with my own family involved? Not just the shooting but looks like there may have been a cover up, and if so why and who is responsible for it. Everything that I have read points to self defense the same way the jury decided. Do you have any reason to come to any other conclusion?

I don't know what to conclude at this point, I just know that something in the milk about this case ain't clean.

But the only witness was this Nikki Parks and, from what you are telling me, she's not in any condition to speak on anything right now, but if there was anything else to know it would have come out in the trial right?

That's another question Strong, we don't know if it came out at the trial or not, there is no record of the trial and it's beginning to look like Nikki Parks was not the only witness that night.

What do you mean?

This Jamie Rice says that he was there and witnessed the entire thing; he's also calling the trial a joke. But then again, his name is nowhere in the case file or on any of the police reports as having been at the scene, he claims he was across the street. Sounds fishy but I believe the guy Strong, from the look on his face he either was there like he says or has convinced himself that he was there, either way he could re-open this case. Tammy can't be charged again due to the double jeopardy laws but maybe there is something else that could come out of it, you know like some skeletons in this case's closet.

Teddy are you sure I can't talk with him before I head back?

No Strong that may not be a good idea right now, he is not in the mood to become chummy with a Prentice. I'll give you a call and keep you updated man. Peace and chicken grease my brother.

Peace Teddy, I'll holla.

53

Hey Consuela, where are Mom and Dad?

Master Armstrong, good to see you sir, your mother is on the tennis court and your father is downstairs in the Den, shall I tell him you are here sir?

No Consuela, I can hear Miles Davis' *"Straight No Chaser"* playing so I know what kind of mood he's in, I think I'll surprise him. Well I say there must be a Prentice in the county because I can smell money, old money Son, old money.

Strong, well Son, good to see you and I might add you do a pretty good impression of your old man, glad to see you. It's been a while since you've been out here to Sandy Grove. Pour yourself a cognac and here take one of these Behikes, I'm sure you don't get one of those too often.

Hennessy Ellipse, Dad what are you celebrating?

I see you still know your cognac, that's only about four thousand dollars a fifth and with the Behikes.

Yes I know Papa, rolled in Cuba on the thighs of virgins and about forty two dollars a piece.

You got it right Son and I am celebrating being Armstrong Prentice, its worthy of celebration in these hard economic times, you should celebrate too Son every day.

Dad, now you know these cigars are illegal here in the United States, for that matter a four thousand dollar bottle of cognac should be illegal everywhere, but I do like your style.

Now, now Strong, take me to jail after I've had a few more snifters and I won't complain Son, I won't complain. So what's on your mind my boy I know you didn't come all the way out to Sandy Grove just to stretch your legs.

Well Dad, I just got back from Savannah and I see that you raised quite a ruckus at City Hall down there. Now you know that I don't get involved in too much of your personal business but this is a legal matter and I can take care of it.

Take care of it, Strong it has already been taken care of, this Rice person or whatever his name is will never reopen that case. I don't know what his motives are but I can assure you of the outcome. That particular case has been closed and there is no way some no account private whatever will stir that pot again, not as long as I live in the fair State of

Georgia. I won't have it, Tammy doesn't deserve to have this thing come back to haunt her, she is your little sister and it's your sovereign duty to protect her.

I know Dad; I had no intention of getting you riled I just want to be kept informed of what you plan to do that's all. The family is more important than this badge, this job and anything else for that matter I just don't want anything coming back to haunt us.

Strong, I understand but while I am the patriarch of this family I will make the decisions concerning this family! The only reason this loose end came back to haunt us is that we didn't know that it existed, I will make sure that it doesn't happen again.

Dad, I cannot sit by and watch you do something illegal; I am still Chief of Homicide you know.

Are you alluding to the fact that I plan to kill the guy or have him rubbed out? You watch too much TV Son, what is this Augusta CSI? I'm just going to make sure he goes on a much needed vacation that's all. I will not have his blood on my hands or the hands of this family, just a vacation Son, trust me. And by the way, does your mother know you're here?

No sir, I wanted to have a few minutes to talk with you before seeing her. Consuela says she's on the tennis court anyway. Does she know about the Tammy situation?

Not really, let me get her.

No need Papa I saw his car outside, so tell me, how are you and Cheryl doing? It's nice to see that you still know the way to Sandy Grove, what has it been three months since you last visited? You can apologize to me later; give your mother a hug and a kiss, you may be one of four but you are my first born and your father's namesake, that means something in this family, so what brings you out here on such a lovely day?

Nothing Mama, just wanted to see Dad about some business that's all.

Well, you never could lie to me Strong but if it's something that I don't need to know about then so be it. By the way, I invited you and Cheryl to join your father and I at the head table during the Mayor's White Ball the week after next, she and I have to start making plans for the holidays and I thought that would be a good time for us to talk since you men always seem to desert us at these events, is that okay with you?

Sure, that's fine, thanks for reminding me. Actually, Cheryl did mention something about the Ball and with everything else going on I totally forgot that it's in a couple of weeks. I might need to get my Tux altered; I have put on a few pounds here of late, so what's the theme this year so that I will know what color tie and cummerbund to wear?

I'm not sure yet but I will let Cheryl know as soon as I find out.

I'm sure you will Mama, I remember how much you relish the holidays and I just hope you didn't decorate too much for Halloween like you did when we were kids.

Of course I did Strong, didn't you look into the great room when you got here?

No, I heard the music and just came straight down to see Dad.

Well make sure you do before you go home, by the way, your father and I were talking the other day and were wondering if you had any aspirations of becoming a candidate for Chief of Police?

Chief of Police?

Yes, Chief of Police.

Dad I always thought you were ribbing me when you mentioned the Chief of Police position; I never took you or it seriously.

Well Son I think it's time you started taking it seriously.

But Dad, I enjoy my current position, I enjoy hands on police work, besides Chief of Police is just a title, it's not really a job. I would just be a gofer for the Mayor. Nope, it's not the job for me but thanks for the consideration I'm cool where I am.

Armstrong Prentice this is not about you! It's about history, you would be the first black Chief of Police in this city and we think it's time.

Who is this we Dad, who is this we that thinks it's time?

Don't bother about that Son; my question to you is whether or not you are ready to take your place in history where this town and the South are concerned? The Chief of Police job is considered a stepping stone for the office of Mayor and I think you would make a damn good one.

Dad you thought the same about Uncle Ed and besides I am not a politician.

I will not have you speak anything negative about Mr. Ed McIntyre by God; he was one of the building blocks of this city and especially the black community, if it wasn't for Ed McIntyre there would be no Riverwalk or none of the businesses enjoying prosperity down there today. And to think there is not even a statue or plaque of that man anywhere in this town, it's a damn shame. There should be a statue of Ed McIntyre right there at the entrance to the Riverwalk holding his hand out to shake the hand of the common man upon entering, besides son every man is a politician when he has the proper backing.

I have no problem with that dad but I want to make it on my own, based on my individual merit, I don't want it given to me on a silver platter like so many after dinner mints.

Nonsense! Do you really think the amount of votes dictates who holds political office anymore? Wake up and smell the vote's Strong, the political machine decides who sits in that office, it's true in local as well as national politics. Hell, you should know by now that the one with the most votes doesn't always win, ask former Vice President Gore. Money pays for votes Son, don't for one minute think that this is a Democracy. Now we asked you a question and we want an answer now?

Sorry sir, I will think hard about the Chief of Police's position but not about the Mayor's office right now. The both of you know that I will do what is necessary to maintain our family's rightful place in this town and in its history, I feel honored that I have met your approval.

That's my boy, that's my boy.

I am so proud of you son; you continue to make your mama proud. Make sure you tell Cheryl tonight, she will be proud of you as well. Nothing will happen right away because we are at least one year away from the next election, we first have to decide who to run for Mayor and make sure they understand who the Chief of Police has to be.

I really wish Dr. Blount would consider running, he is one of the most trusted men in the county and has always had a reputation that is second to none and above reproach.

54

Hi honey, I didn't hear you come in, can I get you something?

No Pud, I'm alright, just a little tired, had to run down to Savannah on a case and then stopped by Sandy Grove to see mom and dad when I got back.

How are they, I talked to mom the other day, did she mention the good news to you?

What good news?

That she was going to have us at the head table this year with the Mayor!

Oh yeah, she did mention that.

What's on your mind Strong, any other time you would have said, head table and hunched your shoulders like you didn't care. So what's up, I know you honey something is on your mind.

Well Pud, they want me to consider taking the Chief of Police's position during the next election. Mom said that they first have to decide who to run for Mayor, can you imagine that, I expect that from dad but now mom is calling shots as far as who runs for political office?

Now Strong, you know that the two of them are a team and can literally finish each other's sentences, they have always been two people with one brain.

Yes I know that it just didn't hit me that hard until tonight.

Well how do you feel about it, you would make an excellent Chief of Police? You have all the right credentials honey, why don't you want the job?

It's not that I don't want the job it's that I haven't really had the opportunity to think about it and all. I mean who wouldn't want the job, it's a major promotion. My only problem with it is that it would take me off of the streets and away from real police work, I'm not sure I want to leave that behind just yet.

Well I'm sure; it would make me sleep a hell of a lot easier at night. Besides if we are to have a family it could help assure me that you are coming home safe at night instead of having me waiting, staring at the ceiling and praying that you are okay when you are out there Strong. I love you honey and would hate for anything to happen to you. You have done your time on the trail man and now a corner office is what you've earned. Besides I would make an excellent Mrs. Chief. I could get a nice blue uniform with medals and all.

I gotta tell you one thing; you should have been my mother's daughter. I have never seen too women so much alike in all my days, status this and status that. The two of you know how to manipulate every opportunity and turn any situation into something that will favor the family. Most notably favor you, but I ain't mad at cha I guess that goes with the territory, you are a Prentice of course. So tell me honestly honey, should I accept the position if offered?

Can you say hell yeah?

I love you Pud.

Me too tiger, now let's talk about that uniform.

55

Where might we find the Desk Sergeant?

Right down the hall to your left sir.

Thanks officer.

May I be of assistance sir?

Sure you can, I am Detective Richard Powell and this is Detective Eric Boyd of the Georgia Bureau of Investigation and we are here to escort a prisoner of yours to Augusta, here's the warrant and transfer authorization.

Thank you sir, right away sir, lockup, bring down a Mr. Jamie Rice for transfer to the GBI.

Have a seat in the waiting room detectives; it may take a few minutes for his paperwork to be completed.

Can you speed the process up officer, we are trying to make it back before it gets dark, and you know what I mean with the wife tripping and all.

Man don't I, hell I haven't made it home on time one night this month and lately it been like sleeping with an Eskimo if you can feel me. I've eaten so many TV dinners this week that I'm beginning to glow in the damn dark and you won't believe what I would do for a Klondike bar.

Yep, I do know what you mean, tonight happens to be the wife's birthday and, well I would just appreciate anything you can do to speed up the process. Thanks.

Will do detective, usually we get advance notice when there will be a prisoner transfer, I would normally have to call it in but it is your wife's birthday so let me go up and get him myself. Hey Connor, watch the desk for me, I'll be right back.

Thanks man, we owe you one.

I am not going anywhere, what's the charge, I haven't been charged with anything, you can't, where are you taking me?

Be careful with him detectives, he fought me all the way down here. So if you will sign right here we can consider the transfer done, I will follow up with all this damn paperwork, have a safe drive back and like I said keep an eye on this one.

Thanks a lot officer, what is it Richardson?

Yes sir officer Lawrence Richardson from Slidell, Louisiana.

You are a long way from home but thanks officer Richardson.

You don't look like much to me Mr. Rice, today is not your lucky day man; as a matter of fact you have to be the unluckiest motherfucker on the planet right now, you are about as lucky as OJ is in Vegas, you got any memorabilia you need to collect?

Man, screw you, Augusta ain't really that bad, so what that asshole Captain decided to press charges, the extortion rap won't stick. I got lawyers that will make this case go away in the blink of an eye and have me back in Savannah by lunch time tomorrow. So laugh now man, this won't take much time at all, as a matter of fact I may just sue the motherfucker for false arrest, I do know a little bit about the law.

What are you talking about Mr. Rice, who pressed charges, what charges? You heard anything about any charges E? And who told you that we were headed to Augusta? Ah man, that's funny as hell, you have no idea what's really going down do you? Take a good look at Savannah Mr. Rice because the next time you see it will be in your dreams.

Where are you taking me, who the hell are you anyway, what is this? This ain't the way to Augusta, where are we going dammit? I promise you that when I get out of this I will hunt the both of you down like the mad dogs that you are; you can't get away with this!

We already have, so shut the fuck up man, we got about three hours to drive and I honestly don't feel like hearing your puck ass bitching the entire ride, so shut up and take it like a man. Hey E, hook him up now man so that we can have a little peace on the way back.

Cool, man I was getting tired of listening to this little bitch whine anyway, hey you want some cheese to go with that whine Mr. Rice?

What are you doing with that syringe, what are you doing to me, helppppppp, somebody helpppppppppppp, look man I got money, I can get both of you straightened out real nice man, I got over three hundred grand in my apartment, it don't have to go down like this, let's talk, lets, talk, lets . . . .

Knock, Knock, Knock.

Come in gentlemen I've been expecting you, where there any problems? Did you follow Mr. Johnson's instructions to the letter? You know he doesn't like sloppy work; you didn't hurt him did you? Is he alive?

Look man it's not like I just busted my cherry on this job you know, I am a professional so put some ice on all that interrogation shit. He's okay, just knocked out, as a matter of fact he should sleep for another hour or so but there are no marks on him or anything.

Okay, put him on the gurney and follow me.

What is this place anyway man, it's dark as hell down here.

You ask too many questions. Here put him in this room for now and strap him down. Mr. Johnson arranged for me to give the both of you these envelopes and to tell you that he will be in touch with you soon. Be sure to ditch the car, take the blue van parked on the side of the building; the keys are in the envelope.

Will do; when sleeping beauty wakes up tell him I said hi, let's bounce man.

Hey E, what the fuck is this place man, talk about spooky. Listen follow me in the van I'm heading back the long way so we can ditch the car somewhere in Louisville.

Well, well, well Mr. Jamie Rice, it seems as if someone has a hard on for you in the worse way.

Where am I, what is this fucking place?

Calm down Mr. Rice, I am Doctor Austin, Doctor Jean Austin and please don't be so dramatic, you should know where you are Mr. Rice, you've been coming here for almost two years now.

Coming where, what is the place?

Are you familiar with the Taj Mahal Mr. Rice? It's such a beautiful work of art and is regarded as one of the eight wonders of the world. Western Historians have noted that its architectural beauty has yet to be surpassed; however it is actually just an elaborate Tomb Mr. Rice. Unfortunately your view won't be that stunning; you see Mr. Rice out of that window over in the main building you can see the rather mundane accommodations of your precious Ms. Nikki Parks. It is my understanding that you prayed to have a life with her, but it seems as if God is not here today. However, now you can have that life with her, for all of eternity, or should I say till death do you part? Who knows Mr. Rice; you might just be able to catch a glimpse of her from time to time. You no longer have to be just a visitor nor will you have to drive so far to see your precious Nikki. Welcome to the Georgia Mental Institution Mr. Rice, or should I say welcome home.

56

Officer Richardson get me Jamie Rice from lockup and bring him down to interrogation room number two.

Jamie Rice?

Yes, what's wrong officer?

Sir, he was transferred to Augusta yesterday afternoon; he was picked up by the GBI.

Transferred! I agreed to no transfer!

I have the warrant right here sir.

Warrant, damn so Strong decided to press charges after all, I still should have been told, isn't there a flag on his paperwork that states that he was my detainee?

No sir, was there supposed to be?

Get me Captain Prentice up in Augusta on the phone officer, damn.

Captain Prentice is on line one sir.

Strong, sup brah, man you should have told me that you were having Rice picked up, I would have brought him to you and that would have given me a chance to come home on the department's dime.

What are you talking about Teddy? I never sent for Rice and if I had you know damn well I would have let you know.

Strong, Jamie Rice was picked up here by the GBI yesterday afternoon, I have a copy of the court order and transfer authorization right here in front of me.

What Judge signed the warrant Teddy?

Man I can't make out the damn signature; you know how these high muckety mucks write.

Teddy, don't tell me that you allowed a prisoner of yours to be transferred from your facility without verifying the information. Man, don't tell me that you just got the both of us front row seats at the world premiere of the latest shit storm.

Strong, I'll call you back, I got to get in touch with the GBI and see if they have this asshole, cross your fingers brah, we might need a prayer.

Prayer would be a good thing right now man, later.

Richardson!

Yes sir.

Now tell me again numb nuts, make me understand why after all your years on the force, tell me why you allowed a prisoner to leave this facility without going through proper procedure? I want you to sit there and come up with an answer while I get the GBI on the phone and Richardson, please understand something, right now your job hinges on the information I receive on the other end of this phone call. How many years have you worn that uniform officer?

Fifteen years sir.

Fifteen years, you mean you screw up just five years away from being eligible for your pension? Let me get a good luck at you officer, let me get a good look at what fifteen years flying out the nearest window looks like. Yes, this is detective Taylor from the Savannah Police Department; I need to talk with the detectives who were responsible for picking up a prisoner down here yesterday afternoon. The prisoner's name is Jamie Rice and they were transporting him to Augusta, yes I'll hold. Are you listening Richardson, can you hear what fifteen years flying out the window sounds like. What do you mean no detectives were dispatched to Savannah for any reason on yesterday or any other day this month? Are you sure? Could you have made a mistake? Thank you. Richardson clear out your locker and wait for me in the squad room. Somebody get Captain Sykes down here. Sir, we have a problem of monumental proportions, Jamie Rice was picked up yesterday by who officer Richardson thought were two GBI agents, it seems that they were imposters, we have no idea of his whereabouts.

You have got to be shitting me Taylor, I hold you totally responsible for this bullshit. Find Jamie Rice detective that is your only responsibility, do you understand me. I don't give a damn if you have to go get three of Clem's bloodhounds but you will find Jamie Rice and I mean yesterday! Get me the surveillance camera's tapes and get the pictures of those two fake ass detectives that took him out of here and I want a description of their car on the wire immediately, you get me detective immediately!

Beep Beep Beep

Who the hell is beeping me? Yes I'm on my way now sir, thanks.

Well don't just sit there looking like a warm turd, get your coat; we have another meeting in the Mayor's office.

57

Send them in.

Good afternoon Mr. Mayor.

Well, well if it ain't the three fucking stooges, do you three idiots take warm showers together or do you all use the same soap because right now I smell quite a bit of shit! Where the fuck is Jamie Rice Chief?

How did?

Don't worry about how I knew, I know everything that goes on in this city Chief Cherry, that's my job, I am the HNIC, and I go by the title of Mayor. Now where in the hell is Jamie Rice or do I need a new Chief, Captain and Head of Detectives down at the Police Department?

Well Mr. Mayor, we honestly don't know where he is at the moment, we were about to go through the surveillance information when we got your call.

Surveillance, I don't give a fat baby's ass about no damn surveillance, where is Jamie Rice?

Excuse me sir Senator Armstrong Prentice is on line three.

Damn, of all the motherfuckers in the entire world today and all the fucking phones on the planet, this motherfucker has to be on mine. Yes Senator Prentice, how are things going sir? May I put you on speaker I have Chief Cherry, Captain Sykes and Detective Taylor in the office.

Go right ahead Otis, nice to talk with you gentlemen again, and Teddy how's the family son?

Everyone is okay sir, I'll be sure to tell them that you asked.

So tell me Otis, what's going on down there in Savannah?

What do you mean sir, everything is under control.

Stop lying to me Otis, I can tell you're lying because your damn lips are moving, tell me about Jamie Rice?

Well sir, there seems to be a little problem.

Problem, there are no such things as problems Otis, just challenges, the real question is whether or not this challenge is a mental one or a physical one. What type of challenge is this one Otis?

Well sir, it could be a bit of both.

I see, well who is going to put the cards on the table down there? Talk to me Teddy.

Well sir, right now we are in the process of trying to locate Mr. Rice.

Locate Mr. Rice; why on earth would that be necessary, you got him locked up down there don't you?

Well sir, there has been a small complication.

Really, tell me about it?

Mr. Rice is currently missing Senator, he was taken from the jail on yesterday afternoon by two men posing as detectives from the GBI and we are in the process of trying to locate them.

Two men posing as detectives from the GBI, I see, so you mean to tell me that Jamie Rice is missing?

Yes sir, sort of.

Was he ever charged with a crime?

No sir, we hadn't gotten around to that, he was still in a detainee status.

And you really can't charge a man for intent can you? You actually have to wait until a crime has been committed, am I correct about that one Mr. Mayor?

Yes sir, you are.

Well then the only thing we need to do is make the paperwork fit the situation is that also correct Mr. Mayor?

Well sir, that all depends.

Depends on what Mr. Mayor?

Well sir, Mr. Rice could be in harms way.

I wouldn't worry too much about Mr. Rice Mr. Mayor. I'm sure he's on a nice vacation probably headed to South Beach in Miami or somewhere exotic like that. My main concern is that he is no longer around to do harm to my daughter Tammy. So in essence I should thank you gentlemen for a job well done.

A job well done, ah Senator Prentice can you hold on for a minute while I clear the office?

Sure go right ahead Otis. Teddy take care of yourself son, hope to see you soon, drop by Sandy Grove the next time you are in town.

Thank you sir, will do.

Now Senator, what is going on here?

Nothing is going on Otis; I just wanted to head off you putting all your energy and resources toward attempting to locate Mr. Rice that's all. Why waste the valuable man hours on yourself and the department, no crime has actually been committed.

Senator Prentice is there something you want to tell me.

Yes Otis there is, I want every mention of that arrest stricken from all records, Mr. Jamie Rice never made it back to Savannah yesterday, you have never heard anything concerning this case and neither yourself, the Chief, that Captain or Detective Taylor received this phone call. We did not speak yesterday, today, and I promise not to call your ass tomorrow is that clear Otis?

But sir, I need to know.

Is that clear Otis?

Crystal Senator.

Thank you Otis, I knew that you would understand, say hello to the wife for me and have a great day Mr. Mayor.

Damn.

58

Yes officer this is Captain Prentice in Augusta, is Detective Taylor available?

Yes sir he has just walked in.

Hey Strong, what's up man?

Teddy, sounds like you just got your ass kicked again man, what's wrong?

Well actually Strong, I am not at liberty to say man, the Captain just initiated a gag order down here and we can't really discuss too much of anything.

Okay, I can feel that but what is the status of Jamie Rice man?

Strong I am not a liberty to speak on that case man; it's a real sore subject down here right now.

Teddy, man we go a long way back and I need to be updated on the situation.

I can feel you Strong but I can't speak on the case, you might want to ask your father.

What does my father have to do with you updating me on the Jamie Rice case?

Strong, gotta go man, probably said too much already; work with me on this one. Peace.

Teddy, Teddy . . . . that Negro hung up on me, what is going on around here? One minute we boys and the next minute I'm left eating a hero sized shit sandwich. Only one person could spook Teddy like that, only one person on the face of this earth. Hello Consuela is my father around?

Yes he is Master Armstrong, just a second.

Why hello Son, I was just thinking about you, have you had any time to consider our offer about the Chief's job?

Dad you know I already told you and Mom that I would definitely be interested in the position if it were to become available.

Good Son, actually that's great, I am indeed proud of you.

Dad, we need to talk but not over the phone, are you going to be at Sandy Grove all evening?

Why, yes Son I plan to kick up my feet and enjoy the chilled air, you know that this is the best time of year for me, I love it.

Thanks Dad, I will stop by sometime this evening, talk with you then.

Fine Son that would be just fine.

59

What tha? What are the television people doing up here, what has dad done now? I'd better park around back, wouldn't want to see myself on channel 12 news tonight.

. . . . And I am more than happy to say that I wholeheartedly endorse Senator Barrack Obama to be the next President of the United States, I think he definitely represents a change in the political aura of this fine country and I am proud to be a part of this historic undertaking. I also promise you all, that the ribs and collard greens will be catered and not cooked at the White House.

Senator Prentice, Senator Prentice, John Ford CNN. Why have you waited so long to endorse a candidate, why now sir?

Well Johnny, as you know I have always been one to speak softly while carrying a very big stick, if you know what I mean. I have watched the debates both Presidential and Vice Presidential and I think John McCain shot himself in the foot by selecting that, excuse me sir, by selecting Governor Palin as his Vice Presidential running mate, let's understand one another, Governor Palin is not ready to be the President of the United States and that is primarily what the job of Vice President was designed for.

Senator Prentice, Benjie Anderson TBN. The state of Georgia has primarily been a Republican stronghold especially where the Presidential contest is concerned; do you see that changing with this election?

Well, it's hard to say Ben, you and I both know that the Bible Belt is a hard row to hoe when it comes to changing the minds of die hard Southerners, now by saying that, I am not saying that this race will not tear the guts out of some of our good ole boys when it comes to their traditional way of thinking because it most definitely will, however even they may have to question their own humanity with this election and that is what's important. It's time for a new way of thinking in this Country, but I do see a shift in the way they are thinking about the changes that Senator Obama has promised and I think it is time for that change, and what better place to start than with the current residents of 1600 Pennsylvania Avenue.

Senator Prentice, Monica Pearson WSB TV Atlanta. You have never really supported a straight party ticket sir, you have instead supported what has been best for your district and your constituents, so tell us Senator with the positions that are rumored to have been offered you by Governor Purdue, are you still a Democrat or have you switched parties?

I am a Georgian Monica, and a real American and I do not require any other adjective or title to modify the noun that is Senator Armstrong Prentice. I am a Georgian first and a American always.

Senator Prentice, Bob Gaye Comcast Community News Atlanta. Will you be campaigning for Senator Obama in the remaining weeks prior to the election sir?

Son, you don't know me do you? By giving Senator Obama my endorsement I have done all the campaigning required for the junior Senator from the great State of Illinois. Johnny educate your colleague and bring him up to snuff, he sounds like he works for Channel 6 or the Chronicle Herald. That will be all ladies and gentlemen, thanks for coming.

Hi Dad, nice press conference, you didn't mention to me that you would be formally endorsing Senator Obama.

Well Son, I wasn't quite ready to but General Milliner crossed party lines and endorsed him this morning and I couldn't allow him to steal all of my thunder, besides it was time so that those that were still sitting on the fence can finally commit.

Dad, can we talk?

Sure we can Son, walk with me out to the stables, I think I know what you are wanting to speak on and it's been a while since we have taken a ride, I want to show you something.

Sure Dad.

You see that ridge over there to your right Strong?

Yes sir.

Well, that is the eastern border of Sandy Grove, I sold off a few acres so that they could build the Jones Creek Golf Club and they probably still do not know that a black man owned it, but that's not really why I brought you out here. Strong, I'm not getting any younger Son and although I think I have done a lot to provide for the family I think it's almost time for me to pass that responsibility on. There is a lot that you don't know about our heritage that I think you are now old enough and mature enough to understand.

Dad, are you doing okay, I mean your health and all?

Sure Son, I'm about as healthy as a bull, don't worry about that I am not about to be put out to pasture quite yet. Son in every family there comes a time to pass the torch and that day may be just over the horizon for me. You are my oldest Strong but you don't have an heir as of yet and the person that I pass this legacy on to must have an heir apparent himself. I know you want to talk about Jamie Rice but bear with me and you will see how all this fits together. Our family wasn't always as prominent as we are now Strong and it took the wiles, imagination and trustworthiness of two magnificent visionaries and the faith they had towards each other to bring all of this about. Land Son, land is the only thing that God is not making any more of. It's the soul of this family and the bedrock on which our future wealth will be maintained. Your mother and I were out here yesterday and she made me understand that my job as the patriarch of this family has run its course. Why haven't you had kids Son? Is something wrong with Cheryl?

Well Dad, it's not that we haven't been trying, I am a Prentice.

Well I want you all to have some test ran and find out exactly what's going on. It must be driving your wife crazy not to be raising kids at her age. I mean she is a Prentice and a Prentice woman is responsible for providing heirs to the legacy. Now get the tests done and get me another grandson pronto.

Okay Dad, what does Jamie Rice have to do with all of this? Where is he Dad? Is he still alive?

Jamie Rice was in the position to destroy all of this, maybe not right away but we cannot afford to have anyone cast a blanket of doubt or suspicion over the Prentice name. First Jamie Rice and then before you know it every year there would have been another Jamie Rice trying to make a name for himself by riding the coattails and attempting to extort or tarnish the name of Armstrong Prentice. No, that can never be allowed to happen. Nip, it, Nip it in the bud I say.

Dad is he still alive?

Of course he is, do you think I'm a murderer? He is fine and in good health, he is just away on a vacation and will never hinder our progress again. I will never allow anyone to hamper the progress of this family Strong.

But Dad I am a sworn officer of the law.

You are a pure blood born Prentice first! If you lost that damn job tomorrow you would still be a Prentice, family and land Strong, that's the only thing that matters, do you understand me?

Yes Dad but I just needed to know that he was okay.

He is fine Son; he is right where he wanted to be and enjoying the view. You see when you decided to become a part of law enforcement I was a bit apprehensive because of its possible contradictions with the importance of this family; I knew that in time you might face a few ethical dilemmas that you would have to find your way through. It is that reason alone Strong that we were considering the Chief of Police position for you and why I wanted you to know that I was considering asking your brother Kelvin to take over the family businesses and manage Sandy Grove.

I don't understand Dad, Kelvin is in Maryland and hasn't been a major part of the family business for years, how do you know he wants to come home and take on such a responsibility? What about Maria and the kids?

That is the reason I need him here because of Maria and the kids. An heir Strong, he has already provided an heir and there must always be an heir. I wanted to know your thoughts because managing the Prentice assets is an all day job. Your mother has been doing it for years and she has a torch to pass on as well. What are your feelings on that Strong and be honest with me Son?

Well Dad, I always thought I would be the one that would take over when you decided to retire; as a matter of fact I thought you were grooming me for that position. I understand why Jamie Rice had to be dealt with and I understand why an heir is necessary. What I don't understand is why all the secrecy, why the cloak and dagger stuff Dad? I want the opportunity to succeed you.

The opportunity is yours Strong but you haven't the guts for this type of undertaking, you haven't the heart for what you may be asked to do one day. You will forever be finding yourself straddling the fence and there must never be a question when the family is pitted against the rest of the world. But listen, I do owe you this much, you get the test done and if you can put one in the oven that has a handle on it instead of a hole in the next sixty days then I will reconsider. If not, I want your full cooperation in convincing Kelvin to take the position. Is that understood?

Yes Dad and thanks but what about Martin?

Now Strong, you and I both know that Martin is about as ready to take over this family as a bull is to shooting basketball. Before you knew it we would have more illegitimate Prentices than you could shake a stick at, why take that chance?

Okay, Dad, see you at the Ball, what was the theme again?

I think your mother said it was Autumn Metamorphosis, something having to do with the leaves changing colors, so we are to wear accoutrements that reflect the colors of the leaves.

So all of that means what?

It means wear what your wife puts out for you Son and don't ask any questions.

Okay Dad, I get it.

60

Now arriving, Senator and the lovely Mrs. Armstrong Prentice.

Connie, why do they always make such a big deal when we arrive I mean all these cameras, the red carpet and carrying on, I just want to get to my seat.

Wave and smile Papa or I will make this the longest evening of your life.

Yes Connie . . . . hello , , , , hi . . . glad to see you, hello.

Welcome to the Riverwalk Marriott this way to your seats Senator, may I take your shawl Mrs. Prentice?

Sure, but please be careful its Starlight White Fox.

Sure Mrs. Prentice I will take personal care of it Madam.

This is your table Senator the Mayor is holding court on the balcony.

Has my Son arrived Peterson?

No not yet sir, any instructions?

Yes Peterson, when he arrives tell him to join me and the Mayor on the balcony, by the way who else is out there with him?

The Chief of Police is out there along with Judge Fleming.

Thanks Peterson, where is the Mayor's wife?

She went to powder her nose sir.

Thanks Peterson.

Connie, why don't you go and find the Mayor's wife, she is in the powder room and I'll join the Mayor on the balcony.

Work it Armstrong, work it.

You also my dear heart, do your society thang.

Mr. Mayor, Mr. Mayor and hello Judge, haven't seen you in a while, how are things on the bench sir?

Why Senator Prentice, glad to see you sir and nice tie, what color is it?

I haven't the faintest idea, how are you gentlemen?

Just fine Senator, we were just talking about your impromptu press conference the other day.

Oh, my endorsement of Senator Obama?

Yes, Armstrong, we were wondering what side of the fence you would fall on?

Yeah right, and I also believe in the tooth fairy gentlemen, anyway, I hope I'm not interrupting anything, I thought the Chief was out here.

He just went back inside to interrogate the bartender, seems his Martini was shaken and not stirred.

Well Mr. Mayor, what do you plan to do when your term here is over, do you have any aspirations beyond city government?

As a matter of fact Senator I was about to speak to you on that very subject tonight, Judge Fleming thinks it may be a good move for me to consider a run for a seat in Atlanta.

I think that's a fine idea your honor, but Deke you would have to be a bit more specific; I personally feel that a House seat may be more enterprising than one on the Senatorial side of the aisle, another thing you might want to definitely consider is what Party you will represent, it will be almost impossible to get an independent elected in Atlanta but I'm prepared to put up a real fight on your behalf. I've seen the accolades and seats Sonny has been throwing your way but please don't let him make you a Republican, he only has a couple of years left in office and we are working on putting a Democrat back under the Dome so be careful because Democrats can be vultures too, anyway rest assured that whatever decision you make just know that I got your back.

Good evening Gentlemen.

Oh Judge Fleming and Major Reynolds, you both know my son Armstrong; he is Chief of Homicide for our fine Police Department.

Yes I have heard good things about you and the Department lately Armstrong. Keep up the good work and who knows what your future may look like.

Well thank you sir. Dad, Mom is looking a little restless we might want to make it back to the table for a bit.

Alright son, I'm right behind you, well your honor I will see you later on in the evening sir and we can talk more about this young Mayor's future, see you back at the table Deke.

61

Well my goodness Cheryl you do look lovely tonight, is that Vera Wang?

No Mom, I can't exactly justify Vera Wang, not yet anyway, it's a knock off but my lips are sealed.

That's the way you do it honey, look like a million bucks even if all you want to spend is two hundred, it's been a while since I've had to fake it but I do remember those days. Don't worry sweetie, your day will come, it would come quicker if you had some kids, now darling what is the problem?

I don't know Mom; I'm doing all that I can, I think Strong and I should probably go and see a fertility specialist but how do I approach him with the subject?

Not sure you will have too, his father already has, at least he mentioned to me on the way over here that they had a very extensive conversation the other day and the subject came up, so just pretend you never thought of the idea and carry on.

You are so smart.

Got to be girl in this family, I didn't get to be Mrs. Armstrong Prentice by giving a damn what other people thought, I have always been discrete but I will scratch a bitch's eyes out about my man and my position. I didn't get to the head table tonight by being a prude okay and you need to follow suit and take control of your proper place in this family. The only way to do that is to have another male Prentice Cheryl, now go home and get your freak on, if not Mrs. Maria Prentice will find herself right at home in Sandy Grove.

What are you talking about Mom, right at home in Sandy Grove?

Child haven't you been paying attention to anything these past few years? Strong is the oldest and by all rights should be the successor to his father and that would make you the successor to me. The only reason it has not taken place yet is simply because Armstrong hasn't made the decision as to who his heir will be and that heir must be a man child and you don't have any male heirs Cheryl. Armstrong doesn't give a damn about rights he is interested in heirs, somebody to past all this magnificence on to. This family will not perish just because Armstrong and I die off you know. Oh, hell no, we will not allow that to happen, listen Cheryl, sista to sista, Armstrong is ready to hand the reins on to the next generation, he is ready to relax and we want to do all the traveling that we planned whenever we talked about retirement, we have to pass the torch before any of that can happen. I have no problems with Maria, I think she is a nice girl and maybe if I got to spend more time with her I would feel even more enamored but right now you get my vote but don't screw it up by not becoming pregnant in the next sixty days, like I said, get your freak on because quiet as its kept, Mr. Armstrong Prentice is already putting things in place to pass the torch, you better get your name in the hat before it's too late.

Wow, I didn't know it was that crucial, I have been trying and I take that damn test every month to see if I am pregnant. Oh Mom, what if I can't have kids, what if Strong can't have kids, what are we going to do?

Now see, you are out of my league with that one but I will tell you one thing, if I were you, and I hope I am not letting my horns show, Strong is my son and all, but if I were you I would make an appointment so fast it would make your head swim. Find out now Cheryl, because none of us are promised tomorrow, do what you have to do and keep in mind that Sandy Grove is not just an address it's a destiny child, handle your business before it is too late.

What do you mean before it's too late? If we can't have kids we can always adopt.

Have you lost your mind all together girl? You can adopt all the fucking kids in that, thirty cents a day can change their lives commercial if you want too, but they will never be an heir to this empire. As long as Armstrong Prentice draws breath the heir to this family will be of pure blood. Oh no wifey, it's got to be one hundred percent Prentice blood running through the veins and none of that diluted shit. Sounds to me that you got some work to do, oh and by the way, there are more secrets to Sandy Grove than even I know, but you must admit the crib itself is to die for, I just hope Maria, ahem, I mean whoever ends up there doesn't change my decor. Here come the boys, smile girl, looks like you just ate some Castleberry's chili and got heartburn.

Well how have the ladies of the family been since the breadwinners have been rubbing elbows with the city's elite?

We have been fine darling, just making arrangements for Thanksgiving dinner and the remainder of the holidays.

Okay, whatever you ladies decide will be fine with us, we just want a little more football than usual and we should be able to get all the games this year with that new high definition contraption, as long as I get one of Maria's sweet potato pies I am in heaven. Mr. Mayor, I was wondering when you would be joining us.

I know Senator, every time I turn around somebody else is grabbing my arm. I just stopped by for a minute, I have to give this speech and then we can chat for a bit, I have some of that good cognac in a suite upstairs, I need to talk with you concerning our earlier discussion.

Sure Mr. Mayor, you don't mind if my son joins us do you?

If you think it wise, let me get through this speech then join me in suite 1116.

62

Nice speech Deke, if I didn't know better I would swear you just threw your hat into the State political ring a year early.

Not exactly Senator, but as I said before it has crossed my mind. This is what I was thinking of; if we can put together the requisite financing I could launch a bid for the State House or Senate seat as early as April of next year, that's why I decided to bring you in.

Bring me in! Listen Deke; let's not forget who drives the political train in this State. The first thing you have to understand is that you do not make the decision, as an individual, to run for office especially not in the 12th or 22nd district here in Augusta, you are chosen to run and that does not necessarily have anything to do with having held prior political office, you can ask Carver about that. Now do you want to start this conversation over again?

Sorry Senator Prentice, what I should have said sir was, if you would recommend running me for Statewide office I would appreciate it, and whatever good word you could put in for me at the Capitol level would be greatly appreciated as well. I know I can bring a lot to the table Senator and serve our constituents better than who we currently have in Atlanta today, look at Howard sir, he is a rookie and hasn't been in office long enough to really get any legislation proposed more or less passed, and Carver is a rookie also who has never held political office until now, he's still cutting his teeth. Let's agree Senator that had it not been for Senator Walker's debacle, Carver would not have ever been heard of at the State level. What I'm asking from the powers that be sir, albeit not taking anything away from Senator Walker's accomplishments. His deeds for Augusta and for the State of Georgia will not go unnoticed and I can promise you that. His work speaks volumes for his constituents here but I am asking the powers that be for a chance to amass the power that Senator Walker had and I can promise you a better district then we have ever had and not only that, I feel that I can assist in making Augusta not just Georgia's second largest city in size but in scope as well.

Now, now calm down Deke, the decision to move your office to Atlanta was made over a year ago and that was quite a nice acceptance speech you just gave but this is politics, and when it comes to politics I play hard ball! Before we can even think about this move strategically we have to decide who to run for Mayor after you leave office, which happens to be step one, then we can move on and see what it will take to get you to Atlanta. The question is what can you do for us once you are in office Deke? What's in this thing for us?

Well what would it take Senator?

I'm not sure quite yet but I want you to know that this job will come with some concessions for the people that get you the job. That is how politics is done in this country, I scratch your back and mine will have no reason to itch, do we understand each other? The first thing I want examined before I go any further is for my son Armstrong here to be considered for the job of Chief of Police. You get those wheels turning and by next year this time, when we are ready to launch your campaign, I want him selected for that position, will that be a problem Deke? Will we ever have any problems Mr. Mayor?

Senator there will never be any problems between us and I want to thank you for taking the time out of your busy schedule to meet with me.

Well I'm not leaving yet Mr. Mayor; if I remember correctly you offered me a snifter of Cognac, oh and by the way I just happen to have three Behikes in my pocket, enjoy Mr. Mayor enjoy, oh, and you too Son, or should I say Chief, enjoy.

63

Driver let's take the scenic route back to Sandy Grove. Connie you know I haven't been down in this part of town for a minute, let's drive past that statue they have of James Brown down on Broad Street. Well, well, well, they did an excellent job on that statue don't you think Connie?

Yes Papa looks just like him; they could have made him a little taller though he looks like a midget with a microphone. I still remember the last time he stayed at Sandy Grove; he said the road was beginning to be a little too much for him. When was that back in 2004 I believe, may have been earlier, that was the year he sold the rights to his music catalog for one hundred million dollars and they haven't been able to find a dime of it.

You're right, it's a damn shame that they can't find a paper trail of all that money, and it's not like James was broke before that. I tell you between what the Kings are doing to tarnish Martin and Coretta's legacy in Atlanta the Browns are doing as much dirt destroying James' legacy right here in Augusta, at least Martin and Coretta are in a tomb, I think they still got James in a living room with air conditioning somewhere, it's such a shame.

Driver lets go down Ninth Street.

It's James Brown Boulevard now Papa.

Oh yeah that's right, remember when H. L. Green's was on that corner Connie? Remember when we participated in the Sit-Ins at the counter just because they would not serve black people? That seems like it was a million years ago and who would have known that one of those protestors would become the most prominent person in this entire State? Thanks H. L. Green's for being such assholes and for being such motivators, it may be the Board of Education now, as it should be, they definitely gave us an education of another sort back then. Wasn't the AMVETS on that corner Connie? It sure is a shame that they tore down Bethel AME Church, but at least they moved it over to Crawford Avenue I believe, I'm surprised Dents Funeral Home is still open when so many of the other buildings around it have been torn down, and look Connie, there are only a few people left that can remember when the Lennox Theater sat on that very spot. I can remember going there to see "Imitation of Life" years ago. Driver, make a right turn onto Laney Walker Boulevard past where the Paramount Supper Club once was and a left on 12ᵗʰ where Pilgrim Health and Life Insurance Company was, they call it the Walker Group now, Gephardt Drug Store was once in that building, Driver make a left on Perry Avenue and park for a minute, look Connie, remember this house? This was the house that my parents owned, right here at 1116 Perry Avenue. Not a soul knew that the old man was nurturing a multi-millionaire even in this neighborhood. I have quite a few memories of that house and the Silver Dollar Café that set right next to it. I wonder what happened to the guy that ran this place "Kool Papa" they called him, and the girls that lived next door, Linda, Doris, Beverly, Deloris and Debra. We sure had good times when I came back home from school, and I hear that "Cuts" is still open on the corner down there on Wrightsboro Road, remember his son Reese and I were good friends. I think Barbara Few still lives in the house next door and our cousins Jackie, Janet and Andrea lived across the street, ok Driver take me to my son's school. Look Connie, that new building right there is a part of Tabernacle, have they opened A.R. Johnson back up yet? What they have done with the outside looks great.

Papa, Dr. Blount still has his office right there, right in the district where it belongs; he has done such a service to this neighborhood, his office never seems to have changed; it's nice to see that they are revitalizing this old neighborhood, thank you so much Papa for having such a prominent hand in that and for helping them get the funding to finish the Stadium.

Oh it was nothing Connie, nothing that any other man would not have done. I can remember Dr. Blount and I standing in the front of his office and talking about this very thing over ten years ago and now look at it. Dreams do come true Connie but first you have to wake them up.

64

Wow, glad to be back home, that was some event, what did you think sweetie?

Well, the usual Strong, but it did make a difference sitting at the head table, I mean everybody that was anybody made sure they stopped by and spoke with mom, me and the Mayor's wife when she could drag herself from the powder room. But Strong there is something that I want to discuss with you honey and please don't let this ruin the evening for us.

Okay Pud what is it?

Strong, would you mind if I scheduled an appointment with a fertility doctor for us to get examined? I can't see why I haven't been able to conceive as of yet, Strong you know how much I love you honey and you know that I would do anything for you; I just want you to do this for me. I want to have your kids Strong, your kids, we would make great parents and this family deserves a legacy that includes our kids, not just Kelvin and Maria's. I want kids Strong, please honey, can we go see a Doctor?

You know Pud; I have noticed that when Maria and the kid's names are mentioned you seem to go to a faraway place, is it because of the kids? I know you and Maria get along great so what else could it be. Our time will come sweetie; we just have to wait a bit.

I know Strong but I am tired of waiting dammit! All I ever seem to do is wait! I am over forty years old Strong, I've waited so long that I have developed a monthly ritual. Make love to my husband as often as possible then on the first of every month go and get an early pregnancy test and when it shows negative go into a four day depression. I am tired of waiting Strong!

Wow, Cheryl, well I never thought you wanted kids that bad sweetie and yes if you want us to go and get checked out its okay with me. Just think about it, we could be parents. I'm gonna look forward to the pitter patter of tiny feet around this camp. Maybe we could get a Nanny to give you a hand; actually I don't see why we can't start practicing right now if you get my meaning. Come here Tiger.

Strong, wait, Strong, I got to, Strong , , , , damn baby . . . . damn.

65

Welcome home honey.

Where are the kids?

In the family room downstairs.

Well let's just go down there and share the news.

What news Kelvin?

Family attention, may I have your attention please, as of this moment we are on orders to report to Ft. Gordon, Georgia in April of next year.

Wow, Kelvin that's amazing honey, did you put in for it or did it just happen?

That is not the only good news Maria, I am also finally going to get my Command, take a look at the new Commander of the 67th "Lighting Force" Signal Battalion, and kids, guess what, you get to spend some time with Grandma and Grandpa.

Yeah!

Maria, can I see you in the bedroom for a minute honey?

Sure, right behind you, what's on your mind babe?

Maria, I just know that my dad had something to do with this I can feel it in my gut.

Kelvin you don't know that, I mean you are a Signal officer, it would make sense that your first Command would be with a Signal unit. You have spent two of the last three years in Afghanistan so they wouldn't send you back overseas so soon would they? Honey this could be a good thing besides who said your dad had that much power?

Maybe you're right; to finally have my own Command is probably out of dad's reach. Wow, April of next year back in Augusta, I really can't wait to spend some time with the family, my crazy brothers Strong and Martin and of course Tammy, this could be a good thing.

Does that mean that we won't be going there for Thanksgiving this year?

Nope, one has nothing to do with the other; as a matter of fact do you think we can keep the secret until next month? It's gonna be hard, I mean dad probably already knows but we can try and keep the surprise from the rest of them, we can share it at the dinner table when the entire family is there.

Oh honey, I am so proud of you and you are not the only one with a secret.

144

What is that Maria?

Well I was going to wait until later to tell you but I don't want you to have all the glory.

What is it?

Kelvin you're going to be a daddy again, honey we're pregnant!

66

Good morning my darling, I brought you some fruit in case you wanted to lie in bed for a bit, I mean here it is Monday and I have a little down time on my hands for a change. This is the first day in about two months that I have had any time off. I thought about what we discussed last week and I found a Doctor Screen up on Chafee Avenue and printed his information off of the internet, he happens to be a fertility specialist and he was the guy that was able to help Detective Carr and his wife conceive, he comes heavily recommended and is at the technological forefront of his field.

Oh thanks Strong, thank you so much, I have done nothing but think about this for the past week, let's give him a call and make the appointment.

Anything for you Cheryl, anything at all.

Yes, this is Cheryl Prentice and I would like to make the earliest appointment possible to see Doctor Screen. My husband and I would like to have a fertility test, no there's no history of that in my family. Today, oh great, yes, they have an opening at three Strong, yes we can make it. Do we need to bring anything, yes we have our insurance card but that is not what's important, what is important is now we will know. Thank you so much Strong, I never thought you would agree to this but thank you honey.

It's all good Cheryl, my primary responsibility is to keep you happy, if all it takes is a visit to the Doctor then so be it. You are my wife and I love you more than life itself because without you I have no life, just a mere existence, if making a family is that important to you then I am all in.

Oh Strong, I have an amazing husband and each day I awake in your arms is a blessing. When I think back on my life and re-evaluate the decisions I've made I realize that the most important decision I have ever made it to say "I Do" to you, I love you so much Armstrong Prentice.

And I love you back Pud.

67

It has been a lifetime since I have been to the fair, James H. Drew Expositions, nice to see that some things never change. I know I will not risk my life on any of these rides, I just heard that a ride operator over in Columbia got killed when the ride he was working on hit his ass. Just point me to the turkey leg booth and I will be on my way. Excuse me but are you in line?

Yes I am.

Tameka?

Yes do I know you?

Quit trippin, I'm Martin, Tammy's brother; I see the two of you together all the time and I know that you are not out here at the fair all by yourself.

Why can't I be here by myself, I just came to get my turkey leg on.

So did I, I'm a little too old for any of the rides, so would you care for an escort while you are here?

Hadn't really thought about it, are you offering your services?

Maybe, what were your plans for afterwards?

I was going to probably just go back home and chill-lax; it's been a long week.

I know what you mean, listen Tameka, I may as well put my cards on the table, let's take a walk, we can always get the turkey legs on our way out, but if you are hungry right now how about we share a corn dog and some lemonade, would that be cool?

Yeah, that sounds like fun.

Cool, look I actually asked Tammy about you the other week when I was over at her place talking to her about all that craziness, you know what I mean? Let me have one foot-long corndog and two large lemonades please. Thanks, keep the change.

Yep, we talked, you know Tam is my girl and all which is why I worry about her all the time, she has been through an awful lot these last couple of years and she needs to know that somebody's got her back. You're the new Principal over at Laney right?

Yes, but all work and no play make Marty Mall a dull boy.

Something tells me that there is nothing about you that could even remotely be called dull Martin; by the way your sister told me what you said about my breast and stuff.

Well, do you have a problem with your breast and ah stuff?

No I don't.

Well I don't either, look Tameka, I run into a lot of ladies all the time and some of them are lucky enough to have me take them out and things. The problem is that I don't have a special lady in my life right now and, well, I would really like to get to know you better and maybe, I mean who knows what might happen.

Listen Martin, the last thing I need in my life right now is another playa, if you are serious, and I'll be able to tell if you are, then maybe we can hang out for a minute that is if Tammy doesn't have a problem with it, but you have to understand that I will not be a member of your harem nor your stable. I can do bad all by myself and if you are just looking for a roll in the hay then holla at a sista on that level just don't be wasting my time or playing with my emotions.

So what are you trying to say?

Bottom line Martin, a sista can be a playa too just another type, if you get my meaning, I just want you to understand that game peep game. The last thing I want to do is cause your little ego to explode because you could find yourself in the same boat as a few other brothers that thought they wanted to ride this train.

Meaning?

I mean that just because you buy the ticket doesn't mean you can get off this ride when you want too or decide when the ride is over on your own, now do you really want to ride this train Martin?

You got issues Tameka.

Nope I don't have issues Martin, that's what most men can't understand, you all like to prey on women so much that when you get preyed upon its hard for you to put your timid little minds around it. Martin I grew up an only child but I have five uncles, so there is no line, paragraph, or page in the book that I don't already know. Why is that so hard for men to understand? I like to get my freak on just as much as any man, probably more. Look around you Martin, look at all these men; there is not one of them that wouldn't rather be balls deep in a good piece of ass right this minute. When a man sleeps with multiple women he's considered a playa but when a woman surveys the field looking for her Adonis she's considered a whore, screw double standards Martin, I just choose to live my life by my own set of rules.

Wow, I never really looked at it from that perspective Tameka; ah may I have a bite of corndog? Look I hope I haven't come on too strong but I really thought you had a nice air about yourself and I was intrigued, now that I have had the opportunity to speak with you I can understand why I was so attracted. Can I give you a call from time to time?

I don't do anything on a from time to time basis Martin. Are you looking for an excuse to end this conversation? Do you feel as if you have bitten off more than you can chew? I understand and it's not your fault. Look at me Martin; look at the way that I carry and take care of myself, I don't consider myself high maintenance but a sista likes to look nice, not for myself but for that special man that I haven't even met yet, can you be that man to me Martin?

What are you asking me Tameka, what do you want?

I want to be Her?

Her?

Yes Her, I want to be the woman that you think of whenever the concept of female enters your mind. I want to be the one that makes you shiver every time I lay my hands on you, I want to be Her. Can you honestly put all your bullshit and arrogance aside and be the man that I need in my life? Because if you have answered no to any of those questions then my answer to you is no as well. I own my house, I drive a Benz that I pay for, and I work forty hours a week to make my paper. Therefore I don't need a damn thing from any man except his companionship, his respect, and a high hard one every now and then. Again, if your answer to any of those questions is no then I have enjoyed talking to you and I'll holla.

Well I must admit that I haven't had a woman break it down like that before and yes it could be a little overwhelming, if I were any other man that is. I guess I do need to digest what you just fed me; the one thing that I do know is that I want to see you again and maybe we can explore some of the things that we both enjoy. Look, maybe I did bite off more than I can chew but you don't see me spitting anything out do you?

Alright Martin cool, I'll meet you half way on this, here's my card and this is my private phone number, now let's walk back to the turkey legs, the corn dog was cool and thanks for letting me have the stick but I have had my sites on a turkey leg for over a week.

Don't you want my phone number?

Not really, I don't see a need for it at the moment, besides you will pursue me, court me, sweep me off my feet, and date me like a real gentleman should. Remember that the next time you decide you want to lay the rap down on a real sista. Make sure you are prepared to handle the truth.

What do you mean handle the truth?

Its simple Martin, I came to the Fair for two reasons.

And your reasons were?

Because Tammy mentioned that you might be here.

Yeah right, what about the turkey leg?

Oh that was reason number two or was it number one? You see Martin; you were not the only one that had an interest. I quizzed Tammy about you a long time ago and as you can see, I do my homework. You thought you were being the aggressor? This is what it looks like when that shit gets turned back on you. You see Dr. Martin Prentice I had already planted my seed in the recesses of your mind and knew that all I had to do was wait for them to germinate and that one day you would come around. You are a Prentice Martin and you will always need more than just an average woman, you need a dime piece that will ride or die for your ass, so let me know when you are ready to ride this train and by the way.

Yes.

Two turkey legs please in separate bags, you will walk me to my car, now pay the man Martin, I am a girl after all.

68

Knock, knock.

Tammy it's me Martin, open up.

Martin what are you doing here at this time of night.

Well I just left the Fair and thought you might want to share a turkey leg with me.

No you didn't bring me a turkey leg.

You're right I brought us a turkey leg, take the cork out of that bottle of Chardonnay and get the napkins.

Martin what is this all about, you seem to have something on your mind?

Tammy, I ran into Tameka at the Fair and we had a great conversation, as a matter of fact I haven't been able to get her off my mind since walking her to her car.

You walked Tameka to her car? You have got to be kidding; I told you Tameka ain't no joke Martin, that sista got all of her shit together, you didn't hit on her did you?

That's what confusing Tammy I think she hit on me but I'm not sure, so what's her story?

Martin I'm not going to be giving you the 411 on Tameka, all I can say is when I grow up I want to be just like her, a lot of men can't handle Tameka because there is no gray in her life, you are either on one side of the fence or the other, there is no in between with her which is why I dig her so much. She is a "tell it like it is" kind of person and deserves to have somebody unique in her life.

And?

And what Martin? I just told you that I am not about to spill the beans on Tameka, I will tell you that she graduated Magna Cum Laude from Spelman then got her Masters from Mercer and is currently a Doctoral candidate, oh she also teaches Psychology at Paine College, of course up there they call her Professor Tameka Allmond.

Professor?

Yes Professor, see you never would have guessed it, I told you Tameka got all of her shit together and is paid in full, the last thing she needs in her life is another playa.

Now where have I heard that before tonight?

From Tameka I'm sure.

Tammy, I'm serious about wanting to get to know her better, I meet loads of women, you know that, but I feel like Tameka is different.

The only reason she seems different Martin is that the two of you are both intellectuals and those other chicken heads couldn't underline the verb or circle the noun if their lives depended on it.

So how would you feel if the two of us decided to date?

Martin do not screw over my girl, Tameka and I have been best friends since our Spelman days and we are both members of Delta Sigma Theta Incorporated okay, so I don't want to be in the position to have to choose between you and my Soror. So just leave my girl alone and go back to your whorish ways and everyone lives happily ever after.

I wish it were that easy Sis, I think cupid has me in his sites and I don't know which way to run.

Maybe it's time you stopped running Martin.

I do want to stop Tammy; God knows I do.

You are serious aren't you?

Yes Tammy I am, like I told you something about this is different.

Well while you try to figure it out pass me the hot sauce.

69

Good morning Mrs. Bradford and how was your weekend, did you make it to the Fair?

Yes Onika and I had a great time.

My weekend was great as well.

So I see.

What do you mean by that Sonya?

You'll see.

Whatever, oh my lord, Sonya where did all these Roses come from?

You tell me big Pimpin.

There has to be twelve dozen here, was there a card or anything?

No sir, not at all, I figured you knew who sent them.

Ahem, excuse me is Doctor Prentice in? Is that his office, no problem I will let myself in.

Ms. you can't go in there!

Good morning Martin.

Tameka?

Excuse us Mrs. Bradford and hold my calls.

70

Consuela get all the girls on a conference call for me, I will take it in my office.

Will do Mrs. Prentice.

Hello Divas, is Maria there?

Yes Mom.

And Cheryl?

Yes Mom.

And Tammy?

Yes Mom.

Now Divas, the reason I got all of you together is to try and make some formal arrangements for Thanksgiving, is there anyone who will not be able to make it this year?

We can all make it Mom.

Thanks Tammy. That's good because Consuela will not be here and we will have to prepare the meal ourselves. Now on Wednesday we should be finished with the bulk of the cooking and I have scheduled a small cocktail party for the four of us and I plan to invite the Mayor's wife and Phyllis Jones from Human Resources at the college and a few other prominent ladies. The colors for the cocktail party will be Maroon and Beige. I think the guys will either be away from Sandy Grove watching that dreaded game on television or down in the sub-basement with Armstrong. Anyway, they will be out of our hair. This is what I propose, Cheryl and I will take care of the turkey this year and I believe Consuela will do the ham before she leaves. Maria you will be responsible, as always, for the deserts. Armstrong is still crazy about your sweet potato pies; you must leave Consuela the recipe. When will you and the family be getting in?

We should be there around Tuesday Mom, Kelvin is taking a few days off and Tuesday at the latest should be good for us.

Great Maria, you and your clan will be housed in the Johnson Wing of the estate, Tammy you will have to help me with the vegetables and the dressing, get with Consuela if you need help with any recipes, you will be housed in the Main House in your old room.

But Mom I can go back to my house after dinner.

DAVID K. DREW II

I will not hear of it.

Yes Mom.

Cheryl you and Strong will be housed in the Brown Wing. I will have a few cases of wine brought up from the wine cellar and we can be prepared to sit down formally at about 3 pm on Thursday. Dress for dinner will be Dressy Casual with the colors Black and Cream. Are there any questions? Anybody, any questions at all? Is there any news that the family needs to be made aware of? Excellent, isn't it great being a Prentice? Thank you Divas, I look forward to having a wonderful and grandiose holiday season as usual. Maria get my grandbabies here as soon as you can, I will have a formal dinner menu delivered to each of you no later than next week.

Sounds like you are planning a great day Mrs. Prentice.

We will try and make it without you Consuela; it's been a couple of years since we have all been here together, this year is special because you know Kelvin has been away for the last two Thanksgivings in that dreaded war, so we must be thankful that he is back and safe and I can't wait to see Eleanor and Boregard, those two get taller each year. Who knows in a couple of more years they will pour us some Sherry Consuela; it is the holidays you know. Asking Armstrong for a new car. Oh well, the toil of being a Prentice, who knew? Pour us some Sherry Consuela, it is the holidays you know.

71

So tell me Dr. Allmond what brings you to the hood? Slumming?

Cute Dr. Prentice, I was just in the area to drop off these stems, some fool bought all the Roses.

Well allow me to say thanks and note that you have made my day, now I have to figure out a way to explain this to my staff so that I will not look whipped.

Oh no Doctor, you aren't whipped yet, as a matter of fact I am capable of redefining the definition of the word itself for you, while on that note I wore something today just for you.

Well your London Fog trench is snapping I like that.

Oh no Doctor it's not the coat, it's what's under the coat.

What tha, Tameka, you can't be walking the streets with nothing on but a trench coat.

Don't forget the stilettos, garters and the teddy, you like?

Well, of course I like, I can't believe you pulled a stunt like this.

Oh Martin this is not a stunt, just getting your attention, I actually have to leave, but before I do may I have the pleasure of taking you to dinner tonight?

Where too?

Charleston!

Charleston? How are we going to get to Charleston and back, I have to work tomorrow?

Well actually, I chartered a Jet that can have us there in just under an hour and there's a great restaurant called "*Hermes*" that not far from the Battery that I would love for you to see, now is that a yes or a no? I'm sorry Doctor Prentice didn't your teachers tell you to project your voice, man up; you act like the cats got your tongue.

Yes Tameka, I would love to have you for dinner.

Cute choice of words Doctor, cute choice of words.

I'll pick you up here at five.

But won't I need another suit.

Why, if things go as I have them planned you won't have that one on for long.

72

Are those the results Pud?

Yes.

Well open the envelope and let's find out.

I'm scared Strong.

Don't be sweetheart; you wanted us to take the test so now let's see the results, whatever it is I'm sure we can fix it if need be, at least we will know what the problem is.

Okay Strong, but hold me okay.

Sure Pud.

What does it say?

It says that you have a condition called Oligospermia.

Oligo who mia? What the hell is that?

It's a low sperm count Strong and they want you to come back in for more test so that they can find out why your little soldiers aren't standing all the way up.

Cute, when do they want me to come back?

Next Wednesday at 3:00 pm?

Okay, no problem, I told you we would work this thing out, we need more Prentices anyway, and Armstrong Prentice the third is on the way.

I love you Pud.

73

Nice restaurant Tameka, thanks for bringing me.

Well Charleston happens to be one of my favorite getaways and I wanted to do something special with you Martin, something special that would create memorable moments.

That's nice; I must admit that this is the first time I have been treated to a dinner in a place like this after having been flown down here on a chartered Jet, what's a man to think?

Think what you want to but the dinner is on you, I took care of the Jet so don't get it twisted, I just wanted you to see that there are some women who are capable of handling their own business, you are a Prentice and everybody knows that all of you Trust Fund Babies got deep pockets which mean absolutely nothing to me. I want to know the real Martin Prentice not the Dr. Martin Prentice or the Playa Martin Prentice that everyone seems to be so enamored with, like I told you before I want to be Her and if I am to be Her then I have to do something that She is not capable of doing and that is showing you something different and unique. I have been Tammy's best friend for a long time and I hear stories about your escapades and who in Augusta doesn't know it's most eligible bachelor. You see Martin I knew that one day you would get tired of telling all the lies, and evading all the truths, I knew that one day you would look into the mirror and realize that as long as God makes women there will always be vaginas. I have to bring more to the table because all women have the same magic between their legs if they know what they are doing with it. So if I want you to love me then it has to be for me and not for anything that I can do for you physically, can you feel me Martin?

Yes Tameka, but you did catch me off guard with all the Roses; it took me forever to come up with an excuse for that.

You see that right there is what I'm talking about Martin, why was it necessary for you to make excuses? You could have just told the truth, any real woman would have understood and would have probably clapped if you told it real, I saw the stares that I got when I left there Martin and I am willing to bet you that Macy's sold at least five London Fog trench coats today and don't get me started on the money Victoria Secrets made tonight. You see Martin a real Diva knows a real Diva when she sees one and maybe for the first time they witnessed one today, so we have at least five happy ass men in Augusta tonight wondering what the hell got into their ladies. Check out the smiles they'll have on their faces tomorrow.

Are you ready to order sir?

Yes we are, bring the lady and I, a dozen raw Oysters on the half shell and we will have the Oysters Rockefeller along with some top neck Clams, a Garden and a Caesar salad, also a bottle of your best Sardinian Carignano would be nice.

We have the 64 sir.

Great year, yes we will have that.

Hmm, a Wine connoisseur I see, do you always order dinner for your dates?

No not at all, I just thought you would like what I like, these are memorable moments we're creating remember?

Why the Sardinian Carignano?

Well I prefer Red Wine with Seafood and the Sardinian is rather acidic which brings out the flavor of the Oysters as well as the Clams.

So you are a connoisseur?

Not really, my Dad has a rather extensive wine cellar, we played there as kids and as we grew up we developed a taste for the grape.

Impressive, I like a man that takes charge of a situation as long as he knows what situations to take charge of.

And what situations would those be?

I think you will be able to figure that one out Doctor Prentice. Tammy has told me quite a bit about the Prentice clan, so what do you all do for the holidays?

Well my Mom usually goes all out for the holidays no matter what holiday it is, I mean Halloween, Thanksgiving, Midgets day, whatever. I'm sure you know her Constance Prentice; she was once the Associate Dean at Paine.

Everybody knows Dean Prentice Martin; I think I may have met her once during my initial interview at the College. Of course at that time I already knew Tammy so let's just say I know of your mother. What about your father the great Senator Armstrong Prentice?

Well now you are standing among high cotton my dear, that's what my father would say after being asked that question. Has Tammy ever taken you to Sandy Grove, the family estate?

No she hasn't taken me there, but I saw it as we flew over when I took a helicopter from the airport to the campus last year, it was one of those publicity stunts put on by the college during homecoming. I remember when we flew over the place every eye was glued to it, that has to be the largest estate I have ever seen in my life, it looks like Michael Jordan's place outside Chicago. It must have been great to grow up in a place like that.

Well I wouldn't say it was great, it's not like we really had anything to compare it too at the time, but it was great growing up surrounded by the love that we still share as a family. I'll tell you what, are you going to be in the area for Thanksgiving?

As far as I know I will be, why?

Well that settles it, why don't you accompany me for dinner at Sandy Grove?

Martin I would love to, are you sure?

Yes Tameka I'm sure, I haven't been this sure about anything in my life. Wow, here comes the waiter hmmm this smells delicious.

Yes this Wine will be fine.

So that's why they pour such a small amount in the man's glass first?

Yes, so that we can taste and approve the wine. Become accustomed to your life changing right before your eyes Tameka, I know I will. Bon appetite!

74

Good morning Ladies.

Good morning Dr. Prentice.

Why so formal today Sonya?

Well sir I was just making sure you were the same man I once knew.

Meaning?

Well after yesterday morning and all the roses we kind of figured you might be off the market.

Sonya come into my office I want to speak with you on something, close the door. Look Sonya we've known each other since high school at Richmond Academy and we've always been able to talk about anything and right now I need your honest opinion about something.

Sure Martin, anything.

What did you think about that woman that came in here yesterday morning?

You mean Queen Diva.

Why do you call her that?

Look Martin, for once in my life I was kind of proud of you, you finally stepped up your game, it was about time you left those skeezers alone and found somebody that was worthy of your attention and sister girl seems to have her shit together. I'm just glad Macy's had that Trench Coat on sale yesterday, who is she anyway?

That's not important but I can feel you on the stepping up my game deal, I just may have bitten off a little more than I want to chew right now.

What, did the Pimp get Pimped? Wait a minute let me get a closer look, yep you do look a little different truth be told, you looked whooped!

No, I'm just a little tired that's all; I was up kind of late last night.

With Queen Diva?

Yes, you could say that, we had a late dinner.

Where did you go, the Olive Garden or T Bones?

We went to Charleston.

Charleston, is that a new restaurant, I haven't heard of that one yet, where is it?

No, it's not the name of a restaurant she flew me to Charleston, South Carolina for dinner.

Flew you? Okay wait a minute, the two of you flew down to Charleston just for dinner?

Yes, she chartered a private Jet and we flew down to Charleston for dinner at her favorite restaurant near the Battery.

You have got to be shitting me, I kind of figured she had a few bucks, I mean those stilettos were the bomb and that coat.

Actually all she had on was that coat.

Gone sista, get ya freak on.

I invited her to Sandy Grove for Thanksgiving dinner.

Martin I haven't even been to Sandy Grove and I've known you for over twenty years, so just how long have you known this woman?

Well she is actually Tammy's best friend so I have known her for quite a while I just haven't known her if you know what I mean.

Well after dinner did she get you desert?

No it wasn't like that at all; that conversation never really came up, after dinner we just walked along the shore at Isle of Palms Beach, played in the sand for what seemed like hours just gazing at the moon and getting our feet wet. I was so involved that I can't tell you one thing that we talked about, it was just that surreal.

Damn, it was like that?

Yeah, when I first met her getting into her pants was all that I could think about but I held out because she was Tammy's best friend, now that I know her better that's not even an issue anymore, I just enjoyed being around her, she is really a fantastic lady.

What does she do for a living?

She's a Professor at Paine.

Look at you man, eyes glistening, permanent smile, you look like a kid in a candy store Martin. Bulletin, bulletin, Augusta's finest could be off the market, you look good man, just remember one thing, you teach people how to treat you and don't forget that the pendulum swings both ways. If she is the right one you will know it and believe me there will be nothing you can do about it if it's real. We can never tell our hearts what to do, I always thought that one day you would see the light and now that you have I'm gonna miss the old Martin Prentice but I think I might like the new one. Talk with you later Casanova, I got work to do.

Thanks Sonya.

75

Come on in here girl and give me the scoop.

What do you mean Tammy?

Tameka I know you ain't finda trip, so what is really going on between you and my brother?

You cool with that Tammy?

Actually I think the two of you make a good couple, a good couple of what, the jury is still out on but yeah I can roll with it.

Great then sit down and take a deep breath, Tammy we had the best dinner last night you could ever imagine, we had Oysters and Wine and we walked on the beach, it was fabulous girl.

Walked on the beach, what beach Tameka? Newsflash! Augusta doesn't have a beach?

Okay, you know Cal Ripken, Jr. with the baseball team? Well he keeps a plane at Daniel Field right, well when he is not using it you can charter it, anyway I chartered it last night and flew Martin down to Charleston and we had dinner at that restaurant near the Battery that I told you about and girl the rest is what dreams are made of!

Okay let me get this straight; you flew my brother down to Charleston just for dinner, girl no you didn't, tell me everything, I mean everything I even want to know the waiters name okay!

Just keeping it real Tammy your brother is a great guy, I mean he still has playa tendencies in him but that's to be expected, I have never felt this way about possibilities before but Martin makes my nipples hard.

TMI Tameka, TMI.

It's just the way that he talks and the way he smells and the way he seems to actually listen to what I have to say and, well, he made no move toward the goodies which he probably could have indulged in right there on the beach but we connected on an entirely difference level.

Tameka, look at you girl, have you fallen for the old Prentice charm?

Girl I don't know what it is but it feels good and I'm gonna flow with it, oh and guess who got an invitation to Sandy Grove?

What! Martin has never brought a woman to the estate, when are you going girl?
Thanksgiving.

What, for real, Tameka that's great, that is terrific, why don't you come with me
to the party.

What party?

Well my mother always gives a cocktail party just for the girls on the night before
Thanksgiving. Oh Tameka please come girl, you can stay with me in the main house,
and it will be the bomb girl. My sister in laws will be there, my brother Kelvin and
his wife Maria and the grandkids from Silver Spring, Maryland will be there and who
knows who else my mother has invited but you may have to help us cook. Mom said
Consuelo would not be there this year because her twins would be home; my Daddy
got them into the University of Georgia.

Sounds like fun, tell me about Sandy Grove Tammy.

What exactly is there to tell, Sandy Grove is my father's crowning achievement, I
actually think they went a little bit overboard with the place but you would have to be
Senator Armstrong Prentice to understand.

I've flown over it and was impressed, how many rooms are in that place.

On which Wing?

What do you mean on which Wing?

Well at Sandy Grove there's the main house, and then there is the Johnson and the
Brown Wings which are attached to the main house by corridors that extend from each
side, each corridor has an elevator that takes you either to the main floor of the main
house or to one of the three sub-basements, behind the main house and in between the
two wings sit the swimming pool and at the front of the estate is the statue of General
Sherman.

General Sherman, what's up with that?

No idea, he's always been my father's favorite; there's even a picture of him in the
main hall, then there's my father's Study which actually sits in the middle of the second
sub-basement but you need a special code and clearance to get in there, even I have
never been in there.

You have never been in your father's Study?

Nope and then there is a four lane bowling alley and a fifty seat movie theater; two
kitchens, servant's quarters, the stables, and well you know the usual.

Yeah right, usual my ass, girl I could get lost in a place that big.

You really become accustomed to it after a while, when Consuela, our cook, first
moved in it took her about six weeks to learn her way around the estate and almost that
long to see every room, thank God for golf carts. The estate has a total of sixty three
rooms, of that sixty three; twenty five are bedrooms with fifteen bathrooms and yada
yada yada. Now about the party can you hang?

Ok, if Martin doesn't have a problem with it.

What do you mean if Martin doesn't have a problem with it?

I was just.

Whatever, the colors are Maroon and Beige girl.

Colors?

It's a Mama thang girl ok.

Ok.

76

Hello.

What's up sis, this is Strong, listen Maria, first of all its great that you guys are going to make it down for Thanksgiving this year, we are all looking forward to it. Let me just say this, Dad is going to want his own sweet potato pie and I just wanted to put in a bid for mine, ya heard. Sis, I don't know what you do to it but just plan on making an extra one for me.

You are so crazy Strong, let me get Kelvin.

Sup brah?

Hey man, just wanted to touch base with you guys, haven't heard from you in a while and just wanted to holla.

Cool man, looking forward to coming home next month.

Yeah, you know Mom is looking forward to spending time with the kids, as a matter of fact it's gonna be hard for you all to take them back to Maryland with you, Mama has assigned them a permanent room at Sandy Grove and the baby pictures you guys sent are now tapestries in those rooms now man, it's crazy but you know your mother. So brother man, tell me what's going on with you?

Nothing out of the ordinary Strong, what's going on in the Garden city?

Well we just had an episode with some guy that wanted to bring all that negative shit on the murder case back on Tammy but we took care of it. It was just some Crazy trying to get paid but not to worry, other than that everything is Kool and the Gang.

How is Dad really doing man? He's not a spring chicken anymore.

You know Kelvin, Dad is hard to peg man, he always seems to have something on his mind but he also seems to be waiting for the right moment and things, he worries me sometimes but he is still Armstrong Prentice at his best, he is getting older Kelvin and it's beginning to show, but his vigor is still prevalent however I think he needs his family around him right now, who ever thought the old man would age, I know I didn't.

I know what you mean, Maria's mother passed away two years ago at the age of sixty and it really threw us for a loop, anyway let's not even talk about that, did Mom do all the decorations again this Thanksgiving?

No, she hasn't done Thanksgiving decorations yet but Kelvin; you should see what she's done for Halloween, it's spooky as hell at the estate man.

How are things going with her is she alright?

Mom hasn't changed a bit, she is still the Belle of the Ball and more importantly she is still running Sandy Grove like some prison warden.

I hear some woman is trying to slow Martin's ass down, what's the scoop on that?

She's actually a best friend of Tammy's and they've been kicking it pretty heavy these last few weeks but you know Martin man, he easily gets bored with women but maybe this time it's different.

Well let's hope so anyway, look got to run but looking forward to hanging out with you when we get into town. Expect us the Tuesday before Thanksgiving and Strong; we got a bombshell to drop on the family man, so keep it tight until I get there.

You can tell me bro, I can keep a secret.

Not gonna happen man, you have to wait just like everybody else.

Aright bro, kiss the wife for me and hug the kids and help me work on that sweet potato pie, peace.

77

Well you seem to be in a good mood this morning, let me guess . . . . you've spoken with all the kids and all of them are going to make Thanksgiving dinner this year, am I right?

Yes Papa you are, you seem to know me so well, it's going to be an amazing time for the family, Kelvin and Maria should get in on Tuesday and they are bringing the grandkids, Papa I think I'm going to cry.

Now, now Connie, just relax sweetie, these are the days that we dreamed and talked about when we were planning this family. This estate and our kids are the real fruits of our labor and I am proud as punch to have been blessed with the lot of them.

I spoke with Cheryl, and Strong has to have some more tests run since the Doctor says he has a low sperm count, which is the reason they haven't been able to have children Papa but let's just pray that everything works out alright. Did you mention anything to him about making Kelvin your successor?

Well we spoke on the matter for a minute and I gave him sixty days to put one in the oven or I will have no choice. I'm still not sure how to convince Kelvin to take the position, his physically being on the property could wait, he has about another five years before he is eligible for retirement and I don't plan to be put in the ground no time soon so it could all work out.

Let's hope so, I know you are about ready to pass that torch so that we can move part time into the Coconut Grove property in Miami and spend the day on the boat.

The boat Connie, it's a one hundred and ninety seven footer and sleeps twelve comfortably and can get up to speeds exceeding fifteen knots; it's a Yacht sweetie, not a boat, that's like calling Sandy Grove a house.

Whatever, but I do miss those days Papa.

So do I, we have put so much into this family and I think we have done an excellent job, it's gonna be hard fading into the background but that's what leaving a legacy is all about, to be able to sit back and watch them take over the family business. I might just take up golf Connie; imagine me being an old Tiger Woods, are you planning the party the night before Thanksgiving as usual?

Yes as always, I think by then the girls and I will be exhausted, especially since Consuela will be with her family this year and we will have to do most of the cooking.

Remember those days before we had the staff Connie, you did all the cooking then and we had no problem.

Yes I remember Papa, but who knew that Sandy Grove would take two years to build and you almost need a degree in computer technology just to cook an egg around here now.

Well anyway have a good time, I think me and the boys might just go up to the cabin and get in a little fishing.

Fishing Papa, no not the night before Thanksgiving, I won't hear of it, the last time the four of you went up to Helen you almost drank yourself silly and got back here two days late. No you will stay downstairs in the sub-basement out of my way and watch that dreaded football.

Okay, whatever you say.

I hear that Martin is starting to get serious about a friend of Tammy's.

Is that so, well it is about time? I figured he would be finished sowing his oats years ago but the boy is a Prentice, I got to give him that.

And what does that mean Papa?

Oh, nothing honey, just being silly, I meant ahem nothing.

Tammy said I have met the girl; she is a Psychology Professor at Paine, Dr. Allmond I believe her name is, anyway she will be here for the party with Tammy and she will be Martin's guest for dinner on Thursday.

Really, that serious is he? Should we have her investigated?

No Papa, I don't think it will be necessary with this one; I'll just stop by the college and spend a little time in Human Resources if you know what I mean, but I am sure she will check out okay, I hear she's a Doctoral candidate.

Well, that's my boy, there is nothing like an educated woman, I didn't do so bad myself now did I?

No Senator Armstrong Prentice you hit the jackpot. Ka Ching!! Oh Papa you are a Gem.

78

I am sorry Mr. and Mrs. Prentice but it would seem that the condition is more serious than we anticipated before, the Oligospermia is simply a symptom and we think the cause may be deeper still. What we would like to do Mr. Prentice is subject you to an MRI or Magnetic Resonance Imaging scan of your cranial area, what this will do is rule out the presence of a pituitary or some other form of tumor. We may also want to conduct a testicular biopsy to try and determine the cause, have you been having any major headaches that you can remember? Do you smoke or drink beyond reason?

No Doctor I haven't had any headaches that I can remember and no I don't smoke but I do have a nice Cognac occasionally but nothing that could even remotely be considered excessive, is this something that could be hereditary or what might be its root cause?

Well Mr. Prentice I am not one to speculate at a time like this, let's get the test done and move forward from there. I can actually have the MRI done today if that fits into your schedule.

How pervasive is the procedure?

Not pervasive at all Mr. Prentice, what we will do is place you into the machine and it will take digital pictures of your brain, this can rule out any type of tumor or pituitary abnormality.

And if there is a tumor what would our course of action be at that time?

Well Mr. Prentice there are myriad of treatments for tumors of this nature if they are present but what would be important is whether or not the tumor is malignant and its position but we are not at that place yet.

Doctor let me ask you something, let's say we do this test and there is no tumor, what then?

Well at that point we will probably proceed with a testicular biopsy. In looking at your blood work results from your last visit I can see where your ACTH, testosterone and LH levels may have to be further examined, they look to be a little abnormal.

Okay Dr. Screen you got me man, in layman's terms my ACTH, LH and testosterone levels?

Sorry Mr. Prentice, your hormone levels.

Bottom line Doctor, if everything works out when will we be able to conceive a child?

Mr. Prentice is that such a worry at this point; there are batteries of test that we would have to run to find out the exact cause of your problem, this is not something that could have a one stop shop for a cure or result. There are hormone replacement therapies that we could try and other things that might solve the problem but we will need to run, like I said, batteries of test to be sure and this could take a little time.

Oh Armstrong, tell him that we do not have that much time, all we have is sixty days.

Excuse me Mrs. Prentice, what do you mean you only have sixty days?

Don't worry about that Doctor, let's get the MRI done and behind us and move forward from there.

Good call Mr. Prentice, let me get that scheduled, I'll be right back.

Cheryl you have to control yourself, Dr. Screen comes highly recommended and we came here to find out what the problem was, I want kids as bad as you do but this is going to be a process and we have to play by the rules, now you were quiet up until that last outburst and I expect you to maintain your composure while we get the rest of the news, can you do that for me?

Yes Strong I can, it's just that?

It's just what Cheryl?

Ok, Mr. Prentice, if you would go into the next room with my nurse we can get you prepped for the MRI and once I have had time to go over the results I will be giving you a call. Nice meeting you again Mrs. Prentice.

Same to you Dr. Screen.

79

Well, how have you been Dean Prentice and what brings you back to the slums?

I am doing just fine Phyllis and how are things going up here with you in this snake pit?

Well you know how it is in Human Resources, always something else to do.

Tell me about it, Phyllis I was wondering if I can see a file concerning a Professor we have on staff here, there seems to be something familiar about her but I don't want to just go up to the child unless I'm sure, can you help a sista out?

Sure Dean anything for you, besides if it wasn't for you I wouldn't have moved up the professional ladder as fast as I did, what is the Professor's name.

Her name is Tameka Allmond and I believe that is with two L's.

Tameka Allmond, oh here she is, I remember her, she has quite an impressive resume and a 3.6 GPA from Mercer, and she's also a Doctoral candidate.

Thanks Phyllis, I'll just sit over here and peruse her file for a minute, her name sounds so familiar to me, I believe I may know her parents if they are the same Allmonds I remember, thanks I won't be but a minute.

Take your time Dean, I have to go downstairs anyway, you can use my desk if you need too.

Thanks Phyll, hmm Tameka Kyle Allmond, so she's from Atlanta, that would explain the Spelman and Mercer connections. She seems to be an overachiever which is excellent. What about her references, hmm, they all seem to check out. Delta Sigma Theta Step Master, Big Sister, she made the National 100 People under 30 to watch list, you go girl. Everything seems to be in order here but wait a minute she's almost too perfect but so was I, anyway I trust Tammy and if she has her as a best friend then she will just have to do. In my opinion she is worthy of the Prentice name if it comes to that but I will definitely keep an eye on her, I can spot a gold digger from thirty thousand feet in the air at midnight in a dense fog.

You don't have to get up just because I came back Dean, take your time.

No need Phyllis I am done, I just thought I knew her parents from our times in Atlanta but it looks like I was wrong. But thank you so much for your time.

Anytime Dean, you are welcome anytime.

80

Tammy.

Hi Mother, what are you up to today?

Well I was just up at the college and just wanted you to know that I am taking you to lunch and to the precinct to vote today so up and atom my dear.

What time today are you talking about Mama, I just got out of bed?

Well that's good because I am just turning onto Broad Street and should be in Harrisburg in about twenty minutes, and be ready Tammy I do have other things to do you know.

Yes Mom, I will be ready. *I wonder what Mama is doing downtown today, and more importantly, why does she want to take me to lunch?*

So tell me where do you want to have lunch today Tammy?

Well, you didn't really give me time to think of anywhere, it's not like we planned to have lunch today, what's so urgent?

Let's do Fujiyama's' Japanese Steak and Seafood on Washington Road, it's been a while since I've been there; they always have the freshest seafood.

Ok, that's fine but you didn't answer my question, what is so urgent?

Well Tammy, your father and I heard that Martin is getting a little serious about your little friend Tameka and we just wanted to know a little bit more about her, what is her pedigree and does she really qualify to become a Prentice?

If I didn't know that you were serious I would probably laugh at you mother, you know that Tameka is a great person and what do you mean qualify to be a Prentice? I didn't know there were certain qualifications that one had to possess except to breathe on their own and walk on two feet instead of four.

Well sweetheart that is true but your father and I aren't getting any younger and we must ensure that the family legacy is not only intact but that all of you are happy and content before we relocate to the great beyond.

Don't be silly Mama what are you saying?

It's simple child, it is our responsibility to make sure that no gold diggers get their hands on any of the Prentice assets and those assets include our children. Oh come on Tammy, not only is this a family but it is also a business and it must be managed as such.

When each of you turned twenty-five years old you were able to access your trust funds. How many other people do you know that became instant millionaires upon reaching twenty five? Don't worry I'll wait, well then my point is made and it is quite obvious that upon your father's and my transition there are loads of cash and property that must also be managed. This legacy must continue Tammy; it has done so for over one hundred and fifty years and will not be squandered during my watch, do you understand?

Yes Mama but Tameka is your least worry, she and Martin have been having a great time and she is really looking forward to celebrating Thanksgiving with us. The hard part of our job is to keep Martin focused, what I didn't know was that they have had a thing for each other for over a year but both of them were too shy to make the first move, and you can rest assured that the last thing I would do would be to hook my own brother up with some skeezer. Besides Mama, Tameka was with me every day during that mess I went through and it's because of her that I have come as far away from that as I have. I'm still a little apprehensive about going out and dating but I feel that I can at least walk to the edge of that bridge and maybe one day cross it. All of that is because of Tameka so rest assured that she would be a prime mate for Martin, as a matter of fact Mama I think Tameka is just what Martin needs.

Well great Tammy, I will not only take your word on it but her personnel file speaks volumes as well.

Mama no you didn't?

Tammy, yes hell I did, and it's not the first time and won't be the last.

Why do you say won't be the last.

Well you aren't married yet are you? I did the same thing with Strong and Kelvin, the only problem with Strong is that Cheryl's files were destroyed during Hurricane Katrina so I wasn't able to get it all but I got enough.

Mama you are crazy.

Crazy like a fox, oh, here we are, see talking to you made me pass the restaurant.

No problem, just make a right turn into the skating rink parking lot and turn around, thanks for picking me up.

No problem Princess I just didn't want you to be standing in that voting line on an empty stomach.

Mama you tricked me and what about you?

Child, your father and I were number one and two in line this morning; we are Prentices and had to set the standard, besides, your father is off doing his thing all day today so we had to get that small matter taken care of. I just wasn't going to let you come up with some excuse not to Barrack the vote, so I'm bribing you with lunch, so be it, tar and feather me tomorrow but you will vote today my dear, Barrack it.

So are you telling me who to vote for Mama?

Hell no, as long as his name is Barrack Obama you can vote for whoever you want too, now don't make me go behind that curtain with you.

No Mother that will not be necessary I was going to vote for him anyway.

General William T. Sherman

Exit 154 off of Interstate 20 to Warrenton

Miss Jane's Restaurant

The Knox Theatre

Johnsons Church

Johnson Church Marker

Hut on Johnson Plantation

Johnson Road enroute to Sandy Grove AME Church

One Room School House

Sandy Grove AME Church

Augusta, Georgia

The Augusta National Golf Course

Amanda Dickson Toomer

Amanda Dickson Toomer's House on Telfair Street

Amanda Dickson Toomer's Tombstone

Augusta, Georgia's own Diva the Great Jessye Norman

The Jessye Norman Ampitheater

Mrs. Lucy Craft Laney

Lucy Craft Laney High School

Paine College

Springfield Baptist Church

Statue of the Godfather of Soul, James Brown in Downtown Augusta

Tabernacle Baptist Church

The Bethlehem Community

The Bethlehem Community (2)

The Famous Lenox Theater

The Honorable former Mayor of Augusta Ed McIntyre

The Pinched Gut Community

The Pinched Gut Community (2)

81

Well Hello Martin, funny hearing you answer your own phone, I was expecting one of the hired hands.

Watch it Tameka, Sonya and I have been partners every since high school and she was hired here because she has always had my back and helped me with some of my papers during my college years so she is more than what one would call a hired hand.

Like I care, anyway Martin, how about lunch today will you have any time?

Yes as a matter of fact I can do a late lunch; I took the afternoon off so that I could take care of a few things like voting.

Oh great, I was going to vote as well, tell you what, my last class starts in about fifteen minutes and will last about forty five so let's vote first and then meet for lunch, I have to go downtown to Walton Way since that is my district, where would you have to vote?

Not too far from where I live, the precinct is on Wheeler Road, make sure you take a book with you looks like it might take a minute.

Tameka thanks for inviting me to lunch and for the record I can't get Charleston out of my mind and anything about you for that matter. I think you were right when you said that one day I would get tired of all the lies and of evading the truth, if this is how truth can make a man feel than truth be told.

No Martin it's you that I have to thank, you have restored my faith in relationships and in doing so you have also restored my faith in me. I was a little gun shy for a minute; I guess that's why it took me so long to put my cards on the table, but I am glad that I did, if my shyness had continued I would have missed the chance to smile again so thanks goes out to you Martin Prentice. Look I don't have time for all this mushy stuff; you just call me when you finish voting. And you better vote, remember the key to my heart today lies with that little peach sticker that reads "I voted", hugs and kisses Martin.

Same to you Tameka.

82

Well I'll be dipped in buttermilk, where did the wind blow the two of you in from?

It's been a long time man, but even the other side needs a hair cut every now and again Thomas.

Armstrong how long has it been since you've been down here on Brown Street and you brought Doc with you. Boys I want you to take a good look at two of Augusta's finest gentlemen and I am proud to have them back in my shop and in my chair, is this a business call guys or is it one of those?

It's one of those Thomas but we promise not to take up too much of your time. It's just so nice to see that you haven't changed the place at all, you need to have that picture of James Brown framed, he won't be making anymore, I promise. This is one of the last bastions that have remained the same since I was a little tyke myself.

Yes, and I can remember when it was just Blount's Barber Shop, now The Blount's but I'm just glad you've held out and remained stalwart in the community. The three of you are a testament to entrepreneurship and you would be surprised how many lives you have touched but we do have to ask you to close up for about an hour so that we can have a discussion.

Anything for you all and you know that, let me put the sign on the door, and if you customers don't mind can you please come back in about an hour and if you have a voter registration card your haircut is on the house. What can I do for you Armstrong?

Well we need you to keep your ear to the ground and let us know who we might run for Mayor in this next election. I came here because you have your hand on the pulse of the streets as always. I can remember when myself, the good Doctor here and Ed McIntyre would come here just to find out how things were faring in the community and I don't see that changing anytime soon. We want to move Deke to a post in Atlanta but we are going to need someone in office here that will not rock the cradle if you know what I mean, are there any up and coming community leaders that we don't know about or someone we can make a community leader in a hurry? I am not impressed with the current City Council so we may have to go outside the box on this one.

No one comes to mind right away Armstrong but I will be more in tuned to that from now on. What about W. A. Hussein, he hasn't exactly pissed off everybody downtown has he?

He pissed off enough with this school superintendent debacle the other year; I don't think he can recover from that one. Every time there was something negative in the paper concerning anything, his name was the first one uttered and we can't afford to have a loudmouth in the Mayor's office, nope, is there anyone else?

Well Mort, I really wish you would consider running we can almost assure you the job is yours if you want it.

I appreciate it Armstrong but I am a Dentist not a Politician, besides I am seriously considering retiring and raising horses on my place in North Augusta. I don't however think I will ever totally give up the dentistry but I want to rest a while and visit my kids in California.

Tom do we still have those busses on the road ferrying people to the polls? I want them on point until the polls close tonight. We need to insure that we go door to door if necessary to ensure that everyone that is registered also gets to the polls to vote. I will pay all expenses out of my own pocket. There will be no excuses this time, in addition Mort lets confirm that we have our own undercover security at each polling place, my son tells me that the police department and SWAT took refresher training in Riot control just in case the Republicans pull another Florida tonight and also to be prepared for too much celebration. I can definitely understand what you mean about taking a break you've earned it as well as I have. That's why I will be glad when the family gets together at Thanksgiving this year; it's time to pass the torch to the next generation but you all must admit we had a great time living the hell out of this one didn't we. We had better than most and have forgotten more than most will ever know. We are Augusta gentlemen and we must make sure that history recognizes that. I might as well get a cut while I'm in here Wayne, what do you say Doc?

I could use a little trim myself.

Here's to Men.

Men like us.

Damn few left.

83

Hi Papa, I didn't hear you come in how long have you been here?

Just got in a few minutes ago I've been keeping an eye on this election, we have over three hundred of our people in place just in case they try to pull another Florida. People have been in line since four thirty this morning Connie, it was a sight to see, Mort and I went up in the helicopter to look at the lines after we dropped you off and it was amazing. It actually brings tears to my eyes when I think that this is actually happening in my lifetime, I just wish our parents were alive to witness this, just think Connie, tomorrow morning we could wake up to a black man in the White House doing something other than cleaning up or kissing ass.

I know Papa; it hasn't been far from my mind all day and to watch the kids carry on as if nothing spectacular is happening is just awful. They just don't remember the racism that once plagued the South, they don't know about J.B. Stoner, Lester Maddox, and that George Wallace of Alabama and who could forget that Theodore Bilbo creature out of Mississippi. They can't wrap their modern minds around the multitude of lynching's that took the lives of many a generation in the name of segregation especially here in the South. They will never hear those black voices that were silenced before they could even develop a foothold on this earth. I ought to go downstairs right now and make them watch "Eyes on the Prize" so that they can remember Papa.

Calm down Connie, when you really look at it, those tickets of hope we as a people were forced to buy back then in the name of racism, those same tickets can finally be redeemed tonight! The tears, the beatings, the water cannons, and even Bull Connor's vicious dogs, yes those tickets of hope can finally be redeemed tonight! The families that were torn apart during the midnight rides of the Ku Klux Klan and the dreams that were destroyed under the guise of Jim Crow can finally be redeemed tonight! Tonight our Redeemer has a face, we have a man that has vowed to take all the checks that were previously returned stamped insufficient funds from this government, this man has pledged to redeem even those checks Connie. America has a chance to start anew and to wage a battle for equality that can insure that all of its citizens can have a chance to enjoy the freedoms fought for in physical as well as economic War, now is the time

Connie and I am proud to be a part of it, that is why I have made a decision concerning passing my torch to our next generation.

What is that Papa?

Connie, later on this evening I will have a meeting with the boys, we can conference Kelvin in, and I need to explain to them why it is time, they will have to understand that this must happen now while I am still around to give advice and guide my successor.

But Papa you promised Strong and Cheryl sixty days, you have never gone back on your word and now is not the time to start. The name Armstrong Prentice stands for honor and integrity; those qualities still ring true even here at Sandy Grove.

I know Connie, I will not make a decision until the sixty days are past, and I just want the boys to know that a decision is on the way and that the decision may change the landscape of this entire family, because once that decision has been made the secret will have to finally be shared with my heir and I can relieve the burden of carrying it around with me.

I'm sure they will understand and do the right thing Papa, I just pray that whomever you choose is ready for the sacrifices that being a Prentice curtails, and I just hope he's ready.

He has lived his entire life waiting for this sliver of time to come Connie, it is his birthright, and he was born ready. What's all that noise I hear outside?

It just might be the boys Papa they said they would be here with you tonight, is Strong bringing Cheryl?

Nope he said she wasn't home with he got there.

Okay, let me head downstairs to see my boys and where did you say Cheryl was?

I didn't Papa; I said she wasn't at home.

84

Hey Millicent, I need to talk with you about something girl and I need to know that you are still my friend and that I can trust you.

Sure Cheryl, sup girl?

You and I go all the way back to the "Big Easy" and I need a friend right now.

Spill it.

Well Strong and I went to a fertility specialist and the reason that we haven't had any kids is because his sperm count is not up to par and they are running some test to find out why, anyway those results could take weeks and I can't just sit around and wait. Then they will have to come up with some action plan and by the time they get around to doing whatever it is they do a whole lot of time will have passed and time is something that I do not have right now.

What do you mean do not have?

Millicent, Strong's father has given us sixty days to get pregnant or he will turn over the family business to Strong's brother Kelvin, the one with the two kids in Maryland.

And why is that a problem Cheryl, it's not like you and Strong are destitute.

I know that dammit, listen to me! Strong is the oldest and by all rights the family business should go to him, the only stipulation is that his father demands that another male heir be in place to take the reins from his son when the time comes.

So you don't only have a problem getting pregnant you also have a problem ensuring that your baby is a boy.

Yes, what should I do?

What should you do? Not a damn thing Cheryl just let nature take its course, when it's time for you to get pregnant it will happen, until then don't try to rock the boat. Wait a minute, oh hell no, Cheryl what's on your mind? Don't do anything stupid that will jeopardize your entire situation. What is their family business anyway?

I'm not all together sure about that but whatever it is its worth millions and I don't mean one or two, we have got to be talking millions in the nine figure range girl.

And you want to screw that up! Cheryl you need the worst kind of therapy you need white peoples' therapy, you said that Strong's trust fund made him a multi millionaire so what is your problem? You already struck gold girl.

Yeah but Strong doesn't act like it Millicent we haven't even bought a bigger house since we got married and I still drive that old car.

Newsflash! You don't need a bigger house Cheryl, hell it's just you and Strong, and your car might be old but it's a Benz bitch, a Mercedes Benz 500 SEL and a convertible at that, the best I have ever done is a damn Toyota Camry okay, it's so old it don't even say Camry anymore, I drive a Toyota amry Cheryl.

You just don't understand how important it is that I get pregnant! I know what the doctor said and all but that does nothing to help my situation. I will be the next star to shine at Sandy Grove and not that little prissy ass Maria.

What the hell is Sandy Grove Cheryl?

Sandy Grove is the estate that Strong's family lives on and it is one of those Blake Carrington type of places. Strong's family is like a modern day Dynasty and his mother is the real black Crystal Carrington and I will be Dominique Devereaux up in that spot! I refuse to let anything including lack of a pregnancy destroy my chances.

Looks like you're planning to destroy them on your own, listen Cheryl, you already got it made girl, now I know how devious you can be but now is not the time. If you are destined to be Queen Bee up in there then it will happen but don't screw your future up by being greedy.

I don't know Millicent; I am at the end of my rope, I will not just stand by and watch Maria take over all that I have planned for. The first time Strong took me to meet his family I knew that one day the estate would be mine; I have already re-decorated the damn place in my mind.

Cheryl, please home girl do not do anything stupid, you are my girl on the real but if you fuck up that gold mine you call home I will have to cut your bitch ass loose and pursue Strong my damn self. I said it! We didn't go through all that Katrina bullshit for nothing Cheryl; you remember, making sure we created new identities, getting new credit files and erasing our criminal records, thank God for your boy at Equifax not to mention your cousin at the New Orleans Police Department, and who could forget sleeping in that infested ass Super Dome for six days, just so you can screw it all up now! Cheryl we are not the people we were then, I thought you had put that Ninth Ward project mentality behind you, those people are gone forever; they drowned in all that filthy ass water remember! Don't ever forget where you came from just be thankful that God gave us a one way ticket out of that spot! Now your stupid ass wants to go back. See ya! You are married to a millionaire police Captain now stupid, you haven't been hungry in years and I'm sure you haven't turned a trick in ages. Don't do this now when all that hard work is finally paying off, promise me Cheryl? I want you to promise me dammit!

Ah, girl I was just trying to see what you thought about the situation that's all, I would never put all of this in jeopardy, besides like you said if it is to be it will be. Okay Millicent, thanks I'll talk to you later.

Peace out Cheryl but ah and can a sista borrow some paper for a new car? Ok how about another used one. Cheryl , , , , Cheryl? How about the C? Can you help a sista buy a C?

Bye girl I got another call to make.

Yes, this is Cheryl Prentice is Dr. Screen available?

85

I thought I heard you boys down here.

Hi dad.

Martin it's good to see you son, Strong will it be safe on the streets of Augusta tonight? Who knows what might happen during this election, it's been a while since you have made your way to Sandy Grove but I am happy that both of you made it out here to watch this historic election with your old man.

Where else would we be tonight of all nights dad and yes the streets should be safe tonight?

Do you think Obama can take Georgia?

Good question Strong, when we were in Atlanta for David Franklin's funeral I had a chance to speak with Reverend Lowry, Ty Brooks, John Lewis and Andy Young on that very subject. Georgia is a progressive State but neither of us feels it has progressed to the point of electing a black man just yet. The problem is really two fold; first we haven't supported a Democratic President since Clinton won the state in 1992. That itself is going to be major to overcome especially with a Republican Governor under the Dome. Then there's the racism that still resonates here in the South, I have it on good authority that the only southern State Obama can count on is Florida with North Carolina becoming a battleground State which makes it a tossup.

Wow Dad, looks like you're up to your old self again.

Martin, I have had my hand firmly on the pulse of the political acumen of this State from as far back as I can remember. Over the last forty years I have become the man that can get things done in this great State of Georgia. It means something to have that type of power but remember you must never abuse such strength and I am saying to the two of you that whoever takes the reins from me in the next few months will also wield unimaginable power just because you are a Prentice. Listen boys, let's go down to my study, I want to discuss something very important with you. The polls will close in about another half hour and I want to have both of you here with me. Thomas and Dr. Blount should be here later on but I want to talk with my boys first.

But dad we have never been allowed down in the study.

Martin, things are changing son and it's time you were made aware of a few things, hit the intercom and tell your mother that we are retiring to the study.

Yes sir.

Mom, this is Kelvin, dads taking us down to the study so we will probably be there for a minute.

He's taking you where Kelvin?

To his study mom.

His study?

Yes, mama are you okay?

I'm fine son just wondering where I was when your father lost his mind.

86

Dad this place is huge, and who are these men in these old pictures on the walls and looks like you kept all of our baby pictures too.

In time all three of my boys will understand everything Martin, in time it will all make sense. Sit down guys, Serge pour the boys a cognac and give them a Behike, make mine a double; you should be able to get Kelvin on the monitor from Maryland, and then make sure we are not disturbed.

Right away sir, will there be anything else?

No, that will be all. Strong and Martin two of the three Prentice men, I must say that I am proud of all three of you but for different reasons, tonight marks change that will cause ripples across the world once again.

Master Kelvin is on the monitor sir.

Kelvin, how goes it son? As you can see I am here with Strong and Martin and we are in my study.

Your study, Dad what's going on? We were never allowed to even come near your study.

Well Kelvin, things change and tonight is the beginning of that change. This country has the opportunity to finally live up to its creed that all men are created equal. Some of the men on that wall behind you believed in that creed but only a couple lived long enough to at least dream about it and we have lived long enough to see it come to fruition. Yes they had more than most, thanks to a man that you may hear about later but they were never really able to grab a hold of the American dream but that didn't stop them from dreaming. As a matter of fact their dream included most of what you will find in this room and throughout Sandy Grove. Their dream has now been entrusted to the three of you, follow me. This first picture you see here is Armbruster Brown who was my Great, Great Grandfather, not much is known about him except for the fact that he was born around the turn of the nineteenth century and lived as a slave his entire life, he is renowned for bringing my Great Grandfather Boregard Walker Brown Johnson into this world in 1834. Boregard was a little over thirty years old when General Sherman burned his way from Atlanta to Savannah; he is who your son is named after Kelvin.

But who is the white man next to him dad?

I was getting to that Strong, that white man is the most important man on that wall. It's because of him that we are who we are; boys meet Massa Franklin Johnson of Warren County, Georgia, Massa Johnson was the owner of our ancestors', he was their slave master.

How can you say that a slave master is the most important person on the wall dad? That sounds stupid to me.

Let me continue and then maybe you might understand a little better Martin. The man in the next photograph is Prentice Walker Brown Johnson who was my Grandfather and one of the proudest men I have come to know in my lifetime. He was born in 1856 and was just eight years old during Sherman's march but he was a great horseman and a crack shot even at such a young age. Grandfather was always up to something it seemed and in time I would come to find out why. Grandfather would become heir to the legacy of this family at a time when lives were being changed and lifelong friendships were being forged. Son it was my Great Grandfather who was first informed of the true meaning and heritage of this family and it was he who would set the wheels in motion that would cause my Grandfather Prentice and my father Benjamin to become two of the most powerful forces in the South, more powerful than Jim Crow, racism, and segregation combined. You see the name Benjamin Walker Brown Johnson would become synonymous with power son but it was a quiet power, a power that was only spoken of in a small hut off of the Gibson Highway in Warren County.

What is that vile that all of them seem to have around their necks dad? That is all of them except Boregard; even this Johnson guy is wearing one.

Kelvin in time that vial will mean the world to you or whoever my successor is but not now. The photo next to that is of my father Benjamin who was born in 1880 and of course the last photograph is of me and I got here in 1938. I was my father's last child and the only survivor, the space next to my photograph is reserved for my successor.

But dad there's only one space provided for your successor, there are four of us.

That's true Martin, but only one of you will succeed me and become the patriarch of this family and that person will be named in early April after we crown a new President, hopefully a black one for the first time. That wall is one of only two places on earth where your ancestors are displayed. Their history does not reside anywhere but within the confines of this room, there is a reason for that and it will be revealed to you at a later date. I am open to questions at this time and this time only from the three of you because after tonight only one of you will be allowed to return to this study and that one will be my successor. To him and to him only will all the other secrets of Sandy Grove be revealed.

So like I asked before how can a slave master be the most important person on the wall?

Franklin Johnson was much more than just a slave master son, he was also an honest and God fearing white man, he was a man of his word and a man among men. It was he who was responsible for solidifying the legacy that became this family. Boys, years before the Civil War was fought a free man by the name of Fessa Brown from Philadelphia

214

fell in love with Eleanor Walker Johnson, he made a deal with Massa Johnson to help him turn a profit from his farm at a time when the Plantation wasn't providing much income and the Johnson clan was little more than white trash. In return for allowing Fessa to marry Eleanor he made him agree to work on the place for six months out of the year and then return to Philadelphia for the remainder of the year. Fessa Brown was an excellent farmer in that he knew about crop rotation and irrigation and things that were new to the South, he also taught the Johnson clan to read and write. In thanks for this, Massa Johnson decided one day that he would give Fessa Brown and his relations part of the profits from the Johnson Plantation. Those profits son and much more has led to what you now know as Sandy Grove and much more, much, much more. You see Fessa and Eleanor Brown were my Great, Great Aunt and Uncle. Boregard and Eleanor were brother and sister.

Why did the last name change from Johnson to Prentice?

In honor of Prentice Brown Johnson son, you see Strong after the war was over and the slaves were freed Prentice stayed on at the Johnson Plantation and it continued to prosper but he couldn't get over the vision of what he had seen slavery do to a lot of his people out of his head. Growing up on the Johnson Plantation was a benefit in that Massa Johnson treated his slaves humanely, but that didn't necessary hold true for the rest of Warren County. Prentice wanted nothing to remind him of the toil and strain that he saw so many blacks suffer; he started making plans to move to the city but changed his mind in order to provide for his next generation. He made sure that his son Benjamin would lead a much better and more rewarding life. Benjamin eventually graduated from Howard University and became a member of the first class of pledges to the Omega Psi Phi fraternity of which I am a proud member and why it was so important to me that all of you became members as well. Your photographs along with your Grandfather and I being awarded our crest are on the walls on the other side of my desk. Prentice's father and Massa Johnson decided that one way to disconnect from the past would be to change the last name of his son Benjamin. As far as the world was concerned Benjamin's official last name became Prentice in honor of his father. They named me Armstrong Walker Brown Prentice in honor of Armbruster Brown and my Grandfather Prentice.

Dad why all the secrecy, I can remember that while we were growing up mentioning our ancestors was taboo in this house, it was almost as if we didn't really exist, then Maria mentioned putting together a family tree a few years ago and you almost lost your mind, why was all that drama necessary?

It wasn't drama son it was self preservation, only two people outside of this study knows the legacy of our family and I find it necessary to keep it that way. There are no records to trace or ancestral documentation to uncover. What I have told you is all you will ever need to know about your legacy, I will not allow some naysayer to try and erroneously document our existence; it is of the utmost importance that it never be known. I only shared the information with you because you are my sons and you have a right to know. You also have a right to keep this information to yourselves for reasons that I cannot explain to you right now. Just trust me and try and understand, by the way I have something for each of you. On the table behind you Strong are three boxes one for each of us, Kelvin yours should have been delivered today with my instructions not to open it until now.

Yes dad, I have it.

You may open it now boys.

Thanks dad, wow, this is a Rolex Oyster Perpetual, this had to set you back about what sixty or seventy five thousand dollars each, why such an extravagant gift?

Because I love you guys and want tonight of all nights to be one that you remember and from this day forth I want you to understand that it's not important who takes over this study as my successor, what is important is that we are family and nothing must ever be allowed to come between that. There will always be enough money to go around, let's just understand that no one, no wife, no outsider, or anybody must break the bond that we have between us. Oh by the way, give me the last box, it holds my Rolex, I've always wanted one myself. Heed the words that I have shared with you my sons, your future will remain intact as long as you remember that land and family are the backbones of our heritage and nothing can ever be allowed to get in the way of that. Now put on your Rolex's and join me in the den so that we can watch the election results come in, your mother is probably worried about us and I was expecting Mortimer and Thomas Blount to come over. Kelvin, I look forward to seeing you and the family in a couple of weeks for Thanksgiving, take care son and remember what you have witnessed this evening.

Here's to men.

Men like us.

Damn few left!

87

I am definitely in the wrong place, what is this? Three Prentice men, a Dentist, and a Barber together in one place at the same time, only in America.

Very funny, Connie very funny.

What is it looking like Papa?

Well its ten thirty five and they said that we should know something around eleven. There is no way that McCain can win and not even voodoo economics can make the math work for him as far as the electoral vote is concerned and he is also behind in the popular vote.

Right you are Mortimer; it's just nice that you and Thomas could make it out for this historic undertaking, my only regret is that my mother and father are not here to witness this historic evening.

As I sit here I am reminded of a time right here in Augusta when a black man's only wish was to make enough money to just feed his family, it was unimaginable for him then to even wrap his mind around anything other than the basics. Now here we are witnessing a moment in time that we will remember for the rest of our lives. From now on people will ask where you were when Obama crossed 277 and was declared the winner. I hope you all don't mind but I have to turn this up a bit, I'm recording it as well.

What channel is that Armstrong?

CBS.

(Television)

10:40pm: The action is rapidly shifting a little over to the Senate races where several remain unsettled. Democrats are expected to pick up a seat in Colorado, a tight race in Georgia could result in a runoff after the election if no candidate gets over 50 percent (Georgia is the only state with that law on the books) and in Minnesota, comedian Al Franken is trying to unseat incumbent Republican Norm Coleman, add in a special election in Mississippi, and GOP incumbents in Oregon and Alaska and we might not know the makeup of the Senate until tomorrow morning—or beyond.

11:03pm "No matter whom you voted for, you'd have to agree that this is an incredible milestone in the history of this country," is how Katie Couric put it after saying that CBS News estimates that Barack Obama will be the next president of the United States.

Historic is almost a tame word to describe the election of the first black man to hold the highest office in the land and it's going to take a generation or more before the full meaning is realized.

But that's for later, right now it's time to find out just how big a victory Obama can roll up by the end of the night. Several key States remain to be decided and Obama will want to pick up at least several more big targets to claim a mandate, there's still a lot of the story left to be told.

11:10pm: Right on cue, CBS News estimates that both Florida and Virginia will be won by now President-elect Obama, he's now at 323 in the Electoral College and counting with Colorado, Missouri and Indiana still out as big States.

Papa, are you okay?

I'm better than I have ever been Connie, I am better that I will ever be again, America is once again beautiful and is once again my Country tis of thee. Serge cognac for everyone and make sure it's the good stuff.

Right away sir.

So dad, what exactly do you see happening in the next few months now that he is President-Elect?

Well Martin first of all an awful lot of assholes just puckered up in Washington and across this Nation, but realistically speaking it will take at least two years before he can filter through all that's terribly wrong with the economy, the auto industry and Wall Street, then it may be another two years before whatever changes he makes filters down to the common man. His first actions will include the economy and bringing those boys home from the war, after that it's any ones guest but tonight is definitely historic and I am glad I had you boys and two of my best friends to share it with. I think I'll head upstairs now if you don't mind and sit on the balcony for a bit, I'll see you all tomorrow.

Same here Armstrong, I think I'll head back to town.

See you tomorrow Mortimer and drop Thomas off at his house this time and not Mr. J's.

No problem at all Armstrong, I will be sure to take him home.

Good night dad.

Mama, let me know when you come up.

I will Papa, just let me see everyone off.

Take care Connie and take care of the old man, tonight is a special night for him.

I will guys, I promise.

Mom is dad okay?

Yes Strong, he just a little sentimental this evening, that's all, you both know that your father has had his hand on the political climate of this State for most of his life and the fact that Obama did not win Georgia just upset him a little but he will be okay believe me. Tonight is a night that will go down in infamy for your father, tonight is a win for all Americans son, not just those of African descent but for all Americans.

I just hope the election of an African American President in this country can bridge some of the racial divide that still exists; change has to start somewhere, let's hope it started in Chicago tonight. Now the both of you run along and I look forward to seeing you both next week.

88

Papa do you need anything I brought you some tea, looks like it may get a little chilly tonight and I do not want you to catch cold out in that midnight air.

Thanks Connie, the tea will be fine.

The boys are worried about you Papa, they can see that you are aging and they show concern.

Why concern Connie, aging is a part of life and we all must eventually get old, there is just something special about tonight, this is still Augusta tonight but what will it be tomorrow? What has just happened hasn't really sunk in yet, it's when the ruling elite wake up tomorrow and realize that tonight was not a bad dream but was in fact reality, that's when I wonder what will happen. I wonder if this Wall Street and auto industry debacle happened arbitrarily or was it a calculated ploy to disrupt whatever progress Obama would have made in his first term, you can never trust politicians at that level Connie; they can do things today that will not have an immediate impact, it could take years before its effect is felt. I just hope they let him lead from the front and not from behind a bunch of bureaucrats.

Papa that was a nice gift that you gave the boys I was so proud of the way they kept glancing at them all evening but why a watch Papa?

Because it's time that I want them to remember the most Connie, it is this time in their lives that I want them to reflect back on long after we're gone. I want them to remember that this is the start of a new day in America. I want them to remember tonight each time they look down at their watches, each glance at their wrist will remind them of this night, the night America became whole again.

Armstrong Prentice I do like your style, I do like your style. Let's go inside Papa and get some rest, tomorrow will be one hell of a day.

Okay Connie but I am feeling a little frisky tonight can you scratch an itch for me?

Sure Papa, let me pour us some wine.

89

Consuela what time are the twins going to arrive I would love to see them before they leave.

They should be leaving Athens now Mrs. Prentice I will expect them around five this evening, what time will Mrs. Maria and Master Kelvin be getting in?

I am expecting them at any time now they left Silver Spring late yesterday and stopped in Fayetteville overnight I believe, anyway they will be here before five I'm sure.

I certainly hope so, I would hate to miss them but rest assured that I have taken care of everything as far as their accommodations are concerned. I also baked the Ham and made the Canapés for your party on Wednesday, all you have to do is warm things up. I also had three cases of the Chateau Lafite Rothschild Pauillac 1996, three cases of the Dom Romane Conti 1997 and five cases of the Petrus Pomerol 1998 along with five cases of the Veuve Clicquot brought up from the cellar and placed in the chiller.

Consuela you are a gem, thank you so much for taking care of that, well it seems like all bases have been touched so we can have us a cocktail. Join me on the balcony my dear, I'll get the good stuff from the bar.

Mrs. Prentice, this is a different concoction what is it called?

It's called a Mojito and I make it with fresh mint leaves.

I was wondering why you ordered those mint leaves, now I know.

I hear a car coming, oh my God Consuela, its Kelvin and the kids hold the elevator for me, let me run and freshen up.

Oh, my God, come here Kelvin and give your mother a hug, oh you look so good and who are these two angels, did you find them on the side of the road someplace? Come here and squeeze your Grandmother, oh Boregard you are getting so tall and Eleanor, you are the splitting image of your beautiful mother. Maria, how have you been sweetheart? All of you welcome back to Sandy Grove, Consuela aren't they just lovely?

Yes they are, welcome home Mrs. Maria and Master Kelvin, little Master Boregard and Ms. Eleanor, I know where there are some homemade cookies and fresh apple cider, come with me. Master Kelvin leave everything right where it is I will get Serge to take care of the bags and the car.

The both of you must be tired after that long drive, why don't you freshen up and then join me downstairs in a couple of hours. Maria you know we have to catch up girl, I am so happy to have you home Kelvin, so what's on the grapevine in the DC area since Obama won the Presidency?

We're really not that tired Mama we did stop and spend the night at Ft. Bragg. The same buzz that is going around the country is also what's going around inside the beltway, it's amazing and many can't believe it happened but it did so all we can do now is wait until January 20th to crown our new first family.

Good Maria, come with me sweetie, looks like you could use a Mojito after that drive, so much dust on the road nowadays. Kelvin if you need anything Consuela will be here for another couple of hours, we'll be on the balcony.

90

Is a Mojito all right with you Maria?

No mom, I can't take any alcohol right now, I think it was the drive; I'm a little dizzy already?

Really well I made me the Mango Mojito which has Havana Rum, fresh mint leaves, sugar, and lime juice with a spritz of mango juice and club soda topped off with a slice of mango.

Sounds terrific, a couple more of those and you won't be any good.

Well I'll look forward to being no good then because I have just gotten started. I hope you feel better later, anyway relax girl and enjoy the ambiance that is Sandy Grove.

This place really is magnificent mom, the design is so unique what did dad have in mind when he built it?

I haven't the faintest, there are some things that defy the imagination and you decide to just go with it but you can believe there is symbolism to everything Armstrong Prentice does.

Do you need my help with anything for the party tomorrow? I can remember the last one I made it too was the bomb.

No, all is done really, I am expecting just a few people, maybe twelve or so but they are all leaving early and then us girls can have a little bit of fun.

I have really missed you and the family for the last couple of years while Kelvin was in Afghanistan so we have so much to catch up on. What's going on with you and the babies?

Nothing really but we do have a surprise for dinner Thursday, I think you will all be pleased especially dad.

Come child, no secrets, what's the big surprise?

I'm so sorry mom but Kelvin made me promise and besides I can't wait to see the look on your face, my lips are sealed.

Sealed, that means I need another Mojito, I'll get it out of you if it's the last thing I do.

91

Hey Serge, what's up man?

Nothing really Master Kelvin and welcome home sir, how was your drive?

Not much to talk about man, Serge how do you do it?

What is that sir?

Serge I have known you for almost what thirty years and you never seem to age, whatever you are using hang on to some for me, I just might need it later, is my old man still treating you alright?

Of course Master Kelvin, your father and I will never have any problems sir, not as long as we both breathe the same air; he has been like a father to me and my family as well. Had it not been for your father my family would still be in Croatia trying to pick up what was left of our lives after the war.? Your father has shown my family a new life here in American and I will always be thankful to him for that.

Good deal, come walk with me Serge, the ladies are doing their thing and the kids are with Consuela, let's get a cart and just ride for a minute.

Fine sir, right away.

I am forever amazed at how big this place is even as kids it looked massive but you would think that once you grew up it would shrink a little but not Sandy Grove it is still quite a massive structure.

Yes sir, even after your father sold off the lower acres for the golf course it still seemed to have grown. He had the helipad put in last year so that he could fly his special guests here first class. Tell me Master Kelvin has your taste for war changed now sir? Was going there really worth leaving all of this behind? I know that when the Serbs invaded Croatia the entire mindset of a country, that had recently been liberated, changed and the climate of peace was once again destroyed. It's really quite stupid for men to think that you must have war in order to maintain peace.

Well Serge, I have to give you that one man, war is hell regardless of the territory you are fighting for, or the cause for that matter. I once enjoyed going to the beach and playing in the sand, now all I can see when I go there are the faces of some of my men. I can no longer enjoy what was once a pastime for me, that happiness has been replaced with fear.

Fear sir?

Of course Serge, any man that finds himself in the middle of a battle has to be frightened, it's only natural. It's the guy that isn't afraid that I keep my eyes on because he has already crossed the line mentally and that can be some scary shit especially when he can't find his way back.

It's good to have you home sir your father will be pleased.

What do you mean by that Serge?

Master Kelvin even though your father did not approve of your joining the Armed Forces, once you made that decision he was very proud of you, not only for standing up to him but for putting your life on the line in service to your country. He may never admit it to you sir but trust me I saw the old man glued to the television night after night hoping to catch a glimpse of you.

So the old man has gotten a little soft over the years?

No sir, he hasn't changed at all, he remains dedicated to family sir, and it's always been about family.

92

(Telephone ringing)

Hey girl, what's up?

Nothing much, I was just calling to see what you were up too.

Chill laxing right now trying to decide whether or not to go out to Sandy Grove to see my mother, I just know she is wandering from room to room making sure everything is perfect for Thanksgiving; I might help her finish decorating.

Let's go girl, I have been waiting to see that place for a minute, besides I know that there is at least one bar in there somewhere.

Funny, you wouldn't believe how many, and Mama is always trying to pawn some new drink off on her guest, the other year it was Apple Martinis then it was Gorilla Farts.

What is a Gorilla Fart Tammy?

You don't really want to know, it's a mixture of one shot of Bacardi 151 rum and one shot of Wild Turkey I believe, can't really remember how to make it and I don't remember much about that night or the day afterwards to be honest. There's no telling what it will be this year but it is the holidays, I'm surprised you and Martin aren't kicking it.

We were earlier; we had a late lunch after driving around town looking at all the Christmas decorations and it's not even Thanksgiving yet, I am trying to take this thang slow girl but your brother makes my knees itch. So let's do Sandy Grove and get our drink on, besides I want to formally meet Queen Bee.

Queen Bee?

Your mother, girl once it got out that I was seeing Martin it looks like everywhere I go somebody is talking about your family in a good way. I was at Avery's Hair Emporium yesterday and Konica was talking about how it was your mother and father that got the Laney Walker district renovated and how Mr. Armstrong Prentice himself put up the money to get the voter's rides to the polls on Election Day.

Well when it comes to politics my father is the one to talk too, he could have continued to hold any office in the State that he wanted but he was more content with being behind the scenes instead of being in the spotlight after retiring. You might get to meet him as well tonight, he's usually down in the study but with family at Sandy Grove the old man will be smiling from ear to ear and holding court. Okay, let's do it, I'll pick you up.

93

Yes Mrs. Prentice, how can I be of help to you?

First of all Dr. Screen thanks for meeting with me today on such short notice and I really wish you would keep this meeting between you and I, I really don't want my husband to know that I met with you.

And why is that Mrs. Prentice?

Well Dr. Screen the matter is one of a sensitive nature and I just want to know that I can trust you.

Sure Mrs. Prentice but I don't know if doctor patient confidentiality extends to one's spouse so I will have to be very careful here.

Dr. Screen my husband and his father are worth more money that you and I could earn in ten lifetimes and it is his father's intention to pass over Armstrong and past the family business down to his younger brother Kelvin simply because Armstrong and I do not have an heir, that is why it is so important that we be able to conceive as soon as possible.

Oh I see but Mrs. Prentice, when the test results get back I'm sure we can fix whatever the problem is and I'm almost sure we can get the two of you pregnant sometimes next year.

That's it Dr. Screen, we must become pregnant with a son within the next sixty days in order to have the estate turned over to us.

Mrs. Prentice I don't see how I can make you that promise and I definitely can't predict the sex of the child.

Do you find me attractive Dr. Screen?

Mrs. Prentice I can't answer a question like that professionally. Now listen, getting back to the problem at hand here, there is no way that I can predict the sex of the child even if we can get you pregnant in the next sixty days, that is just impossible.

Dr. Screen if you don't find me attractive would you find one hundred thousand dollars attractive? And let's just say another fifty thousand if it's a boy? I've seen the way you have looked at me Dr. Screen and yes I am quite desperate, I see my entire future being ruined just because of a simple pregnancy.

Mrs. Prentice I could lose my license just for having this conversation with you, did you say one hundred thousand dollars?

Yes Dr. Screen I did and another fifty thousand if it's a boy.

May I call you later on tonight after I have made certain arrangements?

Sure Doctor and just to make sure you make that call here's something for you to remember me by and for you to think about.

Mrs. Prentice, you can't, ah , , , , wow.

94

So tell me girl, what are your intentions for my brother?

I intend to screw his brains out but I am trying to hold out for that special moment, but it's hard out here for a pimp.

You are so silly Tameka, but on the real because I will be asked that question at least half a dozen times when we get to Sandy Grove. I already gave you a clean bill of health with my mother but if my nosey ass sister in laws get a whiff of big pimpin turning in his platinum player's card she will want to know what you working with and if we should name you the new "super-head" because you tamed that beast.

Look girl, I can feel you and I feel the same way about my peeps but I think this can really work between Martin and I, and I don't give head . . . . all the time. We make each other laugh and he can make me feel like whatever and whoever was missing in my life has finally arrived. At first I thought he was just showing me his representative, you know how men are girl, but I see that the Martin that he introduced me too was the real Martin and not some façade. Tammy thank you so much for not having a problem with me and Martin seeing each other because if you had I would understand and back off but since I got your okay it's on like Oprah girl.

That's cool with me I just don't want to end up looking like the cat that swallowed the canary. I guess I should say congratulations, you could do much worse. I literally hated all those chicken heads he went out with when we were in school, all they wanted was to be seen riding in his Lexus but I knew that one day he would find somebody that was worthy of his time and affection and who knew that the someone I was talking about would be you, my best friend. So yes its cool with me, just keep the details to yourself, just thinking about it makes me wanna throw up in my mouth.

You are a fool girl.

Girl times are changing, who ever thought we would have a black President Elect? Michelle better hold on tight because I can see the sistas and the chicken heads lining up in the White House trying to get their Bill Clinton on.

What do you mean get their Bill Clinton on?

Bill Clinton girl, you know play hide the salami with the most powerful man in the world?

Tammy you need help real bad, look I am a Psychologist and you need to lie down on my couch for a minute.

Minute my ass, I need at least four hours a day and if I lie down on your crazy ass couch it will be because I had one too many Margaritas cause I ain't telling you shit.

Whatever, where are you going Tammy?

Oh this is the back way to Sandy Grove, this is the family entrance.

So where's the estate?

You have been on the estate for about twenty minutes now Tameka.

But I didn't see a gate or anything.

That's why dad made this entrance the way that he did, look at it as if you are entering the bat cave.

Bat cave my ass, oh my God is that the main house on top of that hill? What is it two, three stories? What about security?

I'm not supposed to be telling you or anybody else this but there is a device similar to a Lojack installed in all of the family cars that lets the electronic beam back at that last corner aware that it's one of us. Just wait a few when we get to the outer border the retina scan will appear and let us pass, if not you would be surrounded by gun carrying security in about twenty seconds. See that pole, watch this. Tamlar Prentice.

Welcome to Sandy Grove Mrs. Prentice, voice recognition accepted, please prepare for scan. Scan accepted, please proceed and again welcome home madam.

Get the fuck outta here, that was some James Bond shit right there, what does your father have up in here that would require that kind of security?

Just his family, dad is very serious about his family, nothing is more important to him.

And where is this tunnel going to take us?

To one of the garages, we will pick up a golf cart from there and drive the rest of the way to the main house.

Okay but don't leave me anywhere at any time okay, you already got me lost ya heard. You sure I won't need a passport to get in here?

Tameka, you stupid, we can park right here.

Welcome home Ms. Prentice and madam; this cart is ready for you, is there any other way I may serve you?

No Serge, thanks.

Serge, who the fuck is Serge Tammy? He was kind of cute, he can serve me but who the fuck is Serge, Tammy?

Serge is my father's right hand man; he does odd jobs around the estate and keeps an eye on things for my father.

Keeps an eye on things for your father? Tammy why do I hear Godfather III music playing in the background? Is your father the black Don Corleone?

Don't be silly Tameka, it's just the way that things are around here so roll with it, you wanted to see Sandy Grove; okay you get to see the shit in 3-D panorama so chill. You might want to hold on it's been a while since I drove one of these things.

Are you going to drive inside the house Tammy, oh hell no, this is just too much for me.

Not all the way just inside the elevator to the middle floor of the main house, there's a rack for the golf cart there.

Talk about a foyer, oh there's Mama and my sister in law Maria that means my brother Kelvin made it. Hello Diva's, we'll be down in a minute.

95

Mama and Maria this is Tameka, Tameka this is my mother and this is my sister in law Maria. Come here girl and give me a hug, where are the kids? Maria you look so good girl, no one will ever believe that you have had two kids.

The kids are with Consuela.

Good day ladies, glad to meet both of you.

So you're Tameka.

Yes Mrs. Prentice.

Oh hell no, don't yes Mrs. Prentice me I am not that old, especially without a drink in your hand. Welcome to Sandy Grove Tameka I've heard quite a bit about you and have been looking forward to meeting you as well. Maria this is the Diva that has taken Martin off the market. Tammy pour me another Mojito and sit down Maria has a secret.

Pour you a what?

A Mojito, it's my new drink for the holidays this year, that's what's in the pitcher on the bar.

And what is your secret Maria?

I can't reveal it until Thanksgiving dinner when we do the round robin at the table.

What's a round robin?

That's when everyone tells why they are thankful and we get to share in everyone's good fortune, it's a Prentice family tradition.

Yeah, yeah, whatever, I am the Queen Prentice and I demand to know the secret right this moment.

Mama, now you can't play the Queen card on your own daughter in law if she wants to wait until the round robin we will just have to wait.

Okay Tammy I'll chill, now back to you Tameka.

What are you doing to my son that makes him smile as if he always has some juicy gossip that he is keeping to himself?

Nothing really Mrs. Prentice we just enjoy each other's company and we do seem to have quite a bit in common, we like the same foods, the same music, the same shows on television, we make a good team. Martin is a great guy and I am lucky to have him.

Well I have to agree he is a great guy but I have four great kids. So where are you from Tameka?

Well I was born and raised in Atlanta; I am one of the Grady baby's that survived. I graduated from Spelman where Tammy and I became best friends. I then went on to Mercer to complete my Masters and I am currently a Doctoral candidate and as you know I am a Psychology Professor at Paine.

Did you pledge?

Yes I pledged Delta Sigma Theta.

Actually I knew that already, you see I pledged DST as well and I am notified whenever one of my Soros joins the staff. Actually back in my day you would have been considered too dark or too black to pledge anything, especially AKA.

I have heard some rumors about that but never really understood it.

Rumors my ass, it was the truth.

When I was growing up I always heard about the paper bag test.

Let me tell you about the real paper bag test child? Tammy hand me that brown paper bag on the counter. Look child, back in the day in order to enter some colleges and join most sororities and fraternities you had to have skin that was lighter than this paper bag here. That's how they screened out what they called the undesirables. You always hear about how the white race discriminates against black folk but we were our own worst enemies because we are the only race in history that discriminated against its own people because of skin color. Other races may discriminate based on the caste system or some status ethic but we did it based on how light or how dark our skin was. Check out your history child, in order to be considered a member of the black elite you had to have a certain skin tone and straight hair and what they called European facial features. Look at the history of Howard University and Washington, D.C. for that matter. Howard once required that you include a photograph of yourself with your college application. Some white night clubs would have what they called black "spotters" at the door to screen out those that could usually pass for white. It wasn't just the colleges or the sororities and fraternities but even some of the churches and the social groups. Groups like the Links, Jack and Jill, the Lotus and Monocan clubs and quite a few others. Dunbar High School in DC was designed to filter students, the right students, into Howard University. They would even shine a flashlight on your profile and if your mouth or jaw extended beyond your nose you were considered "too black". You see many of these black elite groups thought they would one day be accepted by whites as equal partners on this small planet. Sadly some of them still believe that horse crap today. Sorry about that venting but it still gets under my skin when I think of how petty we have become and after all that we went through, now look at us reducing ourselves to the point where we willingly discriminated against our own people. And when you think of how silly it was because "the one drop rule" always applied anyway. Now do I need to explain the "one drop rule"?

No, mama, you've done enough explaining.

So Tameka, what professions are your parents in?

My mother is a Psychiatrist in private practice in Atlanta and my dad is in research at Crawford Long Hospital also in Atlanta. I am an only child which could explain why Tammy and I are so close.

I really wish I had finished college.

Nonsense Maria, college is not for everyone and besides you're still young and already a Prentice. Therefore you have already accomplished more than most women ever will. Besides being a Prentice is a full time job by itself. Anyway Tameka, welcome to Sandy Grove once again and I want you to make yourself at home here and drop the Mrs. Prentice, call me Connie, everyone else does. There you are Consuela come and meet Martin's companion Tameka.

I am quite pleased to meet you madam. Mrs. Maria the kids are asleep in their rooms and should be out for a couple of hours. I am leaving now, is there anything I can do prior to my departure?

No Consuela, have a lovely holiday and tell the twins to stop by and see Armstrong and I before they go back to Athens and there is an envelope in your box at the top of the stairs and I demand that you get something special for yourself this year, I insist upon it and have a lovely vacation.

Tammy how is our supply of Mojitos, it's much too early for us to run out you know.

96

Tameka lets go up to my room for a minute there is something I want to show you.

Girl is your mama going to be alright, she knocking down those Mojitos like they are kool-aid?

Sure Queen Prentice will be just fine; her grandkids are in the house so she is in heaven, she will talk Maria's ears off before the evening is over then both of them will fade into the woodwork. Maria normally takes a drink when she is here with Mama but things do change, give me your hand.

For what Tammy?

Because if I don't swipe your palm on this machine you won't be able to get from one floor to the other and you will get too tired of walking up and down all those stairs, it's another security precaution of my dad's. Someone from the family must initiate the swipe to make it go through and if you don't clear it before you leave the estate the security gates won't open.

Go ahead, Bond, James Bond, I want my Mojito shaken and not stirred.

Tameka cut it out, anyway this is my room and the one next door is yours tomorrow, come on in; I have a bar in here too.

Tammy you got to be kidding me, this room is bigger than my apartment, why do you have your own place in Harrisburg when you got all of this out here? You better pack up your things and move back to Beverly . . . . Hills that is.

You stupid, this was where I grew up and my mom hasn't changed anything; it's just the way it was when I left for college.

What is in there? What a view! I can see Dwight David Eisenhower Medical Center on Fort Gordon from here.

Oh that's my closet but be careful you could get lost in there; I've hidden from my mother back there many a day.

Tammy I knew you were spoiled but I see now that it wasn't your fault, that picture of you looks like you are about to just step out of the painting.

My mom has a portrait like that in all of our rooms and just commissioned two more for the grandkids. Each room will eventually belong to a Prentice heir, I guess that's why there are so many rooms. Right now there are twenty five and less than ten are being used, less than that when we are not here, don't ask, it's a Prentice thing.

What's that noise?

Somebody just arrived.

97

Man it is good to see you, when did you get in.

We got here a couple of hours ago, where did you come from?

I just got here, I spoke with Tameka and she is supposed to be here with Tammy have you seen them?

No man, I been out back with Serge since I arrived talking about the good ole days, Serge still looks like he is about twenty years old; I told him that whatever he is using to save some for a brother and who is this Tameka I keep hearing about?

We'll talk later, is dad here?

Not to my knowledge.

Where is mama?

She's probably on the lower level with Maria and the kids.

How you been bro, ya looking good, looks like family life is treating you right Kelvin. I'm happy for you because you got everything you always said you wanted, a beautiful wife and a house full of kids.

Wait a minute bro, hold off on all the kids, the two we have are enough right now.

Hey man can I holla at you about something?

Anything baby brother, speak on it.

Well Kelvin, when did you know that Maria was the one man?

Oops, this is going to be one of those conversations, well little brother, for that we will need a drink, let's head to the den.

I never thought you would come to me with this type of conversation. Strong was the sensitive one so we just might have to close the door and put on some Harold Melvin and the Blue Notes.

I miss you man.

Same here baby brother.

Now what'll you have?

Let's say a tight brandy on the rocks, for the good times.

Okay I can roll with that.

So man, answer the question, when did you know she was the one?

You never really know Martin, to a certain extent, all women are the same, there are small things that distinguish them from one another but they are basically the same, Maria and I just clicked, she doesn't seem to worry about things that are out of our control. When I left to go to Afghanistan the first time, I wondered how she would be able to handle being alone with two young kids but she stepped up to the plate and hit a home run.

But when did you know that she was worth taking the time to get to know and what made you want to climb through all her issues? And you and I both know that all women come with a certain amount of issues, they call it baggage.

That could be because they have been running into and wasting their time with men that don't have any idea what it is they want themselves, so how will she ever know how to please him if he is the one that's confused? Then there are those that are dogs who will never really commit to one woman, they're the ones that make us real men look bad. Kelvin you must first understand that a woman is God's most delicate flower because she has the ability to evolve in order to fit into any situation especially where her kids are concerned, that is, of course, until she gets fed up and when a woman's fed up that's when you get smoke in the city. There is no such thing as a perfect relationship or perfect marriages, Maria and I have well defined roles in our household and as long as we both stay in our lanes we steer clear of most problems.

What do you mean stay in your lanes?

Look at it this way; I am responsible for putting food on the table and ensuring that there are enough assets to keep the bills paid, in addition, I am responsible for providing security for my family and, let's not forget, taking the trash out, well defined roles like that. Maria is responsible for raising and taking care of the kids, preparing the food that I put on the table, and managing the household. As long as we understand our roles we don't run into conflict, she doesn't tell me how to take out the trash and I don't tell her how to manage the household, so we stay in our individual lanes.

Wow, that makes perfect sense but what happens when you want to cook or do something that falls in her lane?

That's cool too; that's when we engage the benefits package, in other words there are times when it's okay to share a lane.

Benefits package?

Yes, it's okay to give her a break every now and again and she does the same for me. We enjoy working together Kelvin and I guess that's when you'll know. This is about Tameka isn't it?

Yes it is.

Martin let's keep it real, are you really serious about this woman?

We've known each other for a while with her being Tammy's best friend but we never really knew each other until we started dating which hasn't been that long, we haven't even had sex yet.

What? This calls for a refill, make mine a double, Martin it's not the quantity of time that you spend with a person that makes that person special, it's the quality of that time you spend together. I became infatuated with Maria about two weeks after meeting her but I wasn't in love with her, that came later. So don't let the time issue become an issue, love at first sight is alive and well my brother.

Ah hell, the two of you down here with an unguarded bottle of brandy, let me call backup . . . . pimp down, pimp down.

Strong, what's up with you man?

It's cool and the gang Kelvin, how was the drive man, is everything okay?

It's all good and I can see you're wearing your Rolex.

So what are you guys down here talking about?

I was just giving Kelvin a little advice on women you know, looks like our baby brother is smitten with this Tameka.

Or so I heard anyway, Martin and Tameka sitting in the tree, k I s s I n g.

Man cut it out.

Like I said Martin, if you are serious then let her know and that way neither one of you will be wasting your time and neither of you will end up heartbroken, but be sure you are ready to give up the Playa's card for real and for good. No woman deserves to be caught off guard when after a few months you decide it's not what you bargained for, in the meantime have fun man. Smile, laugh, sing, share a corn dog, and cook breakfast naked. You're only young once, relationships are serious things but that doesn't mean you have to stop having fun, as long as that fun is with each other, and believe me brother, it's so much better that way.

Pour me a drink Kelvin.

Are you off duty Captain?

Man if you don't pour me a darn drink.

Be right back man, Tameka is here with Tammy somewhere and its time I found her; we will finish this conversation when I get back.

Can you say whooped boys and girls??

Yep, Kapow.

98

Well, like I was saying Tameka, there are no real eligible bachelors anywhere just a dog pound on every corner.

I heard that? Hey sweetie, how long has my sister been holding you hostage?

Long enough for me to miss you Martin, baby this place is fabulous, like you said you could never appreciate it unless you saw it for yourself. There are no words that would have been appropriate enough for you to describe Sandy Grove to me.

Tammy do you mind me stealing Tameka away from you for a minute, I promise to bring her back in one piece.

Whatever, I'll be in the den.

Hey Tameka, let's take a walk; have you ever ridden a horse?

I did once but it's been a long time ago, it was back when I was a Girl Scout.

You were a Girl Scout?

Yes Martin I was, and yes I still have all of my cookies.

For now Tameka, for now, let's walk down to the stables there is someone there I want you to meet.

Okay Martin but you promise to be good to me today.

I'm always good to you.

I mean since we are around your family, some guys trip when they get around their peeps and I don't want to have to go "Kill Bill" on you in front of your parents.

Sup Serge, can you have Alfred bring Brown Betty around.

Right away Master Martin.

Tameka Allmond meet Brown Betty.

Should I bring around another mount sir?

Yes Alfred, one befitting of a lady, how about Prima Donna?

Fine choice sir.

Oh Martin, she is so beautiful, what kind of horse is she?

Well, Brown Betty is an Arabian; they are theorized to be the oldest breed in the world and were used primarily by the Bedouin tribesmen of Arabia who relied on them for survival during their movements around the desert. Thanks Alfred. And this lovely creature here with the spots is Prima Donna she is an Appaloosa, the Spanish introduced

240

them to Mexico in the 1500s, and spotted horses have been depicted in images as far back as prehistoric cave paintings, however it wasn't until the 1700s when horses first reached Northwest America that they gained recognition in the United States. My dad raises Arabians and Appaloosas, the Appaloosas remind him of the old west.

Martin this is wonderful, can we ride?

Sure we can, Alfred.

Take her slow at first sir, she has already been put though her paces for today.

Oh Martin, this is some Hollywood stuff right here, where are we going?

Just keep up will you; I want to take you to my favorite place here on the estate, it's a place where I spent so much of my youth, it's the one place where I went to in order to be totally alone and sometimes to just lie back and look at the stars when I was a child. Okay, I still catch myself looking at stars each time I glance towards you.

That was corny, anyway Martin, how much property is out here? I can't even see the house anymore.

Girl, you have no idea, we can ride for the next hour in one direction and you still won't reach a fence except eastward of here where the golf course starts.

Is it always this peaceful out here?

That's what makes it special to me.

Wow, there's a lake and everything.

This is the place I was telling you about; this is my most favorite place in the world, welcome to Lake Flora, Tameka, let's stop, here let me help you down.

Martin Prentice I do think you have just swept me off my feet.

Then hold on to the wind Tameka, come closer looks like you have something on your, Muah . . . .

Martin Prentice you didn't have to steal a kiss, I have waited for this moment since I lost myself in your brown eyes.

It wasn't the kiss I was stealing, it was the moment; remember the memorable moments we were creating? And I hope you don't mind if I do this.

Martin you can't undress me out here somebody might see us.

Then you better hurry up and get in the water.

Martin this is crazy and this water is cold.

Then you might want to get closer to me and let this body heat keep you warm.

Martin can it always be like this, can we always have special moments like this?

Tameka believe me, you have no idea what I have in store for us and the answer to your question is yes.

What about my hair Martin?

Your hair is your least worry.

Is that a fact?

Yes, that is a fact.

99

Hey baby girl.

Strong, I didn't know you were in here; I thought it was just Kelvin.

Hugs, hugs, hugs, where did Martin go anyway?

He took Tameka somewhere, who knows what those two are up too.

Which gives us a little time to quiz you about this Tameka?

What is it Kelvin, Tameka is my girl, she is real good people and she's not a gold digger which is very important, anyway she and Martin have been kicking it for a minute and they seem to be having a great time. What's scary is that they both seem to be taking this thing kind of seriously.

Well let me play devil's advocate here.

What do you mean Kelvin?

Well, the first question Mom and Dad are going to want to know is whether or not she is Prentice material. I can hear Dad now, does she have the proper pedigree, who are her parents, what do they do? Are they old money or are they Nouveau Riche.

Well she is a Psychology Professor at Paine; does that qualify her to be Prentice material as you say?

Don't get testy little sister; you know that I am telling the truth, I remember what they put Cheryl through when she and I started dating and I could have sworn that they were having us followed.

Sad but true Strong, when I first mentioned to Mom and Dad that I had met someone and that her name was Maria they almost lost their minds until I assured them that she was not Latino, and even then I just know they did a background check.

Okay, I get it, but they only have our best interest at heart, it's not just what we can put on the table it's all this, Sandy Grove and the estate and who knows what else dad has his claws into.

Speaking of claws, when are you going to start dating again little sis? You can't let that one episode put a damper on your future, I hate to say it but you would make some man a half way decent wife.

Half way decent?

Yes, half way decent.

Strong you and Kelvin both know where you can go with that half way decent crap.

We just want to see our little sister with a man that deserves her that's all, he just has to know that he will be responsible for all the cooking, all the cleaning, taking care of the kids . . . .

Cut it out guys, I can cook . . . . a little besides I am a Prentice and if I want to eat out every day of the week I can make that happen. Besides I can always hire me a Consuela to take care of all those domestic things. He won't be marrying me for my cooking anyway; I have yet to have a man kick me out of bed because his eggs were runny.

You just haven't met the right man yet but that doesn't answer the question Tammy, what's the hold up?

I'm not totally sure; I'm just a little gun shy I guess, I might start going out in a few months. I went out for a minute while in Atlanta with Mom and Dad and I still got it but I am not in any hurry, it's all good.

Okay Tammy, just know that we are here for you sweetie, whenever you need us.

And Strong, thanks for getting rid of that creep, he had me scared for a minute.

You are quite welcome Madam Prentice.

Whatever let me go and find Tameka.

100

Martin we better be heading back, I'm sure Tammy is looking for me and remember that I am her guest this evening and tomorrow, you can have me all to yourself after dinner okay?

I guess so but don't be surprised if I happen to sneak up to your room tomorrow night for a little night cap, that way you can finish what you started.

What I started? Hmm, that doesn't sound half bad if you are ready to buy that ticket, just try and keep it under your hat; I definitely don't want all my business out in the street.

Well if that's the case, good luck on explaining why your hair is all wet, I'm sure Tammy will get a kick out of that, mount up and let's head back.

You know Martin, this really is the golden time of day, right now when the sun is going down and the crickets are chirping, and look there's a fire fly.

Yeah, it's my favorite time of day as well but right now we'd better hurry or it will be dark when we get back.

That's the plan Martin I don't want everybody to see me when we get back, you will have to sneak me upstairs to Tammy's room so that I can get my hair back in some sort of order, better yet you just go and get Tammy, she will know what to do.

Okay Professor whatever you say, of course I could sneak you up to my room and ah . . . .

Never mind Dr. Prentice just get me your sister.

Back so soon sir?

Yes Alfred, it was beginning to get dark.

Here Madam may I assist you in dismounting?

Thanks Alfred.

Tameka, I have been looking for you all for about an hour, where have you been and what happened to your hair?

Look girl, you can interrogate me all you want to when we get up to your room, right now just know that I have had a fantastic time with your brother.

Martin, I will talk to you later, this is what I was afraid of; you have let the freak come out of you already and what did he do to your hair? I cannot have you walking around here with that permanent grin on your face so let's take the back elevator to my room.

What are you talking about Tammy?

You don't really want to know, trust me.

Tammy, get me upstairs!

Tameka, girl you got some explaining to do!

Tammy get me up to your room so that nobody will see my hair the way it is please, you can do all the interrogation you want to but get my ass behind closed doors.

This has got to be the funniest crap you have ever done even funnier than when you flipped that crab leg behind us and into that white man's salad while at Red Lobster on Gordon Highway, now that was funny but this takes the cake. What I want to know is how can your hair be wet and your clothes be dry? That's what I want to know, wait a minute, Tameka no you didn't!

Didn't what girl? I didn't do anything.

Tameka Allmond, look me in my eyes and tell me that you did not get in that dirty water with Martin.

What dirty water?

The dirty water in Lake Flora!

Lake Flora, where is that Tammy?

It's in the lower forty and named after an esteemed family member, I had to always ride out there and get Martin, that was his favorite spot when we were growing up, he would go down there and camp out for days sometimes.

Martin is a fascinating guy Tammy, you should cut him some slack and we did not have sex.

Okay, you all must be calling it something else these days; you got in the lake naked with my brother and didn't break him off?

No it wasn't like that we just held each other and played around, he is quite the gentlemen believe it or not. I must admit it was hard to just hold him in my arms with all his manhood exposed, he has a nice package too.

Oh, please not again, TMI.

You got some clothes I can put on? And direct me to the towels so I can take a shower and freshen up, where is your hair dryer?

All of that is in the bathroom, look in the first closet on the left for the towels and things and you can find anything in the world inside my closet to wear so have fun. I'll see you back downstairs when you're done, if you get lost just use the intercom to find me and don't be coming all the way out here to Sandy Grove to let your inner slut come to the surface, don't forget that you are a professional woman, but I guess most hookers are.

Who are you calling a hooker Tammy? Don't make me read you okay! It's not like you have never got your slut on, don't make me bring up Acapulco?

No you did not dig up Acapulco, call it what you will girl, Rodrico was the bomb. E'se had a sista speaking ancient Spanish, he did not get the name Rod Rico from his mother, okay! Besides it was Cinco de Mayo and I was just celebrating Mexican independence, that's my story and I am sticking to it.

I know you girl, prissy my behind, I can spot a slut one hundred miles away in a snow storm even under those curls.

Rodrico can remember the Alamo anytime he feels like it, and it takes a hooker to know a hooker, and I know you.

Girl you are a fool.

Whatever, hurry up girl it's almost time for a drink.

101

Well welcome back Casanova, you have been gone for a minute, you must have found Tameka?

Yep and we rode down to Lake Flora and had a nice talk.

Let's just hope that's all he had.

Pour me a drink man, where is Cheryl anyway?

I have no idea bro, but she knows that I am out here with the family; she's probably resting up for tomorrow night when the Diva's do their thang. What has dad got planned for us?

Not sure Kelvin, but after that Helen caper we pulled a few years ago we'll probably get locked downstairs.

Let's go and hit Club 706 for a minute.

Martin that is easy for you to do, we are married men and there is no way in the world Cheryl and Maria are going to go along with that. Tameka might go along with it right now but later on she'll have a problem with it too especially with this being our home town and we are Prentices don't forget that.

Why not man, don't your wives trust you?

It's got nothing to do with trust Martin, you'll find out soon enough, it's about respect and honor. I actually have the best time when I go out with my wife not with you two hard heads, besides when have the three of us ever been out together and didn't run into trouble?

I know what it is; the two of you are whopped that's it, I never thought I would live to see the day when both of my brothers would show up wearing pink panties. I knew that you had some female tendencies Strong but Kelvin I am shocked.

Screw you little brother, just keep on living and loving and one day we'll chip in to buy you a pair. Where is Ms. Tameka anyway, why are you keeping her hidden?

I'm not, she's upstairs with Tammy they'll be down here in a minute.

Give me minute guys; let me find out what my lovely wife is up too.

102

Well hello Mrs. Prentice.

Nice room, the Marriott has come up I see, and feel free to call me Cheryl, after all we are about to get to know each other rather well, so I trust you've had time to ponder my proposal, can you get with this?

I'm not sure at the moment, by the way my first name is Charles; now let me understand what is actually going on here Cheryl, would you like for me to pour you a drink?

Wow a gentleman, yes a drink would be nice, thanks and we'll see how long this gentlemen shit lasts.

Whatever, it is my understanding that you want me to impregnate you and if it's not a boy, then what? And how do I know that you will not end up blackmailing me for child support and shit after the baby is born?

Listen ah Chuck is it? I am the one with everything to lose in this mess so don't get it twisted; this is not an emotional transaction. The last thing I need is for you to start catching feelings and shit like that, just be a man and do the damn thing as usual with no emotion whatsoever, most men are accustomed to that so it should be no problem for you. I just need for you to handle your business and then just go about your way and carve another notch in your bedpost or whatever men do to celebrate new pussy, when my pregnancy is confirmed I will have your money.

Wait a minute Cheryl I thought we agreed on . . . .

I know what we agreed on Chuck but I am not stupid, here take this envelope, inside you will find fifty thousand dollars. You must understand that this may not be the last time we have to do the damn thang and for this kind of money you will be at my beck and call with a heavy hard one, now if you don't mind can we get undressed and do this?

You didn't answer my earlier question Cheryl, what if it is not a boy, what happens then?

Well Dr. Charles Screen at that time you might just have to go where no man has gone before. You see Chuck you will announce the sex of my child at the proper time and you will ensure that I leave the hospital with a boy, whether I deliver it or not, now do you understand?

Mrs. Prentice, you have got to be out of your mind, there is no way I can insure that the baby you may carry will be a boy. What if your husband wants to be in the delivery room? You can't mean that if it's not a boy you want me to switch babies. How am I supposed to make that happen? Besides where would the other baby come from? And how much do you think that might cost?

Well actually Chuck, money is no object and switching the babies will be plan B, but the ball is in your court on that one. I heard that men are responsible for the sex of the child so you can ride this ass as hard and in as many positions and directions as you like, just get the job done and we won't have to cross that bridge at all. Isn't this the nicest ass you've ever seen Chuck and look at these tits, yes they are all natural? In the meantime I noticed earlier that you have a decent package, can I play with it for a while? Why don't you just lie back and let me finish what I started and then we can see what you can or can't handle just don't pull my hair the way you did before, I still have other things to do tonight, like my husband. Move your hand I'll get the zipper, well hello there . . . .

Ringgggggggggggggggggggg
Ringgggggggggggggggggggg

103

Hmm that's strange.

What's that Strong?

I just tried to call Cheryl and there was no answer, she always has her phone with her.

Ah man, she could be anywhere and she'll call you back as soon as she notices that she missed a call, she could be in the ladies room you know.

Yes, I guess you're right.

Well look at what the cat just dropped off, sup sis.

It's all good, so what do we have here, the three black musketeers or is it three the hard way?

Whatever Tammy, so where is Tameka?

She's still upstairs, thanks to you she messed up her jeans playing cowgirl, she'll be down as soon as she changes clothes, she shouldn't be but a minute, did Cheryl show up?

Nope, not yet, but you know Cheryl she could be anywhere and doing anything.

Well as long as she shows up tomorrow early so that we can get dinner finished and prepare for the party. I know Mama is gonna want to get an early start but knowing Consuela most of it is cooked already. So what did I interrupt, what were you three geniuses talking about?

Nothing really, just glad to be home is all, so Tammy how has Dad been looking to you?

What do you mean how has Dad been looking? I can't see any difference, he's aging but so are all of us, Dad will be Dad and even death can't cheat the great Armstrong Prentice.

He just seems to always have something on his mind and looks like he's about to burst waiting to get it out, he's still on top of his game but I think he and Mom should probably head down to the place in Miami for a break.

I agree they could use a nice vacation away from this place for a while.

I could mention it to Mama during girl's day tomorrow if you think it would help.

Sure Tammy that sounds like a great idea, do that Diva stuff yall always do to get your way? Mama just might fall for it. Why don't you go up and get Tameka, I am dying to meet my future Sister-in-Law.

No you did not say Sister-in-Law Kelvin, whatever; you might want to talk with Martin about that.

My lips are sealed and I have nothing to say besides I haven't given up my platinum card just yet.

Given up your what card Martin?

Oh, Tameka, it's about time you made it down here, Tameka this is my oldest brother Strong and my other brother Kelvin from Maryland.

I'm pleased to meet the both of you; I've heard quite a bit about the Prentice men and I must say the information was on point, but what card were you speaking of Martin?

Oh, girl we were just talking about probably playing some bid whist later on that's all.

Whatever Martin, just remember I was born at night but not last night and as far as the card is concerned fellas, he didn't give it up; I took the damn thing and have chosen to wear it as a dog tag, any questions Scooby Doo?

Rut roll, no questions at all Ms. Tameka, no questions at all.

I like her already Strong.

So do I my brother, so do I.

Welcome to Sandy Grove Tameka.

So this is where all of you have been hiding, I have looked all over this place for my husband and you all have him corralled down here.

It's about time you got away from Mama Maria, girl if I didn't know better I could swear you have a glow about yourself.

Alright Tammy, don't start none and won't be none.

Maria this is Tameka who just put Martin in the dog house, literally.

Yes I know we met earlier, sup girlfriend, I could swear you had on a jean outfit earlier.

I did girl, I just got it messed up riding around the estate with Martin.

Did Mama talk your ears off sweetie? One thing is for sure you won't have to worry about Eleanor and Boregard for the rest of the time that we're here Mama got them both on lock down.

I know Dad has kidnapped his grandson and heaven only knows what the two of them are up too.

Well, it's good to have all of you home man, we really missed you the last couple of years, it's just a blessing that you made it back from all that madness unscathed Kelvin.

I'm not sure about unscathed but at least let's hope it's all over, we have a new man headed to the White House and maybe he can get the rest of our troops home. The hardest part about the war is being away from home during the holidays. I can remember spending two Thanksgivings, two Christmases, and two Birthdays looking up at the same Moon that I was hoping Maria was looking up at; it can be a bear just counting the day's man. But that's in the past, now let's head to the bar, I need a tight one. Prentice men join me please.

On the way, my brother, on my way.

104

I just heard a car pull up that must be Cheryl.

Well it's about time, where have you been sweetie? We've been waiting for you for hours, is everything okay?

It's all good Strong, I just stopped off and did a little bit of window shopping, I am still putting together a few ideas for the holidays.

But I called you sweetie and you always return my calls.

Silly of me, I must have overlooked it in my hurry to get here, anyway none of that matters because I am here now and Kelvin and Maria, so good to see the two of you again, give me a hug girl and Martin, what have you been up too?

Cheryl this is Tameka, Martin's girlfriend.

So this is the new Diva . . . . pleased to meet you Tameka, and Tammy you are looking great girl, how do you do it. Tameka you will definitely have to let me know how you put the brakes on the ole pimp Principal here, so where are Mom and Dad?

Upstairs with the grandkids, we may not see them for a while, Mom is with Eleanor and Dad has disappeared with Boregard.

Well that calls for a drink I guess, window shopping has a way of making a girl thirsty, at least I can still have a drink, for the time being anyway.

What do you mean for the time being Cheryl, are you pregnant?

No Tammy, not yet, Strong and I are giving it the old college try for real this time, we are not getting any younger so if it is to happen we are trying to make it happen sooner rather than later.

Well congratulations to the both of you anyway, I need more nieces and nephews.

Well thanks Martin; I just wasn't expecting my lovely wife to spill the beans in front of everybody now we have nothing to talk about at the dinner table Thursday.

Ah Strong, cut it out we are all family so if not us then who? I think it's great that the two of you are finally ready to start a family. Bravo, I say Bravo.

That calls for some of the good stuff, look in the chiller Kelvin and pull out a bottle of Cristal, this calls for a toast, come on everyone get a flute.

Nothing for me Tammy, sorry but I have been a little under the weather lately, I'm still kind of groggy from the drive down here. Maybe I'll have something later, I can still join the toast but with a little soda not champagne.

What! Is my toast not good enough for you to join Maria?

No Cheryl, that's not it at all, it's just that I have not been feeling well lately and probably just need a little rest that's all.

We do understand Maria, here's to my big brother Strong and my sister Cheryl, may you be successful in your quest to add rug rats and curtain climbers to this clan. Believe me when I say that we can always use more kids in this family, besides somebody has to fill up all the rooms in this house because God knows that I ain't about to have shit. If you all start now we could have it full by next year this time and that would mean that all of you women would have to have twins so let's get it crackin up in here.

Tammy you are a fool and looks like you got started before the rest of us so would you please back slowly away from the bar.

Here's to my brother Strong and his lovely wife my sister in law Cheryl, may the remainder of your days be spent surrounded by as many little Prentices as you can handle and add three more to that for good measure.

Here, here, and to my brother Armstrong Prentice II, may your twilight years be filled changing diapers and heating baby bottles for as long as the both of you shall live.

You got a crazy family Tammy.

Call it crazy if you want too Tameka looks like you just might be a part of it before long.

Cheryl you better take it easy girl, what's that your fourth glass of champagne? Keep it up and you might not be able to break Strong off later on tonight it does take two to tango you know.

Don't even worry about that Tammy, that's why they call me Strong.

You go Cheryl, nobody needs to know what goes on behind closed doors girl as long as he doesn't try to turn a whore into a housewife it'll be all good.

And just what is that supposed to mean Maria?

What do you mean what is that supposed to mean? I was just kidding with you Cheryl; I didn't mean to step on any toes.

No, you didn't step on any toes bitch! I just want to know what that was supposed to mean, you need to keep your mother fucking mouth shut and talk about what you know!

Keep my mouth shut and talk about what I know! And who are you calling a bitch Cheryl? It takes one to know one and from where I sit, bitch would be a promotion for your country ass, it is still one level above whore you know?

Hey, hey, the two of you cut that out, what brought all this on? We always tease each other like this, that's why they call us family remember?

You tell that bitch to remember Martin, just know Maria; just because you have two kids already doesn't mean you will ever outdo me where this family is concerned. The day will come Mrs. Prissy when you will look up to me and grovel at my fuckin feet.

Grovel at your feet! You need to get Mrs. Kim or one of those Korean motherfuckers to grovel at your jacked up ass feet Cheryl, let's not forget that I am from 8 mile bitch, 8 mile, that's Detroit for those of you that get it twisted and I haven't had my foot knee deep in a slut's ass in a minute. Don't make me break that record tonight Cheryl because I can, believe me, I can do this and don't let my having kids fool you, please don't make that mistake because I will stomp a mud hole in a bitch at the drop of a hat then go straight to Church and talk to Jesus about it, I am not the one to be fucked with tonight Cheryl; I am not the one to be fucked with ta night!

Strong you better take her for a walk man looks like she has had a little too much to drink it's all good man; just take her for a walk.

Ok Kelvin, I'll take a walk, yes I will take a mother fucking walk, but Maria know that this is not over by a long shot, you want to be me bitch; well you don't have enough class to be me.

Class, school is out Cheryl didn't you get the memo? You can't buy or marry class you either have it or you don't. Class not ass, see you got it twisted again.

I'm sorry Maria, you didn't deserve that, and we'll be back in a few.

It's all good Strong, I can hold my own and will ride or die for mine, just make sure she's okay, maybe we can talk tomorrow or later on tonight. She probably didn't eat anything and you know some people can't hold their liquor on an empty stomach; the bottom line is I got nothing but love for all of you. Here Strong, don't forget her purse.

Maria are you all right sweetie?

I'm fine Tammy, thanks for asking and allow me to apologize for that episode of "Love Always Charleston", I truly apologize.

Where the hell did all of that come from?

Girl, I just had an 8 mile flashback and went back to Detroit; it was cold as hell there too.

No need to apologize, we could all see that you were provoked but Maria, I would have never thought you had all of that inside of you girl.

Well Martin it just goes to show that you can't judge a book by its cover.

Damn Kelvin, I see why you didn't want to go out, it's not the going out you were worried about; it's the coming back in, Negro I will pray for you for real.

You lay off my husband Martin, it's not like that and Kelvin knows it, we are a team and there is no permission given for anything that we decide to do, it's the mutual respect that we have for each other that keeps up focused and we both know when to stay in our lanes.

There goes that stay in your lane thing again, okay; okay I know what you mean.

Anyway I think I could use a little fresh air as well, would you care to join me on the verandah my darling.

Don't mind if I do sir, glad to be in your company Colonel.

Yall need Jesus.

Hush Tammy.

Right away Ms. 8 mile.

105

Honey are you okay?

I'm great Kelvin, you know that I love it when we come down here to Sandy Grove; this place holds a lot of memories for us.

Yes it most certainly does, this view is amazing; you can almost hear the leaves changing colors, the fall and winter are the two seasons that I really miss down here in the South, there's so much concrete in Silver Spring that you can hardly find a tree let alone the leaves, but when I asked if you were okay I was referring to the baby and that episode back there with Cheryl.

Well honey, if I embarrassed you then I do apologize but you know that Cheryl did cross the line and my hormones are crazy when I'm pregnant so pray for a sista okay, I will apologize to Cheryl tomorrow, right after she apologizes to me! And what did she mean that one day I would grovel at her feet? What did she mean by that Kelvin?

I have no idea sweetie who knows? Hey I'll talk with Strong about that as soon as I can but it seemed to me like there was a bit of tension between the two of you where did that come from?

No idea sweetie, Cheryl and I have always been able to get along, I have no idea what's on her mind but I will keep an eye on her from now on since she did draw first blood.

Maria, keep that first blood stuff to yourself, we are family and there is no way a conflict between the two of you will ever take place so pull in your claws and let's make this negativism go away okay.

No problem with me Colonel as long as she stays in her lane it's all good, you know I can handle mine. So tell me, what did you think about Tameka and Martin?

They look like a nice couple I just hope Martin is ready to commit and settle down, he talked with me earlier about Tameka and the boy just might be sprung, I hope so anyway. A real man doesn't know what he is missing when he's playing the field; the real passion comes from being with the same woman for a long time and growing together, that is of course if the two of them are headed in the same direction and willing to make sacrifices for each other when necessary. Love is a two way street but some people tend to put up red lights on some of the most awkward corners, love should be an expressway not a parking lot.

I love you Kelvin.

Now as much as I love you because I loved you first.

Whatever Colonel.

106

And who is that Grandpa?

That is your great, great, great grandfather Boregard, the man who you are named after son, you actually look a lot like him, he was a smart man too; he was almost as smart as you will be one day.

Grandpa can I come and live with you here on Sandy Grove?

Why sure you can and one day you just might own the entire estate, that's why Sandy Grove was built Boregard so that we can all live together as a family and never have to worry about anything. You see Boregard over one hundred and fifty years ago a couple of real wise men thought they would be able to live together regardless of the color of their skin and bring a new meaning to the word brotherhood, we are legacies of that way of thinking, if two men really trust each other then skin color has no reason to ever come into play.

Grandpa I want to be big and strong when I grow up so that I can ride one of the big horses next time, I love my pony but I want a big horse so I have to be a big boy to ride it right?

Right you are, right you are, you should be ready for school by next year and if your daddy has no objections we might want to put you in a private military school so that you can start learning how to lead men. I can see you riding a big horse probably leading a group of men that look up to you because you are a Prentice son, Boregard Prentice.

Are we rich Grandpa?

Well, that depends on your definition of rich, now when most people say the word rich they are speaking about how much money they may have in the bank or tied up in property but when a Prentice talks about being rich they are forced to think on an entirely different level because the number itself is more than any mortal man can imagine in one single thought. No my boy, when a Prentice answers that question they have to talk about stepping in higher cotton, as far as land is concerned we own and control over fifty thousand acres spread across five states with a fifteen hundred acre spread on the coast of Texas, prime grazing land Boregard. We also have holdings in South America, Grand Bahamas, Florence, Italy and over four hundred thousand acres right here in the State of Georgia. In addition to that we also own or have controlling interest in six banks located in three countries and let's not even add stocks and bonds to that number. We are diversified Boregard that way we can insure this family's prosperity remains long after you have lived your life. That's why land and family are the two most important resources we have and of those two, family is the most important. That you must remember Boregard, that you must never forget. Family will sustain you no matter what society brings to bear, just remember that no woman or anybody living can ever be allowed to break our bond of family.

Grandpa when I grow up I want to be just like you and my daddy.

You already are Boregard, you already are, Grandpa will see to it that nothing ever changes that.

107

Cheryl you care to share with me what just went on downstairs; what has gotten into you?

What do you mean gotten into me Strong?

Cheryl you just attacked Maria down there for no reason, as I told you before for some reason you seem to change when you are around her, is something going on that I should know about?

Nothing that I can think of besides that bitch needs to know her place.

And what do you mean by that Cheryl? Explain know her place?

Well first of all I meant what I said about her groveling at my feet, I can't wait to take over this estate then you will see what I am talking about.

So that is what all of this is about? Cheryl I promise you that Maria is not even thinking about Sandy Grove or taking over when my mother retires, she is busy thinking about taking care of her kids, they are the real treasures of this family.

What about our kids Strong?

Cheryl we don't have any kids and whether we have them or not it will not change the fact that Kelvin and Maria already have two.

I know that Strong but when the test get back and we become pregnant then your father can make you the leader of the family and then we can move out here to Sandy Grove and the world would be our oyster Strong, don't you want that honey?

Cheryl, the most important thing about being a Prentice is family; there will always be enough money and material things to go around. Whomever my father chooses to be his heir will be fine but that is his choice and his alone.

I know that Strong but we are so close honey; we are so close to being selected to take over this estate, I can't believe that one day this will all be ours.

By ours I hope you mean the family Cheryl, this place and all of our holdings belong to the family regardless of who sleeps out here at Sandy Grove.

I will sleep at Sandy Grove Strong, by any means necessary.

Cheryl you are sounding a little crazy honey, why don't you lie down for a while and get some rest, I will stay up here with you but you will lie down right now and get those thoughts out of your head. I will not have you planning any treachery that will involve anyone in this household. This is my family and I will ensure their safety at all cost, do you understand me Cheryl? I mean that, at all cost.

I understand Strong, I'm good but I am beginning to feel like I made a perfect ass out of myself tonight.

Well not perfect but if you turn it just right, buyer beware.

I don't know what got into me; Maria has never done anything to me that would make me go off on her like that. I feel so bad Strong, I am so sorry honey, can you please forgive me?

It's not me you should be asking for forgiveness, what you need to do is take you a nap, get refreshed, then go downstairs and apologize to Maria, can you imagine what the temperature in this house would be if you all don't tackle this before Thanksgiving? You do need to cook tomorrow and then there's the cocktail party, you need to apologize to Maria, Cheryl.

What's sad about it Strong is that I meant everything that I said, if I don't hurry up and get pregnant Maria will be running Sandy Grove before we know it.

You have got to be kidding me; Sandy Grove belongs to the Prentice family Cheryl. It's not a fiefdom that is run by some King or Queen. No matter whom my father chooses nothing between us or the rest of the family will change. Sandy Grove is a family, not just a building made of brick and mortar, this is the legacy of my family and it goes back over one hundred and fifty years and will go forward regardless of who is left as patriarch. There has never been an argument stemming from succession in the history of this family and that is because family is the most important aspect of our very survival. This could all be gone tomorrow but the Prentice family will still move forward, it's the way of all things Cheryl; we all go forward no matter what.

But Strong, I want to stand in your mothers shoes when she retires; I want to be the Queen of Sandy Grove, I have dreamt of nothing else since the first time I saw this place. It's just not fair that your father has mandated that an heir be in place before his transition, it's just not fair.

It doesn't have to be fair Cheryl, it is what it is, my father has decided that the transition will go down the way it always has. He has it planned and that is the way that it will be, now let me tell you something. My family, meaning you and I, will not be responsible for bringing any discord into this household, my parents must never know what happened here tonight. There will always be peace in this place regardless of what else happens in the rest of the world. Sandy Grove will know peace Cheryl and for that I must put my foot down, there are no ifs or ands about it, do you understand? You need to find a way to deal with your greed and your sense of self worth. I am Armstrong Prentice II, the son of the most important man in this State and that makes me one important man in my own right, don't let the train leave the station without you Cheryl and please understand that the train will leave the station. Get your shit together or build your house in the sand, do the math yourself and figure that one out. You are my wife not some girl from the streets who has never had a taste of the good life now act like it.

I'm sorry Strong, I do apologize to you honey and I will apologize to Maria, and can you forgive me?

We'll see Cheryl, we'll see.

108

Whoa, what just went down Tammy, it almost looked like they were going to come to blows, what's up with your sister in laws girl.

Tameka your guess is as good as mine but I have to agree that something in the milk ain't clean, I have never seen Cheryl go off before in my life, she has always been the "no drama" type, or at least that's the person she has always portrayed.

No drama my ass, she almost had her head handed to her by 8 mile, sista girl ain't no joke and was about to bring the pain.

I know, little ole Maria got a dragon inside of her. "I'm from 8 mile bitch, that's Detroit for those of you that get it twisted". Well I guess we all got a little bit of ghetto in us, must be in the DNA because I have never lived nowhere near the projects.

Sandy Grove is almost big enough to be a project girl besides project is a state of mind not just an address and Maria was all up in the zip code okay.

So when are you going to take me home Tammy, it's getting late?

Why don't you hang Tameka besides you were going to stay tomorrow night anyway so what's the difference? I'm sure Martin would like for you to hang around.

He sure would, what's up Divas?

Where did you come from Martin, I thought I left you in the den with Kelvin and Maria.

I know but they went out to the balcony remember and Strong and Cheryl went upstairs so that kind of left me alone with Mr. E&J Brandy so I decided to find the two of you because he only had one thing on his mind.

Martin tell Tameka that it's okay for her to stay here tonight instead of me driving her back to the city, that's unless you want too?

Sure sweetie, it's okay to chill; besides you can keep me company and I promise to be on my best behavior.

I have already seen your best behavior Martin but it is getting kind of late so I may as well hang out, thanks Tammy, it's almost midnight anyway so I'll meet you upstairs, I need some time with my man now if you will excuse us.

No you didn't just dismiss me Tameka, you got some nerve girl, you really got nerve but you two love birds have a nice evening, I think I'll make me a nightcap and call it a night. Tameka your room is right next to mine and make sure you sleep there tonight, this is Sandy Grove and not the Dew Drop Inn, you feel me.

Good night Tammy.

Shut up Martin.

109

Martin I want to thank you for making this one of the most memorable days of my life, I have thoroughly enjoyed spending today with you and your lovely family, and thanks for keeping your promise.

What promise was that Tameka?

The promise you made not to perpetrate with your peeps, I actually felt like I was a part of the family tonight, that was until the fireworks went off, that was bananas man.

Yeah, the both of them have some explaining to do tomorrow but I am confident that whatever it was will work itself out; they have too much history to be tripping like that. Cheryl just had one too many that's all; but I know that she only has everyone's best interest at heart, the same is true with 8 mile, I mean Detroit, I mean Maria.

Shut up Martin, you are crazy man.

Crazy about you Tameka, so what do you ladies have planned for tomorrow?

Not sure, I just know that Tammy was saying that we have to get up early so that we can finish what's left of the cooking and prepare for your Mom's party tomorrow night. I believe she said the Mayor's wife and some of the people from the college were coming by, it should be fun actually, I haven't had the pleasure of meeting the Mayor's wife yet.

It's all good; the Mayor's wife is actually a nice person. From what I understand the men have been regulated to the other den in the second sub basement, right under my father's study so that we will not disturb the festivities. Dad had mentioned us escaping up to the cabin that we have in Helen but after what happened a few years ago Mom would not hear of it.

What happened a few years ago?

Well it's like this; it was the Thanksgiving before Kelvin was to leave for Afghanistan about three years ago. He and Maria arrived the Sunday before Thanksgiving so Dad suggested that the guys get away to the mountains and come back either late the night before Thanksgiving or early Thanksgiving morning since the ladies would be preoccupied with the party and cooking and girly girl things. Anyway, Dad knows the Mayor of Helen and told him that we were coming, he was having a cocktail party which we crashed upon arrival; it was a real good time. The next day Dad and the Mayor decided to go trout fishing and the guys and I went up to Blairsville to do some horseback riding, by the time we got back that night some of the Mayor's people from Texas had arrived and that's when it all went south. Come to find out the manager of our ranch outside Houston is married to the first cousin of the Mayor's sister in law so they are connected somewhere down the line by marriage. This became the excuse for a party that went on for what seemed like forever. Long story short, we never did make it back in time for Thanksgiving. It was actually the Saturday following that we made it back to Sandy Grove.

I bet your mother was pissed.

Pissed is not the word, she wrote a brand new book on pissitivity. Dad pleaded with all of us to stay there at Sandy Grove so that he wouldn't lose his head over the whole mess and that's what we did but Mom never lets us forget it and we haven't been allowed outside of the estate during the Thanksgiving holidays since.

I don't blame her one bit; you all should have known better Martin, what were you thinking?

I am the youngest and was just following the crowd, now that's my story and I am sticking to it.

Anyway all of you needed a good spanking after that.

Believe me we got one; we got a good one then and still get some of what's left every Thanksgiving.

So this is what it's like spending holidays with the Prentices?

Pretty much, we are like any other family Tameka we just happen to do things just a little bit different.

Different my ass Martin, everyone I have met here tonight are millionaires and you all act as if that's no big deal but believe me Martin for ninety percent of society that is a very big deal.

Okay so what would make you happy me giving the money back?

Hell no, I didn't say do stupid, continue to do you, but it's nice to see just how normal you all actually are and you have your parents to thank for that, just look at all of the sad Hollywood stories about trust fund babies killing themselves or being arrested for murder or for killing everyone in the house. That's crazy man but you all seem to have good moral character on lock.

Well we do have Mom and Dad to thank for keeping us grounded and things. It's just that from day one we all knew the value of a dollar and even as kids we had to earn what was given to us, it's not like we would go shopping with credit cards that had no limits. I was tasked with mowing the lawn on this place for a long time and Strong had to take care of the cars while Kelvin had the Boy Scouts and the Rotary Club to contend with so it's not like we had it handed to us on a silver platter.

Ok, genius, what kind of platter was it when you turned twenty five.

Oh, that platter was made of solid gold. It's all good Tameka, just one of our family rites of passage I guess you could say, anyway I still have it all and basically have had no reason to touch it, everything I own I have earned with my salary at the school and I plan to keep it that way.

But Martin those Rolex's that all the guys were wearing had to cost thousands, how do you explain that?

Oh this little thing, it was a gift from Dad, he gave it to all of the guys a few weeks ago on the night of the election, and they came in at around seventy five thousand dollars each.

And he bought one for all of his boys?

Yep, that's my Dad; he always does things over the top, but for a reason. He said something about wanting us to remember how historic election night was and that the watch was supposed to remind us of the history that was made on that night, also to remind us that family is the most important element of our existence, land and family is something Dad continually hammers into us.

I see, I have heard Tammy say some of the same things, I am getting a little sleepy Martin, I think I will head upstairs and call it a night.

Would you like a shoulder to lean on?

Nope, I have a pillow but good try; we'll have our moments Martin, so don't be in such a hurry for your life to change.

What makes you think my life will change?

Because mine has and I like to return the blessings that I receive and Martin Prentice you have become a blessing to me, I just wanted you to know that.

Same here Tameka, lets head upstairs and if you need me just dial my number or knock three times on the pipes.

Old school again Martin, besides you all don't seem to have any visible pipes in this place, maybe I should knock three times on the marble.

Actually all you have to do is think about me and before you know it I shall arrive to rescue my damsel in distress.

You are a fool Martin Prentice.

As long as I can be your fool I don't mind.

110

Well good morning Maria, you are up with the hens I see, is everything alright?

Yes of course it is Mom, I was just up having a cup of coffee while checking on the kids, they had a ball with you and Dad last night I don't even remember them being put to bed.

That's because I put them to bed after we finished watching Charlie Brown and Rudolph. That Eleanor is something else; she called herself playing the part of Lucy on Charlie Brown's Christmas last night, anyway we had a ball with them Maria and I've arranged for a Nanny to keep an eye on them this afternoon and tonight so that they will not be underfoot, besides we have quite a bit of arrangements to make before the party tonight.

I don't think a Nanny will be necessary but as usual, if you insist.

And I do darling I most certainly do; besides they will be in good hands and will probably have a better time than we will and they won't actually leave the estate they'll just go down to the all purpose room in the third sub basement, there they can have ice cream, play on the jungle gym or do whatever their little heart's desire.

Thanks Mom I appreciate all that you do for them, you are a real Godsend.

Nonsense I am their Grandmother and I adore the little brats. I see you're up early as well Cheryl, good morning, let me pour you a cup of coffee, you look awful didn't you sleep at all last night?

Good morning everybody, and no I didn't get much sleep last night Mom, probably had one too many glasses of Champaign as well, hey Maria girl, can we talk later?

Sure we can Sis and here take these Tylenol for your headache, they work wonders for me.

Thank you girl, I can really use them right about now.

They won't hurt the baby will they?

What baby, what baby are you all talking about? Cheryl are you pregnant?

Not that I know of Mom, I just mentioned to everyone that Strong and I were really going to try this time.

What did the fertility doctor say about the situation?

Well he just said that when the results of the MRI and the blood test get back he would be able to determine what the problem is and what they have to do in order to correct it, in the meantime he said for us to go on as usual.

When do you have to go back to see him?

Not sure but it will probably be next week or right before Christmas.

What's his name Cheryl maybe I can give him a call and pull a few strings?

That may not be necessary Mom; we can handle it from here.

That was not a request Cheryl, what is the Doctor's name, I just want to know in case anything happens and we have to call him due to an emergency.

His name is Dr. Screen and his office is up on Chafee Avenue.

Oh, I know Dr. Screen, his mother, Mattie and I went to Paine together; she is one of my Sorors. His first name is Charles right, about six feet four inches tall, muscular and actually kind of cute in a Vin Diesel kind of way.

Yes he is, Mom you seem to know everybody.

That's everybody who is worthy of my knowing them child. I don't think it's fair to have a man that good looking touching you all over your body and you are not supposed to feel anything. That's almost like having Denzel as a Gynecologist, there is no way in hell I could just lie there and not get excited I would be in for a pap smear every other day.

Mama Constance, no you didn't.

Yes hell I did, just because you can see some snow up on my roof don't mean there is no fire left in my furnace. As a matter of fact I just broke Armstrong off the other night so he should be smiling at least until New Years.

I can't believe my ears Mama Constance; you shouldn't be talking like that somebody might hear you.

Girl, what did Eddie Murphy say? This is my house Lillian.

Well it looks like we got up just in time for all the juicy gossip, I can see that Mama got that devious look on her face, she must be talking either about sex or Denzel or both.

And good morning to the both of you, don't look so shocked, just sit ya ass down and have a cup of coffee Maria made it fresh this morning.

Good morning Mrs. Prentice's, I guess that could mean all four of you, anyway thanks for having me stay over last night and I am ready to do whatever you might need help with today.

Welcome child but I told you yesterday to call me Constance or Connie; I am not accustomed to being so formal in my own house.

Okay Mrs. Connie, I can do that.

Tammy where did you get this child from and how can a future PhD, anyway, just call me Connie child.

So what's on the agenda for today Mama and what time do we get started?

Well first of all I want us to prepare a fabulous breakfast for the guys then we can lock their asses downstairs, I already made sure they have enough beer, wine, or whatever they might want. I also arranged for lunch to be delivered to them at around two this afternoon, they should be knee deep into that dreaded football or whatever around then. Get a good look at them at the breakfast table because when breakfast is over you will not see them again until after the party tonight and if I planned things correctly you will be seeing them through blurry eyes because tonight it is definitely on Diva's. So Maria and Cheryl get to work on the bacon and sausage, I have some of that turkey bacon for those of you who pretend not to be from the South and real bacon for those of us that really are. I will do the home fries and hotcakes and Tammy and Tameka can do the eggs and toast. You can also start on the fresh squeezed orange juice Tammy. I would let you try bacon this year but we will need the kitchen for the rest of the preparations, besides we've tasted your home fries and I am glad you got a nice ass and tits because your kitchen skills are lacking.

Mama no you didn't clown me like that!

Tammy let's keep it real! We do remember when you tried the turkey a few years ago and forget to take the packet out of the inside, so please keep it real.

I was young then and besides nobody told me that there was something inside the damn bird.

So Mom what else do we need to get together for tomorrow? I saw where Consuela did the turkey and the ham and I can see greens, mashed potatoes, gravy, and a shrimp cocktail, so what do you need for us to prepare?

Well Maria still has to do the pies, the ingredients you said you would need are in that brown bag in the pantry Maria and I want to do some cabbage and maybe some more of the oyster dressing that your father in law craves and some macaroni and cheese, besides that I think we got it all taken care of.

What about for the party tonight?

Consuela has already prepared the canapés and I have a bartender who should arrive at about six, I also have a caterer from Sconyer's Barbecue dropping by to top the menu off. So let's "get er done" and get it over with so that we can start our day. The 2008 Constance Prentice pre-Thanksgiving Diva's Delight Throw Down has officially commenced.

111

Mom and the rest of you ladies breakfast was great and thanks for not allowing Tammy to cook anything.

That's not funny Martin.

Boys, I want all of you to meet me back at the stables and let's take a ride around the property, I want to talk with you all about some things that have been weighing heavily on my mind, let's say in about fifteen minutes?

Sure Dad that would be fine, that gives me time to steal a hug from Tameka.

Oh yes, Tameka, welcome to Sandy Grove young lady, it is indeed an honor to have you here to celebrate the festivities with the family but watch Martin, he's a slick one, reminds me of me when I was his age.

What was that Armstrong?

Oh, nothing Connie, just welcoming the young lady to the estate, that's all.

All of you get out of my kitchen; the girls and I have a few more things to take care of this morning now shoo the lot of you. That means you too Martin, Tameka will be here when you get back now poof, be gone!

112

Thanks for everything Alfred, we should be back in a few hours, how's the family and are you okay for the holidays?

Yes sir, the family and I are squared away Mr. Prentice, thanks to you sir, we just want to let you know that our affiliation with a man such as yourself is worthy of giving thanks within itself sir. You all have a nice morning ride; the air is brisk so keep your jackets on.

Will do Alfred and make sure your family knows that I asked about them.

I will do just that Mr. Prentice and may I say that it's good to see the four of you together again sir; it's been a couple of years. Welcome home Master Kelvin, we really missed you sir.

Thanks Alfred you were missed as well.

Man, it's been a while since I've ridden this early in the morning, feels good, but why do I feel like one of the Cartwright's?

That's because you all were born into a Bonanza boys, which is why I asked you all to join me this morning, let's ride down to the lake and then take a little walk.

Yes sir, anybody want to race?

No son, I want to just take it leisurely and smell the fresh air, look around you boys and see what I have prepared for you and our subsequent generations.

What's on your mind dad?

Strong, Kelvin and Martin first of all let me say that it is one hell of a pleasure to have all my boys with me here at the same time for the holidays, who knows when or if we will have moments such as these in the future so let's take full advantage of them now. And if I remember correctly Martin it is your turn to sneak in the strippers so let's not forget that later on tonight.

That was funny dad but you are not going to get me shot, what's on your mind for real?

Well I have made a decision that I think concerns all of you and I wanted to discuss it before we got back to the ladies. My boys there are some things that men must keep to themselves, this is not to be confused with keeping secrets, nope it has nothing to do with that, but if a man is to continue to prosper and, as they say, walk softly and carry a big stick, then there are some things that he just has to manage himself without the opinion of a woman or anyone else for that matter. Hell, if we had to get our wives' permission to do half of the things that need to be done than nothing would be done at all. Strong, Kelvin and Martin I have decided to retire boys and turn over the reins of the family business to one of you. I mentioned most of this to you during our teleconference on election night. There are some secrets to this family that only two people know on the face of this earth and that is myself and Mr. Johnson, whom you might remember back in Warren County. The only definite criteria about this transition is that only one of you must know the secrets and that person must keep them for the sole purpose of turning them over to his heir, and that heir must be a son. Right now the only one of you that qualify for the position is Kelvin of whom I am very proud, however I did make Strong a promise that with him being the oldest, if he and Cheryl should get pregnant with a boy in the next, let's see, now its forty five days then by right of him being the oldest I would turn over the reins to him. There is also something that I want all of you to know that is very important and it is something that whomever takes over the reins will need help with. Boys, this family is worth close to one billion dollars. This was due to the investments that were made years ago by my father and grandfather and the land holdings that are currently in my name and in the name of the family business, Prentice Enterprises. Those figures are the only thing that I have ever kept from your mother, that and the secrets. The bottom line is I plan for that fortune to remain in place for my grandchildren's grandchildren. Can I have your pledge on that?

Well sure dad but how?

How is not important right now boys it's only important right now that you know the "what" of this thing? The how and the why will be explained to my successor. Regardless of whom takes over I want the three of you to know that there will always be enough money to go around. Effective immediately the three of you will begin to draw an additional stipend of ten percent bi-annually of the interest on five hundred million dollars which will automatically place each of you into another tax bracket but no one other than the accountant that I assign to each one of you will know where the funds are disbursed from. The only other criteria is that you cannot quit your current jobs until you are either eligible for retirement or find other suitable employment and you cannot let your wives know about this disbursal or how much you are really worth. Of course my successor will probably have to retire immediately, but I will leave that decision up to whoever is chosen. You see boys once some women realize that she has struck pure gold, instead of that plated shit, they will begin to let the money, and not their love for you make decisions for them and, at that point, you will become just a little bit more than an ATM with eyes, and I don't care who the woman is or how much she has professed her love for you. Remember boys, a woman is the most treacherous creature on this planet and that is because of what she possesses most of all, not her body but her mind and with that she can put in motion some of the most scandalous scenarios ever known to man. Money means power my boys and when you walk in tall cotton you must learn to respect and not abuse that power and the three of you have just been presented your ticket into tall cotton. Taller cotton than most men will ever see and the kind of cotton that most men would kill or die for, and somebody said that pimpin wasn't easy. Everything is easy to Armstrong Prentice, welcome to the club my boys welcome and while speaking of your new accountants, I want you to know that they are answerable to no one but yourselves and will not ask any stupid questions about what you do with your money. They are also certified financial planners and also specialize in a new field called Forensic Accounting. In other words if a dollar is out of line they can trace it back to its source at a moment's notice. I have had them looking into your financial affairs for the past three months. If you have a problem with that then here's a bridge, get over it.

Do you think all of that was necessary dad? We are responsible adults, you taught us the value of a dollar before we could stand on our own two feet, why is it so important now?

For this reason Strong, none of you have ever seen the kind of money you are able to control at this point. I taught the three of you about money because it is important to have a working knowledge of what wealth is all about. Some people can't get their minds around the word wealth because they think it has something to do with being rich, which happens to be the poor man's answer. I believe Chris Rock said it best when he said that "Shaq is rich, but the man who signs Shaq's check is wealthy". Look at some of the professional athletes; let's take that fool Michael Vick for instance, they are reporting in the Atlanta newspaper that he has gone through over three million dollars in the past couple of years. You may ask how that is possible, well my father Benjamin had a saying that went "the money is good and the money is fast, with no business mind the money won't last". Think about it boys, the man was worth over one hundred million dollars less than seven years ago and he is now filing for bankruptcy all because of some stupid ass dogs and the white people who love them. What kind of fool is that? A stupid one that's what kind it is, I feel that there should be a mandatory class given by the NFL and the NBA or whomever to teach these college recruits how to handle the kind of money that they are throwing at them at the age of twenty-one or shortly after college if they stay around long enough to graduate. You hear about it all the time, they lose their minds right away and buy expensive mansions, eight or nine cars, and enough jewelry to make Liberace blush, it's crazy. The smart man would ensure that no one on the outside knew how much he was worth on the inside which is why I have made it my business to insure that the three of you were trained on how to handle wealth as opposed to handling being rich. We Prentices are wealthy boys; we haven't been rich in almost one hundred years, and after this day you as individuals will be wealthy. If you remember nothing else, please remember this, to whom much is given much is expected, I want to see this family thrive beyond my years and I think I have put things in place to ensure that. You may ask why I am doing this now, it's simple, I am not getting any younger and I don't want any of you to destroy what I have built by fighting over a few dollars. Financially, when I die whatever is left, and it will be a substantial amount, goes to Prentice Enterprises and Sandy Grove. Your funding will continue however so you won't have to worry about that. I love you boys and what I have given you today I want you to pass on to your kids and grandkids when you feel the time is right. That is my only criteria, that and for you to have fun and enjoy this money.

113

Okay I do believe that everything is either on the stove or in the oven and it smells delightful up in here, Mom where are you headed?

To the bar child, its past twelve somewhere on this planet and I want to make sure that I drink to that, can I get anyone else a cocktail while I'm in a retrieving mood?

Tameka and I will go with you Mama, I could sure use something to clear up this dust in the back of my throat and Tameka you can either watch me or join me girl.

I'm right behind you and Mrs. Connie, let a sista have one of those MoFritoes you were making yesterday.

That would be Mojitos, PhD; they told me you were brilliant I just didn't believe them.

Maria can we talk for a minute? I am so sorry about last night, I must have had one too many and I just wanted to apologize.

I understand Cheryl but you know what they say, when you have had one too many the truths usually comes out. Is there anything that I should know? If you and I have crossed the line somewhere than please holla at a sista, the last thing we need to be doing right now is ignoring this big elephant in the room, we are family Cheryl and the last thing I need is to be watching my back when around family, so what's up girl and keep it real.

Well Maria, the problem is that Strong and I are having a problem having children and daddy Prentice has decided to retire and turn over the reins to Sandy Grove and the business of running the estate to one of the boys.

Well that happens to all families Cheryl, nobody lives forever besides I have heard that they have a slamming place on Coconut Grove in Florida that mama Constance can't wait to get back too, so what's the problem?

It's not really a problem girl but the son that takes over the reins to the family business has to have a male heir already in place before the transition can be made and believe me Strong and I have been screwing like a bunch of rabbits but the Doctor said that Strong has a low sperm count and it may be a while before we can conceive but I am not accepting that drivel, I rebuke that Doctor in the name of Jesus. I am putting nothing but positive energy into the universe and I have already claimed a son. Armstrong Prentice the third is already in the mix.

I can see you've read the "*Secret*", good for you Cheryl, but regardless of who dad puts in the driver's seat we will always be family. According to Kelvin and from what I have seen since becoming a part of this family is that family itself remains most important, besides it's not like we're broke ya heard.

The bottom line Maria is that if he doesn't choose Strong and me it will most likely be you and Kelvin since you have Boregard to carry on the legacy.

Is that what last evening was all about Cheryl, Sandy Grove and a few dollars?

Maria not even your crazy ass can call millions, a few dollars.

What do you mean millions Cheryl?

Maria look around you, does this place look rented? The Prentices are worth millions girl, and I mean somewhere up there near nine figure millions. I know you are not naive and that you are just as greedy as I am, Maria this place is big enough for both of our families' girl and I have already done some mental re-decorating so are you with me on this?

No Sis that's where you got it twisted again, I am definitely not greedy and what do you mean with you, with you on what Cheryl?

Well what I mean is if for whatever reason Strong and I cannot get pregnant in the next couple of months tell me that we can still move to Sandy Grove and live on the estate.

Cheryl you are talking some crazy shit girl, I have never been able to tell Kelvin what to do and if he is the chosen one and if he decides to live here on the estate then he is the one you, or better yet, Strong needs to talk too about that. I have no idea whether or not he and Strong have discussed this thing, besides the money belongs to my husband not to me, as long as he continues to love me and take good care of our babies then I really could care less where we live as long as the roof doesn't start too leak. I am satisfied with our tri level town home on Carriage Square in Silver Spring, yes it's small enough to fit into one of the bathrooms here but it's our first real home Cheryl and I wouldn't change it for the world.

So you want me to believe that you don't care about the money?

I didn't say I didn't care about the money Cheryl what I said was that the money wasn't mine. Now it may not be mine but since it's in my house I have to be aware of all predators and low lives, are you one of the low life's I need to be aware of Cheryl?

Low life? Who in the hell are you calling a low life bitch?

Sister-In-Law pump your brakes for a minute, and let's understand one another. Now ahh, I was your bitch a couple of times last night and maybe three or four more times after that because, ahh I thought about it a few times on my way to your ass but please know that I have no intentions of being your bitch today. Now you have a quick decision to make, you need to either turn bitch into a term of endearment or twitch your nose and disappear because if I hear anything else that comes out of your mouth that even remotely sounds like bitch I can promise you on my mother's grave that the next time you take a breath it will be through a plastic chest tube while in the horizontal position, now here's where you get to shine Cheryl, you get to make the call!

Okay Maria, keep up that goody two shoe role but I got to give it to you, for such a small thing, you do have a lot of swagger so I'll back off for now, but understand me Mrs. Maria Prentice I will be the next Queen of Sandy Grove, by any means necessary, so yes this would be a real good time to start watching your back.

In the words of the great Mya Angelo "when people show you who they are, believe them". Thanks for the head's up Cheryl, now pass me the nutmeg so that I can finish my pies.

How can you take this situation so calmly and not be concerned about your own place in this family Maria, what makes me and you so different?

Well Cheryl if you must know home girl you already failed test number one. Now I am not a skeezer or a gold digger but I have been acquainted with a few of them in my past and I did pick up, I mean overhear, a few tips from time to time. Let me make this lesson easy for you, one of the first things a woman does when she realizes that she is in a situation that can produce and then surpass the kind of money that ordinary people think is the limit, is to ensure that she never allows herself to be put in any situation that could cause her current reality to come to an end. One way she can always insure that she has a seat at the table, whether the table is theirs, or one that the courts provide for her, I'll explain that one to you later, that's in lesson number two and I don't want to confuse you. As I was saying, to ensure she always has a seat at the table, she makes sure she buys at least one matching baby chair to go with the decor. Now you must understand that I love my husband to death and would crawl through molten lava to keep our shit tight but I am nobody's fool. You see Cheryl I was born with a smoking gun sweetheart, as all women are, and I know how to load, cock, and fire mine, you obviously need more target practice.

And just what is that supposed to mean?

Chill for a minute, you might just accidently learn something; now let's understand what the law means when they say standard of living. Cheryl I was raised in one of the seediest parts of Detroit, they call it 8 mile, and I can live in a tent if it came to that but I won't have that for my babies. You see they are heirs to all of this and because of that their standard of living would blow the average person's mind. So the bottom line is my babies will live in this type of environment always and it is my job to make sure of that. You see Cheryl I don't ever get too tired to serve some of this good loving up to my man. Ain't no mountain high enough or valley low enough for me to not have the time to serve him and having a headache is definitely out of the question because every time he hits this there is a chance that I can have another mini-me and in this family that's just like giving birth to the Hope Diamond, holla if you hear me. See you've been wasting time Sis, if after the first six months I hadn't become pregnant I would have found every Doctor this side of John Hopkins to find out why not, but you stood there expecting a miracle. Miracle my ass, what you did was slip, now you are trying to prepare for a marathon without even knowing the fundamentals about running. Good luck and good looking out. You see Cheryl I will always be your sister-in-law and I got nothing but mad love for you but let's not make this personal because I am not to be fucked with when it comes to my family or its place. I understand you got forty five more days to make something happen, good luck and if I were you I would be fucking my man right about now and claiming that miracle, it is the holiday season you might want to try sitting on Santa's lap or some shit like that, if not just know that it's just pimpin, Pimpin.

114

Dad you never really talk about your childhood, what was it like growing up as Armstrong Prentice?

Well boys, my childhood was anything but normal. It always seemed to me that I was being prepared for something great, I never imagined anything like Sandy Grove, or the money, or the power, I just knew that I was being groomed for something great.

But how did all of this happen dad, was it passed down to you from granddad or did somebody hit the lottery? What made all of this?

Son, if I told you all of that you would know more than you need to know unless you are my successor. Just know that it was totally legal and happened at a time when black men were not wielding the kind of prestige and power that we enjoy today.

So what exactly was your childhood like?

From as far back as I can remember there were always lessons son, history lessons, lessons in finance and lessons in the psychology of man. My earliest memories were of being on the Johnson farm right off the Gibson highway in Warren County and with my grandfather over on Bray Street. Those were the days when family really took care of family and I mean across the board. The next thing I remember was being sent off to boarding school at the age of about eight. My studies took me to England, France, Italy, Egypt and finally Boston, Massachusetts. I would always come back to Richmond County during my vacations and things like that and we had a house at 1116 Perry Avenue in Augusta. On my eighteenth birthday I received a golden box and inside that box were the title and deed to two thousand acres of land, an astronomical amount of money, and land holdings across this nation and other places. This and my education were my inheritance from my great, great, grandfather Boregard. In addition to that I became affiliated with the same people that my successor will become affiliated with and there is a group of professional people in place to assist you with any questions or circumstances that may arise. In other words boys when I said high cotton I knew what I was talking about.

Wow, so what turned the inheritance that you received then into almost a billion dollars now dad and how could our great, great, great grandfather amass such a fortune?

If my math is correct slavery was still in force back then, how could all of this have occurred during those days?

Martin you were always the most astute of all of my boys and I hope that one day you may find out the answer to that question but not today, just know that it is what it is and let it ride my boy, let it ride.

Dad what was grandfather like and why were you the first to live the way that you do? We know that he was a college grad at a time when only the elite black men were attending college but other than that we don't know much of anything.

Boys, your grandfather Benjamin was a man of very few words but you can rest assured that when he did speak everybody listened. You see my father knew the secret and he also knew that he was the last generation that was to go through life the old fashioned way. Imagine commanding millions but not being able to enjoy the privileges of being wealthy. He made a decision to sacrifice all that he was in order to lay the foundation for all that we are today. He was a humble man; he was also one of the smartest men that I have ever known. My father was the reason for our political affiliations that have stood the test of time and transcended generations. It is also important to do everything that you are involved in the legal way. If you do it all the legal way then no one can come back from your past and wield any power over you. So remember, even when it comes to friends, do everything the legal way the first time and that way you can put the matter to rest for good. My father was a visionary and although he never lived to set foot on what is now Sandy Grove he had the idea long before I was able to pronounce the words boys. He was a true visionary. Here's to men.

Men like us.

Damn few left.

115

Good morning Papa, how did you manage to sleep last night after all that partying you and the boys did downstairs, you should have seen that place this morning, even Serge and Alfred looked to have had one too many.

Fine one to talk Connie; we had to keep the shots going just to drown out the revelry of your shin dig upstairs, how did that go anyway?

Well, once we got the Mayor's wife out of the powder room we were able to engage in great games of Bid and Pinochle. It was also nice to hear from Mya who thought she would be able to make it but something came up at the last minute.

Well, I must admit that being with the boys has already made my holiday worthwhile; I really think that I have laid the ground work for the transition, I've given them all the information that I can without breaking the rules and I think all three of them are eager to come on board, it's good that Serge and Alfred were able to join us for the festivities. I thought I had some stories but you should hear Serge and Alfred after they have had a few.

Papa you don't usually rub elbows with the employees.

You can't really call them employees Connie; they are more like members of the family, each one of them has been with us for over twenty five years and that's a long time for anybody to be on one job, besides they are as much a part of this family as they are of their own. Do you have everything you are going to need for tomorrow? By the way you may have to explain to Maria where that fifth pie went.

Papa, you didn't!

You are right my love, I didn't and that is my story and I am sticking to it.

Armstrong Prentice I just might have to spank you.

Come on baby girl, it's been a while since I have had a spanking and if I remember the last time correctly, as they say, hook a brother up.

Really, and what are you feeling about Tameka, Martin's date?

Well I didn't really have a lot of time to evaluate her one way or the other, she seems to be articulate and not bad on the eyes if I may say so myself. Let's just get through the next couple of days then hit me again with that question. I just want to gauge her intent, besides once you have had a Prentice it's hard to go back to ordinary.

116

Gracious Lord we are gathered as a family once more in your presence. Father we are humbled and find ourselves in continued awe of your grace as you have made this day a memorable one by bringing my entire family together once again. We are aware of those that are not able today to look along their fine tables and make that comment and for them Father we ask extended mercy. We revel at the growth of this family and know that we are blessed beyond measure, and for those blessings we are again humbled. Bless my boys Armstrong, Kelvin and Martin and my lovely daughter Tammy as they embark on a journey that will one day find each of them healthy, wealthy and wise oh Lord. And with their blessings Father shower your grace on Cheryl, Maria, and Tameka and of course my better half Connie, but don't stop there Lord since we know that you are in the blessing business. Bless subsequent generations of this family Lord as their future parents sit at this table and wonder what tomorrow may bring. God bless Boregard and Eleanor who will continuously praise your name as they will one day sit at the head of their own tables oh Lord. We ask these blessing in Jesus' name. Amen.

Amen.

As tradition would have it, this is the time where we go around the table and tell the rest of the family what we as individuals are most thankful for, we will start this year with my eldest boy Armstrong.

Dad, I would like to say that I am so proud to be a part of this family first of all, you and Mom continue to lead by example and I am honored to be one of your most faithful students. I would also like to thank the powers that be for considering me to become the next Chief of the Augusta Police Department and the fact that I will be the first African American to hold that position is reflective of the history not only of this town but of this family as well, I am indeed honored.

Well said Son and congratulations, Kelvin we will hear from you next.

Well Mom and Dad, and the rest of the family, my first blessing is to be here with my family this year because as you all know for the last two Thanksgivings I have been in Afghanistan and missing the family and this good home cooking. I plan to catch up on all that this afternoon, and also to let you know that I have received orders for my first

Command and Maria, myself and the family should be here at Fort Gordon sometime around April of next year, family we are coming home!

My, my, that is great news Kelvin, don't you think so Papa.

I find it to be fantastic news Son and your home is awaiting you and the family as well, Martin it's your turn.

Well Mom and Dad, I guess what I have to be most thankful for is the fact that I have finally found someone that not only believes in me but has found a way to keep a permanent smile on my face. I am thankful for Tameka and I want to thank her for sharing this holiday with me and my family. Tameka is the first woman I have ever brought to Sandy Grove and I'm planning also for her to be the last, and I also want to thank God for this family, Mom and Dad thanks for doing whatever you did to ensure that God gave me to you because on the day that I was born my spirit could have gone anywhere so thanks for whatever good deed you did to get me here.

You are a fool boy, okay Tammy you're up.

Well it's going to be hard to deal with what has already been said here today. I am always thankful to have a family full of strong black men who continue to set the example for all to see and it's refreshing to know that when I look for a black man to look up too I can always come to this very table and find at least four. Mom and Dad thanks for all the blessings you have bestowed upon me and thank you for giving me three brothers who have made it their business to always take good care of their little sister, thanks guys. Also I want to thank my best friend forever Tameka for finding the time in her busy schedule to take care of a little scatter brain like myself and for always being that rock that we all need from time to time and I guess I could thank Martin for showing me a side of Tameka that I didn't know existed and that is the side of her that is reflected when she's in love. Who knows maybe we might have another Prentice Diva in the making.

Bravo, bravo, and she ain't hard on the eyes at all.

What was that Papa?

Oh, nothing Connie, I was just saying how welcome the girl is that's all. Ah, ah, who wants to go next? Cheryl.

Well Dad, along with Strong's good news, I want to add that I too am more than proud to be a part of this family and look forward to the day when Strong and I can continue the legacy by introducing the world to Armstrong Prentice the third.

Cheryl congratulations, we didn't know you were pregnant!

I am not Dad but Strong and I am seeing a fertility specialist and hopefully real soon we will be.

Congratulations anyway Cheryl, Connie and I are looking forward to it as well? Maria you're up to bat?

Well Mom and Dad I might not be able to top what has already been said here today either but I will try.

How is that Maria?

Okay, first of all I am pleased as well to be a part of this fabulous family and I want to thank everyone at this table for the support that you all gave me and the kids when Kelvin was in Afghanistan. God knows that I missed my man and I am blessed that God sent him back to me in one piece, but I would not have been able to make it had it not been for the support that I received from the very people sitting around this table. I am more than happy that we are moving here to Augusta so that all of you can have a hand in the growth of your niece and nephew. Look at me just rambling on, here is the good news, Boregard and Eleanor are about to have a brother or a sister, Kelvin and I are pregnant again!

Well at least now we know why you wouldn't have a drink with us the other day.

You don't say? You have got to be kidding; God is so good, all the time.

Congratulations Son, Connie, did you hear that sweetheart, we are about to have another grandchild.

I am so happy for you Maria.

Cheryl and Tameka, don't you think that's wonderful news?

Sure it is that's wonderful news.

Yes, that's fantastic Maria, just fantastic, I am looking forward to being their favorite Aunt.

Thanks Cheryl, and I mean that.

Oh Papa this is the best Thanksgiving ever, Tameka it's your turn.

My turn?

Yes Tameka, you are spending this holiday with us so you must take a part in all traditions.

Well, wow, so this is what it's like to come from a family that is so full of love. If I wasn't here myself I would swear that black families were not as ritualistic as you are and I am proud to look around this table and see what love can create when all else fails. When I first met Tammy at Spelman I knew that she was something special but I had no idea what that something was, I see it now for the first time, what is special was her definition of the word family. The word family can mean a lot of things to a lot of people, when I would hear the word I would always reflect back to the times that I shared with my family, I remember the good times and the times when I was so alone while my parents made a name for themselves in their respective professions. I can remember being alone so much that I would create imaginary friends so that I would have someone to talk to and to play with. In other words when I thought of family it always started with negative thoughts. In the time that I have known Tammy and now all of you, and definitely not forgetting Martin, I have had to change that definition to include what I have witnessed since I have been here at the estate. I guess what I want to say is thanks to all of you for changing that image of family for me. Thanks for sharing Martin with me and for sharing Tammy with me but most of all thanks for sharing all of you with me, I consider it an honor to break bread with this dynasty.

Well said Tameka, I knew they had to have a reason for considering you for a Doctorate.

Wow, thanks Tameka, we welcome you as well, in conclusion, so that we can eat, my lovely wife and the matriarch of this family, Mrs. Constance Walker Prentice.

Armstrong you will have to answer for that introduction later, I am thankful to look down this long table and see what Armstrong and I created years ago when he seduced an innocent little country girl. I remember we drove up to Clarks Hill in that white Chevrolet Impala with the Batman wings and how he conveniently ran out of gas, we found Strong on the way to the gas station, and then there was the trip to Pawley's Island in South Carolina near Myrtle Beach during Spring break, we were on a private beach and before you knew it when we turned around and Kelvin was just standing there. And who could forget the first night we slept here on the estate, how we roamed these massive halls when the only furniture on the entire place was in the guesthouse. Well anyway, "poof" there's Martin. We should have stopped there because it seemed that every time we would cross into a new standard of living it would come with another Prentice.

Well Mama, you forgot about me, what was the new standard of living that brought me about?

Oh Tammy, I almost forgot that accident, you are the result of a trip to Anguilla off the coast of the French side of St. Maartan, Virgin Islands. Your father just threw a dart on the map in his study and said lets go there. Seventy two hours later we were walking among the luxury that is Cap Juluca. I have never seen a place so beautiful in all my life; we even had our own private pool at our Bungalow. Almost nine months to the day, here comes the love of my life my baby girl Tamlar, so I have all of that to be thankful for and also for the people they have chosen to enhance their lives with, as an addition to this family. Cheryl, Maria, and now Tameka, welcome to Sandy Grove. Happy Thanksgiving everyone now let's eat.

Mama, Tammy didn't help with the bird this year did she?

Of course not Kelvin, I am not crazy.

Mama! Strong, Tameka, can somebody help me get out from under this Bus.? I was a child then.

117

"(Phone Ringing)"

Prentice residence, well yes Sir the Senator is in, who's calling? Yes Sir Congressman Rangel, right away Sir.

Mr. Prentice, a Congressman Rangel is on the phone sir.

Thanks Consuela, thanks.

Well I'll be, Red, it's been a while, how is life treating you on that end.

Life is wonderful Armstrong, just wonderful; I am blessed to have made it through another holiday season, how was your Thanksgiving and Christmas?

Well Thanksgiving was terrific, I had my entire family here at the estate and it's been three years since that has happened. You know my middle son Kelvin has been overseas in the war for the last couple of years and he and his family made it home this year. It was wonderful and we are about to be grandparents again, so I have nothing to complain about. We didn't do much for Christmas, Connie and I went down to Miami to the Florida estate and just made it back last week. Now Red we have known each other since we were rubbing elbows with Adam at the Abyssinian Baptist Church back in Harlem, you don't usually make casual calls, what's on your mind Congressman.

Well Armstrong, believe it or not I don't need anything right now I just wanted to invite you and Constance to be my personal guest during the Inauguration of President-Elect Obama. I can promise you a spectacular weekend and even get you accommodations at the Hay Adams which is where the Obama's will be staying prior to Inauguration Day and before moving into the White House, besides I have convinced him that if he is to wield significant power in the South that you are the man to know below the Mason Dixon line. I also have it on good authority that he had heard about you and wants me to set up this meeting. So tell me Armstrong can you do me this favor and let me be the one to make the formal introductions?

Why Red, Connie and I would consider it an honor, I though tickets to the events were long gone and we hadn't really given much thought to making the trip. But I tell you what, consider it done, you make all the arrangements and the introductions are yours.

I can get you an audience with the President-Elect on the 19th which will be the day before the Inauguration, how does that work for you?

How appropriate for Martin Luther King Day, that would be fine Red, we can fly in the night of the 18th and stay the entire week, that will give us some time to see Kelvin, Maria and General Milliner I'm sure will be in the area. Thanks again Red, you are a gem.

I'm looking forward to seeing you and Constance again Armstrong, thanks a million.

Connie, Connie, you will not believe our good fortune sweetie.

What is it Papa is everything okay? You sound more excited than you have been in a while, what's going on?

Well Connie that was Red Rangel and he wants you and I to be his personal guest during President-Elect Obama's Inauguration, he has us staying at the same hotel with them across from the White House. He has also set us up an audience with the President-Elect the night before the Inauguration, Connie I think we have arrived.

You mean the Obama's have arrived. I can't wait to give Michelle some fashion tips, did you see that dress she wore while in Grant Park on election night. No, no, that can't be allowed to happen again. That fashion mishap was far worse than anything Janet Jackson could have done at the Super Bowl a few years ago. Oh Papa, you are more than I ever could have dreamed of, you are the best.

That's what they tell me Connie, that's what they tell me.

Who tells you that Papa, who is they?

Was that the door Consuela . . . .

118

Damn, it is still negative, what the hell am I doing, nothing is going to work. I have bought enough of these damn tests to wallpaper a room with; I can't believe that after all of this I am still not pregnant. And that Maria just had to announce that she was pregnant again, I wish I could have been behind her while walking down those stairs. There is no way I will let that breeding factory sit in my seat at Sandy Grove.

Hey sweetie, why are you looking so down, that lovely face of yours does nothing for you when it has a frown on it? So tell me what's on your mind.

Strong, we are negative again sweetie. I just don't know what to do, you have been on the medication since early December and I am still not pregnant. You would think that by now the shots would be working. I have no idea where to turn right now or what to do.

We will do what we normally do Cheryl; we will continue taking the medication and what will be will be sweetie besides we could always adopt if you want a child that bad.

No Strong, we can't, I want to have your child. I want to have Prentice blood running through the veins of Armstrong the third. Oh Strong, promise me that whatever happens that we will always be together, I need you to promise me that you will never leave me just because I could not give you an heir can you promise me that honey, can you Strong?

Stop talking crazy sweetheart. Sure every man wants to be fruitful and multiply but that's God's work and I definitely can't blame him. We are still relatively young Cheryl and with today's technology we can continue to have kids well into our fifties. So let's just give Mother Nature a hand by continuing the medication that Dr. Screen prescribed and give it another shot next month. And yes I can promise you beyond the shadow of a doubt that we will always be a team Cheryl. You are my wife and I worship the very ground that you walk on. Now I have to get to the station, whatever you decide to do today do it on me here take this card and paint the Mall red.

Oh Strong, you do know how to turn a gloomy day into one filled with the warmest sunshine even if it is just 32 degrees outside. By the way Strong, I didn't really know how to ask you honey but can we go house hunting. We have been in this place since we got married and it is getting a little small don't you think?

I will keep that in mind Cheryl, but do you think the market is sound enough for us to be considering such a major purchase? But as I said I will keep it in mind, love you sweetie and will see you for dinner.

Love you too Strong and thanks for making me feel a little bit better. Yes this is Mrs. Prentice may I speak with Doctor Screen? Tell him it's urgent.

119

So, how long do you think this will take.

Well the first thing we have to do is the oil change and we will check your windshield wipers, battery, belts and hoses, tire pressure and change the anti-freeze.

What does the windshield wipers have to do with winterizing my car?

It's just one of the courtesy checks we make to insure that if a problem arises that the vehicle is in the best condition across the board. The entire process should take a little less than an hour so you can wait if you wish.

Thank you I will wait, it's not like I have anything else to do today.

Did you really have to give the man such a hard time?

I'm sorry but I could swear you were trying to get all up in my business.

Whoa, lovely lady I was just trying to start up a conversation that would probably get your mind off the reason you came here today. These places can be a bit overwhelming for a female and hearing all of your questions to the mechanic brought out the gentlemen in me that's all. If I have offended you then maybe I could take you to lunch as an apology.

Are you asking me to have lunch with you Mr.?

Oh, sorry, I'm Doctor Screen, Doctor Charles Screen, and you are?

My name is Tammy, pleased to meet you Doctor Screen, however I don't see how we can do lunch with both of our cars being in the back.

Well we could always walk across the street to Ruby Tuesdays if that is not being too forward.

I am a little hungry, well Doctor Screen I think I will take you up on your offer, after you Sir just let me get my coat.

Allow me.

120

Papa, you still seem to have so much on your mind these days, what has you so worried?

Nothing really Connie, it's just that I promised Strong that I would give him and Cheryl two months to get pregnant and I am wondering if Maria being pregnant again will complicate that. It looks as if I have no choice but to turn over the family business to Kelvin.

If that is the case Papa then I am sure that Strong will understand and give you his support.

Their sixty days will be up in about two weeks and I was just remembering how I felt when I learned the whole story about our heritage and the burden that I thought it would be. However in the long run I have adapted to the changes and made the best of the obstacles that were thrown in my way. It is an awesome undertaking but I think I've prepared the boys for the mental aspect of the job.

You've done more than just prepare them Papa; you have made it so much easier for them to step into your shoes, much easier then it was for your father when it was time for him to pass it to you. You have always known that this day would come Papa, embrace it and know that you have done your job.

As usual you are right Connie, so in a couple of more weeks when its time I will make the announcement and all of us can sleep easier. The way I have it figured we may get the chance to tell Maria and Kelvin personally because we will be in Washington for the Inauguration at that time.

I can't wait for the festivities, Papa; I will have to go back to Atlanta to find me an appropriate gown for all the Inaugural Balls and festivities. I wonder who else will be there; maybe we will have a DST representative from Howard or Georgetown in the area, I must get out my rolodex and make some calls. Oh Papa there is just so much to do, do you think we will have enough time to get prepared? And what if there is a Sorority Ball planned.

Connie, twelve months wouldn't be enough time for you to prepare and you know that. But promise me that you will not give the First Lady any fashion tips unless she specifically asks.

I promise Papa but I may throw a hint here and there.

I've seen your hints Connie, and I mean it, off limits unless she brokers the question.

Well, I could dress to the nines that may give her and me something to talk about. If I can accessorize right she will have no choice but to ask me for tips. I will just let my grandeur provide the impetus; remind me to call Oprah to find out where she's staying.

I had no idea that Oprah was going to be there.

Papa, really, this is her President you know, and as Oprah goes, so goes the nation. And I must call Mya, maybe we can get together for Bridge and have Michelle as a fourth, who knows, she might have some game, she did do the fist bump thingy on national television. The girl has heart I must give her that.

121

See that wasn't so bad after all and by the time we finish lunch our cars should be finished and ready for the weather.

I usually ask one of my brothers to take my car to the shop for me but I thought I should get in the habit of doing more for myself; I need to personify the independent woman ethic.

Oh, I see, so all those questions were just getting your independence on? Okay I get it.

Well a girl has to start somewhere. So Doctor Screen, what's up? What's on your mind or do you ask every woman you meet at car dealerships to have lunch with you?

No, and I would never consider you to be every woman, look at you, you are beautiful and quite fascinating and I would be less than a real man if I said nothing. Look upon this as an attempt to get to know you better, besides how often does a man look upon perfection?

Flattery will get you everywhere Doctor so please continue, what type of Doctor are you anyway.

I'm actually a fertility specialist I have a practice up on Chafee Avenue.

Oh, I see, but when Doctors aren't in the office aren't they supposed to be playing golf or something like that?

It's a little too cold for golf right now but for the most part you are correct; I just needed to get the car taken care of so I took a few hours off. So, Tammy, tell me a little about you, for starters what your last name?

I don't think so Doctor, not yet anyway I don't usually talk a lot about myself so you will have to be a bit more specific. I have been told time and time again not to volunteer too much information, it has been known to give people an opportunity to either use your past against you or play on your emotions for personal gain. So which type are you?

Which type of what am I?

Which type of man are you, one that will play on my emotions or are you the type to use my past against me?

I'd like to think that I am neither, first of all I can't see where my playing on your emotions can benefit me in the least, and everyone has a past. I'd like to think that learning from and understanding one's past is necessary in order for us to be molded into the people we were meant to become. Without a past the future has no direction.

Oh, I see, so you are a philosopher as well as a fertility specialist. You must get a kick out of making women swoon Doctor Screen, both professions make for either an extremely interesting evening or one hell of a nightmare. You see Doctor I am quite amused by a man who personifies perfection the way you seem to and I must admit that you are not hard on the eyes. But you are a man and there are just too many scary things that go along with that particular fact.

And what things might that be?

The bullshit factor Doctor, and I am sure you are well aware of it. Allow me to explain, handsome Doctor claims to be single, handsome Doctor drives a Mercedes 500 SEL classic but still claims to be single; handsome Doctor has eyes that could make a blind woman get woozy and a body that makes most women question their morals, but still claims to be single, am I getting warm Doctor Screen?

What are you trying to say?

Let me continue; let me tell you exactly how this day could end. Handsome Doctor decides to take the rest of the day off just so he can get to know Tammy. Handsome Doctor takes Tammy to places that she hasn't been to sexually in quite a while, a place she actually wouldn't mind going right about now. Handsome Doctor wakes up in the morning and miraculously remembers that he does have a significant other and Tammy is left with the memories of one of the greatest nights of her life. Fast forward, Tammy tries to contact Doctor because women develop an emotional bond with the men they sleep with but Doctor no longer has time for Tammy and before long Doctor disappears completely and he is the only one who lives happily ever after. Is it getting clearer to you now Doctor?

Pump your brakes Tammy, ok, for the most part you are correct, in that yes, I would like to get to know you better, and yes I do find you quite attractive which is why I went out on a limb by asking you to lunch. And yes I would take the rest of, not just the day, but the week off to spend that time with you, but you are wrong about me having a significant other. I am a single man, very single, too damn single if you ask me. But what I detect is bitterness in you and although I am not accustomed to rescuing damsels in distress I can make an exception for you this time. I can't imagine who has caused the pain in your life or who has tarnished you this much but I wish I did know so that I could at least explain to the moron what he has created. It's amazing to me how much of the essence of a woman men destroy without even realizing it.

I'm sorry Doctor it's just that I am very particular about who I meet and what I tell them. Thanks for lunch and I hope to see you again.

Wait a minute, you mean you are going to leave just like that. No phone number, no address, no nothing.

Doctor Screen, your mission, should you choose to accept it, is to do what is necessary to find me again.

And that is?

Be, my Knight in shining armor Doctor Screen, rescue this damsel in distress as you called me. Augusta is not that big of a city; pretend that finding me again would save your life, make this your quest to find the Holy Grail. Are you up for the challenge? If you are really interested in getting to know Tammy then that is what it's going to take, you see with me you really have to earn your stripes.

So I see.

For real?

Knight's honor.

We'll see Doctor Screen; have a nice day and again, thanks for lunch.

122

Welcome to the Hay Adams make I take your coat Sir?

No but thanks, that won't be necessary.

Your name Sir?

Oh, sorry, forgot I was not at home, I am Armstrong Prentice, that would be Senator Armstrong Prentice and this is my lovely wife Constance.

Oh, yes Sir Senator, we have you in the White House Junior Suite.

The White House!!

Yes Sir, your Suite has a direct view of the White House.

That would be fine, that would be just outstanding, are there any messages?

Yes Sir, as a matter of fact there is, I will have your bags delivered to your Suite Sir, feel free to have refreshments at the bar complements of Congressman Rangel.

Why thank you and here's a little something for you.

Thank you Sir, but this is the Hay Adams and tips are not required, please enjoy your stay and if there is anything else you require do not hesitate to let myself or any member of my staff know. Sir, Madam.

Yes Sir, welcome to the Hay Adams may I offer you and the lovely lady a cocktail while your room is being prepared?

Why yes, I will have a snifter of your finest Cognac and what will you have honey?

I will have a dry Vodka Martini with an extra olive.

Fine Sir and Madam, I will be right back with your refreshments.

According to this note Connie our meeting with President Elect Obama has been moved to 8 pm tonight and he has left us with two tickets to the Inauguration itself and four tickets to two of the Balls on Tuesday night.

Oh Papa, just look at this place, I mean we have stayed at some of the most luxurious hotels on the planet but who would think that Washington DC would have a place like this nestled right across from the White House itself and the staff is to literally die for.

Like I've said before Connie, you are now stepping in high cotton, high cotton my dear, Prentice cotton.

Your cocktails Sir, Madam.

Thank you lad, thank you.

So Papa, what do we do tonight, should we call Kelvin and Maria or just relax and take in the sights and sounds of the city? I am sure this city will come alive tonight because history itself is swirling around in the air and anyone that is anyone has been drawn to our Nation's Capital to witness what no one thought would happen in their lifetimes our first Black President. Who knew Papa, who knew?

123

Hello Cheryl, sorry I missed your call earlier; I was actually getting the car serviced. What's on your mind today?

You know what's on my mind dammit? We need to meet again for what just might be our last time.

Why would it have to be the last time Cheryl?

Because my trifling ass sister in law is pregnant again and looks like I am the most infertile woman on the planet. How can I be sleeping with two viral men on a regular basis and not be pregnant yet. How long has it been, over a month, and we have been seeing each other at least twice a week and I am still not pregnant.

The results are strange to me as well Cheryl; I thought that by now you would have conceived. I'll tell you what, let's meet tonight at the Marriott again and why don't you wear that purple teddy that you wore the first night we had our little rendezvous. Prepare for a long night because I do kind of miss you and don't forget that cash.

Not a problem Doctor you just make sure you can handle the truth because tonight I am bringing my "A" game with me.

Whatever Cheryl, I will be on my "V" game, V for Viagra. Viva Viagra.

Whatever it takes Charles, whatever it takes; if this is to be our last evening together then let's make it mean something other than just sex. I must admit that I never planned on developing any feelings for you but I guess I just can't help myself.

Listen, Mrs. Prentice this is a business arrangement and nothing else, I can't allow myself to look at this as anything other than that so if you don't mind can we keep it on that level?

Sure, ah, sorry, I have no idea what came over me, I will see you tonight and don't forget to bring your "V" game.

Oh I won't forget, see you tonight.

124

And I Barrack Hussein Obama do solemnly swear that I will faithfully execute the office of President of the United States, and will to the best of my ability, preserve, protect and defend the Constitution of the United States so help me God.

Congratulations Mr. President.

Wow Papa, we have our first African American President of these United States. I am honored that we could be a part of history in the making. Papa, papa, are you okay.

Just feeling a little light headed Connie, I will be alright, it could be the cold air but I will be okay.

Maybe we should go back to the room for a bit, today has been overwhelming for the both of us and after staying up last night with the Obama's, Oprah, Red and Joe Lowery, maybe you just need a little more rest.

No Connie, I will be alright, what time do we meet Kelvin and Maria for the Neighborhood Ball tonight?

They are to meet us at the Hotel at around eight, let's just go back there and rest Papa, you aren't looking like yourself.

Okay Connie, whatever you say. I just can't believe that so many people showed up for the Inauguration, there had to be over two hundred and fifty thousand just in the ticketed area alone, feels like it did back when we came to hear Martin give his "I Have a Dream" speech.

Washington doesn't seem to have changed much since then; I wonder what he would think about today. Today his dream has awakened and the world will never be the same again. The second coming of Camelot, don't you think so Papa, Papa . . . . Papa . . . . Armstrong . . . . somebody get a Doctor please . . . . Papa!!!!

125

Maria have you seen my bow tie sweetie, the one that goes with the Tuxedo?

I thought you were wearing your Dress Blues to the ball tonight Kelvin I just got them out of the cleaners, did you change your mind?

Well if I know DC and I do know DC, I may have to get loose tonight and my Blues are too restrictive for me to get my Cupid Shuffle on, besides I don't want to stand out in the crowd just in case.

Well I've seen your shuffle and you could use some restriction. Besides you look great in your Blues . . . . but if you insist on looking like a penguin then be my guest. Your tie is in the bottom drawer of your nightstand in that black box . . . in other words my darling, just where it is supposed to be.

I can't believe that Mom and Dad were actually sitting that close to the President, he mentioned that he had a face to face with him last night. That must have been amazing. I'm just glad he was able to get us tickets to some of the festivities.

(Telephone ringing in background)

Is that the phone?

I'll get it honey, put on your tie. Hello, yes this is the Prentice residence, yes he's my husband, just a minute, sweetie, it's the Hay Adams.

Yes, this is Mr. Prentice, may I help you.

Mr. Prentice, this is the concierge at the Hay Adams hotel here in Washington, Sir there has been an incident.

What sort of incident?

Sir, your father, the Senator has collapsed and the ambulance is currently on its way to Howard University Hospital, your Mother is with him and asked me to make this call. Sir, it doesn't look good I think you should meet your Mom at the hospital.

Ambulance, what the . . . . is my Dad alright?

I'm not sure Sir.

What do you mean you're not sure, is he alright?

Sir, again, I don't know.

Thanks I'm on my way.

Kelvin, Kelvin, what is it?

Dad has collapsed and they are on the way with him to Howard University Hospital, I'll bring the car around.

No Kelvin, let me drive sweetie you are too distraught.

126

Hello Martin, I was just about to call and invite you to dinner, so tell me exactly what can I do for you this evening?

You can do an awful lot actually; I was calling to see if I could have you for, I mean take you to dinner.

I would enjoy that Martin but I have already prepared dinner although I am missing a couple of key ingredients that would make this a memorable evening.

And exactly what might those ingredients be?

Well I have the candles on the table already and I could use a strong Omega Man to help me light my fire.

Oh I can help you light that fire and quite a few others Tameka but please don't tease a brother like that, you know how much you mean to me and you also know which buttons to push, so stop teasing.

Martin I told you that when I was ready I'd let you know. I want you to stop whatever you are doing and get your fine ass over here and light this fire.

Look out of the window sweetie, I am already here.

Get your behind in here Martin; keep an eye on the stove for me I will be right back.

Sure, no problem, smells great in here are you sure this isn't take out? Tameka, Tameka?

Over here Martin.

Well, wow, you look wonderful sweetie, you look like . . . .

Stop talking and get those clothes off.

What about dinner Tameka?

Don't be scared now Martin, turn off the stove and get over here, you have earned this evening and I think, I mean I know that it's time for us to take this relationship to another level, it's time for us to become one. So do me baby, make me your appetizer because I plan to certainly make you mine.

Clothes, what clothes . . . . come here baby, get to this.

No you didn't pull a Marvin Gaye on me Martin.

Buzz, Buzz,

Is that your phone?

Yes but who cares, whoever it is can wait.

Martin, this feels funny sweetie, answer your phone.

But Tameka.

Your phone Martin.

Hello, sup Kelvin.

Martin, Maria and I are on the way to Howard University Hospital, Dad collapsed and the ambulance is taking him and Mom there as we speak. I wish I had more to tell you but unfortunately that's all I know right now.

Is he going to be alright Kelvin?

I have no idea; Mom had the concierge at the hotel get in touch with me and Maria. I will fill you in as soon as I know something, right now all we can do is pray.

Should I get on a flight and head up there?

Not until I find out more man, right now I need for you to get in touch with Strong and Tammy so that they know what's going on.

Alright man, I will handle things on this end but keep me posted.

Martin, Martin, what's wrong honey?

Not sure Tameka, they are rushing my Dad to the hospital right now, seems he collapsed right after the Inauguration.

Is he going to be okay Martin?

It's too early to tell but if I know Armstrong Prentice, and I do, it's going to take more than collapsing to take him out of here. So yes, the old man is going to be fine, just fine. I got to get in touch with Strong and Tammy.

Honey I am so sorry but you might want to put your clothes on before you do that.

Oh yeah, but I claim my rain check.

Honey you will never, ever need a rain check with me. Handle your business; do you need me to come with you?

Sure.

Let me get dressed, I'll drive and you call your brother.

127

(phone ringing)

Hello.

Hey Strong, its Martin man, listen I just got off the phone with Kelvin in DC. Strong, Dad collapsed right after the Inauguration and he and Mom are currently on the way to Howard University Hospital according to Kelvin, that's all we know right now.

Has anybody had a chance to speak with Mom yet?

No, from what I understand she is in the ambulance with Dad and Kelvin and Maria are on the way to meet them at the Hospital.

Okay Martin, let me try and find Cheryl while you locate Tammy and inform her, I'll get back to you as soon as I figure out what my next move should be.

Okay Man, and Strong, Dad could use a good prayer right now man, so send up the love.

I always do baby brother, I always do.

(Please listen to the music while your party is reached)

That's strange; it seems lately that I can never reach Cheryl when I need too.

Hello, Prentice residence.

Consuela this is Strong, I was just wondering if Cheryl may have stopped out there, she had mentioned the other day that she left something in our room at the estate, have you seen her by chance?

No Master Strong, I haven't seen Mrs. Cheryl since the holidays is everything alright Sir, is there anything I can do.

Actually Consuela, don't get overly concerned but I just got a call from Kelvin in DC and he told me that Dad collapsed right after the Inauguration and he and Mom are on the way to Howard University Hospital as we speak.

Oh my God, is everything going to be alright Mr. Strong?

I'm sure everything will be fine Consuela, as a matter of fact, is Serge on the estate? He might be able to get me to the airport the fastest. I think I need to head to DC just to be on the safe side and to give Mom some support.

Yes Sir, just a minute Sir.

Yes Sir, this is Serge, Consuela just informed me about your father, I am sorry Sir, but I want you to know that I will energize the system here just in case.

Energize what system there Serge?

Well Sir, your father has put certain protocols in place for emergencies such as this and I just want you to know that I will handle what needs to be done on this end.

Ok, whatever Serge, listen I will need for you to arrange the Jet at Bush Field for me so that I can fly to DC in the next hour, can you make that happen.

Consider it done Sir, but the plane is currently at Daniel Field but I will take care of the arrangements.

Great Serge, Daniel Field is a lot closer than Bush Field is anyway and when I get back be sure to inform me of those protocols you spoke of.

(Please enjoy the music while your party is reached)

Cheryl this is Strong, where are you? Listen my Dad has just been rushed to Howard University Hospital in DC and I am on my way to Daniel Field to take the Jet so that I can get there. When you get this message, call me and meet me at the airport for the flight.

Martin?

Yes Strong, what's up man?

Listen, I can't get in touch with Cheryl but I decided to take the Gulfstream V and head to DC, is Tameka with you?

Yes, she is.

Have you been able to contact Tammy?

No, not yet.

Ok, let me try, if you would, can you and Tameka stand by for a minute?

Sure no problem.

Hello.

Tammy this is Strong, how are you Sis?

I'm good Strong, just got out of the shower, you don't sound so good, what's wrong?

Well Kelvin called, Dad has collapsed and is being rushed to the hospital, Mom is with him and Kelvin and Maria are on the way. Listen I can't find Cheryl and I need to fly up there in about an hour; I have Martin and Tameka standing by.

Strong, calm down, what do you need?

I will have Martin drop Tameka off at your place then he can meet me at Daniel Field so that we can figure out what else to do. Could you and Tameka try and find Cheryl for me.

Sure Strong, but I am sure Cheryl is probably at the Mall or someplace.

I know Tammy but for the last few weeks I haven't been able to reach her with I need too. So please take care of this for me and I will call you as soon as I land. I will tell Martin to drop Tameka off at your place, they are headed down Walton Way right now. Talk to you soon and thanks Tammy.

304

Sure Strong, no problem and just know that Dad will be alright, remember we are talking about Armstrong Prentice. He probably got over excited at the festivities and stuff, he'll bounce back, he always does.

Okay Sis, I know. I'll talk with you later.

Hello Martin, I just got off the phone with Tammy, can you drop Tameka off at Tammy's place and meet me at Daniel Field in about thirty minutes? I just need to stop by the house, throw a few things in a bag and get out of here.

Sure thing man, but why didn't Mom and Dad take the Jet?

Because they just finished doing maintenance on it and you know how superstitious Mom can be. Anyway it worked out for the best, at least now I can stop everything and head there to be with them.

Okay man, on my way.

128

I see you remembered the teddy, how about a glass of wine to set the mood and I hope you are not in a hurry because from what I hear we got four hours to make something magical happen.

Four hours, you got me totally wrong honey; I don't want to do anything for four hours regardless of how good the sex is, besides Strong just might miss me if I am gone that long.

Well pour me a glass while you are over there and I'll put on some old Smokey Robinson because tonight I want you to let me be the clock for the time of your life.

Oh it's going to get smoky up in here anyway and I got your miracle but first I want to talk for a minute.

Sure Cheryl, what's on your mind? You're not getting into that feelings mood you talked about earlier are you? We promised that this arrangement would only be a professional one.

Buzz Buzz.

Is that your phone?

Yes but it can wait, it's just my husband, you were saying?

Cheryl you are a fascinating woman and so full of passion but you also happen to be married to the Chief of Homicide whose father just so happens to be the most prominent man in this State if not the entire Southeast.

I know Charles but I can't tell my heart what to do.

Well you better figure out another language because there is no way that I will risk everything I have worked for just to watch it slip through my hands in the process. And there is no way in hell I can afford to compete with the Prentices financially so let's do the right thing and keep this professional, and speaking of professional did you bring the money.

Yes the envelope is on the table, look Charles I don't know if I mentioned it to you or not but Maria, my sister-in-law is pregnant again and this may just be our last tryst so since you already have your money can we not mention the particulars and just pretend for these few hours that there are only the two of us in this world.

Buzz Buzz.

Are you sure you shouldn't answer that.

More sure then I have been about anything lately, continue Charles.

Cheryl there is one thing that I don't understand about this entire situation; you are already married to one of the richest men in the State, why can't you be satisfied with that? There is no place for greed in any of our lives, can you make me understand?

Charles have you ever visited or even seen Sandy Grove?

Sandy Grove, what's that?

See you will never understand. Close your eyes for a minute and imagine this hotel being a private residence complete with all the servants, the best food, the best wine and with all the trimmings. Now imagine that it all belongs to you, imagine that this hotel is your home and you are the master of your castle, imagine that you drive the finest cars and; you command attention wherever you go. Imagine that the Mayor comes by on the regular just to kiss your ass. Now think about what it takes to run a place of that magnitude and the prestige that goes with the address alone. Sandy Grove is the estate of Senator Armstrong Prentice and it's practically run by his wife Constance. I need for my husband to be next in line so that I can manage and we can reside in that mansion man. But the only way that can happen is for me to get pregnant with a male heir like yesterday. I don't see it happening but we just have to try one last time.

Wow, I didn't know it was that deep and maybe my charges were too cheap. But I do understand for the moment anyway, now look what you've done; now you have to wake Killa back up.

And just how would you like for me to do that Dr. Screen.

Buzz Buzz.

I'm sure you remember how to get his attention sweetie, how about a little?

Well we will just have to see about that. I guess we umph . . . . sorry I forgot to relax my throat.

129

Tammy, I'm sure that everything will be all right; your Dad will be fine, now where do you think we should start our search for Mrs. Augusta Mall?

Not sure, but there aren't too many places she can be, she is a Prentice and that image of hers significantly limits the places she can be seen in.

That seems so stupid to me, I just can't put my mind around the restrictions that some people put on themselves.

Well she learned it from one of the best, none other than Constance Prentice herself.

Girl you know you need Jesus.

Okay, let's start in the bottom down by East Boundary.

Why? This is Cheryl Prentice we are talking about and there is nothing on that side of town that would remotely be of her caliber.

Good point, let's just roll by the Mall and see if we see her car but since we are near downtown already, let's stop by Club 209 around the corner from the Marriott for a cocktail, the music there is nice and I think the bartender has a thing for me.

Okay but we will only have time for one; in the meantime I will keep trying to get that girl on the phone. We can park in the Marriott parking lot and walk over. I know how you feel about your family, just know that I have you and your family in my prayers.

Thanks Tameka, but I know that everything will be alright, I just know it, besides my father is in the best of health, this can't be anything major. So let's just go in here and have us a cocktail.

130

I got here as soon as I could Strong, any word from Cheryl yet?

No man nothing at all, Martin this strange man, for the past few weeks I am having trouble keeping tabs on her. This is so strange to me and now that I really need her she is not returning any of my calls.

What time does your flight leave?

In about another fifteen minutes.

Are you sure you don't want me to come with you?

No man, we will need some stability down here for the girls, as soon as I find out what is really going on I will contact you. I just don't know what to do about Cheryl.

Look man, I am positive that nothing is wrong with Cheryl, she just may have lost her phone, or is in a dressing room somewhere, who knows? Women are strange like that.

Oh, so now you are educating me on the ways of women? I have heard everything now, I am sure that we are in the last days.

Whatever man, Strong I am a little worried, I didn't want to show it in front of the ladies but what if this is more serious than we know man, what if Dad doesn't come back from this, what if he dies Strong?

Look Martin, we can't afford to think like that man, Dad will be alright. This family can and will survive anything, we were raised to succeed and that's what Dad would want for us to do so it's going to be cool man.

Mr. Prentice, Mr. Armstrong Prentice.

Yes I am Armstrong Prentice.

Sir your plane is prepared for you to board.

Thanks I will be right there.

Look bro, I have to board now but do me a favor and take care of the girls until we know exactly what's going on with Dad and help them find Cheryl. She had better have a major excuse for my not being able to reach her.

Have a safe flight Strong and don't worry about Augusta, I got this situation on lock. Call me as soon as you can, we will be at Tammy's.

131

Oh Charles, that was the best ever, are you sure you can't hang around for a while. I know I need to probably check in with my hubby but I can find an excuse to come back for a little more of your pampering.

Actually Cheryl, that's not a bad idea, I don't really have anything to do for the rest of the evening and I could order some room service here. How long do you think you'll be gone?

Not long at all, maybe an hour or so let me just go into the ladies room and freshen up a bit.

Okay, look can you throw me the remote while you're up. Thanks. Feeling like a little hellivison to keep me occupied while you are away my dear.

"Retired Georgia State Senator Armstrong Prentice has just arrived at Howard University Hospital after having collapsed right after the Inauguration of President Barrack Obama. Senator Prentice's condition is not known at this time but we will keep you informed as our team gets into place. This is CNN."

Oh my God, this can't be happening.

What is it Cheryl?

Senator Prentice is my father in law, oh Charles this is awful, now how do I justify my absence? I have got to get out of here.

Cheryl, wait, Cheryl, you left your . . . .

The next time we go anywhere Tammy you better make sure you bring enough money to pick up the tab, that's the third time you have stuck me with the check this week, I thought you said the bartender had a thing for you, he had a thing all right, a bill.

Get over it Tameka, I just left my ATM card at home that's all.

Do you ever leave home with it Tammy?

Ah , , , , occasionally, this was just not one of those occasions.

Tammy look over there on the Marriott steps, is that who I think it is.

Who Tameka?

That woman looking all disheveled at the top of the stairs? Well I be dammed, that is Cheryl, but what is she doing down here?

I have no idea, and what is this?

Cheryl, you left your purse, I tried to catch you before you got to the elevator.

Who is that with Cheryl Tammy?

It looks like that Doctor I was telling you about that I met at the Mercedes dealership but it couldn't' be, could it?

Cheryl!!, Cheryl!!

Oh hell no!

Cheryl, we have been looking all over for you, Daddy collapsed in Washington and Strong had to leave, where have you been and why are you here? And who is this man?

Hello Tammy.

What are you doing here?

You do remember me don't you? I'm Doctor Screen, from the Mercedes dealership.

Oh I know who you are Dr. Screen but what are you doing here with my sister-in-law? I didn't know you made house calls.

Hold on, Tammy, I can explain everything to you in the car sweetie, I can explain it all. Let's just get out of here; I have to get to Strong.

It's a little too late for that Cheryl he is on the Jet to Washington he just left and may I ask how you and Dr. Screen know each other?

It's nothing like that Tammy; Dr. Screen is our fertility Doctor and I just so happened to run into him here at the hotel that's all.

And what is he doing with your purse, barefooted and with an unbuttoned shit, if you just happened to just run into him? And Doctor Screen thanks for restoring my faith in men . . . you see Tammy is always right. Looks like the Marriott's dawg policy is a little too liberal for me, oh where are my manners, it is quite nice to see you again and I'll tell my brother you said hi, let's go Tameka.

Tammy I can explain everything.

Explain it to my brother Doctor Screen; I am sure he is more willing to listen to you then I will ever be again.

Tammy, that won't be necessary, like I said we can explain everything.

What's going on Cheryl, are you coming with us or do you have other plans?

We are Audi, let's go Tammy.

Wait Tammy, Tameka, where are you all going to be.

The same place you need to be Cheryl!

132

Hello, may I speak with Mr. Johnson?

May I inquire as to who is calling Sir?

Sure, tell him that its Serge from the Prentice estate, he is expecting me.

Very well Sir, would you please follow me?

Well, Serge, it's been quite a while my good man, you look terrific and how is the family?

Everyone is fine Sir, thanks for asking.

No, it's you that I must thank for getting me the information on Armstrong as soon as you did. We have already put security on at the hospital and he is currently being examined by the crème of the crop. However if things don't start to look up over the next 72 hours I want you to bring his son Kelvin here to Mason Hall so that we can get him installed as the heir to the Prentice holdings since he is the only sibling with a male child thus the next Prentice heir. There can be no mistake about this, Armstrong should have made the decision years ago but I do understand why he could not but that is of no consequence right now. Is that understood?

Yes Sir it is understood and I have made all the necessary contacts on this end based on information provided to me by Mr. Prentice if something like this should occur. I have all the power of attorneys and living wills that he provided.

Great, the only thing left to do at this point is wait, as soon as he is diagnosed we will have the best Doctors in that particular field at his disposal. If worse comes to worse we can have a contingency plan in force at a moment's notice. Did Armstrong mention to you what to do about the accountants if he were to have problems such as this?

Yes Sir, I have contacted them already and they have begun an exhaustive twelve month audit of each account belonging to the Prentice siblings. We should know in about 48 hours if anything has gone awry, will there be anything else Sir?

No Serge, you have been magnificent and a credit to Armstrong, you may leave now. I will be in contact with you as soon as I hear anything. At this point there is nothing we can do about the press but be sure to tell the children that all interviews must be cleared by Armstrong's attorney prior to them going on the air and even then only after all questions have been pre-approved. Have a good evening Serge and thanks for everything.

Same to you Sir.

133

Armstrong, Armstrong can you hear me Papa? Can you hear me Armstrong, Armstrong speak to me Papa, speak to me!

Mrs. Prentice, you must allow us to take him in now, we have our best staff at his disposal, Mrs. Prentice please you must allow us to do our jobs.

I'm sorry Mrs. Prentice; but you will have to wait here in the waiting room until we can find out more information concerning his condition. Please Mrs. Prentice you will have to calm down.

I'm sorry attendant; Mrs. Prentice will not wait in the waiting room she has been summoned to the office of . . . .

Excuse me, are you Mrs. Prentice?

Yes I am Sir, Constance Prentice and who are you?

Mrs. Prentice, please come with me, I am Doctor Ahaghotu, the President of Medicine here at the Howard University Hospital. I can assure you that the Senator is in the best of hands and I am here to see to it that those hands are extended to you as well. You may wait with me in my office. Please Mrs. Prentice, come with me. Attendant can you please bring us a couple bottles of water and two cups of coffee, decaf.

Right away Doctor.

Is Armstrong going to be okay Doctor? They aren't telling me anything, is he going to be okay?

Mrs. Prentice, it is much too early for us to tell at this time; the only thing we know for sure right now is that his vital signs are stable and that he is breathing normally. So let's just take one step at a time, I can assure you that he is in the best of hands.

I must call my family please excuse me.

Yes, Martin, this is your Mother, we are at the hospital, is Strong with you?

No Mom, is Dad okay? Strong is in the air on his way to be by your side, have Kelvin and Maria arrived yet?

Not that I know of, but this is a big hospital, I am with Dr. Ahaghotu who is the President of Medicine here and we are awaiting some word from downstairs.

Are you okay?

Of course I am Martin, I am a Prentice and we normally glide though adversities such as this, but I must admit that I am a little shaken right now but I am sure your father will pull through this little episode, he always does. Just be sure to stay away from the press, you know how they can distort things.

Yep, I got a call from Serge earlier and he told us to avoid them as much as possible which is why Tammy and I are staying out here at Tameka's.

Good for you Martin, listen I have to go now, I have to try and get in touch with Kelvin and Maria to update them, until then know that I love you all and your father could use an extra prayer today so make that happen. Love you, tootles. Hello Kelvin, this is your mother, where are you and Maria?

We are on Georgia Avenue just down the street from the Hospital; we should be there in about fifteen minutes, any word on Dad's condition?

No not yet, when you get here ask for Dr. Ahaghotu's office, they should be able to direct you. Thank God this gentleman saved me from that dreaded waiting room there is no way I could have survived out there with Tom, Dick and Harry. Dr. Ahaghotu was a Godsend Son.

Okay Mom, we will see you there in a few.

Is she okay Kelvin?

Sure she is, you know the great Constance Prentice, nothing shakes her except maybe wearing the wrong color combination at the yearly cotillion, she will be okay.

What tha!!!!

Maria watch out . . . . watch out . . . . oh my God!!!!!

134

FEBRUARY 16^{TH,} 1953

. . . . Armstrong, Armstrong, wake up Son, we have an awful lot to do today, wake up Son.

Yes Sir, but Dad this jetlag is awful, I still feel like I'm still on that plane from England.

I know but today will turn out to be the most important day in your life, it's your eighteenth birthday and today you are legally a man.

I know but other than that what makes you have to wake a brother up at the crack of dawn?

We have to take a trip to the country today and visit the Johnsons; you do remember the Johnsons don't you?

Yes Sir, we spent almost every summer near there, but why so early Dad?

Because of what today is, listen get cleaned up and meet me in the living room, we have a lot to discuss.

Later . . . .

Okay Dad, what is so important that I had to, not only get out of bed, but get dressed at such an early hour, what's on your mind?

Son, I want you to first of all think back on the things that have transpired in your life, things that have separated you from what you have seen others do, can you remember any of those things?

Sure I can Dad, who else from this block can say they graduated from Oxford University in England at sixteen than traveled throughout Europe for two years, heck most of them haven't even left the country but they will remain my lifelong friends. I always wondered how we could afford to pay for all of that but you said it was a part of what my grandfather left me in his will.

That's true Son but that's just the tip of the iceberg, Armstrong I have been waiting for this day all of your life. Your real inheritance has been handed down from generation

316

to generation in this family for over one hundred and fifty years. You were designated the proper heir long before you were even a twinkle in my eyes Son, it is today on your eighteenth birthday when the truth of who you are can really be told.

What are you saying Dad, what do you mean who I really am?

Actually Armstrong it has to do with the family, this family, your family, because after today your family as you have known it all of your life has changed.

Dad, you have totally confused me now.

Get in the car Son maybe I can explain it along the way. No I want you to drive because this journey is one that you must take every year for the rest of your life; I want you to pay close attention to everything I tell you and everything you see. For the first time Son I am asking you to trust me totally because, actually you have no choice, this is your legacy and it begins now. I want you to drive all the way out Wrightsboro Road and hit the Gordon Highway headed towards Ft. Gordon and Evans.

But Dad it would be must easier if I just took Interstate 20.

Armstrong, you must understand something, as I said before I want you to pay close attention to everything you see and everything you hear, now don't question me, go into receive mode and react. Now make this right on Wrightsboro Road headed towards Fort Gordon and when you get to Jimmy Dyess Parkway make another right.

Yes Sir, but Dad at least tell me what this is all about.

In time just pay attention for now, your right is coming up, keep straight until you cross I-20 then make the first left and keep driving.

We've been on this road for about thirty minutes Dad, now what?

Pull over and roll down the windows Armstrong and smell the fresh air, your air Son.

Dad, what is this all about we left the city miles ago and there is nothing out here but wide open spaces.

That's where you are wrong Armstrong; I want to show you something, look around you, because everything you behold in all four directions belongs to you.

Yeah, right and I also believe in the tooth fairy.

It's all here in these documents Armstrong, the reason we must go to the country today is so that all of this can be signed over to you. It's your great, great, grandfather's legacy Son; it has been in this family for over one hundred and fifty years. There is over two thousand acres of prime real estate here, two thousand acres that have been in your name from before you were born. Land Son, the only thing that God is making no more of, land has been and will continue to be the life's blood of this family Armstrong and it's now up to you to do your part. I know this is a little overwhelming but in time it will all make sense, get back in the car I'll drive this time.

Dad you have to understand that I am totally lost, how did all of this happen?

I wanted you to see your land before you found out why and how Son, but believe me when I say that it is your land. I'm going to get back on 278, the reason I prefer not to use the Interstate is because when you travel the back roads you travel a similar path to the ones that our ancestors also traveled, remember there were no Interstates or roads back then.

I know Dad, each time you took us to the country you always had a history lesson to share with us, I can remember the stories well, my favorite was about Fessa and Mammy Brown and how Fessa taught the Johnson family to read and write then there were the ones about the train filled with Gold and the way our family made a deal with the Johnsons and that one day they would keep their word and we would get our inheritance . . . . oh my God you mean to tell me that those were not just stories you told me to keep me quiet as a child?

Son, those were more than just stories they were part of your legacy, each and every one of those stories were true?

How could that be Dad? We lived on Perry Avenue, the neighborhood was nice and we all looked after each other but we were not rich by any stretch of the imagination, if the stories you told were true then why didn't you take advantage of any of the wealth?

Because it wasn't mine to take advantage of Son, I was not the heir; this is your legacy it was never mine.

Okay Dad, let me understand this, I mean Oxford was a little over the top but at least I got a great education in finance and got to travel the world while in Europe, you mean to tell me that all this was orchestrated, even the Economics degree? What else in my life was planned Dad and who was doing the planning?

Calm down Son, you have to view the entire picture before you start down that road, you must understand Armstrong what you represent. Yes Son, there have been things in your life that have been planned from the very beginning and I had a major hand in making some key decisions, then there was your mother prior to her death, and Mr. Johnson had a few suggestions as well. You see Armstrong each family had to have a male heir in order to carry on the legacy and to keep the family secrets.

What family secrets Dad?

Be patient Son, it will all make sense to you after a while.

And if you don't mind my asking, how much money are we talking about?

Ah, as Shakespeare would say "there's the rub". Let's just say that as of midnight last night you became the wealthiest black man in the South. But it's a different kind of wealth Armstrong, it's the kind of wealth that men would live and die for, that's why it became important that you be taught how to handle it. That's why it was necessary to send you to boarding schools in France, Egypt, Tuscany and on to England to attend Oxford. There was a method to my madness, it was necessary for you to become educated on a global scale in order to handle such a responsibility and remember Armstrong that most of all this is a responsibility and to whom much is given, much is expected.

Welcome to Warren County, and as I said you will have to make this trip once a year on Mr. Johnson's birthday, you will be told why, normally I would ride through the town and make a few stops but I want you to make this left right here and when you see the school make another left; this is the Gibson Highway Son.

Wait a minute Dad, its coming back to me now; this was where granddad would bring me when you left us here during the summer vacations. I remember most of his stories too; I can't believe the two of you have kept this from me for all of these years.

It was a necessary evil Armstrong, that church on your right is Johnson Church with all its ornate designs and granite grave markers. Now about fifty yards from here make a right turn onto Johnson Road.

This really is Johnson Road Dad?

Yes Son but that is not what we are here to see, we came here to see the other Church coming up on your left at the fork.

See that Church coming up on the fork that is Sandy Grove African Methodist Episcopal Church and that building next to it is the one room school house were all slaves on the Johnson Plantation went to school, again thanks to Fessa Brown and Massa Johnson's daughter.

Wow, Dad this is amazing, so these are the two churches where the Gold was hidden? Who is buried in the graveyard?

Generations of slaves and their decedents Son, generations, Fessa Brown, Mammy Brown, the Youngblood's, Walkers, Ryans, Cosbys, Drews, Cowins, Curtis's and quite a few others whose ancestors decided to remain on the plantation after the civil war. And yes this was one of the Churches that was built to hide the Gold Son, this very Church along with the Johnson Church, that we passed coming in, really do exist Armstrong, they exist even to this day. This very Church has sustained this family and others like it for over one hundred and fifty years. It's because of these two Churches that our families have thrived all of this time and today is the day that our ancestors dreamt of when they made the decision to assist old Massa Johnson all of those years ago. Come Son, we have a meeting to go to.

135

The Hut on the

Johnson Plantation

Why Armstrong, you have really grown into an outstanding young man and we were so proud of you graduating from Oxford, that was extremely impressive; do you remember my Son Franklin?

Yes Sir, we played together as kids when granddad would come out here to this very hut, he always said that this was the most special place in the entire world for him.

Yes Son, I must say that your grandfather was a magnificent companion to my Father and we honor him today by making good on a promise made to your family by our Great, Great Grandfather over one hundred and fifty years ago. Armstrong there was originally only one thousand acres of land left for you down in Richmond and Columbia Counties but through the years we were fortunate enough to acquire an additional thousand acres which brought it to two thousand acres of prime land that will be yours when you leave this hut today. But that is not all; there will soon be a team of lawyers and accountants that have been put into place in order to assist you with the management and control of such a fortune.

But Mr. Johnson, you must understand how shocked I am about all of this and I guess a bit overwhelmed, how can all this be possible?

It time you will understand Armstrong but right now I have to ask you to hold out your left hand. Franklin hand me a knife and get the jar out of the safe for your cousin Armstrong here. Armstrong I need for you to hold out your hand and look at your father, in this jar holds blood from each of our descendants; this jar holds the legacy of both families, our blood has always been one and shall always remain one. As your blood spills it will become intermingled with that of our forefathers. You must understand that what goes on in this room must remain in this room for an eternity; one day when you are prepared to anoint your male heir with this secret you will do so at this location. Armstrong as I sign this deed I have completed the task that was passed down from our forefathers to honor a promise made over one hundred and fifty years ago between two men, one white man and one black man who just so happened to be brothers, those men were our great, great grandfathers. Armstrong, along with this deed, located inside this golden box, goes the ownership of a bank account that has ties to six countries on five continents. You also own major stock in 27 Fortune 500 companies; I know this is overwhelming which is why you will have your lawyers and accountants readily available to advise you.

Mr. Johnson I don't really know what to say Sir.

Let us toast this day Franklin did you bring the Behikes and the Cognac?

Yes Father.

Armstrong this Cigar and this Cognac are the finest that money can buy anywhere on the face of this earth, from this day on let it be the symbol of our family pride. The sacrifices that were made by your family have finally borne fruit. Keep this vile forever for it contains the framework and DNA of you and this family's future. Welcome home Armstrong and welcome to a brand new world.

THE END

About the Author

DAVID K. DREW II

drewexec@yahoo.com

David K. Drew II is a native of Augusta, GA. He graduated from The Academy of Richmond County High School after which, he joined and spent 21 ½ years in the United States Army. After retiring in 1998 he enrolled and graduated Magna Cum Laude from Georgia Military College (Atlanta, GA) majoring in Education. He is a member of the Phi Theta Kappa honor society, Who's Who among Students in American Junior Colleges, an Eagle Scout and a Bronze Star recipient from Operation Desert Shield/Storm where he served with the "Rock of the Marne" 3rd Infantry Division.

As an Author he experienced great success through the publishing of his first book, one of Poetry and Prose, entitled "Can You Hear the Drums" which is how he became connected with Bob J. Gaye of BJG Productions and first introduced to screenwriting. This alliance has enabled him to work in Community Television for the past ten years. This alliance also enabled him to garner experience both behind the camera as a Producer and Director, as well as in front of the camera as a featured Actor.

David is one of the Executive Producers, writers, directors and featured actors on "Love Always Charleston", (formerly "A-Town East" and Misty"), a Soap Opera drama from BJG TV/Theater Productions out of Decatur (Atlanta), GA. This independent drama is a "first" and is currently the longest running locally produced Soap Drama in the history of Atlanta (Community Cable) TV, airing for ten seasons and is still in production. Love Always Charleston, LAC (*www.lovealwayscharleston.com*) was also on air in Charleston, South Carolina for fourteen months and remains the "only" locally produced Soap Drama in the history of Charleston, SC television thanks to an alliance with Comcast Cable TV.

David's philosophy toward the entertainment business is, "dreams make living worth the hustle".

This production team is committed to helping others realize their dreams in the entertainment business; his personal mantra is "In the game of life even seats on the 50 yard line are not good enough because I came to play."

Although residing in Columbia, South Carolina, David frequents Atlanta, Georgia and Charleston, South Carolina for production commitments.

David is a firm believer that, "If a man wants his dreams to come true, he must first wake them up."

CPSIA information can be obtained at www.ICGtesting.com
Printed in the USA
LVOW08s1019020314

375615LV00004B/566/P